PRAISE FOR JA[M...]

"This dark, edgy tale touches a multitude of human emotions and is filled with sacrifice, loss, and terror. Hang on tight and remember to breathe."
—Steve Berry, *New York Times* bestselling author on *A Blood Thing*

"Wonderfully fast-paced and suspenseful! Hooked me from the first page. I'd recommend to anyone who likes nice, twisty suspense novels."
—Jennifer Jaynes, *USA Today* bestselling author of *Never Smile at Strangers,* on *The Inside Dark*

"This outstanding crime thriller from Hankins grabs the reader by the scruff of the neck and never lets go."
—*Publishers Weekly* (starred review) on *Shady Cross*

"[A] fine, offbeat novel . . . crammed with crackling dialogue and characters who are . . . true to life."
—*Booklist* on *Shady Cross*

"A thrill ride that takes you on a journey that is not for the 'faint of heart.' Wonderful character development, believable storyline, a true page turner, with an ending that I was not expecting . . . five stars!"
—*Poised Pen Productions/Authors on the Air* on *The Prettiest One*

"A prosecutor and a homeless man team up against a murderous conspiracy in this rollicking thriller . . . The two settle into an entertaining dynamic as . . . Hankins surrounds them with a crackerjack cast of bristling thugs, weaselly lowlifes, and beady-eyed feds, and he ties the story together with pitch-perfect dialogue, mordant humor, and action scenes poised exquisitely between menace and chaos . . . A complex, entertaining thriller."
—*Kirkus Reviews* (starred review) on *Brothers and Bones*

A
BLOOD
THING

OTHER TITLES BY
JAMES HANKINS

A
BLOOD
THING

JAMES HANKINS

THOMAS & MERCER

Published by Thomas & Mercer, Seattle

www.apub.com

Amazon, the Amazon logo, and Thomas & Mercer are trademarks of Amazon.com, Inc., or its affiliates.

ISBN-13: 9781503950160 (hardcover)
ISBN-10: 1503950166 (hardcover)
ISBN-13: 9781503900363 (paperback)
ISBN-10: 1503900363 (paperback)

Cover design by Rex Bonomelli

Printed in the United States of America

First edition

For my entire family

CHAPTER ONE

If Sally Graham had stopped at four beers tonight, maybe even five, she might have noticed that the front door of her apartment wasn't locked when she got home, though she always locked it when she left. But she had downed six St. Paulis at the bar and a Heineken in Teddy Mulcahy's truck on the way home, holding the beer in her right hand while giving Teddy a hand job with her left—and by the way, she was getting a little tired of people thinking she was a prostitute just because she engaged in a *minor* sex act now and then in exchange for a little cash or maybe even just a favor—so when she entered her little apartment above Dave Ellison's detached garage, she wasn't thinking about whether the lock had clicked when she turned the key. The only question in her mind was whether she would sleep better if she forced herself to throw up before rolling into bed.

She passed through the living room and barely noticed the shadow in the corner, the one that didn't belong.

In the bedroom, she stripped down to her bra and underwear, almost toppling to the floor when one foot caught on the waistband of her jeans.

She decided not to vomit—at least intentionally—and walked back down the short hall to the kitchen, which was really nothing more than a kitchenette. She popped a couple of aspirin into her mouth, filled a glass with water from the tap, and was in midsip, her head tipped back, when something in the living room caught her eye. A tiny red dot of light. Then it was gone.

It was back a moment later, then gone again.

A blinking red light in the dark corner of the living room? Her drunken mind stumbled through the possibilities: Her TV? The cable box? No, those were in a different corner of the room.

She wished she'd turned on the living room light when she'd come home. The switch was right there by the front door.

She set the glass on the counter and took an unsteady step toward the blinking light. Another step, and she realized that the light belonged to a video camera mounted on a tripod. She'd never seen that camera before. And she wasn't too drunk to know that the blinking red light meant it was recording.

Her first thought was that her landlord had snuck in and set up the camera, hoping to capture footage of Sally he could whack off to later. But why would Dave put the camera in the living room? Why not her bedroom? Or even the bathroom, if he was especially perverted? And why wouldn't he hide it rather than leave it visible in the corner of the room?

As she stood wondering these things, the shadows behind the camera shifted, and one detached itself from the darkness around it. A man stepped into the dim light spilling from the kitchen. If he had looked any less strange, Sally would have screamed immediately. Instead, she blinked stupidly as her beer-soaked mind tried to comprehend what she was seeing.

He wore regular clothes, the same clothes every guy she knew wore: long-sleeved T-shirt and blue jeans. But he had no eyes. Just . . . blackness where his eyes were supposed to be, a white oval where his face should have been. Goggles, she realized, that's what they were, goggles over a white mask that covered his entire head. But it wasn't just a mask, because it had no bottom; it plunged straight down into the collar of his shirt. She saw now that he wore white gloves . . . but she saw no skin at the man's wrists, only white fabric, which made her realize that the gloves were attached to white sleeves that ran under the long sleeves of his T-shirt.

What the hell? Underneath a set of regular clothes, the intruder seemed to be wearing a white suit that covered him from head to toe.

And he was striding toward her.

She realized, too late, that the time to scream had come and gone. She gave it a try anyway, but the man reached her too quickly and clamped a white-gloved hand over her mouth. She tried to back away, but he slipped behind her, his hand tight over her lips. He reached his other arm around and punched her in the chest, on the left side just below her shoulder, and the blow hurt more than she would have thought possible. He'd whispered something as he struck her, two words, hard to understand through his mask, but it sounded like he'd said, "One eye." She wanted to ask him what that meant—it seemed important that she know—but she suddenly couldn't find the breath to speak.

Her head fell forward, and she saw a bloody knife plunge into the other side of her chest, just below her right shoulder, the weapon clenched in her attacker's fist. She was wrong. He hadn't punched her a moment ago; he'd *stabbed* her. He was killing her. He whispered again, and this time she heard it clearly, though she didn't understand it. "Two eyes," he said.

Her legs grew rubbery and weak, but the man held her tightly, preventing her from crumpling to the floor. Her eyes fell on the video camera recording her final moments.

She always used to tell people that her life wasn't much—in fact, it kind of sucked—but it was the only life she had. She realized now how true that was.

The man reached across her body from behind and sank the knife into the left side of her stomach.

"Smile for the camera," he whispered.

It was the last thing she heard in this world.

———

The man looked at Sally Graham's body on the floor again, as he had done a few dozen times since killing her. Then he looked back down at a page in his black three-ring binder, taking a long moment to study the highly detailed pencil sketch he had made of the murder scene.

He was largely satisfied. The position of the body seemed mostly right, lying on its back, one arm down by its side, the other flung out as if the woman had been reaching for something as she died. The bare legs looked close to correct, too, with her left straight and her right bent slightly at the knee. He knelt down and straightened the right leg just a touch. And there were two stab wounds on the body, in just the right places, and that big curving slice across her stomach—just like in his sketch. As planned, the underwear she'd been wearing was in his pocket; he would dispose of it later. The soiled panties he'd brought with him were lying on her ravaged stomach where he'd dropped them, soaking up blood. He picked them back up and slipped them into a Ziploc bag, then stood and stepped back to survey the scene yet again. A quick glance at the sketch told him that her hair was just a little wrong. He stepped close to the body again, leaned down, and brushed a few strands away from her cheek. He nodded. That looked right.

He frowned, though, at the blood that had pooled under and around her torso. The puddle was a different shape than in his sketch. That shouldn't have bothered him. He'd done the best he could. After all, he'd made the drawing weeks before he'd killed her and had managed to get most of the elements of the scene nearly perfect. Perhaps he should be satisfied with how closely the grisly scene before him resembled his preplanned tableau. But after all the hours he'd put into this, after all the effort and planning, he had expected perfection. He deserved for things—for *everything*—to be exactly as he envisioned them. But he couldn't control the way the blood flowed through the carpet's fibers, he realized. He would try to forget about it. It was a small thing, after all, one tiny piece in a vast puzzle he was assembling. One tiny brushstroke in a grand masterpiece. In fact, he could revise the sketch when he got home. Then everything would be perfect after all.

Not surprisingly, the clothes he wore over his bodysuit were covered in blood. He walked over to the camera, leaving bloody sneaker prints on the carpet along the way, and stopped the recording. His feet were sore. The sneakers he was wearing were at least a size too small for him. He slipped a pair of latex gloves over the white gloves attached to his bodysuit, then put the camera, tripod, and binder into a duffel bag. Before zipping the bag closed, he added two Ziploc bags—the bloody underwear in one, the bloody knife in the other.

Then he left, slipping out into the night, without another look at Sally Graham's dead body.

CHAPTER TWO

Vermont Governor Andrew Kane smiled when appropriate, turned serious when warranted, and did a credible job not appearing irritated about the impromptu press conference that had sprouted from what was supposed to be a casual, feel-good event on a sunny Friday morning: the ceremonial ribbon cutting commemorating the opening of the new senior center in Randolph. He stood holding a pair of gold-plated, oversize scissors and, as patiently as he could, answered questions from the reporters who had gathered with other citizens to share in the moment. Invariably, though, questions drifted from the new senior center into more political waters, as Andrew expected they would—with reporters questioning his budget plan; his chosen successor to the retiring state tax commissioner; and, despite strong opposition, his unwavering support of the plan to build new and better low-income housing to replace the soon-to-be razed projects in the city of Rutland.

"I realize that there are people who would prefer a new shopping mall on that land," Andrew said, "or a sports complex, or luxury apartments, but I doubt you'll hear that opinion from the former residents of the projects, folks who moved out because their living conditions had become unbearable, who left one by one while the apartments around them turned into flophouses, or drug dens, or temporary brothels. I bet those people would love to say goodbye to the shelters they're staying in or the park benches they're sleeping on. I bet they'd love to hear that we're putting up newer, safer housing they could afford instead of another shopping mall."

The small crowd grumbled a little before the questions started again. As usual, despite the fact that Andrew was more than halfway into his second two-year term, a reporter managed to slip into his question the fact that he was the youngest person to be elected governor in Vermont's history—he was thirty-one when he assumed office—implying that his age was some sort of handicap. It probably wouldn't be long, he knew, before one of them hinted—as someone did from time to time—that he likely wouldn't have been elected if his surname wasn't Kane, as if his fitness for office were based entirely on having had both a father and a grandfather who were respected senators, a great-grandfather who was a distinguished federal judge, and a great-great-grandfather who'd had the Midas touch a hundred or so years ago when it came to investing. Nicholas Kane made so much money in his day that none of the Kanes to follow had been able to do much to lighten the family's coffers. They weren't close to being Rockefellers or Vanderbilts, but when it came to the net-worth ladder, far more folks in Vermont were looking up at them than down.

Andrew decided the questioning had gone on long enough. He had a busy day ahead of him, as always. And he was behind schedule, as always.

He raised his hands. "Okay, everyone, I've rambled on long enough," he said, as though having to answer a few dozen questions he hadn't been prepared for had been his idea. "Let's remember why we're here. This gorgeous new senior center. Isn't it something? I almost wish I were a senior myself so I could take advantage of everything this place has to offer . . . though that day is still a ways off, which I'm often reminded of." As he said that, he glanced pointedly at the reporter who had referenced Andrew's age a few moments ago, which drew a few laughs.

He turned and handed the big scissors to Jim Garbose, his press secretary, who was standing off to the side, and said quietly, "Remember when they used to love me, Jim?"

"They still love you. They just really want a new shopping mall."

"And for poor people not to get in the way of that."

"Exactly. Now smile and shake hands. You've got a meeting in forty minutes with the secretary of transportation back at the Pavilion," Garbose said, referring to the five-story building that housed the governor's offices, along with a press briefing room, a reception room, and even a small apartment for the governor, which Andrew had rarely set foot in, using it only during a couple of snow emergencies and a two-day stretch when legislative sessions ran late into the night. A 1971 reconstruction of a nineteenth-century hotel of the same name, and on the same site, the Pavilion also housed the offices of Vermont's attorney general and its state treasurer.

"Okay," Andrew said. "I'll try to keep it moving."

He turned and saw the assemblage inching closer, the people jockeying politely for better positions. He smiled at the folks who, just moments ago, had been grousing. Now they were smiling back and reaching out toward him while maintaining a respectful distance—no doubt due in part to the imposing figure to Andrew's right, Mike Burrows, the square-jawed state trooper acting as Andrew's security detail today. Andrew shook their hands and thanked them for coming, looking into their eyes as he did, one after the other, until their faces blended together.

He was moving down the line, nearing the end of the small crowd, making his way toward his black GMC SUV, when he grasped a man's hand thrust toward him and immediately felt something between their palms. The man withdrew his hand quickly, and Andrew was left holding an object. A small black cell phone.

Faint alarm bells clanged in his head, but he quickly relaxed. Plenty of people wanted to use their phones to have their photos taken with the governor. Usually, they held it themselves while taking a selfie beside Andrew. Or they would give their phones or cameras to their friends or family members. Now and then they even tried to hand them to Andrew's security detail, which never went as they hoped. So, although this man had gone about it in odd fashion, most likely he simply wanted a picture he could post on his social media site of choice.

Andrew looked more closely at the phone. It was a flip phone. Small, no bigger than his palm. It didn't even seem capable of taking photos. It looked like a throwaway . . . a burner phone. But what did Andrew know about it? Technology was changing every second. Perhaps this thing was capable of recording in HD and 3D while simultaneously monitoring his blood pressure, issuing stock market advice, and changing the channels on his TV.

He was still looking at the phone when the man leaned closer and said very quietly, too quietly for anyone but Andrew to hear, "Keep that phone with you at all times, Governor. And keep it secret. You're going to need it after the arrest."

The man turned abruptly and hustled away, toward the corner of the senior center.

What the hell?

Andrew's first thought was to have Mike stop the guy, but he hadn't done anything wrong. Had he? Was that a threat? Had he just threatened the governor of Vermont? But no, he hadn't. He'd given Andrew a phone, along with . . . what? A warning? A message? He looked down at the device in his hand. When he looked up again, the man was nowhere in sight.

He tried to conjure an image of the man's face but saw dozens of different eyes and noses and smiles and hair colors. The portrait in his mind was an amalgam of everyone in the small crowd before him.

He turned to the trooper at his side.

"Mike, did you hear what that guy said?"

"What guy, sir?"

"He was here a few seconds ago. He just left."

"No, sir. And I didn't sense a threat of any kind. Is everything okay?"

Andrew nodded. He looked down again at the phone in his hand. Should he give it to Mike? Probably.

What had the man said? That Andrew would need the phone . . . after the arrest? Whose arrest?

"It's an honor to meet you, Governor Kane."

He looked up to see a woman standing in front of him with a baby in one arm and her other arm resting around the shoulders of a young boy, maybe eight or nine years old. She smiled and said, "What do you say, Brian?"

"It's nice to meet you, sir," the boy said.

He held out his little hand. Andrew felt the small black phone in his own hand. With a last look toward the corner of the building where the man had disappeared, he slipped the phone into his pocket, smiled, and shook the boy's hand.

"It's nice to meet you, too, Brian."

Andrew shook more hands, smiled as sincerely as possible, and couldn't stop thinking about the phone in his pocket.

CHAPTER THREE

Henry Kane stood in late-afternoon shadow, leaning against the brick building beside him to steady his aim. He placed his crosshairs on the center of Vermont State Police Detective Thomas Egan's face and watched the cop say something, then shake his head and smirk. Henry didn't typically relish this part of his job, but he didn't think taking Egan down was going to cost him much sleep. The guy deserved this more than most. Henry exhaled slowly . . . then took the shot. Then he took two more in rapid succession before zooming his 1000mm Nikon lens wider to include the man to whom Egan was talking—a lowlife named Billy Milton. Henry quickly switched to the video camera hanging from a strap around his neck, just in time to catch Milton handing the detective a fat wad of bills. Egan stuffed the money in his pants pocket and said something. Milton shook his head, turned, and headed off in the opposite direction. Henry kept recording until they were both out of sight. This photographic record of what looked very much like a state police detective receiving a payoff from a local drug dealer wasn't enough on its own to actually prove anything, but it was certainly strong supporting evidence in an Internal Affairs investigation of a detective suspected of such behavior.

Henry was looking at the screen on the back of his digital camera, checking the images he'd just recorded, when he heard a furtive sound behind him. A shoe scraping concrete. Damn it. He had figured Egan's partner would have been at the other end of the building, watching the entrance to the small parking lot in which the transaction had taken place. Henry turned and raised his hands, the camera in his left, his right empty. The video camera still hung around his neck.

"Don't move a muscle," the young detective said. Acne dotted his face, and he had a particularly large pimple where his left cheek met his nose that looked ready to blow any second. Henry was surprised the kid's voice hadn't cracked when he spoke. The younger man's hand rested on the butt of the pistol at his hip.

"Relax, Detective Simmons," Henry said. "I'm state police, like you. Got a badge and everything. Want to see it?"

A brief pause, then, "How do you know my name?"

"You've been riding around with Egan lately, learning the ropes, doing legwork on a couple of drug cases. Probably hoping it will give you a boost up through the Bureau."

Simmons had been promoted to the Vermont State Police Bureau of Criminal Investigations less than half a year ago. To Henry, he looked green enough to be getting his nutrition through photosynthesis.

"Are those cameras?" Simmons asked.

"Yeah, but don't worry. You're not on them."

"Who is?"

"Guess."

Simmons said nothing.

"No guess?" Henry said. "I'll tell you then. Egan and Billy Milton are on them. But you probably figured that. Just like you can probably figure exactly who I am and what I do."

"Thought you might be a PI when I saw you. But if you're state police, too . . ." Another short pause. "Guess I'd like to see that badge now."

Very slowly, Henry reached into his pocket for his badge, then held it out. Simmons kept one hand near his weapon and took the badge with his other. He gave it a quick look and handed it back. "Tom's my . . . my mentor, I guess," Simmons said, as if Henry hadn't already essentially stated that fact.

"That doesn't mean you have to go down with him."

Simmons blew out an unsteady breath. Henry looked around the empty lot from which Egan had just departed, expecting him to come upon them at any moment. He frowned. He should have been more careful. He never should have let Simmons find him.

"I can try to keep you out of this, Simmons, but if we don't end this little meeting of ours fast, Egan's going to join us. Then he's going to figure out what's going on, what I'm doing here with my camera. And with us standing here talking, he might even think you're informing on him."

"I'd never—"

"Yeah, you and I know that, but does he? He's known you, what? Five months?"

"Almost."

"Okay, so it's in both our best interests for you to back off right now, forget you ever saw me, and keep your mouth the hell shut until this investigation concludes. Otherwise, you'll be hindering an IA investigation. And trust me, you don't want to be doing that."

Henry almost felt sorry for the guy. He clearly had no idea what to do. They didn't have courses on situations like this at the academy. You're supposed to bleed blue, of course; every cop knows that. You're expected to have your fellow officer's back in all circumstances, at all costs. But what if that officer is dirty and the subject of an Internal Affairs investigation? What if the thing you've feared since the moment you learned of his extra source of income is actually happening? Maybe you have a young wife at home—hell, maybe you've got a baby on the way. Maybe you've wanted to be a cop your whole life. And who knows?

Maybe your dad was on the job, too. And now you're looking down the barrel of a suspension, or termination, or maybe even prison. All because you got hooked up with a crooked cop. What do you do then?

Simmons said nothing.

"You hearing me, Simmons?"

The younger cop sighed and nodded. Henry looked around. Egan wasn't in sight.

As if on cue, Simmons's radio crackled. "Jerry? Where are you?"

Simmons looked at Henry.

"Tell him you'll be right there. You're taking a leak."

Simmons nodded, then did as told.

"Hurry it up," Egan responded. "I'm hungry."

"He's probably back at the car now," Simmons said to Henry.

"You're gonna keep your mouth shut, right?"

"Am I in trouble?"

Henry thought a moment. "You taking a cut?" Henry didn't think he was, but he had to ask.

"No, I swear. He's never even told me what he does at these . . . meetings. I just . . . stand lookout, I guess. Pretend I don't know what's going on."

Henry believed him. It confirmed what he'd suspected.

"So, am I in trouble?" Simmons asked a second time, and this time his voice did crack.

"I'll do what I can for you."

Simmons nodded. His radio squawked again. "Jerry, you taking a leak or a squat? Get the hell back here."

"Roger," Simmons replied. He looked into Henry's eyes. "Will I have to testify against him? Because that would be . . . I'm not sure how the other guys . . ."

"It's probably not gonna be my call."

Until now, it had been just Henry's investigation. He could expand it to include Simmons if he wanted to. He pretty much called the shots in Internal Affairs in all of Vermont, both state and local forces. The local police departments didn't have their own IA units. They usually chose to investigate minor allegations themselves, like complaints of officer rudeness or other various petty rules infractions, but for more serious complaints, or sensitive matters best left to outside personnel—especially allegations of criminal conduct by officers—departments usually involved the state police Internal Affairs Unit, or IAU. And while similar units in some states—particularly the larger ones—might consist of several officers and civilian support staff, in the Vermont State Police, the IAU was a one-man show. And for the past seven years, the sole star of that show had been Lieutenant Henry Kane. So if Henry wanted to sweep Simmons into the investigation, he could. But he didn't. Still, that might not end the officer's involvement.

"Really, Simmons," Henry said, "if I had the final say, I'd leave you out of it if I could. But that's gonna be the state attorney's call." Having personally seen Egan engaged in criminal activity of which he now had photographic evidence, he would have no choice but to involve the state attorney's office. "But like I said, I'll talk to them, do what I can for you."

Simmons looked miserable. "I'd better get back to the car."

Henry nodded. "Seriously, you understand the kind of trouble you'll be in if I learn you've breathed a word about this, right? Egan may be your mentor—who knows, maybe he's even your BFF—but he never should have put you in this situation. You don't owe him. So don't do anything stupid. He's not worth it."

Hell, he didn't even cut you in, Henry thought.

Simmons nodded. "I hear you."

As he watched the young detective walk away, Henry felt conflicted. Investigating his brothers in blue wasn't always easy on his soul, nor did it get him invited along for after-shift drinks very often, but someone had to do it, and he'd decided years ago that it might as well be him. Every now and then, one of his investigations actually cleared a local cop or fellow trooper, and he was able to submit his final report to his supervisor with the word *unfounded* beside every allegation. Those were the good days on the job.

This one wasn't. As Henry watched Simmons disappear around the corner of a building at the far end of the lot, he wondered whether the younger man would survive this, or whether Henry's investigation would lead to him getting chewed up in the prosecution's case against Egan. Either way, it would be out of Henry's hands.

He was heading back to his Ford Taurus, parked two blocks away, when his cell phone rang. Caller ID told him the governor of Vermont was trying to reach him. He'd have been more impressed if the governor weren't his older brother.

As he answered, it occurred to him that the last time Andy had called him during traditional business hours was six years ago to inform him that their mother had died. He sure as hell hoped for better from this call, but for some reason, he had a bad feeling about it.

CHAPTER FOUR

Molly Kane ran like hell, her legs and arms pumping, her feet pounding the pavement, inhaling for three strides, exhaling for two, in for three, out for two. Her elbows were bent at ninety-degree angles, her hands open as they passed her body precisely at the height of her hips. She was a machine, every body part in perfect sync, running as though her life depended on it, like starving wild dogs were nipping at her heels . . . the way she always ran, even when she was just out for a late-afternoon run, as she was at the moment. No leisurely jogs for her. After a thorough stretching, she would start off briskly, then increase her speed rapidly until she was practically in a dead sprint, a pace she maintained until she neared home again and was ready for a brief cool-down trot. She had no interest in spending an hour listening to tunes, nodding to other joggers. She didn't have the time or the patience. So she ran hard and fast, always the same three miles, and she tried to improve on her time every single day. She actually hated running. But she loved being able to run. She loved being in shape. So she hadn't missed a single day's run in the four years since she'd left the army.

As she neared home again, she strained to reach one last gear, pushing for a strong finish. She passed the street sign closest to the end of her driveway, blinking sweat from her eyes, and checked her fitness watch.

She'd missed her personal best by twenty-three seconds. *Damn.* She'd do better tomorrow. She had no doubt.

She passed through the gate in the wrought-iron fence that surrounded the property and started up the driveway toward the grand Victorian house that she refused to call a mansion, though most others described it that way. Twenty-three rooms and a $5 million valuation would do that.

She bounded up the porch steps, grabbed the towel she had left draped over the railing, and used it to wipe away the sheen of sweat from her neck and arms. She pushed through the heavy wooden door and entered the dim foyer. She didn't even glance at the dark, polished wood trim and gracefully arched doorways; or the fine oil paintings hanging over William Morris wallpaper with a delicate green leaf and soft pink chrysanthemum pattern; or the ornate wall sconces that had been converted to electricity during the Taft administration.

When Molly was a child, this had seemed like a magical place, a home from a storybook about a little girl who had endless adventures with her brothers in its endless number of rooms. Today, though, the magic was gone. It was just a house. Undeniably handsome, admired by many, but too big for her taste, too dark, and too empty. Many years ago, she'd lived here with her parents, her two older brothers—Andy and Henry—and her twin brother, Tyler. And, of course, there was Mrs. Gallagher, who lived in a small suite of rooms on the third floor, and who cooked and kept the house and read the children stories and taught three out of four of them to play the piano at least passably. These days, though, it was just Molly and Tyler in the house, along with Julie Davenport, who lived in Mrs. Gallagher's old suite and earned her keep by helping out with Tyler. Molly had met Julie almost two years ago at the University of Vermont, where they both were working toward graduate degrees, and had taken an instant liking to her.

Andy, known to everyone outside the family as "Andrew" or "Governor Kane," had gone to college and never moved back into the house. Henry had moved into an apartment near the state police academy he was attending at the time and, like Andy, never moved back home. Molly herself had been gone for eight years after enlisting and serving in the army. Patrick Kane, their father and the patriarch of the respected Kane family, had died twelve years ago, and their mother, Emma, had followed six years later. But when Mrs. Gallagher passed three years ago, Molly and her brothers knew one of them would have to live with Tyler.

To Molly, she was the clear choice. She and Tyler were twins. They'd always had the closest bond. It was as though she was his lifeline to the rest of the world, so much so that she had almost decided not to enlist to avoid feeling as though she were abandoning him. But serving was something that had been important to her. She'd always felt a sense of duty—first to Tyler, then to her country. And she hoped one day to serve the people of Vermont as a state police officer, as Henry did. So she enlisted, believing Tyler would be okay without her for a few years. For the most part, he was. But then Mrs. Gallagher died and Molly, whose enlistment was up by then, returned to the house in which she'd grown up.

She followed the sounds of gunfire and explosions down the hall to what had been called the music room for as long as Molly could remember. In one corner sat the baby grand piano on which she had learned countless piano pieces. It was also where she learned that she would never be a very good pianist. In another corner sat Tyler, piled into a leather armchair, a wireless video game controller in his hands, his eyes glued to the TV hanging on the wall above the cold red marble fireplace. Not surprisingly, he was playing a first-person war game. North Vietnamese soldiers fell under his withering fire. As she watched her brother's fingers deftly manipulate the controller's buttons and joysticks, the thought struck her that if her fingers could have moved like that, she might have made a decent pianist after all.

"Still trying to reach your final objective, Sergeant?" she asked him.

Without taking his eyes off the screen, he said, "Only two more missions left, then I'm done with this game, and I can start on the next *Smilin' Jack* one. I already own it, too. Henry got it for me for Christmas."

Great job, Henry.

"I don't suppose you did any reading today?" she asked loudly so he could hear her above the sounds of battle.

"Ummm . . ."

"How about that book we got you on ancient Egypt? You said it looked good in the store."

"I tried. The pictures were cool, and I looked at all of them. But the words were boring."

Molly knew what that meant. Perhaps the vocabulary was too advanced. Maybe the ideas were too difficult to grasp. Whatever the case, the book, targeted toward eighth graders, was too difficult for twenty-nine-year-old Tyler. The nasty fall he had taken when he was seven years old had permanently damaged his brain. He hadn't been formally tested in years—no one saw the point any longer—but earlier tests had placed his IQ in the low seventies. His mental age was that of an eleven-year-old boy, a fact that would likely be true for the rest of his life. So unless books were filled with pictures and easy reading, he had no interest in them.

"Well, we can try to find a better book this weekend, okay?"

He shrugged. A huge explosion, far louder than all the preceding ones, filled the room from the surround-sound speakers in the corners, startling Molly. She turned to the TV and saw the following words appear: *Mission Complete. Way to go, Smilin' Jack!* Dramatic music played for a moment, followed by blissful silence.

Tyler turned to her, looking at her for the first time, and beamed a terrific smile.

"Mission complete," he said.

"I see that. How long have you been playing?"

"Today?"

"Today."

He shrugged.

"Tyler?"

"A few hours."

"Did you do anything else today? Did you get out of the house at all?"

"Not really."

"You didn't have to work?"

"I don't work on Fridays."

His "work" was volunteering at the local animal shelter two days a week, four hours each day.

"I forgot," she said. "So you just played video games all day?"

"Not *all* day."

She waited.

"I went to the bathroom a few times. I ate lunch."

She sighed. "Don't you get tired of only playing war games, though? You have sports games, racing games—"

"I wanna be a war hero. Like Jack Smiley."

"I've watched you play those *Smilin' Jack* games a little. They're pretty violent, buddy."

"Jack Smiley's a good guy. A hero. Same as you, Molly."

"Oh." What could she say to that? She couldn't contradict him. She believed that everyone who served in the military was a hero. Besides, he had seen her Bronze Star. She'd even let him wear it around the house one day. But she didn't like him romanticizing war. "Well, how about calling it quits for a while, okay, Sarge? Maybe give that book another try?"

"Hmmm. Maybe I'll take my motorcycle out for a ride."

His "motorcycle" was a black electric bicycle with a 750-watt motor that limited the machine to a top speed of twenty miles per hour. In Vermont, he didn't need a license to ride it.

"That's a good idea," she said. "You have an hour or two before it gets dark."

"I also have a light on my motorcycle," he reminded her.

"Well, be careful anyway, okay?"

"You always say that."

"I mean it."

"I know. And I'll wear my helmet, so you don't have to tell me to, because you always do that."

"I tell you that because I love you."

"I know you do."

"And?"

"And what?"

"You know what."

He sighed dramatically. "And I love you, too, but you're not gonna get me to say it. You always try, but I'm not gonna do it."

She smiled and headed back down the hall, then started up a grand wooden staircase to the second floor. Ten minutes later, she stood in a claw-foot bathtub beneath a rainfall showerhead that issued little more than a light sprinkle because of inadequate water pressure in the 150-year-old pipes. At one point, she thought she might have heard the ring of the doorbell through the drizzle and poked her head around the curtain to listen. She didn't hear a repeat of the sound, though—and Tyler rarely answered the door—so she dismissed it and returned to her carefree daydream of a better shower.

CHAPTER FIVE

The working office of the governor of Vermont was located on the fifth floor of a contemporary steel-and-glass wing that had been added to the Pavilion in the 1980s. Its modernist design stood in contrast to the French Second Empire style of the main structure, which was decked out in brick facade, topped by a mansard roof, and wrapped on two sides by an impressive two-story veranda. Henry preferred the more elegant look of the older part of the building, though he couldn't deny that the location of the office in the newer wing offered his brother a dramatic view of the gold-domed State House. Backed by tree-topped hills, it sat just to the northwest, but Henry couldn't see it just then because it was dark outside, and his back was to the window anyway. His attention was on the simple black cell phone inside a plastic sandwich bag on the governor's surprisingly utilitarian desk, which looked like it had come from IKEA. Henry figured it was part of his brother's effort to maintain an "everyman" persona, though every man certainly hadn't grown up as privileged as Andrew had. Maybe his desk was a small display of frugality following the stunning lack of that quality his predecessor had displayed. Former governor John Barker had an eye for nice things and wasn't above letting the people of Vermont foot the bill for them. Sometimes the legality of such expenses was questionable, and though nothing had ever been proven—in fact, no official investigation had ever been launched—the widespread rumors of corruption, rumors that folks didn't even bother to limit to whispers, contributed in large part to Barker's political upset at the hands of the younger and reputedly more honest Andrew Kane.

Henry picked the plastic bag up off the desk and looked at the phone inside. "Glad you had the sense to put it in a bag. You did touch it with your bare hands, though, right?"

"I thought I was just shaking his hand, like I did with everyone else."

"I'm not blaming you. Just clarifying."

"Yes, I touched it."

"Anyone else touch it?"

"Just the guy."

"Not that big trooper who follows you everywhere?"

Andrew shook his head. "I didn't even tell Mike about it."

"Why not?"

Andrew took a moment to answer. "Not sure. It was just . . . odd. I wasn't sure what it was about—I'm still not—but it seemed personal, you understand? I felt like I should keep it quiet."

"Good. I'd have done the same thing. We don't know what the hell this is about, who that guy was, but it seems like we should keep it between us for now. And you're sure the guy wasn't wearing gloves?"

"I'd have noticed that."

Henry nodded. Should be fingerprints on it then. He put the bag back on the desk. "Remind me again what he said."

"That I should hold on to the phone. Because I'd need it after the arrest. And that was it. He was gone."

What arrest? Henry wondered for the hundredth time since Andrew had called him. *Whose arrest?*

"And you didn't get a good look at him?"

"Sure I did. Looked him right in the eye. Just like I did dozens of other people there. And a hundred people after my remarks at the high school yesterday. And a thousand last week. They tend to blur after a while."

"Yeah, but this guy handed you a phone and gave you a creepy message. Seems like you'd remember that."

"By the time I realized something strange was going on, he was already gone."

"So you don't know what he looked like?"

"Sure I do. He looked like everybody else."

Henry nodded, thinking that the current governor of Vermont could be an idiot sometimes.

"Can you narrow it down at least a little?"

Andrew took a moment to think. "White, medium height and weight, middle-aged. Average-looking as hell."

"Apparently."

"Might have been wearing a blue jacket. Could have been black, though. Possibly green. That's all I've got."

"Very helpful. That narrows it down to half the population. Andy, we need to—"

He was interrupted by the ringing of a phone. Neither he nor Andrew glanced at the landline on the desk; the distinctive chiming clearly came from a cell phone. They looked down at the black phone in the plastic bag. The ring sounded again, and Henry exhaled, realizing it was the phone in his pocket ringing. He shook his head as he pulled it out and saw Molly's name on the screen.

"Hey, Molly. I'm here with—"

"Did Tyler call you?"

"Tyler? No, why?"

"Just wondering if you heard from him in the last hour or two. I'll call Andy."

"I'm with him right now. What's going on?"

"Ask him if—"

He looked at his brother. "Has Tyler called you in the last few hours?"

"Why?"

To Molly, he said, "What's going on, Molly?"

"Probably nothing. He said he was going to take a bike ride. That was almost three hours ago. It's dark out now."

"His bike has a headlight. He's ridden at night before. You need to give him a little more—"

"Henry, I just went out to the garage to get something from my car, and his bike is there."

"He probably went for a walk then. Did you call his cell?"

"I dialed, then heard it ringing somewhere in the house. I found it in the music room. But you know Tyler. He never goes anywhere without it."

That gave him pause. "Did you ask Julie?"

"She's not home, but I called her. She had no idea."

"What's going on?" Andrew asked.

"I'm sure there's nothing to worry about," Henry said to both siblings. "Call the animal shelter, Molly. See if he came in for some reason."

"They're closed now. I'm going to drive around the neighborhood and look for him."

"Want me to head over there and do the same?"

"You busy?"

"Nah. See you in a bit. Give me a buzz if you find him before I get there."

He hung up and explained the situation to Andrew.

"I'll come, too."

"I thought you have a business dinner tonight with some visiting bigwig."

"The lieutenant governor of New Jersey and his wife."

"Whatever. Don't worry about it. We'll find him. He's probably at a friend's house."

"I don't think he has any friends, Henry."

Henry thought a moment. "I don't think so, either. But you have your dinner. I'll text when we find him."

He glanced down at the black phone in the plastic bag on his brother's desk. For a brief, irrational moment, he was certain it was about to ring. But it stayed silent, and he turned and left.

CHAPTER SIX

Tyler was tired of answering questions. He was especially tired of answering the same questions over and over. It made it harder for him to pretend he didn't know the answers to some of them.

"I should probably go home now," he said.

"Now?" the smaller cop said. He seemed short for a policeman, Tyler thought. He was definitely shorter than the cops on TV. "Are you sure? Because if you insist on leaving, we'll take you right home, like we promised. But you said you wanted to help us out, and I don't think you've helped us as much as you can."

It was true. When they'd come to his house a while ago and asked for his help on a case, he thought it would be cool to assist the police on a real investigation. He'd been excited. The car they'd driven him in was a regular car, though, not a black and white with lights on top, which was disappointing, but they'd bought him McDonald's food on the way to the station, which was good. But the food was gone now, and the questions just kept coming. And they were getting harder to answer without talking about things that Tyler didn't want to talk about.

At first, they'd been easy: about what he did most days, where he worked, what he had done three days ago in particular, and later that same night . . .

He'd begun to seriously wonder how all the questions about *him* were supposed to help them on one of their cases. So he told them that he was starting to get tired of talking.

"Look," the taller cop said. He had hair on his face, though not a full beard. Tyler thought he should either shave or let it grow; one or the other. "We told you before: anytime you want to go home, we'll take you home. You're here voluntarily, aren't you?"

When Tyler didn't answer right away, the cop added, "That means we didn't force you to come. We invited you, and you agreed to come with us."

"I know what *voluntarily* means," Tyler replied. He realized then that they thought he was stupid. He didn't want that, so he decided to stick around a little longer and answer questions in ways that showed he wasn't dumb. A bit later, when they started asking him about someone named Sally, he told them he didn't know anyone named Sally and said that his sister was probably out of the shower now and was going to wonder where he was. Then the shorter one said, "You told us nobody was home when we came to your house. Did you lie to us, Tyler? You're not supposed to lie to the police. You know that, don't you?"

"I know that," he said. "I forgot, that's all." But that wasn't true. Once they'd told him that they wanted him to come to the station and help on a case, he didn't want them to know that Molly was home because she might have said that he couldn't go. He could tell, though, that they thought he might be lying. So after that, he not only wanted to avoid seeming stupid, he wanted to appear honest because he definitely didn't want them to think he was a liar. And to do that, he'd have to answer more questions.

But then they did something that surprised him. They showed him a photograph of a woman and asked if Tyler recognized her. If he'd ever met her. Her name was Sally, which Tyler hadn't known. At first, he lied and said that he hadn't ever met her, but he was positive they could tell he was lying, so he finally admitted it, that she'd come into the animal shelter just before closing the other day.

"That was Tuesday?" the short cop asked.

Tyler told them that, yeah, it was Tuesday, and said that even though he'd *met* the woman, he didn't actually *know* her. He promised himself that even though he'd admitted that he'd met her, he definitely, definitely wouldn't ever tell them anything about what he did with her. No one could *ever* know about that. It was *wrong*. His life would be ruined.

"I know you want to go home soon, Tyler, and I get that. But if you can help us out just a little more, I think maybe we can wrap this up soon. With your help, we can get this over with. Okay?"

He liked the sound of that. If they could be done with this conversation before he said anything stupid, before he let on that he had done anything wrong, then maybe he could go home and pretend none of this had happened. No one would have to know about any of it.

So they asked more questions, and he answered very carefully. Finally, the shorter cop said, "Look, Tyler, it's time to be honest. We know what you did. We've known all along."

Oh, no. That was bad. That was terrible. That changed everything. They would tell Molly. And Molly would tell Henry and Andy. He dropped his eyes. How could he look his sister and brothers in their faces again? He couldn't even look the officers in the face. His cheeks felt hot. How could they know what he'd done?

"Why don't you admit it to us now?" the stubble-faced cop said. "I think you want to. I think you're feeling guilty about it. Who wouldn't? I know I sure would. So why don't you tell us all about it? You'll feel a lot better. I promise."

But he wouldn't feel better. He knew that.

"Tyler," the cop said, "your coworkers at the animal shelter saw you get into her car after you left the other day. They saw you drive off with her."

Tyler said nothing. His heart was beating harder than it ever had. And he had to pee worse than he ever had to in his whole life.

"We already know what you did, Tyler. So what harm could it do for you to admit it?"

He felt like crying. He hadn't cried in years. Not since Mrs. Gallagher died.

"Tyler? Are you ready to talk about it?"

He was really tired of answering questions.

The cops had seemed really nice at first, but he didn't like them anymore.

"Look, Tyler, I'm sure you had your reasons, right? If it makes you feel any better, you're not the first person who ever did what you did. You understand that, right? Other people have done the same thing. That doesn't make it right, but it's not unusual."

For some reason, that actually did make him feel a little better. Not much, but a little.

"Just say you did it, Tyler. Tell us all about it, and we'll take you home."

"If you're already so sure I did something," Tyler said, "why do I have to admit anything?"

"You're a smart one, aren't you?" the short cop said, and Tyler felt a tiny flush of pride. "You're not going to let us get you to admit anything more than that you got into her car with her, are you? You're too smart for that, aren't you?"

"If you say so." He almost smiled when he said it. He was feeling pretty clever now.

"So that's all you'll admit then? That you did know Sally Graham, the woman in this picture?"

"Yup," Tyler said.

"And that you met her at the animal shelter on Tuesday?"

"You got it."

"And that after your volunteer shift ended on Tuesday, you got into her car and left with her? That's really all you're going to admit? That's it?"

"Yup," he said a little proudly. "That's all I'll admit."

They didn't think he was stupid any longer. They'd even said so. He knew he should quit while he was ahead. "It's time for me to go home. I definitely want to go home now. Can you take me home? Like you promised."

The cop with the hair on his face said, "Sure, Tyler. My partner here just has to type something up real quick, then make a phone call. After that, we'll hit the road."

The short cop stood, picked up the notepad he'd been writing on the whole time, and left the room. The other cop turned off the recorder that had been running while they talked. Tyler had forgotten about it. "Want me to grab you a Coke from the machine down the hall?" the cop asked.

"No, thanks. I just wanna go home now."

CHAPTER SEVEN

It was a little early to get too worried, Henry thought. Tyler had his issues, no doubt, but he was a big boy. A grown man, in fact. He went out when he wanted to and came home when he was ready. He could get around on his electric bike. He knew enough to eat at mealtimes, to stay out of the rain, to sleep in his own bed at night. He was responsible enough to keep track of his schedule at the animal shelter. And so if he decided to go for a walk, that wasn't a big deal. He'd done that before. Sometimes he'd end up at the park, sometimes the video game store, sometimes the high school, where he'd watch the football team practice.

"He always takes his phone with him," Molly reminded Henry, as if reading his thoughts.

They were sitting in what their mother used to call the drawing room. The upholstered chairs were Victorian and uncomfortable, but because their mother had loved them, they would never have considered getting rid of them. Henry had chosen the sofa, which, to him, was slightly less uncomfortable than the chairs. But only slightly.

"Maybe he forgot it, Molly."

"Maybe. But it would be the first time I know of."

"I'll drive around again for a while longer. If I don't find him, I'll make a few calls—my headquarters, the local PD. You wait here in case he shows up."

He had almost reached the front door when it opened and Tyler walked into the foyer. He closed the door behind him, then turned and smiled when he saw Henry.

"Hey, Tyler," Henry said. "Where you been? You told Molly you were going out for a ride on your motorcycle, but it's still in the garage."

"Um, yeah . . . well, I was gonna go for a ride. I wasn't lying, I swear . . . but then, um, the police came and said they needed my help."

"The police? What police?"

"They didn't have uniforms on, just regular clothes, like you wear to work, but I knew they were real cops because they showed me their badges. I made them show me. And the badges were real. I could tell because I've seen yours."

Questions shot through Henry's mind. What cops had been here? What had they wanted with Tyler? Did they know his brother was in law enforcement? If so, why—

Molly joined them in the foyer and said, "*There* you are. We were getting worried, Tyler."

Tyler studied the tops of his shoes for a moment. "I just wanted to help the police."

"Police? What are you—"

"It's okay," Henry said, cutting her off. He threw her a quick look that said, *Let's keep calm.* "We're not mad at you. We were just a bit concerned, that's all."

He stepped over to a window and saw a black sedan parked on the street near the end of their driveway. The windows were dark, but he thought he detected movement in the front seat.

"Right," Molly said in a steadier voice. "Of course. We just want to know what happened, that's all. We want to know what this is all about."

The car outside rumbled to life, then pulled in to the driveway. When it stopped near the house, the doors opened, and two men stepped out. One of them was a bit short in stature. The other held some papers in his hand.

"We're about to find out," Henry said.

He pulled the door open before the bell even rang. Two state police detectives, guys Henry recognized but whose names he couldn't recall, were standing on the porch with their badges out. The taller one, with the Indiana Jones stubble, said, "I'm Detective Ramsey. This is Detective Novak. We're with the State Police Major Crime Unit. We have a warrant to search the premises."

Henry knew how it must have gone down. It was common practice. Bring a guy in for questioning. Convince him he's there voluntarily. Tell him he can leave anytime, but that if he answers a few questions, they might be able to wrap things up without a lot of fuss. Then get him to admit to something, *anything*, on which they could hang a search warrant. Call your favorite judge, day or night, then knock on his door with the application in hand and watch while he signs it in his bathrobe and slippers. The application in Novak's hand had probably been signed on their way here from the police station. Henry wondered why the detectives hadn't escorted Tyler to the door, but perhaps they'd wanted to discuss something in private before serving the warrant. Of course, it was also remotely possible that they had decided to allow Tyler and his family a moment alone together before bringing the hammer down on all their lives, but Henry was betting on Door Number One.

The warrant meant that Tyler must have said something incriminating.

But what?

"I know who you are, Detectives," Henry said. "You know who I am?"

"We do, Lieutenant Kane. We know who your brother is, too. And we assume you realize that we aren't in the most comfortable position right now. That we're just doing our jobs. And we also assume you real-ize that, given the situation, we're going to have to follow the book on this as though it's the Bible itself and God is watching."

The guy was almost convincing. He nearly managed to look and sound as though this was a regrettable situation from which he was deriving no pleasure. But Henry could only imagine the satisfac-tion he was feeling, knowing that he might get to arrest the brother of Governor Andrew Kane—the same governor who had recently trimmed the budget of the state police in order to shift funds to pub-lic welfare initiatives he was pushing. The governor who had cam-paigned on the promise to rid Vermont of the corruption that had grown under his predecessor's tenure like black mold in several of the state's offices and agencies, including the Vermont State Police. After former Governor John "Jackpot" Barker suffered an embarrassing defeat in the election and Andrew took office, he began to make good on his promises. He'd brought in the FBI to investigate the depart-ment, and eventually, two members of the VSP had been punished for engaging in illegal conduct—a detective in Special Investigations had been arrested, while his captain, the Special Investigations commander, had been fired. Only two bad apples found among hundreds of good ones, yet the public's confidence in the state police had taken a punch in the face, and when the dust settled, not many state troopers were enamored with Andrew Kane. So Henry would have been surprised if Detectives Ramsey and Novak weren't feeling a little warm and fuzzy about having drawn this case.

It probably didn't hurt, either, from their perspective, that Tyler's other brother was in the state police Internal Affairs Unit. In fact, Henry *was* the IAU. He knew, of course, that the naked contempt that TV and movie cops had for Internal Affairs was more of a TV trope than a reflection of reality. Though no one liked being the subject of an IA investigation, most people in law enforcement accepted the need for the unit, understanding that there had to be checks on police power. No honest cop or trooper wanted his or her department tarnished by the behavior of coworkers who used excessive force, trampled civil rights, took bribes, or colluded with suspects. Still, even though people on the job acknowledged the need for Internal Affairs, IA detectives were almost never the most popular people in the room. Another reason that Ramsey and Novak likely weren't as uncomfortable in this situation as they were trying to make it seem. But Henry played along.

"Is there a crime here, Detective?" he asked.

"There is."

"What is it?"

"The murder of Sally Graham."

Behind him, Molly sucked in a sharp breath. Henry almost did, too. He hadn't expected that. Not murder. Not Tyler. He looked back at his brother, whose eyebrows were knitted in confusion. Henry tried to imagine what was going through his mind. The name *Sally Graham* had been in the news the past few days. Murder was far from a common occurrence in Vermont, which had one of the lowest homicide rates in the country—often less than one per month across the entire state—so the young woman's death, and the level of violence involved, had made a lot of headlines. The news reports had stopped short of labeling the victim a prostitute, but the implication wasn't hard to find written between the lines of the stories. Could Tyler have personally known Sally Graham? Could he have . . . engaged her services? Would he even know how to do that? It was hard for Henry to imagine his innocent brother—

Novak handed the search warrant to Henry, who reluctantly stepped aside, allowing the detectives into the house. He quickly scanned the warrant. On its surface, it looked valid. But that didn't mean it would hold up in court.

"You obviously know that Tyler's not your average guy," Henry said.

Ramsey nodded. "We know. Your point?"

"My point is that I don't know what you got him to say, but this warrant will never stand."

"Recorded the whole thing, audio and video. And it was textbook. It'll stand. Now, is there anyone else in the house?"

Henry drew in a long, slow breath, then let it out. "Just us."

"Okay. This is a big place, Lieutenant Kane. Some Manchester Police officers will be joining us shortly to help execute the warrant. Is there somewhere you three would like to wait while we do our jobs?"

"There's a drawing room at the front of the house," Henry replied. "Okay with you?" Ramsey looked at his copy of the search warrant for a moment, then nodded. Henry said to Molly and Tyler, "Go on in. I'll be right there."

When they were gone, Ramsey looked at Henry. "I assume you want to say something to me."

"What's the basis for the warrant?"

Ramsey shook his head. "We'll be filing it in the clerk's office Monday morning, along with supporting docs and the return inventory. You can find out then."

"Exactly, Ramsey. I'll find out Monday anyway. What's it gonna hurt to tell me now?"

The detective seemed to consider that for a moment, then said, "Okay, yeah, what's it gonna hurt? I can tell you one thing, Kane . . . this is legit."

"How so?"

"Coworker at the animal shelter where your brother volunteers saw him get into the passenger seat of the victim's car hours before she was killed. And your brother confirmed that for us."

"That all?"

"Nope. Also got a call from a neighbor of the victim. Says he saw a man leave the scene around the time of the murder riding what appeared to be an electric bicycle."

"Any chance the neighbor gave his name?"

"It was an anonymous tip," Ramsey said with a dismissive shrug.

Henry scoffed. "So you mean you got an *anonymous* call from someone *claiming* to be a neighbor, and *claiming* he saw—"

"Whatever, Kane. His description fit your brother like a glove. That was enough for the judge."

Henry nodded. He probably should have thanked Ramsey for his small breach of protocol, his tiny display of professional courtesy, but he wasn't in a grateful mood. He turned away and headed into the drawing room. Thankfully, his brother and sister had left the sofa for him. After all, this would take hours.

Molly turned to Tyler. "Do you have any idea what they're—"

Henry interrupted. "Better not to say anything at all right now."

"I don't understand," Tyler said. "I answered their questions. I helped them with their case. Why are they here?"

"Please don't say anything else. Okay? Let's not talk. It's important."

Tyler nodded. A moment later, he asked, "Can I go play *Smilin' Jack*?"

"Sorry, buddy. No video games. We all have to wait here. And not talk for a while. Okay?"

"I guess."

"You could read the Egypt book," Molly said. "I bet they'd let you do that."

"Ummm . . . I'll just sit here."

Out in the hall, Ramsey walked past. He was wearing latex gloves now and carrying empty clear-plastic evidence bags.

Henry figured the detectives' bare-bones working theory was that Tyler had met the woman at the shelter, spent time with her in her car, and then, after she dropped him back off at the shelter, followed her to her apartment on his e-bike, where he killed her later that night.

Which was patently ridiculous. His bike couldn't possibly have kept up with her car. More important, Tyler wasn't a killer. He was the gentlest of souls. The only violence he ever exhibited occurred during his video games.

Ramsey walked past the doorway again. This time, as if on cue, one of the evidence bags was no longer empty; inside, Henry saw several war-themed video games, including one Henry had bought for his brother. And he saw clearly how they could be used to portray his gentle brother as a dim-witted, impressionable man who so enjoyed fantasy killing that he was eventually driven to commit real live murder. If that was the most damning thing they found, there was little to worry about.

Several local cops in uniform arrived, and Henry could see them huddling with Novak, receiving copies of the warrant along with verbal instructions before dispersing with evidence bags of their own.

Henry glanced at Tyler. He couldn't read his brother's face.

What did you say to them, buddy? What are they going to find?

CHAPTER EIGHT

Andrew Kane chewed on a bite of medium-rare filet mignon with burgundy mushroom sauce and chuckled politely at something the lieutenant governor of New Jersey said, not because it was funny but because everyone else at the table had chuckled. Andrew had no idea if it had been funny because he hadn't been listening.

He was trying, though. He'd been fully present for much of the dinner he and his wife, Rebecca, were hosting in the elegant eighteenth-century Colonial they were calling home while Andrew served as governor. Vermont was one of the handful of states that did not have a governor's mansion, so unlike newly minted governors in many other states who moved into swanky residences vacated by their predecessors, Andrew and Rebecca had to hit the classifieds to find a suitable residence near his office. And because Vermont did not provide its governors a housing allowance, either, they had to pay the rent on the 4,800-square-foot Colonial themselves. That was fine with Andrew, though, as the house was just two miles from the Pavilion, which put it over fifty miles closer than their own house in Norwich.

Though Andrew had played the good host through cocktails and appetizers, he was starting to become preoccupied. He had expected to hear from Henry or Molly by now, letting him know that Tyler had turned up safe and sound. At first, he hadn't been overly concerned. But as the evening had worn on . . .

His eyes met Rebecca's across the table. Those hazel eyes—sometimes green, sometimes brown, always striking—locked onto his, and when they were sure they had his attention, widened ever so slightly. It was unlikely that anyone else would have noticed, even if they had been looking directly at her, but Andrew noticed and knew what her expression meant: *What the hell, Andrew?*

She was right, of course. He was being rude, even if their guests weren't aware of it, which he hoped they weren't. He hadn't told Rebecca about Tyler. First of all, there hadn't been much to tell. He'd figured his brother would show up soon. Second, Rebecca doted on Tyler—he was her clear favorite among Andrew's siblings—and Andrew hadn't seen the need to worry her. At least not yet.

He had just resolved to engage more fully when his personal cell phone vibrated in his pocket. Rebecca didn't like him bringing it to the table, and she would have been horrified to know he had done so when they were entertaining, so he didn't dare answer it at that moment. But he had to learn who was calling.

"Please excuse me," he said as he stood. "I'll be right back." He folded his napkin and placed it on his chair. "My apologies."

He avoided his wife's lovely eyes as he left the room. As soon as he was out of sight of the dining room, he pulled the phone from his pocket, even though it had stopped vibrating a moment ago. He was about to check the smartphone's call log when a notification popped up on the screen informing him that he had a voice mail. It was from Henry.

"I hope you're sitting down for this. Tyler was questioned by the state police today. About a murder. That woman killed this week. They're searching the house right now. Can't imagine what they could possibly find here, but who knows? The mystery phone that guy gave you this morning? You might want to keep it handy. I'll call you again later."

Andrew mechanically backed up a step, bumped into a wooden chair behind him, and sat down. He'd never sat in the chair before, not once in the three years they'd lived there. Neither had Rebecca, at least not that he was aware of. It was old, probably an antique, and oddly positioned in the middle of a hallway beside an antique table they didn't use, either. But it was a good thing the chair was there now, or the governor of Vermont would have been sitting on his ass on the floor.

Tyler? Was it possible that he was going to be arrested—for murder, no less—as the man who had given Andrew the black cell phone now seemed to have been suggesting? Where had the stranger gotten that inside information?

This is ludicrous, he thought. *Tyler couldn't intentionally harm anyone, much less kill someone.*

He wasn't sure how long he'd sat like that, head down, phone in hand, before Rebecca appeared in the hallway. It took just a glance. "What's wrong, Andy?"

He told her.

"That doesn't make any sense."

He agreed.

She placed a comforting hand on his shoulder. "I'll make an excuse for you. I'll get rid of them. Emergency state business or something."

"Don't bother. He's a lieutenant governor. He'd see through that. Besides, there's nothing for me to do right now at the house anyway." No matter where the Kane siblings lived, the Victorian mansion in which they had grown up would always be known to each of them as *the house.* "The police will be searching for a couple more hours at least. We're almost done with dinner now. I can make it through the rest."

"Even if we have to listen to another of Larry's war stories?" she asked with a small smile, referring to the lengthy narratives with which

New Jersey's lieutenant governor had been regaling them all evening, tales from his days as a prosecutor doing battle with the Jersey mafia.

He smiled back, which took some effort. "Go back to our guests, okay, Becca? I'll be right there."

He typed a text to Henry: Dinner will be over in a little while. I'll be there right after.

He returned the phone to his pocket, glanced down the hall at the doorway to the dining room, then hurried in the opposite direction, toward the room at the back of the house that he used as an office. He lifted his briefcase from the floor, snapped it open, and looked down at the black cell phone in the plastic bag resting on top of several files.

The phone in his pocket vibrated again, this time just once. A text from Henry: Probably not a good idea. Don't want anyone—cops, press—thinking you're stepping in to interfere. Sit it out for now. I'll keep you posted.

His first instinct was to resist, to speed through the rest of dinner, wolf down dessert, kick the Jersey blowhard and his wife out the door, then obliterate the speed limit on the way to the house in Manchester. But Henry was right; it wouldn't be a good idea. Besides, appearance— more important than it probably should be in many aspects of life— was absolutely critical in politics. Andrew had ridden a hard-earned reputation for honesty and integrity all the way to the top position in Vermont's government, decrying the corruption, kickbacks, and crony- ism that had all but defined the administration of his predecessor. And if a number of political pundits were correct, he might actually ride that reputation all the way to the White House one day.

That certainly hadn't been Andrew's goal when he'd first stepped through the ropes and into the political ring, but others, including his wife, his political advisors, and the registered Democrats of Vermont had begun to dream of that for him. And, he realized, somewhere along the line, he had begun to share in that dream. He had never sought power for power's sake. The apple had fallen a good distance from the tree in that regard. His father had relished the power and prestige that his long and distinguished career as a senator, and his even longer career as a feared, hard-nosed litigator, had bestowed upon him. But what drove Andrew was the thought of all that he could potentially accomplish as president, all that he had begun to believe he could offer this country. So he had to tread carefully right now. It would border on hypocrisy for him to stride into the criminal investigation of a family member and appear to be trying to intimidate the authorities by throwing around the weight of his office. He needed to trust Henry. He needed to let this play out. It wouldn't be easy, though; Tyler was his little brother.

He typed a reply: I hear you. Call when you can.

He slipped the black phone—still in the plastic bag—into his front pants pocket, then returned to Rebecca and their guests.

He didn't silence the mystery phone, as Henry called it. If it rang tonight, he wanted to make sure he heard it.

CHAPTER NINE

The search continued. A little before 10:00 p.m., Henry called a detective he knew, Ray Hodges, who had retired last year from Major Crime. In a quiet voice, he asked about Ramsey and Novak without saying why he was asking.

"They're all right," Hodges said. "Decent detectives."

"Are they dicks? They seem like they might be dicks. Especially Ramsey."

"They can be dicks. Especially Ramsey. But so can you. Me, too."

"They're good, though?"

"Good enough, yeah."

He paused a moment. "Here's a tough one . . . any reason to think they'd ever manufacture evidence?"

Hodges grew silent. "If you've got an IA investigation going on those guys, maybe I shouldn't—"

"It's nothing like that, Ray. I'm not asking as Internal Affairs. I'm just asking."

Hodges said nothing for a moment. "I don't see them doing anything like that. I really don't. You never know, of course, but I don't see it."

"Okay."

"What's this about, Henry?"

"I'd rather not say right now. Maybe it's nothing. But if it's something, you'll see it on the news tomorrow. Thanks again, Ray."

Around 11:00 p.m., Tyler fell asleep on a divan. Henry thought it was called that, but it could have been a settee. Or hell, maybe it was just a second sofa.

A half hour later, Molly got a call on her cell phone from Julie, who was parked on the street in front of the house. She'd been out with friends and had just arrived home, only to see police cars in the driveway. Molly told her that they were searching the house. It was evident that Julie was concerned, but Molly walked a line between vague and reassuring and advised her to spend the night with another friend. She told Julie she'd call in the morning with an update.

Shortly before 1:00 a.m., Henry sensed a wave of excitement ripple through the cops in the house. They'd found something. He couldn't imagine what—and he knew there was no point in asking—but whatever it was seemed to give them all hard-ons.

A while later, Henry heard a car rumble to a stop in the driveway. He parted the lacy curtains in the window behind him and watched Detective Novak exit the vehicle with more papers in his hand. Henry hadn't noticed him leave earlier. This wasn't a positive development. The front door opened, then closed. Low voices murmured in the foyer. Then Ramsey came into the drawing room carrying the papers Novak had brought, and Novak followed, a small laminated card in his hand.

Ah, hell. This was what Henry had feared.

With something resembling sympathy, Ramsey said to Henry, "You want to be the one to wake him up?"

Henry walked over to his brother, placed a hand on his shoulder, and gently shook him.

"Buddy? I need you to wake up."

"What's going on, Henry?" Molly asked.

"They're arresting him." As he had suspected when he saw Novak returning. Once they'd found whatever it was that had gotten everyone so excited, the detective had slipped out to get an arrest warrant, almost certainly returning to the same judge who had signed off on the search warrant. Novak had probably drafted most of the arrest warrant application hours ago and needed only to fill in a few blanks before getting the judge's John Hancock.

"Arresting him?" Molly said. "For what? *Murder?* That's ridiculous. It's a joke." She looked at the detectives. "This is bullshit, and you guys know it."

"Molly . . ." Henry said.

"No, this is unbelievable. We know you guys don't like Andrew. We know you're pissed because he decreased your budget and got rid of a couple of dirty cops. So *this* is how you get back at him? Through his family? His younger brother?"

"Molly, don't . . ."

To their credit, the detectives said nothing.

"You trump up a murder charge on a guy like Tyler, who can't even bring himself to step on a spider? This is ridiculous."

"Molly," Henry said more sternly. She turned to him. "This isn't the time. This isn't the way."

She clearly wasn't finished. She opened her mouth to say something else, then shook her head and seethed in silence. Henry turned back to Tyler, who rubbed his eyes and sat up.

"You wide awake now, Tyler?"

"I guess."

"You have to go with these men."

"Where?"

"The police station."

"Why? I was already there today. I already talked to them."

"I know but . . . they're arresting you."

Tyler blinked a few times, frowned, then said, "Arresting me? They know what I did? They told me they knew, but I thought maybe they were just trying to trick me so I'd say something stupid. I didn't know they really knew."

What the hell?

"Tyler, you need to stop talking right now. Don't say another word."

"But if they know what I—"

"Damn it, Tyler, *shut the hell up*," Henry yelled. He didn't for a second believe that his brother had killed that woman, but apparently he had done *something*. Whatever it was, he really needed to stop talking about it.

Finally, Tyler closed his mouth. His lower lip trembled.

"I'm sorry, buddy," Henry said, "but this is really important. I need you to stand up. You have to go with these men."

Slowly, with a beseeching look at Molly, Tyler stood. Ramsey stepped forward, a pair of handcuffs in his hand.

"Turn around, please," Ramsey said in a surprisingly gentle voice.

Novak looked down at the laminated card in his hand and began reading the Miranda warning.

"Henry?" Tyler said. "Molly?"

The confusion in his wide, innocent eyes . . . the tremor in his voice . . . broke Henry's heart. Molly gripped his forearm, her nails digging in deep.

"Just go with them, okay?" Henry said, talking loud to be heard above Novak's droning recitation of his brother's rights under the law to remain silent, to have an attorney.

As he watched Ramsey handcuff his younger brother, Henry felt a nearly overpowering urge to twist the detective's arm up behind his back until bones cracked like dry kindling and ligaments snapped like rubber bands. But the guy was just doing his job. Henry had done the same job countless times.

"Listen to me carefully, though, Tyler," he said. "Pay attention now, because this is really, really important. Do *not* say anything. Not one word. You don't talk to anyone but me, Molly, Andy, or your lawyer. You understand?"

"I need a lawyer?"

Both his hands were cuffed behind him now. A tear rolled down one cheek. Novak put the laminated card in his pocket.

"Yeah, Tyler, you need a lawyer. At least until we figure this out. But I need you to tell me that you understand what I'm saying, okay? Tell these men right now that you only want to speak with your lawyer."

"What about you guys?"

"Just say it."

He did as told. Ramsey shook his head, as if he expected more from a fellow officer, but it was just for show. Ramsey would have done the same thing in Henry's shoes. Novak would have, too. As would anyone who knew anything about the criminal justice system.

"Where are you taking him?" Henry asked.

"Manchester PD lockup."

It was Friday night. The courts were closed until Monday, which was the earliest Tyler could be arraigned. Which meant he would spend the weekend as a guest of the nearest jail.

Ramsey guided Tyler out of the room and down the hall toward the foyer with Novak towed along in their wake. Henry and Molly followed.

"Hey, Ramsey, don't forget that Tyler's not your typical guy," Henry said. "Plus, he's the governor's brother. He needs protective custody. Or at least his own cell."

Ramsey nodded, then opened the front door. Henry grabbed his arm, stopping him, and said, "Even though we're all in our nice suits here, don't forget that I wear blue, same as you."

The detective glanced down at Henry's hand on his biceps, and Henry removed it.

"I know," Ramsey said. "We'll take care of him."

"Guys?" Tyler said.

Henry leaned close to Ramsey and said, very quietly, "Any chance I can stay with him through booking?"

"All due respect, Lieutenant, you're kidding, right?"

"No, Detective, I wasn't. But I hear you. I'll get in to see him tomorrow, though. I promise you."

"And if anyone tries to stop you tomorrow, it won't be me. But tomorrow's not tonight. Tonight I have to do things by the book, like I said. And that doesn't include letting the suspect's brother hold his hand through booking. Okay?"

Henry took a step back and watched the detectives escort Tyler down the porch steps and into the back seat of their car. Before Novak closed the door, Henry called, "Remember, Tyler, don't tell them a thing."

Despite a few brief moments of humanity and civility having bled through his cold, by-the-book demeanor tonight, Ramsey shot Henry a hard look as he slid behind the wheel of the sedan. Then they were gone, as were the local cops, who had left not long before.

"Henry?" Molly said. "What happened here? What the hell is this?"

"I don't know. In the morning, you should call Rachel Addison. She's the most expensive criminal defense lawyer in the best firm in the state. Most cops hate her, but only because she's so good."

Henry stepped out onto the porch.

"What are you going to do now?" she asked.

"No point in my trying to get in to see him tonight. Besides the fact that I'm obviously not welcome, it'll be three in the morning before he's processed."

"So where are you going?"

"Into headquarters. I'll stop by the Major Crime Unit. See if there's anyone there who knows anything. It's a long shot at this time of night, but you never know. If I come up empty, I'll try again in the morning."

She gave a tight, nervous nod. "I guess it's time to call Andy."

"I'll do it. Remember, in the morning, call Rachel Addison. Throw money at her. This family has enough."

"What if she doesn't go into the office on Saturdays?"

"Given her reputation, she'll be there. And if she's not, they can find her. Tell her answering service the governor's brother has been arrested and needs a lawyer. That'll get her to the phone."

"What if she's not available?"

"Throw enough money at her, and she will be."

CHAPTER TEN

As soon as he was in the car, Henry called Andrew and filled him in. He reiterated his belief that Andrew needed to stay away from this for the time being, and his brother reluctantly agreed.

"What about an alibi?" Andrew asked, the concern in his voice evident.

"This happened on Tuesday. As best as we can piece together, he was home alone at the time."

"Doing what?"

"He thinks he was just watching TV."

"And what do you think?"

"I don't think he killed anyone, if that's what you're asking."

"Of course he didn't. But you just said that until you got him to quiet down, he kept talking about having done *something*. What do you think that might have been about?"

Henry hesitated. "The victim supposedly got around."

"And?"

"She supposedly got around for money sometimes."

"You don't think Tyler would have paid her to . . ."

"I doubt it. But who knows?"

They ended the call. A little while later, he arrived at state police headquarters in Waterbury, which housed his Internal Affairs office, as well as the Major Crime Unit. Vermont was a relatively quiet state at night, and at close to 2:00 a.m., headquarters was a ghost town. Unsurprisingly, the MCU was empty at that hour, with any calls that might come in being directed to the main switchboard. Henry had clung to a slim hope that he would find either Ramsey or Novak there, perhaps while the other saw to Tyler's booking, but maybe they were both so dedicated as to want to be present for the processing. Or perhaps one of them went home to catch some sleep while the other—probably whichever was junior—handled the mundane task of seeing that Tyler made it into a cell.

Henry took the elevator to the second floor, passed through a common area and into the left-hand wing, and stopped at the second door on the left: the Internal Affairs Unit. He unlocked the door, which had to be kept locked at all times when he wasn't there, and entered the office. He'd seen the space they devoted to IA units in cop shows and in movies, but his version wasn't nearly as impressive: a single, somewhat cramped office; a desk with a computer and printer; two chairs facing his desk; and three file cabinets. He wished his unit's budget could handle the installation of a urinal so he wouldn't have to lock the door just to go down the hall every time he had to take a leak.

He slipped into the chair behind his desk, ignored the files stacked there—including the one on Thomas Egan, the dirty state police detective taking payoffs from drug dealers—and reached for the phone. He called Manchester PD and learned that, yes, Tyler Kane had been booked and was in his cell, and no, Henry wasn't welcome to visit at this time, despite his status as a lieutenant with the VSP. He could call in the morning if he wished and inquire about visitation then. Henry wasn't Tyler's lawyer, of course. They didn't necessarily have to let him see his brother before the arraignment on Monday. But he knew that the decision whether to allow the visit was within the discretion of the cops running the holding facility. He'd call in the morning and hope for a bit of professional courtesy for a brother in blue.

There was nothing more for him to do tonight. If he'd had room for a couch, he'd have slept in the office, but he didn't, so he headed home to get what little sleep he could.

———

Hours later, Molly had given up any hope of sleep. She was too wound up. Too worried about Tyler. She doubted that he truly understood what was happening to him, or why it was happening. He had such an innocent soul . . . and she refused to believe anything to the contrary.

She hated the thought of him alone behind bars. She hated that she couldn't be there with him. She was the one to whom he looked for comfort, and she felt an obligation to provide it as best she could. She would do that for any of her brothers, of course, but Tyler was different. She knew that some people thought that her need to protect him, to live with him and care for him, was simply a womanly, maternal instinct. Others probably thought their relationship was grounded in their special connection as twins. But it was more than that. Far more. Because, though she hated to admit it to herself—and she'd sure as hell never admitted it to anyone else—she felt responsible for the way Tyler . . . was. She never should have let him climb out onto the roof that day. But he was hell-bent on it, on impressing older brother Henry, like he was always trying to do. He had attempted a similar stunt once before, but Mrs. Gallagher had caught him. And she'd scolded him good. And though Molly had tried unsuccessfully to stop him that first time, Mrs. Gallagher had scolded her, too, because she was supposedly "the only one with common sense." She'd also told Molly that if he tried such a thing again and Molly couldn't stop him, she should run and get help from an adult; and if no adults were around, she should tell Andy, because Andy was the oldest.

But that terrible day, when her attempts to keep Tyler from stepping out the window onto the slippery slate shingles of the steeply pitched roof were unsuccessful, she hadn't run to get help. Both their mother and Mrs. Gallagher were out, but she could have run to Andrew. Yet she didn't . . . because when she'd tried to stop Tyler, Henry had teased her yet again for being a girl and told her she was never any fun, and Tyler had joined in. It hadn't been terribly mean-spirited, just kid stuff, really, but she was tired of hearing it from them, and tired of being *the only one with common sense.* So she watched her twin brother climb out onto the roof with Henry and his mile-wide mischievous streak. And she failed Tyler . . . with catastrophic consequences.

Now he was in jail, and she couldn't be there for him. Tyler, *in jail,* accused of murdering a woman.

Which made no sense at all. Tyler could never hurt anyone. He was innocent. To her, that was an immutable truth, like the sun rising in the east or water being wet. So why was he behind bars? She couldn't wrap her head around it. Her mind spun. So sleep was out of the question for now. If she had any hope of getting rest tonight, she was going to have to drive herself to physical exhaustion first.

So now, at three in the morning, in a second-floor bedroom that she had converted into a home gym, she punished the heavy bag without mercy, rapidly landing furious blows and powerful kicks one after the other, breathing heavily, sweating from every pore, refusing to stop for even a brief rest. Her hands and wrists ached. Every muscle in her arms burned. Her feet were sore. Her legs were growing heavier by the second. But she kept at it, imagining that the bag was Detective Ramsey, who had put her brother in handcuffs, before switching after a few minutes to Novak, who had read Tyler his rights. Then back to Ramsey, then Novak, back and forth, again and again. She saw their faces on the bag, driving her to increase the force of her blows. Maybe they were just doing their jobs, but—perhaps a little irrationally—she despised them for it. So she imagined beating them senseless until her limbs stopped responding to her commands. Then she staggered down the hall and collapsed facedown on her bed, sweaty and spent.

After a while she fell asleep and alternately dreamed of Tyler, alone in his cell, and Detectives Ramsey and Novak, toothless and bruised, bloody and in pain.

———

Andrew flipped from his back to his stomach, accidentally untucking the top sheet at the foot of the bed, which he always hated. A moment later, he rolled onto his side. A hand gently touched his back, and from the darkness behind him, Rebecca said, "You okay?"

"Sorry I'm keeping you awake."

"I'm certain he's okay."

"I'm not, Becca. This is Tyler we're talking about. He's not equipped for something like this."

"I'm sure he's scared, yeah, and probably confused, but I'm just as sure that he's safe."

"I should have gone to the jail tonight."

"You know you couldn't have done that. You said yourself that you'd have to be cleared first."

"I'm the governor. They could clear me pretty quickly."

"You also said it wasn't technically allowed. You'd have had to use your position to get in to see him, bully your way in. That's not you. And as you said, even if you were successful in seeing him, behavior like that probably wouldn't help his cause much."

"No, I don't suppose it would," he conceded.

"You should try to get some sleep. You'll need to be at your best in the morning."

She was right about that. This was going to be huge news. A media shitstorm. And justifiably so. The brother of a sitting governor arrested for murder. Andrew was going to have to face this head-on, while somehow being there for his brother. He did indeed need to be sharp. But whenever his eyes were open, he saw the cell phone the stranger had given him, lying on his nightstand. And when his eyes were closed, the image of Tyler behind bars faded into view.

Finally, far too close to dawn, he slipped into a restless sleep.

———

Tyler sat in the holding cell on the bed, which was hard and very uncomfortable, way more uncomfortable than his bed at home. His forearms rested on his knees, which were drawn up to his chest, and his head was down in case he cried again. He wasn't crying at the moment, but he probably would again soon. Who wouldn't? This was terrible. This was worse than anything anybody else ever went through in history. He was in jail. For murder. He understood that now. Everyone had talked about it earlier, before he was arrested, but he'd been worried about the other thing he had done, so he hadn't really paid much attention to all the murder talk. For a while, he wasn't even sure they were talking about him, because he sure as heck hadn't killed anyone, especially not Sally.

He was really sad. He was in trouble for something he didn't even do. And he was lonely. But he wasn't allowed to talk to anybody except his lawyer and his family. He didn't even have a lawyer, though, as far as he knew, and his family wasn't in jail with him, so how could he talk to them? The only people talking to him most of the time now were the guys in the other cell, and all they did was call him a retard and tell him that the cops were probably going to put them all in the same cell later, and when they did, he'd find out what happened to guys like him in jail. Tyler didn't know what he meant by that—*what happened to guys like him in jail*—but they sounded nasty when they said it, so it seemed like something to be scared of.

So Tyler was scared.

And sad.

And lonely.

And it was a good thing his face was hidden because he was crying again.

CHAPTER ELEVEN

Andrew Kane awoke before seven on Saturday morning after far too little sleep. His first thought was of Tyler. He wondered how his brother had weathered the night in his cell. Andrew wasn't certain whether Tyler had ever spent a single night away from home.

He was even more distracted at breakfast with Rebecca than he'd been during dinner the night before. She obviously understood and was content to eat in silence. He had two cell phones in his pockets, one of which was ominously silent while the other, his personal one, beeped or dinged every three or four minutes as voice mails, text messages, and emails poured in, all in response to the news of Tyler's arrest. Numerous members of the news media broke protocol and reached out to him directly rather than go through his press office. Friends expressed their concern and support. Political opponents did the same, though with questionable sincerity. Even former governor Barker sent an email feigning sympathy over "this difficult situation." His lieutenant governor, Lynne Kasparian, left a heartfelt message offering to do whatever she could to lighten Andrew's load until everything was "sorted out." Other than a text to Jim Garbose, his press secretary, asking him to draft a statement to release to the public, Andrew didn't reply to anyone. He stopped checking his messages after two hours.

He did send a text to Henry, though, who responded immediately: Tell the goon out front that I'm coming to see you soon. The goon he was referring to was whichever state trooper happened to be assigned to Andrew's security detail that morning, parked in front of the house, where a cruiser was always parked when the governor was inside his residence.

Henry arrived forty minutes later and followed Andrew down to his home office. "I saw Tyler a little while ago," Henry said.

"You did? How's he doing?"

"Scared out of his mind. At least they had the good sense to give him his own cell."

"What did he say?"

"That everybody at the jail made him nervous. And that he didn't kill anyone."

Andrew nodded. He believed Tyler. He honestly did. But Andrew hadn't spoken with him last night, nor had he visited him in jail today, as Henry had. He hadn't looked him in the eyes, as Henry had. "You really do believe him, right?" he asked. He shouldn't have had to; he truly didn't believe he had to . . . but he asked anyway.

Henry frowned. "That he didn't kill anyone? Absolutely. But I do think he knew the victim somehow." He paused. "Maybe in the way you and I discussed . . . but I don't know. I can't be sure. He didn't want to talk about it. And I had to be careful. We were whispering, but we weren't alone. There were guys in another cell and a cop standing not far away."

"But you think he might have done . . . something?"

"I don't know. Maybe."

Andrew took in a deep breath, blew it out slowly. "But he's okay right now?"

"Depends on your standard for 'okay.' He's scared, like I said. He'd obviously been crying, which probably didn't go over well with the cops' other weekend guests. On the way out, I let them know who I was, my relation to Tyler, and the kinds of things I might do if I found out they hadn't been nice to my brother."

"And you said we got him a good lawyer?"

"The best. Rachel Addison. She's already on the case. Ran into her in the parking lot outside the station a little while ago. She was on her way in to meet with him. I told her about Tyler's issues. She said she'd keep it short today to avoid overwhelming him. She's going back tomorrow, even though it's Sunday. I asked if I could sit in, but she shot that down."

"Of course she did." Andrew thought back to his days as an assistant state attorney, before his turn as the state's attorney general and then his ascension to governor. "I never faced her. She was pretty new back then. But I remember hearing good things."

"I asked her to call me later. I'll let you know what she says." Andrew nodded. "So, I assume the mystery phone hasn't rung, or you would have told me by now."

"Not yet."

Andrew pulled the bag containing the phone from his pocket and put it on his desk.

"I think it's time to take that thing seriously," Henry said. "Whoever that guy was, he knew there was going to be an arrest of some kind. That phone is definitely not a prank. I hoped for a while that it might be, but it's not."

"No, it's not. But what is it then? How did that guy know Tyler was going to be arrested?"

"Two theories: either the guy is a cop or someone with a direct line to the cops . . . or he's the real killer."

"But what does he want?" Andrew asked.

Henry shrugged. "Whatever it is, he obviously wants it from *you*. Maybe because you're rich. Maybe because you're the governor. Maybe all of the above."

"Either way . . ."

"Either way, it might be time to turn the phone in to the authorities."

"You're the authorities. Take it."

"No, I mean through official channels. All signs point to it being evidence in the murder of a young woman, with the prime suspect being the brother of the state's governor. I think from this point on, we should treat it as such. Turn it over to the troopers on your security team today. Tell them what the guy said. They'll get it into the right hands."

"Won't everyone wonder why I didn't do it yesterday when I first got it?"

"Say the guy seemed like a crackpot. You stuck the phone in your pocket and forgot about it. When Tyler was arrested, what the guy said came back to you."

Andrew thought about it. That was probably the way to go. There might be questions about the delay, but the story Henry concocted was plausible. Andrew had no idea whether turning in the phone would help or hurt his brother's cause, but it was undeniably evidence of . . . something, so he had an obligation, legally and even morally, to give it to the proper authorities.

He had just reached that decision when the mystery phone rang.

CHAPTER TWELVE

The phone was on its third ring when Henry said to Andrew, "Answer it."

"Are you sure we should?"

Henry had no doubt about it. "We might not get another chance. He might never call back, and we could lose this lead."

Andrew nodded and took the phone from the sandwich bag.

"Put it on speaker," Henry said quickly.

Andrew did, and said, "Yes?"

"Is this Governor Kane?"

The voice sounded mechanical. Flat, inflectionless, robotic. Henry figured that unless Stephen Hawking was their mystery man, the guy was using a voice-changing device. Those things did a great job masking a person's real voice. They were also easily obtainable. Hell, there were even phone apps that did the job and did it well.

"It is. Who's this?"

"Please don't insult me, Governor. Or can I call you Andrew?"

"Let's stick with 'Governor.'"

After a creepy, mechanical, monotone chuckle, the caller said, "I'm glad you kept the phone."

"What do you want?"

"Am I on speaker?"

Andrew looked at Henry, who nodded. "You are."

"Ah, so I'm guessing your brother is there with you. Hello, Henry."

Henry hated this guy's guts already. "I'm here," he said. "What's this all about?"

"Governor Andy," the caller said, simultaneously dismissing Henry and disrespecting Andrew, "as you know, your brother Tyler is in deep trouble. Nobody yet knows how deep . . . except for me. Because I put him there."

Henry quickly slid his cell phone from his pocket, opened its voice memo application, and began recording.

"What did you say? I didn't catch all of that."

After a brief pause, the caller said, "Go ahead and record this, Henry. I doubt it will do you much good. You won't get any helpful information about me from the call, not with my voice masked. And if you play this for anyone claiming it proves Tyler's innocence, they'll just think you faked it. But knock yourself out."

Henry had once tracked a reluctant witness to a gym. The witness, who hadn't been happy about that, had hit Henry squarely in the balls with a twenty-pound barbell. Henry hadn't hated that guy nearly as much as he hated this caller. Unfortunately, the caller might have been right about the usefulness of a recording. Still, it couldn't hurt to have it. He kept recording.

Andrew said, "What do you mean, you're the one who put Tyler in trouble? Did you call the police about him? Fake an anonymous tip?"

"No, Governor Andy," the caller said, and the monotone robot voice was becoming an ice pick in Henry's ear. "I mean I killed Sally Graham and framed Tyler for it."

Holy hell.

"I did a really good job of it, too. Very thorough. Watched your family's house in Manchester for months, knew everyone's schedules, knew when Tyler would be home, alone, without an alibi. It's a great frame job. A lot of moving parts to it. I'm actually quite proud of it. In my opinion, it's a masterpiece."

"Congratulations," Henry said. "Give us your address, so I can come and shake your hand."

"Governor Andy," the caller said, dismissing Henry yet again, which was starting to royally piss him off, "I know you're wondering what this is all about. Why would someone frame your innocent little brother for murder? What could he possibly want? Well, I'll tell you . . ."

Henry exchanged a quick glance with Andrew.

"Soon," the caller said. "I'll tell you soon. You're not ready to hear it yet."

"Sure I am," Andrew said.

Henry added, "Try us."

"Sorry, not yet. Obviously, I want something. I wouldn't go through all of this for nothing . . . taking the life of an innocent woman . . . ruining the life of an innocent, mentally challenged young man. I felt bad about the girl, by the way. I didn't like killing her, didn't enjoy it . . . but the truth is that innocent people suffer and die all the time. It's just the way it is."

"Listen," Andrew said, "It's no secret that my family has money. How much—"

"I'm only going to say this once so that we don't waste time on it . . . this isn't about money. Don't mention it again. You understand?"

Henry was mildly surprised. He figured this would be at least a little bit about money.

"Then tell us what this *is* about," Andrew said. "What do you want from us?"

"*Us?* Meaning you and Henry? I don't need anything from Henry. Just you, Governor Andy. Only you can give me what I want. But you won't want to give it to me. It's within your power, but you'll be reluctant. And if I tell you what it is now, you'll just say no. I want to wait until you're more likely to say yes."

"And when do you think that will be?"

"When Tyler has suffered a bit more in jail. When it becomes clear to you and to everyone else that he's going to be convicted of first-degree murder and sent to prison for the rest of his life."

"Why the hell should I give you anything?" Andrew asked.

"Because I can taketh away, and I can giveth."

"Meaning?"

"Meaning I took away your brother's freedom, and I can give it back to him. I can prove his innocence beyond a shadow of a doubt."

"How?" Henry asked.

"You'll have to take my word for it right now. I can set him free. Or I can bury him deeper. Much deeper. It will be up to you, Governor. Give me what I want, and they'll have to dismiss the charges against him. Refuse, and the case against poor Tyler will become so airtight, even your own mother would vote to convict him, if she were still alive."

God, his mechanical voice was grating. And who the hell did he think he was, mentioning their mother? Henry couldn't wait to find this guy and jam the voice-changer so far down his throat, he'd have no choice but to speak through it for the rest of his life.

"And I should mention," the caller added, "if you fail to answer my calls, or if I even suspect that you shared this little connection of ours with the authorities—brother Henry excluded, of course—then it's over. Your chance to help Tyler will be gone, and I'll give the cops everything they need to lock him up for the rest of his life."

"I don't take threats well," Andrew said.

"Don't sell yourself short. I have the feeling you're going to be great at it."

"Just tell me what you want, damn it."

The caller hesitated, then said. "I honestly don't think you're ready to hear it . . . but okay." He paused again, solely for dramatic effect, it seemed. "There's a prisoner in Southern State Correctional Facility named Gabriel Torrance. I want him released. And I don't just want his sentence commuted. I don't want him to have to stay in a halfway house or shelter when he gets out. I want him pardoned, free and clear. And I want it done in a week."

Henry wasn't sure what he had expected, but it hadn't been that.

Andrew sat back in his chair. He opened his mouth to speak, then closed it again. Finally, he said, "I . . . couldn't do that."

"As governor, you have the power, don't you?"

"Technically, but . . . I mean, only in the most extraordinary circumstances . . ." Henry wasn't used to seeing his older brother struggle for words. "I just . . . I couldn't do that."

"No?"

"No. And even if I wanted to . . . a week? That's way too fast. There's just no way . . ." He trailed off.

Something like a robotic sigh came from the speakerphone. "That's really unfortunate. But you might change your mind if you have enough incentive. For now, I'll give you a little time to think about it. I'll call you soon. Until I do, think about your brother going down for first-degree murder and spending the rest of his days in prison."

The line went dead.

CHAPTER THIRTEEN

The caller placed the burner phone and voice changer on his desk, where he kept them when he didn't need them: in the far right corner, with the phone on the left and the voice changer beside it on the right, the two devices almost but not quite touching. Perfect.

The call to Governor Kane had gone as expected. The man wasn't close to being ready to agree to release Gabriel Torrance. Not even a little. But that would change before long. First, Tyler Kane had to stew in jail for a while. And the family had to worry. And put pressure on Governor Andy. And the governor would have to start feeling guilty, believing he could do something to end his poor brain-damaged brother's torment.

Yes, all was going according to plan so far.

His black three-ring binder, which he had come to think of as his bible, lay on the desk in front of him, open to Part II, Section B, Subsection 1, "First Governor Call." In a plastic sleeve was a piece of paper with his numbered talking points for the conversation. He had hit on every one. Perfect.

He was closing the binder when, without thinking about it, he flipped back to Part I, Section C, Subsection 3, "The First Death." The first page was a highly detailed plan for Sally Graham's murder. The second page was a list of the daily schedules of people relevant to the plan, along with descriptions of the vehicles they drove, license plate numbers where applicable, and other potentially important details. He was looking at page three now, though, the pencil sketch he had made before killing Sally. He had been honest when he'd told Andrew and Henry Kane that he hadn't enjoyed killing her, but it had been necessary. Sometimes innocents were hurt during his jobs. It was unavoidable. He took solace, though—a little pride, even—in the fact that he had carried out the murder perfectly. Every single scripted moment executed with efficiency and precision. He closed the thick binder, leaned back in his chair, and allowed his eyes to drift up to the wall above his desk. His canvas. His art. His masterpiece.

Photographs taped to the wall. And news stories. And copies of pages from his binder. And a detailed timeline spanning several sheets of paper taped end to end, events written on it in black pen, some that had already occurred, others planned but yet to take place. Thin yarn of various colors—a veritable rainbow—attached to thumbtacks, stretching from one item to the next . . . from a photograph to an event on the timeline, from a news story to a sketch he had made. Dozens of threads, dozens of connections, forming a web across a mosaic that covered an entire wall, the visual representation of a plan he had crafted over the course of more than a year. A plan he had finally put into motion the other day. A plan that was going very well so far.

In fact, it was going perfectly.

CHAPTER FOURTEEN

Andrew stared at the phone in his hand. Henry had stopped recording on his own phone.

"I can't do what he wants," Andrew said.

"He's right, though, isn't he?" Henry asked. "You do have the power?"

He did. As state governors went, Vermont's was one of the least powerful in the nation. There had been studies conducted comparing the power of the country's governors, using various criteria, including veto and appointment power and budgeting authority, that ranked Vermont's chief executive dead last on the power chart, tied with Rhode Island's governor. Nonetheless, as governor, Andrew was the state's highest-ranked politician—as well as the commander-in-chief of its armed forces, its chief legislator, and the voice of the people—and when it came to the power to grant pardons or clemency, his authority actually exceeded that of many of his more powerful counterparts from other states. While other governors, for example, might be prohibited from issuing a pardon except upon the recommendation of a board specifically tasked with evaluating pardon requests, Vermont's statutes granted its governor the exclusive authority to do so, though he could seek input from the parole board if he so chose. In fact, in some states, applications for clemency were required to be submitted to such boards, which might then forward recommendations to their governors, but in Vermont, applications must be sent directly to the governor's office.

"Yes, I have the power," Andrew said. "His deadline of a week would be tough, though. I would have to pull a *lot* of strings to make that happen. These things take months. That's irrelevant, though. It doesn't matter that I technically have the power. I just can't do it. Longstanding tradition in this office has been to grant clemency only for the most compelling reasons."

"I'd say Tyler being framed for murder is pretty compelling."

"That's not what I mean, and you know it. Full pardons are a rare thing in Vermont. Less so in some states, but *here*, people tend to notice."

"It just means his sentence would be over, right?"

"Yes, but it's more than that. *Commutation* is a reduction in penalty. It says the person whose sentence was commuted has been punished enough. A full *pardon* is more like I'd be saying that he probably didn't deserve punishment in the first place. His offense is essentially forgiven."

"I know the difference," Henry said. "I just meant that, practically speaking, the effect would be that his time in prison would be finished."

"What I'm trying to say is that pardons are a bigger deal in Vermont than in most other states. This wouldn't go unnoticed. But that's beside the point. As governor, I absolutely can't let myself be blackmailed. So it's out of the question. Which means that maybe you're right. Maybe it's time to give this to the authorities."

"Wrong," Henry replied.

"What?"

"That's the wrong move."

"Five minutes ago, you said it was the right move."

"Everything changed when that phone rang," Henry said. "We have to find this guy. Without getting the authorities involved."

"*You're* the authorities, remember?"

"I mean officially. Trust me, we want to keep this to ourselves. And we need to find this guy, fast. You still can't remember what he looked like?"

"No."

"Okay," Henry said as he lifted a knapsack from the floor and placed it on the desk. "We'll do it another way." He opened the bag and removed a small case, which Andrew recognized as a fingerprint kit. Andrew didn't need his brother to tell him that Henry had to take elimination prints. Andrew and the man who had given him the phone were the only two people they were certain had touched it, so once Andrew's prints were identified, at least some of the remaining ones should belong to the suspect.

Henry donned latex gloves and took Andrew's prints one by one, then methodically lifted several clean fingerprints from the phone.

"With luck," Henry said, "these won't belong to just you and some store clerk who sold our guy the burner phone he's no doubt using. You're positive he wasn't wearing gloves?"

"I'm positive. Our hands came together, like we were shaking, when he handed the phone to me. I'd have remembered gloves."

"Okay." Henry filed away all the prints he'd taken into a compartment of the print kit before stowing it away. "Now, in case we crap out on the prints, which wouldn't surprise me, we need to try to identify the guy by his appearance."

Andrew knew he had made it clear that he couldn't remember what the man looked like, so Henry was obviously going somewhere else with this. "Video?" he asked.

"If there is any. And photos."

Andrew nodded. It was a possibility. "I'll ask Jim Garbose whether we shot any official video or pictures of the ribbon cutting."

"Which one is Garbose again?"

"Press secretary."

"Oh, right. We'll take anything they have."

"What if they don't have anything?"

"Hopefully, they do. Obviously, we want to keep this quiet, just you and me for now. But if your people don't have anything, maybe Garbose knows which local news outlets had cameras there. Did you see any?"

Andrew hesitated. "Henry . . . are we sure we want to keep this just between us? Maybe we should give some more thought to turning this phone in. The caller just confessed to murder. If we get the state police on it, the Major Crime Unit, they can help. They can do most of—"

Henry shook his head. "Major Crime is already on it. And they think Tyler's guilty, remember?"

"But what's wrong with telling them about this guy? We could probably use their help. Their resources."

"First, I have access to a lot of those resources anyway. And second, I see a few things wrong with telling them. For example, what if the guy never calls back? We look like liars. And worse, what if he finds out we involved the authorities, and he never calls back specifically *because* we did that? For all we know, he's a cop. Or his brother's a cop. Don't forget what he said: if he thinks we've gone to the police, he'll make it worse for Tyler. Which I have to believe he can, like I also have to believe he can actually help Tyler if he wants to. But there's something else wrong with going official with this . . ."

Henry trailed off, forcing Andrew to say, "What?"

"You won't want to hear this, but I have to say it: as soon as we do that, we close the door on an important option."

"Which is?"

"Doing what the son of a bitch wants, if it comes to that. Giving him what he's asking for to get Tyler out of this."

"Henry, I told you. I can't—"

"I know, I know. But hear me out. If we work this ourselves, maybe we catch this guy, and everyone lives happily ever after except for the scumbag behind this . . . and, I guess, Sally Graham. That's the best result at this point. But if, God forbid, it turns out that we can't find him, you can still give him what he wants and save Tyler. Is that the optimal result? Hell, no. But at least that option is available to us as long as we don't turn this phone in. But if we get all official with this, that road is closed forever. You'd never be able to do a quid pro quo and release a prisoner to get Tyler out of jail with people watching. It would be—"

"An abuse of power," Andrew finished for him.

Henry hesitated a moment. "I wasn't going to say that."

"You can't deny it, though."

Henry said nothing. Because Andrew was right. There was no denying that *that* was precisely what it would be. Andrew Kane, who had run a clean campaign against a dirty opponent and pulled off an upset that landed him in the governor's office, would be doing the very kind of thing for which he had criticized his predecessor, the kind of thing he had railed against since his first day at Harvard Law School, in fact.

How could he do it? How could he barter with a murderer for his brother's freedom? How could he use the power of his office to set a convicted criminal free in exchange for services rendered? While at the same time looking the other way as the true murderer disappeared?

He had promised Vermonters an end to government corruption, for at least as long as he was in a position to do anything about it. He had promised to scrub away the slime left by years of former Governor John Barker's administration. The graft and backroom bargains, the greasing of skids, the end runs, the government contracts bought and sold, the scratching one another on the back in the shadows—nothing ever proven, but something about which there was little doubt. Such was John Barker's legacy. It was how he'd earned the nickname "Jackpot" Barker, which he always hated, but which never had stopped him from acting like a slot machine. Deposit money, grasp his hand firmly and shake, and . . . *Jackpot!* A building contract or exclusive manufacturing deal drops out. You can't win if you don't play . . . or pay. And plenty of shady people and companies that were long on money and short on scruples did both. And though Barker's malfeasance eventually became the state's worst-kept secret, he had somehow managed to hide most of his illicit gains behind falsified records and lying coconspirators. He'd made great investments, he'd said. He was untouchable. And so when he left office, instead of taking up residence in an eight-by-eight-foot cell, he'd moved into a 200-year-old farmhouse in Old Bennington, which he'd expanded, renovated, and upgraded at a cost of $4 million—some of which, it was rumored, he'd actually paid for himself.

In truth, that didn't bother Andrew much. Putting Barker in jail hadn't been his focus. He'd been concerned with ending the corruption and polishing the image of the governor's office, restoring the faith the people had in its government before Jackpot Barker took charge of it. So he had run against Barker, of whom Vermonters had grown tired, and he'd won. He'd earned the trust of the people, a trust he had solemnly promised to hold in clean hands.

And now there he was, debating whether to breach that trust.

"And what about you?" he asked Henry. "You're a sworn officer of the law. In Internal Affairs, no less. You're the one who investigates cops who do the kind of thing we're talking about here, concealing evidence of a crime . . . a murder, for God's sake. You're not troubled by this?"

Henry shrugged. "There was probably a time I might have felt more bothered about it. Times change, though, you know? Over the years, you see things on the job, do things, and well . . . let's just say I could probably live with it. But listen, Andy, you don't have to make any decisions right now. We don't even know if he's going to call back. But if he does, I think we should have our options open."

Andrew almost protested, but something made him remain silent. Henry didn't seem nearly as troubled as Andrew about sitting on this evidence. Was Henry simply a worse public servant, or was he a better brother?

"I'm not going to release a prisoner before he serves his time or makes parole," Andrew said. "I'm not thrilled about keeping this evidence to ourselves, but allowing myself to be blackmailed into granting clemency for personal reasons? That's another thing altogether. I just can't do it."

Henry nodded as if he understood, though Andrew suspected he was doing it for show. "I hear you. Let's hope it doesn't come anywhere close to that. You just talk to your press person and see if we got this guy on film or tape or anything, okay?"

"What are you going to do?"

"Run the prints. See if we get lucky. Also, I'm gonna find out who the hell Gabriel Torrance is and hopefully figure out why someone would want him out of jail badly enough to do all of this. Sound good? We on the same page?"

Andrew looked out the window into the backyard of the rented house. A brown and white bird danced along a nearby tree limb.

"Andrew? Do we agree to keep this to ourselves for now, keep our options open for a while?"

Andrew nodded and, for the first time since having taken the oath of office more than three years ago, felt less than clean.

CHAPTER FIFTEEN

"Your brother's hiding something," Rachel Addison said to Molly. "You know that, right?"

Molly noticed the lawyer's perfectly manicured nails, the shade of polish an exact match for the central color in the stylish silk scarf around her neck. The scarf, which might have been Hermès—Molly was never sure about things like that—was the perfect accoutrement to Addison's rich satin blouse. It was evident where the woman spent some of the money she'd earned through her considerable rates. Molly had the money to dress like that, too. She simply didn't have the desire. "I can't imagine what Tyler would be hiding," she said, "if he is."

Addison sipped her coffee and caught the eye of the waitress across the room. She tapped the rim of her cup, and the waitress nodded and headed toward the kitchen.

"As his attorney," Addison continued, "I don't have to know everything for the arraignment on Monday—I actually have all I need right now—but I'm hoping he'll be more forthcoming eventually."

"It's a bit hard to break through his walls, but once he gets to know you and realizes you're on his side and not one of the people responsible for sticking him behind bars, I think he'll open up to you—though he may need a reminder about Henry telling him he's allowed to talk to his lawyer."

"I'm not sure I connected with him as well as I could have this morning," Addison admitted. "You prepared me for him, told me what to expect, but I wasn't as skillful as I probably could have been. I'll be better at it when I see him again tomorrow."

The waitress arrived, topped off their cups, then weaved her way through the room, stopping at a few other tables to offer refills.

"Molly . . ." Addison began before trailing off.

"Yes?"

She looked down into her coffee a moment before continuing. "There's only one time that I ever put a defendant on the stand, but I think it might help Tyler's case, if this goes to trial."

"You think it'll go to trial?"

The lawyer did a slight shoulder shrug, combining it with a face Molly interpreted as *I'd love to tell you otherwise, but . . .*

"And if it goes to trial," Molly said, "you might want him to testify?"

"He came across to me as very sympathetic. The jury would like him."

"That's good."

"It is. But I'm wondering whether . . ." She trailed off again.

"Whether he's capable of it?"

"That's right. I'm just looking for your impressions here. I'm really wondering how you think he might hold up under questioning, whether direct examination by me or cross-examination by the prosecution."

Molly thought for a moment. "I'm not sure. When he's scared or nervous, he gets flustered. He might say the wrong thing."

Addison nodded. "Might not be the best thing then. I'll think about it. And we'll have him undergo complete medical and psychiatric evaluations."

"What for, exactly?"

"A variety of things. Mostly capacity to be culpable if it were proven that he did, in fact, do what he's accused of. And depending on the medical and psychiatric evaluations, we may be able to get a helpful concession or two from the court if we need them."

"Like what?"

Addison paused. "You know, I don't need to bog you down with all of this right now. Your plate is full. Let's get through the arraignment and worry about the rest later. But, Molly?"

"Yes?"

"Eventually, you'll get to visit him, and when you do, we might need whatever connection you have with him to figure out what he's not sharing with me."

For the next few minutes, Addison discussed what to expect at the arraignment, their chances of the judge agreeing to bail, and conditions the court might attach to any such agreement. She asked questions, taking notes, and patiently answered Molly's questions in return.

Finally, Addison asked, "Anything else I can tell you before Monday?"

"After the arraignment, will Tyler be going back to jail?"

"Most likely."

"All the way until trial?"

"Maybe."

"That could be months, right?"

Addison nodded.

"He'll never survive that," Molly said. "You met him. You saw how he is. He wouldn't . . ." She trailed off, shaking her head.

Images came unbidden—not memories, exactly, but snippets of them . . . putting ice cubes into Tyler's steaming soup; huddling on his bed with him in the dark, in their footed pj's, riding out a thunderstorm together; showing him over and over how to tie his sneakers; resting her hand on his hot, feverish cheek; telling him that he wasn't stupid and that anyone who called him that was nothing but a bully.

"He can't stay in jail," she said emphatically.

"I'm going to argue for bail," Addison said. "It was a violent crime, so the judge might deny it, or he might set bail so high that there's no chance of you guys paying it, even if you're as rich as everyone thinks you are."

"But there's a chance?"

"Judge Finley's reasonable. Plus, there are a lot of extenuating circumstances I can argue. So yeah, there's at least a chance I can get him house arrest. He'd wear an ankle monitor, be restricted to the house, probably, but he'd be home."

Molly thought for a moment. "That would be good. That would be really good. He needs that."

"I'll do my best." She paused, waiting. "No more questions?"

"I guess not."

"Okay." Addison stood, dropped a twenty on the table. "I'll see you in court on Monday." She started to walk away.

"Rachel?"

Addison turned back. "Yes?"

"That defendant you put on the stand? How'd that turn out?"

After a brief hesitation, Addison said, "I still believe it was the right thing to do."

Molly wasn't sure the cryptic reply was what she wanted to hear. She watched the lawyer leave the café, then spent the next half hour staring blankly down at her cold cup of coffee.

CHAPTER SIXTEEN

Henry sat at his desk in the IAU, ignoring the files stacked on its surface, as he'd been doing for the past three hours. His active investigations could wait; he was busy with other things. First, he'd looked into Gabriel Torrance. Squeaky-clean record prior to his conviction for a nonviolent crime. No known criminal associations. There was simply no obvious reason why anyone would go to such extraordinary lengths to secure his early release from prison. Henry would go over it all with Andrew and see if his brother—a former assistant state attorney and ex–attorney general—could see something that Henry couldn't.

Second, he was striking out in his efforts to identify their unknown caller. He'd eliminated Andrew's prints from those taken from the mystery phone; then he'd run the remaining ones through the FBI's integrated fingerprint system, all of which led to . . . nothing. No hits, which meant their caller didn't fall into any of the numerous categories of people whose prints end up in the Feds' database, including those who had been arrested, been employed by state or federal government, served in the military, applied for a gun permit in states requiring them, worked in professions requiring government licenses or background checks, and a few other categories that likewise didn't apply.

Henry took a sip of his coffee, sweetened with four sugars—he didn't like coffee all that much, but he needed the caffeine and he loved the sugar—then leaned back in his chair and thought a moment. He lifted his phone off the desk and looked again at the texts he'd exchanged with Andy an hour ago, as if they would somehow contain new information.

Henry: Any photos or video of our guy?

Andrew: No. I checked. Only of me.

Henry: Nothing of you mingling with the masses after your speech?

Andrew: No. Small turnout. They don't film the crowd unless it's big enough to make me look important.

Henry: Did your press guy check with the local newspeople?

Andrew: Yes. No luck there.

Another dead end.

He'd already driven back to the new senior center to look for exterior security cameras in the vicinity that might have captured the area where the ribbon cutting took place but hit a figurative brick wall. Dead ends appeared to be the day's blue-plate special.

He sighed and reached for his coffee mug, only to find it nearly empty. He locked the door behind him and headed for the break room. Just before he reached it, he heard Andrew's voice. He turned the corner and found a handful of cops sitting at tables or leaning against walls, all facing the TV on the wall in the far corner of the room. On-screen, Andrew was standing behind a podium looking grave.

"I understand that you all have questions," he said. "The public has questions. And I'll do my best to answer them, given a little time. But for now, I'm going to ask you to—"

Offscreen, a woman called out, "With respect, Governor, you're right. The public does indeed have questions." Henry recognized the voice as belonging to Angela Baskin, a reporter with one of the local news stations. "And it seems as though you—"

"Ms. Baskin, I'm standing before you today specifically so I can answer questions. I will do so as your governor . . . one who happens to be in a fairly unique and, yes, tragic situation. Tragic for Sally Graham and her family, of course. But also tragic for my brother Tyler, who I believe in my heart to be innocent. And tragic for our family, as well. So I'll respond to questions in my official capacity, but at the same time, I'd like to ask you to respect our family's privacy at this extraordinarily difficult time."

"Governor . . ." Henry heard Baskin call out.

Angela Baskin wasn't a friend to Andrew Kane. To Henry, it seemed as though an undercurrent of disapproval always flowed just beneath the surface of her coverage of him during his campaign and the gubernatorial race, and even more so since he'd won the election. Perhaps she was suspicious of any politician around whom no hint of a scandal had ever swirled. Maybe she'd been on Jackpot Barker's payroll, like so many others had been. Henry had heard she was driving around in a new Jaguar lately, which seemed a bit of a reach for a reporter on a local news station. Whatever the reason, her stories about Andrew never had the same impartial feeling as stories by other reporters. Henry could only imagine her satisfaction, her outright excitement, about this story.

"Ms. Baskin, please . . ." Andrew said.

"Gonna be a rough ride for our beloved governor," someone in front of Henry said. Sean Duhon. Henry had never liked him.

"My heart bleeds for him," another detective said. Kelsey Watroba. She was smart. Henry had almost asked her out once or twice. He sure as hell wouldn't do so now.

"Karma's a bitch, ain't it?" Aaron Rydell that time. Henry actually liked Aaron.

He understood where they were coming from. Though Andrew's investigation into the Vermont State Police—as part of his larger efforts to scrub away the stain of Jackpot Barker's administration—had yielded only two bad apples, even that minor result contributed to an erosion in the public's trust in the VSP, which didn't endear the new governor to anyone in the department. Most believed that Governor Kane could have gone about the entire affair a little more quietly.

Though Henry understood their animosity, and their satisfaction at seeing the governor squirm under questioning, it pissed him off that no one gave a thought to their brother Tyler, whom Henry likewise believed was innocent. He reluctantly admitted to himself, though, that if his last name weren't Kane, he'd probably be saying the same things they were saying.

On TV, Andrew said, "And while I continue to believe Tyler is innocent, my office and my family are interested in finding the truth, whatever it may be, and seeing that Sally Graham's murderer is brought to justice . . . whoever he may be."

Henry knew Andrew well. He was doing the best he could up there. He looked strong, forthright, and determined, and still managed to seem fairly sympathetic. But Henry knew he was struggling inside. Henry was witnessing his brother's worst moment in the public eye.

"Oh, I'm sure you want to see someone brought to justice," Duhon said to the TV, "as long as it isn't your retard brother."

Aaaaand . . . that did it. Henry began to squeeze his way through the others, heading for the coffee machine. "Excuse me," he said once or twice. As he passed Duhon, he bumped him a bit harder than necessary. "Excuse me." He reached the coffee maker and filled his cup. "Hey, Duhon, I was just thinking about you the other day."

"Yeah? Why's that?"

"I can't remember. I'll have to think about it. I'm wondering if something crossed my desk recently with your name on it. I can't be sure, though . . ."

Everyone in the room knew what that would mean. On TV, Andrew kept answering questions, but all eyes were on Henry and Duhon now.

"Bullshit," Duhon said.

"Yeah, probably." Henry added four sugars to his coffee. "But no big deal if it did, right? You're probably squeaky clean, aren't you? There's nothing I'd find if I looked into you, asked around about you a bit, is there?"

Duhon tried to scoff, but it sounded more like an aborted sneeze. "You're no better than your brother."

Henry nodded. "You got that right. And you know what? Neither are you. Or anyone else in this room."

He shouldered his way back across the break room. At the door, he turned and put on a thoughtful expression. "I'll see if I can figure out where I saw your name recently. When I do, you may hear from me. Till then, have a nice day."

He left and had gone no more than four steps when he heard Duhon refer to him in a terribly unkind way. Someone told him he'd shut the hell up if he was smart. Someone else said no one had ever accused Duhon of being smart. The last thing Henry heard was someone say, "I don't know about you guys, but I can't wait to see how Kane's brother committing murder plays on social media."

That last comment slowed Henry's steps. He thought a moment. Then he hurried back to his office, trying not to spill his coffee.

CHAPTER SEVENTEEN

On Monday morning, a mere two and a half days after his arrest, Tyler looked a year older to Molly. Led by a sheriff's deputy, he shuffled into the courtroom in the same clothes he had been wearing when he was arrested. His hands were cuffed in front of him, attached to a chain around his waist. The deputy directed him to an empty chair at the defendant's table next to Rachel Addison, who sat waiting, her suit conservative yet undeniably chic, her posture perfect. Molly hoped he would turn and see her, see that she was there for him as best she could be, but he simply sat beside his attorney. The deputy took up a position five feet behind him, just in front of the railing separating the gallery of onlookers from where the action would take place.

Molly knew it must have been her imagination, but Tyler's skin looked gray, as though sunlight hadn't touched it in months. A three-day growth sprouted in patches across his chin, cheeks, and neck. He was a creature of habit—rituals seemed to soothe him—and from the day he was old enough to shave, he'd done it with great care every morning. He didn't always lift the toilet seat when he urinated, or wipe it clean when his aim was off, but when it came to shaving, he was meticulous, so she knew the hair on his face must have been bothering him. And knowing that bothered her.

She watched him sitting with his shoulders slumped, his head bowed. It pained her not to be able to walk up to him, tousle his hair, and let him know that she was there for him and always would be. At least he wasn't completely alone, with Rachel Addison seated beside him.

The room was packed with spectators, the seats filled with members of the media as well as citizens looking for an interesting alternative to one of the daytime courtroom reality shows. For those in attendance, the arraignment of the governor's brother on a murder charge was obviously a must-see event. Despite the crowd, though, other than the defendant, Molly was the only Kane in attendance. Andrew had thought it would be a mistake to be there. He didn't want the whole affair to become more of a circus than it was already likely to be. More important, he didn't want to appear to be trying to influence the proceedings with his presence, a move that would play very badly in the press, and worse, wouldn't look good to Judge Finley, with whom he'd been friendly since Andrew's days as an assistant state attorney. That made sense, she supposed. Henry, too, was absent, saying that he was working on something related to Tyler's situation and couldn't be there. She had no reason to doubt him—he loved Tyler *almost* as much as she did—but she still wished he were there, for both Tyler and her. Instead, she sat utterly alone in the packed gallery and watched as Judge Reginald Finley read the charges against her dear twin brother and asked how he pleaded.

Rachel Addison stood, and at her gentle urging, Tyler did, too. After a discreet nudge, he said, "I'm not guilty." Then he sat down.

A murmur rippled through the room, as though this were something no one could have foreseen, as though such a plea was shocking and unheard of, despite the fact that this was how nearly every arraignment played out.

The judge wrote something down, then shuffled a few papers up on the bench. He looked toward the defense table.

"Ms. Addison, where do we stand on competency? Though I don't have specifics, Mr. Tyler's general condition isn't unknown to me. I don't see a motion here on the issue. Are you planning at this time to raise competency to stand trial as an issue?"

"I'm not, Your Honor. He's innocent, and he wants his day in court to prove it."

"He may be innocent, Counselor, but he won't be in my court if he isn't competent to stand trial."

"Of course. I believe it may be common knowledge that my client suffered a traumatic brain injury when he was a child, just seven years old, which left him with intellectual deficits. But he can recall and relate, and I believe he has sufficient depth of understanding of both his situation and these proceedings to assist with his defense. And he is highly motivated to do so. If the situation changes at any point, Your Honor, we will of course notify the court immediately."

The judge nodded thoughtfully, then looked at Tyler. "Mr. Kane?"

"Yes, sir?"

Addison said something softly to him, and he stood again.

Finley said, "Son, one of my jobs is to make sure you're the kind of person who should face a criminal trial."

"Oh," Tyler said. "Well, if you ask me, I'm not."

A few titters sounded from the gallery. Finley ignored them.

"I don't think you understand. I'm not asking whether you are innocent or guilty. What I mean is, I have to decide whether you fully understand the charges against you, and whether you understand these proceedings and those that will follow, and whether you will be able to converse with your lawyer so as to assist in your own defense."

Tyler had been nodding through all of that. "I do. I mean, I can."

"Mr. Kane, I need to believe that you really understand what's going on here. This is very important. Take your time and really think about it, please."

"Okay."

Tyler lowered his head. And kept it lowered. After nearly a full minute, the whispers began.

Finally, Judge Finely said, "Son?"

Tyler looked up and said, "I'm still thinking." After a nudge from Addison, he added, "Your Honor."

It looked to Molly as though Finley almost smiled. "I appreciate that, Mr. Kane. And now that you've had some time to consider, what do you think? Do you fully understand what's happening here?"

Tyler nodded. "I do. I really do. I know I'm not smart, Your Honor. Everybody else is way smarter than me. But I understand what you guys think I did. You think I killed a lady. I didn't, but you guys think I did."

Finley listened.

Tyler continued. "And I know why we're here today. So you can tell me what you think I did, and I can tell you I'm not guilty. I already said that, and I'll say it again. I'm not guilty. And trial? I understand that, too. That's where we make you guys see that I didn't do it. If we win, I can go home. If not, I'll go to prison for a long time."

Finley nodded. "Go on, Mr. Kane."

"What was the third thing?"

"Whether you can talk with your lawyer and help her defend you."

"Oh, yeah. Well, I've talked to her a couple of times already, and we get along great. She's nice, and she's really smart. She asks questions, and I answer them. She says I'm being helpful, so there's your answer right there, Your Honor."

Finley thought a moment, then said, "You can have a seat now, son." Tyler sat as the judge directed his gaze toward the prosecution's table. "Mr. Phillips?"

Assistant State Attorney Reed Phillips rose to his feet in his precisely tailored suit. "Your Honor, if the defense isn't claiming a competency issue, the state has no problem with that. But we wouldn't want the claim to be raised later."

"I'm sure you wouldn't, Counselor. But you're aware, of course, that the issue of competency can be raised at any time. In fact, if the defendant somehow becomes incompetent to stand trial at any time, Ms. Addison would be ethically bound to raise the issue with the court."

"Of course, Your Honor." Even from twenty feet away, Molly imagined she could hear Phillips swallowing uncomfortably.

Addison, still standing, said, "We'll stipulate to my client's current competency to stand trial, Your Honor, if the court agrees with our assessment on this issue. Capacity to commit the offense, of course, is another matter, and the defense reserves the right—"

"We're not talking capacity here, Ms. Addison," Finley said, "just competency."

Addison nodded and fell silent. Phillips was still standing, mostly, it looked to Molly, because he wasn't sure whether he should sit.

Finley rubbed his chin and regarded Tyler. Finally, he said, "The defendant has convinced me of his competency to stand trial." More murmuring in the courtroom. "Now, what are we thinking about bail?"

In the gallery, Molly sat forward.

"Your Honor," Phillips began, "the charges against the defendant couldn't be more serious. The heinousness of the crime is evident. The facts of the crime indicate that it was preplanned, premeditated. Everything about it suggests that the defendant presents a very real threat to everyone around him. The state asks in the strongest terms that bail be denied. Thank you."

The man and his expensive suit folded neatly back into his chair at the prosecution table.

"Your Honor," Addison said, "for a variety of reasons, most of which are no secret to the court, my client is not your run-of-the-mill defendant. He—"

Judge Finley interrupted. "Should he therefore be given special treatment, Counselor?"

"Of course not, Your Honor. What I'm saying is that there are special circumstances here that mitigate in favor of granting bail."

"I'm listening," the judge said, though from Molly's view in the gallery, that looked far from certain.

"To begin, he's the brother of the sitting governor, as you know. And no, he deserves no special treatment for that reason, but I think he does merit special consideration."

Finley said, "Are you requesting that he be sequestered in jail for his protection until trial? That seems reasonable under the circumstances."

"Not exactly, Your Honor. I'm saying that his familial relationship with the governor makes him unusually recognizable, especially after all of the media coverage of his arrest. Someone as well known as he is would have a very difficult time getting far without being recognized, were that person to jump bail . . . which Mr. Kane would never do, of course."

The judge nodded, almost imperceptibly, and Molly decided that he might have been listening after all.

"My client also has certain . . . limitations, which we have already discussed here, that would make it hard for him to function for long on his own, were he inclined to try such a thing. He's never been outside of Vermont other than in the company of his family. He lives with his sister, and they allow a graduate student to live in their house in exchange for her assistance in helping Tyler when he needs it. And according to his family, though he is fairly comfortable getting around locally on his own, until he was arrested three nights ago, he had never spent a single night away from home—again, without being in the company of his family."

Addison paused, and Phillips seemed on the verge of interjecting but apparently thought better of it.

"The charges against my client are of the most serious nature, to be sure, but he has not been proven guilty of them, and he has, in fact, pled his innocence. More than once today, in fact." A few more titters, which Finley ignored again. "He has no history of violence. He doesn't have the skills to survive on his own, ensuring his adherence to conditions of bail should Your Honor see fit to grant it. And, quite frankly, he would suffer in jail." A murmur rose this time, tinged with annoyance, and Addison quickly added, "We are mindful, of course, of the suffering of others right now. The victim's loved ones in particular. But a man is innocent until proven guilty in this country, and putting Tyler Kane in jail until trial would do him irreparable harm. And if the court needs expert opinion on that, the defense would be happy to provide it."

"Do you have expert opinion to that effect at this moment?"

"No, Your Honor, we haven't had the time, but I can say with confidence that it would be easy to obtain. We're hoping that won't be necessary, though. The defendant's . . . condition is relatively well known, as Your Honor has noted. As the governor's brother, it has been mentioned a number of times in the news. And I daresay the court can see it with its own eyes."

Molly looked at her brother. His head was down. It looked as though he might have been picking at his thumbnail, one of the only activities in which he could engage with his hands secured to the chain around his waist. When he was younger, after the accident, he used to do that when he was in an unfamiliar place or an uncomfortable situation. Sometimes he did it until every one of his fingers bled. She wanted to tell him to stop. She wanted to tell him not to be scared, even though she herself was more scared than she'd ever been, even more than in Afghanistan.

Judge Finley took a deep breath. He scratched absently at a spot on his jawline. "What are you suggesting, Counselor?"

"House arrest. An ankle monitor."

Phillips sprang to his feet like a designer-clad jack-in-the-box. "Your Honor, if I may?"

The judge looked at him. "Are you going to add anything new, Mr. Phillips, or simply repeat what you said earlier?"

"Your Honor?"

"If you're just going to say again that the charges against the defendant are serious and the state believes him to be a danger," Finley said, "I can assure you that you needn't repeat yourself. I was paying attention. I promise."

Phillips hesitated, then said, "Thank you, Your Honor," and slid back into his seat.

"Son?" the judge said, not unkindly.

Addison nudged Tyler, who looked up. "Yeah?" Addison leaned down and whispered to him, and he stood. "Yes, Your Honor," he said.

"You've convinced me that you understand how serious this all is."

"I do, Your Honor. I definitely do."

"Mr. Kane, if I were to let you go home to wait there for trial, which might not be for months, would you be able to stay inside your house, if I ordered that? Stay inside and not leave for any reason at all?"

"What if there's a fire?"

There were a few snickers in the courtroom, but a stern look from the judge silenced them.

"Well, let's say you weren't allowed to leave your property . . . your house and your yard. That way, if there was a fire, you could go outside where it's safe. Could you stay in your house and your yard every day and not leave even once, not one single time, until you have to come back to court? If that's what I ordered, could you do that? I want you to really think about that for a moment." He quickly added, "But just a brief moment, okay?"

There were a few chuckles, and perhaps because they were in response to something of a joke by him, the judge allowed them.

Tyler dropped his head again for a few seconds, then looked up. "I could do that."

Molly saw Reed Phillips begin to rise but apparently think better of it.

"Mr. Kane," Finley said, "if I were to allow you to go home, you would have a device attached to your ankle, and you wouldn't be able to take it off, not even to bathe. It would tell us where you are at all times. It would tell us if you try to break your promise and leave your home. And if you did that, you would be in very big trouble."

"I think I'm already in big trouble."

More snickering, another glare from the judge.

"I'm glad you appreciate that fact, son, but I need you to understand this. If you tried to leave your property, or if you tried to take off the ankle monitor, you would be in even bigger trouble. You would go back to jail immediately, and you would have to spend the rest of your time there until trial. You understand that, don't you?"

Tyler nodded emphatically. "I understand that, sir, and I don't want that. I'd rather be home with my sister, Molly. And my friend Julie. She lives with us and helps me sometimes when Molly isn't around. She makes unbelievable sandwiches."

"They sound delicious. But here's the important part, Mr. Kane . . . you have to come back and stand trial. If you were to run away to avoid trial—"

"I wouldn't run away," Tyler said quickly. "If I ran away, I wouldn't get a trial. And I need a trial because that's where Rachel will prove to everybody that I didn't do the things that you and that guy over there said I did." He pointed at Reed Phillips.

"I didn't say you . . ." Finley trailed off and studied Tyler for several seconds. After a while, Molly finally had to let out a breath she hadn't realized she'd been holding. The longer the judge seemed to be deliberating, the more Molly began to feel hopeful. Phillips must have sensed things tipping the way of the defense, because he again looked as though he might pop up to his feet, but before he could, Finley cleared his throat.

"Given all of the circumstances, I don't believe the defendant to be a significant flight risk. Bail is set at ten million dollars. The defendant will be fitted with an ankle monitor and restricted to his house and its grounds. I believe the Kane property is fenced. He may not step beyond its confines."

Phillips was a blur springing to his feet. "Your Honor—"

"Objection noted, Mr. Phillips."

Addison probably would have sprung to her feet, too, if she hadn't already been standing. "Your Honor, ten million dollars—"

"Is certainly within the means of your client's family. It's no secret they're rich and have been for generations, Counselor. They can afford it. A lower amount wouldn't sufficiently ensure the defendant's appearance at trial."

"Ten million dollars is an awful lot of money for anyone, Your Honor. Even the Kanes."

"The court will accept a ten percent cash bond deposited with the clerk, along with proper guarantees for the balance. I'm hopeful Mr. Kane's family will be able to impress upon him how much they stand to lose from a monetary standpoint should he fail to appear. It's true that I don't consider him a serious flight risk, but a little insurance never hurt."

"Your Honor—"

"Objection noted, Ms. Addison."

After a moment, Addison said, "Thank you, Your Honor," and sat down. Tyler, still standing, looked down at his attorney, then up at the judge behind the bench, then back at Addison. She gently tugged his sleeve, and he sat beside her.

Ten million dollars was indeed a lot of money. Most defendants wouldn't be able to pay it. But the judge was right: the Kanes could afford it, which was precisely why he set the amount so high. As Addison had explained to Molly at coffee on Saturday, though, the family wouldn't necessarily have to pay the entire bail amount set by the judge. In this case, Judge Finley was requiring them to pay only 10 percent—$1 million—provided they could demonstrate that they possessed the assets to cover the remaining $9 million if Tyler failed to appear for trial and would sign paperwork obligating them to do so. When Tyler later showed up in court as ordered, they would get the $1 million back. Molly wasn't concerned about tying up that money until the case was resolved; they could afford it. Nor was she worried about the possibility of losing a total of $10 million, because there was no way Tyler wouldn't appear for his trial. The important thing was that he would be coming home.

The judge and the lawyers covered a few more things, including the scheduling of a preliminary hearing date; then Molly watched her brother stand and allow himself to be led by the deputy toward the door through which they had entered the courtroom earlier. As he walked, Molly willed him to look up, to find her in the gallery, to see that he wasn't alone. Just before he disappeared through the door, their eyes met, and his lit up like flares. She smiled at him and hoped he couldn't see her tears from across the room.

Then he was gone, and Molly was alone in the crowded courtroom.

CHAPTER EIGHTEEN

From his prosecuting days, Andrew was more than familiar with the way bail worked. As soon as Molly called him after the arraignment, he got the firm that handled the family's finances on the phone and set into motion everything necessary to deposit the cash bond with the court and guarantee payment for the balance of the bail amount. Just as he wasn't the kind of man to use his position to apply improper pressure on others to achieve his goals, neither was he inclined to use his family's wealth or name to obtain special treatment. But this was Tyler, for God's sake, so he made it clear that this matter needed to be the finance firm's top priority, and he was assured that it would be. He texted Molly back to tell her that Tyler would be home soon, though it probably would be tomorrow at the earliest. It wasn't as soon as he would have liked, but at least Tyler would be out of jail before long.

He put his cell phone on his desk and turned to Henry, who was sitting in one of the chairs in front of Andrew's utilitarian desk. Papers and file folders sat on the desk in front of him. "A million dollars to get him out," Henry said. "Could have been worse, I guess."

"Could have been a *lot* worse. Finley could have denied bail." They pondered that for a moment, then Andrew said, "You were about to tell me what they found at the house."

The search warrant return inventory, which detailed what was seized pursuant to a search warrant, was public information and could be found in the court clerk's case file. Because the warrant had been executed late Friday night, the state hadn't filed the inventory with the court until today. Henry had gone to the clerk's office at 9:00 a.m., but it hadn't been there yet. When he returned at 11:00 a.m., though, he was able to obtain a copy.

"Looks like they found blood on Tyler's electric bike," Henry said. Andrew knew that the inventory would actually have noted a "bloodlike substance," because tests wouldn't have been conducted on it yet. But cops knew what blood looked like. Which meant it was almost certainly blood. "They also found a pair of bloody sneakers in the garage behind some garden tools. Men's size ten, the same size as all the other shoes in Tyler's closet."

"Damn."

"The affidavit supporting the search warrant said that one of Tyler's coworkers at the shelter said she saw him get into the victim's car hours before she was killed, which Ramsey told me the other night. And apparently, Tyler admitted that to them. Also, an anonymous caller claimed to have seen a guy who looked a lot like Tyler leaving the victim's house around the time of the murder, which Ramsey also told me. Along with blood on the bike and the bloody sneakers, that was enough to get an arrest warrant."

"The guy who framed him is obviously the anonymous neighbor," Andrew said.

"Obviously. And he planted the blood on the bike. And somehow got hold of a pair of Tyler's sneakers, bloodied them up, and hid them for searchers to find."

"He's good."

"Let's hope Rachel Addison is good, too. We need her to be."

"Not if we catch this guy. We don't have anything on him yet, but he must have some connection to Gabriel Torrance. So who is Torrance? What's his deal?"

Henry pushed aside a copy of the search warrant inventory and opened a manila file folder.

"He's nobody," Henry said, referring to the contents of the file. "Gabriel Torrance, thirty-eight, has been a guest at the lovely Southern State Correctional Facility for the past four years and five months, serving a fifty-eight-month sentence for leaving the scene of an accident resulting in serious injury. The other driver broke both his legs."

Andrew did the math. "Hold on a second. This guy only has five months left?"

Henry nodded.

"And someone is willing to kill, and frame an innocent man, to get him out sooner?"

"Looks like it."

Andrew considered that a moment. "And not to minimize his crime, but . . ."

"Yeah, all he did was leave the scene of an accident. And by the way, a witness said the other guy caused the crash. Sure, leaving the scene was a felony, given the seriousness of the injury to the other driver, but still . . . he's not exactly Al Capone. According to the statement he gave when they picked him up ten minutes after the accident, he'd had a beer, so he panicked, worried about a DUI charge. The thing was, they gave him a Breathalyzer right away, and he barely registered. Nowhere near the legal limit."

"How about priors?"

"Up until the accident, Mr. Rogers could have taken good citizenship lessons from this guy. Gandhi was a thug by comparison. Torrance volunteered at a hospital, as well as a homeless shelter, where he also kept the books."

"Don't tell me he's an accountant," Andrew said. Henry nodded. "Before you told me anything about this guy, I was expecting him to be . . ."

"Not an accountant."

"Definitely not. What's he have for family?"

"None. No wife or kids. No siblings. Parents both died years ago."

"So no loved one on the outside who just can't bear to wait another five months to see him again?"

"No one who shows up in his file, anyway."

Andrew hadn't been sleeping well since Tyler's arrest, so maybe he wasn't thinking clearly, but none of this made sense. "Henry, can you see a reason, any reason, why someone would want Torrance out of prison so badly less than half a year before his sentence is up?"

"Nope. Not a one."

Andrew sighed. He rubbed his eyes, pressing the heels of his palms against his closed lids. The intercom on his desk sounded.

"Yes, Peter?" he said to his administrative assistant.

"Sir, I just wanted to remind you that you have to be in the conference room in twenty minutes for—"

"I know," Andrew snapped. A moment later, he added, "Sorry. Thanks." He sighed again.

"Andrew?" Henry said.

Andrew looked at him. Then shook his head. "I don't care if this guy is the next Dalai Lama, I'm not letting him out of prison. I'm not giving in to blackmail. I can't."

Henry nodded but said nothing.

"You don't agree?"

"It's your decision. I'm just thinking about Tyler."

"And I'm not?" Andrew said, heating up. "I'm just as—"

"Relax, Andy. That came out wrong. I just . . . I'm wondering whether it matters all that much if you let Torrance out a little early. He's a nobody who didn't do much wrong, and he's got less than half a year left anyway. Giving him five extra months of freedom is a small price to pay for a lifetime of Tyler's freedom."

"Assuming the caller does what he says he will and gives us the proof of Tyler's innocence he claims to have. If he even has it."

"Yeah, but . . . why not take the risk? If our jack-off caller is on the up-and-up, Tyler's in the clear. If not, a nonviolent offender is back on the street a tiny bit ahead of schedule. Low risk, high reward."

Andrew regarded his brother a moment. Years ago, when Henry was still relatively new to the force, would he have arrived at such a recommendation so easily? Maybe, but Andrew wasn't certain.

"You don't get it," he said. "It wouldn't matter if Torrance has a week left. If he was nothing more than a jaywalker. I can't allow myself to be coerced into letting him out early. Once a blackmailer has you, he'll never let go. Besides, it's a slippery slope. If you take that first step over the line, it's too easy to take the next, then the next. I'm sure Jackpot Barker started by taking a single bribe. Look where he ended up."

"You're not Jackpot Barker."

"Not yet. Listen, Henry, I just can't give in to blackmail. It's about my oath. My integrity."

"It's also about Tyler."

Andrew nodded. "I know that. Believe me, I know. But Tyler didn't kill that woman. We have to trust that the system will work, and he'll be acquitted."

It was Henry's turn to nod. He did it slowly, as if to prove a point. "I'm a cop. You were a lawyer. Do you trust the system completely? Do you trust it with Tyler's life?"

Andrew shrugged. "I have no choice. I have to. But hopefully, it won't come to that. Hopefully, we'll identify our caller soon and find whatever evidence he claims to have that will exonerate Tyler. So where are we on that?"

Henry closed the file on Gabriel Torrance and slipped it into his bag, then pulled out a second file and opened it on the desk.

"The fingerprints got us nowhere," Henry said. "Not in the system. And neither you guys nor the local press seemed to have caught our guy on film or video."

"So we've got nothing?"

"I'm not saying that. Because I'm brilliant and had a flash of inspiration." He paused as though expecting Andrew to weigh in one way or the other on the issue of his brilliance. After a moment, he continued. "I hopped on the Internet and trolled all the big social media sites, trying various hashtags and keywords. *#Ribboncutting. #Governorspeech. #Newseniorcenter.* Whatever. I was at it for hours. And hours. Finally, I got some hits. Apparently, to some people, it's a big deal to see you in person."

"To some people, I think it is."

"They haven't seen you naked like I have."

"You haven't seen me naked in decades. Last time was probably in the bathtub when we were toddlers."

"Well, I wasn't impressed. Anyway, a few people posted and tweeted pictures of you speaking, and some even took shots of you shaking hands with the crowd."

Andrew sat forward. "You got our guy?"

"Maybe."

He slid three photos across the desk. They were printed on plain copier paper.

"These were the only possibilities," Henry said, "based on your fantastic powers of recall. Any of them look familiar?"

The first picture, taken from at least a dozen feet away, showed Andrew shaking hands with a middle-aged man in a baseball cap. He didn't think their guy had worn a hat.

The second picture . . . Andrew froze. *That was him.* Taken from a mere three or four feet away, the photo showed a man reaching toward Andrew's outstretched hand. The man was in profile, but his features were plainly visible. Brown hair, a nondescript face that Andrew nonetheless instantly found familiar. He wore a navy windbreaker. Andrew looked more closely at the man's hand, the one stretching toward his own, and saw something dark and angular, the corner of a black object. A cell phone. Andrew's eyes slid over to the mystery phone sitting on the desk beside his computer.

He didn't even glance at the third photo.

"This is the guy," he said, turning the second picture around for Henry to see.

"You sure?"

"No doubt. See the phone in his hand?"

Henry nodded. "I saw that. Wanted to see if you did before I said anything about it."

"Can you find out who he is?"

"Already did." For each of the men in the photos, even though they had all been photographed in profile, Henry had used computer software to create head-on renderings. From there, he used another handy program available to law enforcement personnel: facial recognition software. It had taken a little while, but he'd been able to find solid possible matches for all three men.

He opened his messenger bag, thumbed through a few folders inside, and removed one. He took a quick look inside, then slid it across the desk. Andrew opened it and stared into the now easily recognizable face. "That's Alexander Rafferty," Henry said. "According to the Department of Motor Vehicles, he has a clean driving record. According to various social media sites, he's got a wife and two daughters and likes brewing his own beer, camping with his girls, and attending backyard barbecues. Nothing about him being a dickhead or a blackmailer, but dickheads rarely admit that they're dickheads, and blackmailers are even less likely to talk about their little hobby."

Andrew studied Rafferty's driver's license photo. He didn't have the slightest doubt that he was looking at their guy. "Does he have a criminal record? Wait, stupid question. His prints weren't in the database."

"Right," Henry said. "The guy's as clean as they come. Except that, in reality, he's a dickhead blackmailer."

"Do we know anything else about him?"

"Again, from Facebook, we know that he's a manager of a local Chili's. I called. He's not scheduled to work today. His wife's a schoolteacher."

Andrew nodded. "So what now?"

"Now I go talk to him and ask him very politely to give us whatever evidence he has that will clear Tyler."

"Very politely?"

"Best to start off polite, anyway."

"Are you going to arrest him?"

"If I can."

Andrew understood. He'd have to admit to something that would give Henry probable cause to arrest him. Or he'd have to invite Henry into his house, and something incriminating would have to be lying around in plain sight. Neither of those things seemed likely.

"And if you can't?"

"Don't worry. Whatever it takes, I'll get what we need to get Tyler out of this mess."

Andrew didn't like the sound of that. The implication of Henry's words. And Henry could sense that.

"Andrew, I'm not gonna cross the line . . ."

"Unless you have to. That's what you're not saying."

Henry sighed. "It's Tyler, you know? It's family."

Andrew didn't want to be talking about this. He didn't want to think about it. He was the governor, for God's sake. He was above talk of vigilante justice. He had always railed against the abuse of government power. How could he now condone—

"I'm gonna talk to the guy," Henry said. "See where it leads. And if it looks like I have to . . . well, it's all me, understand? My decision. My action. Not yours. In fact, you know nothing about it." Andrew opened his mouth to speak, but Henry cut him off. "I know what you're going to say. Don't bother. You couldn't stop me if you wanted to."

He gathered his file and the photographs and stuffed them into his messenger bag.

"Remember, Andrew, if things go sideways, you had nothing to do with anything."

Then he walked out of the office, leaving Andrew to wonder when Henry's blacks and whites had become mere shades of gray.

A moment later, the phone on Andrew's desk emitted its distinct intercom ringtone.

"Yes?"

"Governor Kane," his assistant said, "I just saw your brother leave. You have ten minutes until your meeting downstairs with HUD. I left the file on the corner of your desk before you came in this morning."

Andrew thanked his assistant, then sent Henry a text: Call me when you have news.

Rather than use his ten free minutes to review the file about the controversial housing project he'd be discussing with a room full of people very shortly, Andrew spent the time calculating the odds that his brother wouldn't have to cross the line over the next couple of hours, and wondering whether it would irrevocably change him if he did.

CHAPTER NINETEEN

Henry drove his state-issued Ford Taurus past the gray ranch house, circa mid-1960s, that DMV and property records said belonged to Alexander Rafferty and his wife. No cars were in the driveway or on the street in front of the house, but there was an attached garage with its door down, so a vehicle could have been parked inside. Henry looped around the block, parked two houses away, and walked down to the Rafferty residence. He moved quickly up the driveway, peered into the window in the garage door, and saw a silver Hyundai. Alexander Rafferty appeared to be home. If so, Henry was just moments away from coming face-to-face with the man who had framed Tyler for murder—and another moment after that from knocking the guy flat after he resisted arrest, which Henry planned to make sure he did . . . at least a little.

He stepped over to the front door, keeping his hand near the butt of his pistol, and prepared to ring the doorbell. The door had no peephole, but there was a vertical column of small windows on either side of the door, so Henry would know if Rafferty took a peek at him. He had obviously done his homework, calling Henry by name on the phone, so he mostly likely knew what Henry looked like. If he did, and he didn't open the door right away, Henry planned to kick it in if he could. And if he couldn't, he'd break the window nearest the deadbolt, unlock the door, and run Rafferty down, hopefully before he could get his hands on a weapon.

Henry took a breath and rang the bell. A few seconds later, he was about to ring again when he heard footsteps inside. Not running, not retreating, but approaching calmly. The door opened, and Alexander Rafferty stood just inside.

Henry's initial instinct was to take the guy down immediately, then start asking questions, but the man's demeanor was so calm, so relaxed, that Henry hesitated.

"Yes?" Rafferty said.

"Mr. Rafferty, do you recognize me?"

Rafferty squinted at him. "Should I?"

He was either a hell of an actor, or he had no idea who Henry was.

"I'm Lieutenant Henry Kane, with the Vermont State Police." Keeping his eyes on Rafferty, he pulled out his badge and flashed it with a practiced move. "Any idea why I'm here?"

That was when Henry saw the first crack. In Rafferty's eyes.

"You do," Henry said, "don't you?"

After a moment, Rafferty nodded, and Henry felt a surge of triumph. "I didn't think I was doing anything wrong," the man said in a soft, defeated voice. "It didn't seem like it would be against any law. And to tell you the truth, it wouldn't have mattered if it was. I didn't have a choice. I swear to God, I didn't have a choice."

A tear slipped from the man's eye, and Henry sighed. Alexander Rafferty wasn't their mystery caller.

———

"I was standing with everyone else, waiting for the governor to arrive," Rafferty said. "We're interested in the senior center because my wife's mother died a few months ago, and her father is . . . well, he needs to start getting out of his apartment, you know? And Donna, my wife, she had to work that day, so I said I'd go check it out."

Henry nodded. They were sitting at Rafferty's kitchen table. Rafferty had a cup of coffee in front of him that he hadn't touched since he'd poured it. He'd offered a cup to Henry, who had declined.

"Anyway," Rafferty continued, "I'm standing there waiting when somebody said there was a car in the parking lot with its driver's door open, a silver Hyundai."

"Do you remember who made that announcement?"

"It wasn't a formal announcement or anything, nothing over a loudspeaker, just someone calling out."

"Did you see who it was?"

"I think it was a kid, actually."

Henry nodded again. There was no way that it was a kid who had been calling them, voice changer or no. Someone must have told him to make that announcement.

"I didn't think I'd left my door open, but I had to check, right? Who wouldn't? So I walked back to my car and saw that the doors were all closed. And that's when . . ."

Henry gave him a moment.

Rafferty took a deep breath. "That's when I suddenly felt someone behind me . . . I mean *right* behind me . . . but before I could turn, he said into my ear, 'If you turn around, your family is dead.'" He paused a moment. "I almost turned around anyway, without thinking. Just a knee-jerk reaction, you know? Thank God I didn't."

"What happened next?"

"He said something like, 'I've been watching you for weeks, Alex. You and your family.' Then he named my wife and kids. *He knew their names.* He said he'd watched Isabella at soccer practice. And went to one of Megan's swim meets. He said he sometimes drove by Donna's school at recess just to watch her with the children. It was the most chilling thing I'd ever heard."

Rafferty finally reached for his coffee, but his hand was shaking badly and he withdrew it, resting it in his lap again. Henry looked down at his notes, pretending not to notice.

"I can't imagine how frightening that must have been."

Rafferty nodded. "And this was the worst part: He said he had people watching them all right then, at that moment."

"Did you believe him?"

"Why the hell wouldn't I? He knew their names, what they did, where they went, where Donna worked."

Henry thought about how he had found Rafferty on Facebook, and learned where he worked, and his wife's name, and where she worked, and his daughters' names, and how he'd seen photos of their soccer games and swim meets. It was all so easy, once you knew his name.

"No reason you shouldn't have believed him," he said. "I'm just asking."

Rafferty reached out a hand that looked a bit steadier than it had a few seconds ago and took a sip of coffee.

"I did believe him, yes. I had to."

Henry made a note in his little black notebook, mostly to give Rafferty a moment, then said, "So, the guy is standing behind you, tells you not to turn around, threatens your family if you do. Then what?"

"He told me I had to do one simple thing for him, something that wasn't even illegal, and if I did that, he'd leave my family and me alone forever. As long as I never told anyone about any of this."

Henry already knew, but he asked anyway. "What did he want you to do?"

"He put something into my hand and said, 'Shake hands with the governor, and when you do, give him this.' It was a cell phone. He said, 'When you give it to him, you have to say something to him, something very specific, so listen carefully. You have to get this exactly right or . . . well, you know.' He actually said that. 'Well, you know.'"

"Do you remember what he wanted you to say?"

"Word for word. I was terrified of getting it wrong, so I made sure I got it right. I'll never forget it." He paused, then said, "I was supposed to hand the governor the phone and say, 'Keep that phone with you at all times, Governor. And keep it secret. You're going to need it after the arrest.' And I did it just like that. I handed him the phone and said those exact words. I had to. For my family. I didn't know there was anything wrong with it. Was it illegal? Did I aid and abet anything? Am I an accomplice or something?"

"Don't worry, Mr. Rafferty. We don't blame you for doing what you did. You're not in any trouble."

The man's relief was palpable. His entire body seemed to relax. "I was so worried," he said. After a pause, he added, "I've been wondering . . ."

"Yes?"

"Is this about the governor's brother?"

"I can't discuss that. Sorry."

Rafferty frowned. He seemed to be thinking about something; then his eyes widened a tiny bit, and Henry figured he had just remembered Henry's last name and connected the dots.

"I understand, Lieutenant," he said. "I get it. Listen . . . do you think my family is in any danger now? I've been beside myself. We have an appointment on Wednesday to have a home security system installed, but that's two days away."

"A security system is never a bad idea, but I think your family is safe. You gave the man what he wanted. He has no reason to harm any of you. My guess is that once you served his purpose, he forgot all about you."

"I hope so. I . . . haven't told my wife about any of this. I didn't want to scare her. And, in case anything terrible happened . . . well, I didn't want her to know I had any part in it."

"That's understandable. Mr. Rafferty, can you tell me anything about the man based on his voice? Age? Race? Education? Anything at all?"

Rafferty thought hard for a moment. "I was pretty scared, I have to admit. And he was sort of half talking, half whispering, you know? It made it hard to pick up on anything." He thought a moment longer. "Honestly, I don't think his voice told me anything about him. It was a man, I'm sure of that. But . . . that's about it."

Damn.

Henry stood and gave Rafferty his card.

"Please call me if anything else comes to you. Anything at all."

Rafferty promised that he would, then said, "Lieutenant? I hope everything turns out okay. You know, with your brother."

"Thanks," Henry said, while thinking, *Join the club.*

CHAPTER TWENTY

Wyatt Pickman sat in his basement, at the desk in his war room, as he thought of it, his eyes on the beautiful mosaic of photos, threads, papers, and sticky notes covering one entire wall. His mind was elsewhere, though. He was thinking of Tyler Kane's arraignment, which he had witnessed from the back row of the courtroom's gallery. He'd been surprised when the judge granted bail, even with the requirement that Tyler wear an ankle monitor. Pickman hadn't expected that, had thought it unlikely, in fact. But he had anticipated it, of course. He anticipated everything.

He walked over to a row of file cabinets and stopped in front of the first one, which held files for his most recent jobs, including his current one. These days he took only one job per year. He could afford to do that because of all the money he'd made during the first two decades in a profession at which he excelled, though he would have had difficulty describing to anyone exactly what that profession was. He had killed people for money, but he wasn't a hit man. Killing, when necessary, was sometimes his main objective, and other times it was incidental to the primary purpose for which he had been hired. He also blackmailed people, but he wasn't just a blackmailer. And he framed them, utterly ruining them. So he was something of a jack-of-all-trades. In his mind, what he did was make wishes come true—the wishes of those who hired him—though he had to admit that those wishes were, without exception, extraordinarily dark.

Years ago he would take the highest-paying jobs, regardless of what they entailed. He would do anything, literally anything, for the right price. And he took as many jobs as he could handle and still execute to his exacting standards. These days, though, given how profitable the wish-granting business had been for him over the years, he didn't need to base his decisions solely, or even in large part, on his remuneration. As long as a minimum monetary compensation threshold was met, he accepted the jobs that seemed the most interesting.

And because he restricted himself to one assignment per year at most, he could put his absolute all into it, devote himself utterly and entirely to it, plan it to the last and most minute detail, then watch with immense satisfaction as everything played out exactly as he had envisioned. It was his passion. His art. Really, it was the only reason he had for getting out of bed each morning. The only reason he bothered to breathe and eat. He had nothing else. What else was there? He had no use for companionship. People bored him. He couldn't remember the last person he'd met worth his time, with whom he could converse without feeling disdain. Travel? To travel, he'd have to mingle with countless others for whom he felt nothing but contempt. He had neither the desire nor the patience. Sex? He had always been able to satisfy himself more fully than anyone had been able to do for him.

No, he lived for his jobs, thankful that he was in a position to give each the attention it deserved. He could plan it meticulously and execute it with precision. Like Michelangelo painting the ceiling of the Sistine Chapel, lying on scaffolding, paint dripping into his eyes, blinding him, for more than four years. Every color, every brushstroke, absolute perfection.

With his hand resting on the file cabinet drawer, his mind wandered to last year's job. As always, it had gone exactly as he'd planned.

Every gear turning when he'd wanted, all the actors in the play he'd choreographed unaware that they were doing his bidding, believing their choices were the product of free will when, in fact, their behavior had been scripted by him months before. He'd put things in motion, and the people involved reacted as he'd known they would. And in the end, the powerful CEO of a Fortune 500 company had been laid low and was serving thirty years in federal prison for his part in an international child pornography ring. It didn't matter that the man had never exhibited even the slightest unhealthy interest in children, or even pornography in general. All that mattered was that his wife wanted to see her husband punished brutally for some transgression about which Pickman didn't care, and that she could pay handsomely to see that accomplished. What attracted Pickman most to the job was that the wife left the punishment entirely to him. He loved when that happened, when he could let his creativity soar. So he'd spent months laying the groundwork, planting seeds on the Internet, hiding files on the CEO's computers at home and in his office. For good measure, Pickman had broken into several homes where young children lived and stolen underwear from their hampers. Only a pair or two from each house, not enough to alarm anyone. Just before he was ready to involve the police, he hid the garments in the CEO's expansive walk-in closet at home, on a high shelf, in a box containing dozens of photographs that were highly illegal to possess. Then he sat back and watched it all unfold exactly as he had meant for it to.

His favorite job, though, had been seven years ago. It was actually two jobs in one. A wealthy woman in Boston who'd had a long-term affair with a well-known local television newscaster wanted him dead after he had, in her opinion, used her and tossed her aside. And a high-powered lawyer from the tony city of Weston, Massachusetts, a dozen miles from Boston, wanted to punish his wife for infidelity and wanted her out of his life for good, but he didn't have the stomach to have her murdered. So Pickman took both jobs, was paid well for both jobs, and murdered the Boston newscaster and pinned it on the Weston wife.

Now, *that* job had been interesting. He'd had to fabricate evidence of a relationship between two people where none had truly existed. Notes, flowers, motel receipts, everything lining up with both of their schedules. He could have taken care of either of his client's requests separately in a matter of weeks, perhaps even days, but where was the excitement in that? Where was the artistry? So instead, he laid the groundwork over a period of seventeen months, and when he finally shot the newscaster to death, and all of his meticulously crafted evidence came to light, the jury voted in less than three hours to convict the wife. It was sublime.

Pickman had waited years for the chance to do something like that again, something truly worthy of his skills. And then *this* job came along, and he immediately saw its potential. It would be his best work yet. He knew the level of planning that would be required. He foresaw the challenge and the potential pitfalls. He understood how many players would be involved, how many moving parts he would have to track and guide, how many juggling balls he would have to keep in the air. He envisioned how the numerous pieces would have to be crafted to mesh together perfectly. And he'd known almost immediately that he would take the job. How could he not? It would be beautiful. He'd been so excited about it, in fact, that he had agreed to do it for a mere $325,000, well below what he would normally charge for any job, much less one that he'd known would be as complex as this one. Then again, that complexity was the reason he'd taken the job in the first place.

He pulled open the file drawer, found a thick folder labeled *Tyler Makes Bail*, and carried the contingency plan to his desk, where his bible lay open. He flipped through the book to Part IV, Section B, Subsection 3, labeled *Tyler Goes to Jail*, and removed the entire section, replacing it with the pages from the folder, pages he had already run through a three-hole punch.

With Tyler awaiting trial on home arrest instead of behind bars, the revised overall plan was far more complicated. And riskier. And bloodier. But, he admitted to himself, it was also far more interesting.

He wondered idly if Andrew and Henry Kane had found Alexander Rafferty yet. He figured they would, eventually. Did they know that the voice on the other end of their phone call had never heard of Alexander Rafferty before that morning? That he had chosen him as he'd exited his Hyundai, then called a source at the Montpelier PD—whom he had secured through blackmail years earlier—to run Rafferty's plates and obtain his name and address? Then found Rafferty online and obtained everything he needed right from his various social media accounts? All in a matter of minutes as he sat in his vehicle four parking spots away from Rafferty's car? He doubted they'd figured all that out, but he wouldn't have been surprised if they'd been able to identify Rafferty through photographs or video. Pickman had expected that, of course, and it didn't trouble him in the least.

He knew he should probably email his client with an update, give an assurance that Tyler Kane's house arrest wouldn't impact the plan, but Pickman wasn't interested in hand-holding. He'd been hired for his expertise, and his client would simply have to trust in it.

He reached for the burner phone on his desk, though, and for the voice-changing device beside it.

CHAPTER TWENTY-ONE

Andrew stood outside one of the five-story apartment buildings known collectively as the Rutland Projects, located on the outskirts of the city that gave them their name. The projects were an embarrassment to the state, a scar on its face, and Andrew was sick to death of them. Every meeting in which the subject of them came up grew heated. Every time they were mentioned by the media, a new storm of controversy raged for a week. Every press conference in which Andrew was asked about them grew tense, despite his best efforts to avoid that.

The seven buildings were big, dilapidated, graffiti-decorated eyesores. Worse, inspections had revealed them to be structurally dangerous. Their only occupants for the last dozen or so years had been squatters, drug users, and prostitutes. More crimes were committed inside the abandoned apartments than probably occurred in the rest of Vermont combined. Other than the people using them illegally, most folks agreed that the projects had to be torn down and the land repurposed. The problem was that no one could agree on what its new purpose should be.

According to a city councilman, the citizens of Rutland wanted a new shopping mall. A city planner, purportedly speaking on behalf of the city's mayor, said His Honor wanted a new sports complex. A lobbyist advocating on behalf of local business owners was pushing for high-end apartments, which would bring hundreds of upper-middle-class families into the area, families who would spend money in their establishments. A major campaign contributor, who had been trying for two weeks to get a meeting with Andrew to discuss the issue, had ideas of his own on how the properties should be used, ideas that he had yet to share with Andrew but that would no doubt benefit the contributor far more than anyone else. No one seemed to want what Andrew wanted, though, which was to replace the old, run-down, crime-ridden low-income housing with new, safe, affordable low-income housing.

"This place really does suck," the woman beside Andrew said.

He looked over at Louise Landry, Vermont's commissioner of housing and community development, who was staring up at the building in front of them with something bordering on horror, as if she feared it might topple over at any moment and bury them in rubble.

"I can't argue with you on that," Andrew replied. No doubt Landry registered his slight emphasis on the final word of his sentence. He and Landry had been clashing over this issue, among a few others, for months. She concurred on the need for more low-income housing but disagreed that it should be located here. Andrew hoped he was wrong, but he harbored suspicions about the basis for her opinion, specifically about whether it had been paid for. Probably by Clifton Barnes, he figured, a wealthy property owner and developer with reputed connections to organized crime. Barnes's representatives had been among those pushing for high-end apartments to be built here and additionally for Barnes's company to build them.

"I want to go inside," Andrew said.

He'd asked his security team to take a handful of cops through this building a few hours ago, and to do so loudly, knowing it would clear the place out for this visit. Since then, officers had stood guard at each corner of the building to make sure no one slipped back in until they were gone again.

The two state troopers comprising today's security detail led the way into the building. They each turned on a powerful flashlight and handed one to Andrew and to Landry. Electricity to the buildings had been shut off years ago.

They stepped through the front doors into the vestibule, where the dim light spilling in from the outside illuminated a wall of mailboxes, several of which were missing their little bronze doors. With a tilt of his head, Andrew indicated that he was ready to move on, and the security team walked farther into the building, crossing into the dark lobby. Flashlight beams sliced through the darkness, crossing and recrossing as the group directed the light at their surroundings. The walls and both elevator doors, which were closed, were covered with profanity and gang symbols spray-painted in a variety of garish colors. Andrew's beam found a used condom, an empty Rolling Rock bottle, and a syringe with a needle attached.

"Lovely," Landry said.

Andrew turned to Greg Ramos, today's security team leader. "When you cleared the place earlier, did you go inside any of the apartments?"

He nodded to the other member of the security team and said, "Paul and I each went through quite a few of them personally. Maybe a third. Local cops did the rest."

"Was that safe?"

"Probably not."

"And what did you see?"

"Same as in here. Graffiti. A lot of empty bottles. Too many used needles to count. Some rooms had dirty mattresses in one corner and a bucket with used condoms in another."

"Any people living here?"

"Looks like it. At least a dozen apartments seemed occupied. Piles of clothes, boxes and cans of food, buckets with human waste in them. You could tell that people had been there not long before we started knocking on doors. We could hear footsteps in the stairwells. People trying to be quiet. We left them alone, per your instructions."

"I hope this doesn't sound insensitive," Landry said, "but thank God they're finally starting demolition next month."

The buildings had become so unsafe that the civil engineers brought in to assess them had determined they needed to be completely razed, and the sooner the better.

"No disrespect intended, Governor, I swear," Landry said, "but please remind me why we're here."

"We're here because I wanted to see this with my own eyes. And I thought you might want to see it, too. And I wanted to see the surrounding community. We need to make a decision on what we're doing with this land, Louise. It's time to settle this. The people here need to know—"

One of the cell phones he now took with him everywhere vibrated in his pants pocket—his right one, where he kept his personal phone. He pulled it out, saw that Henry was calling, and said, "I need to take this. Sorry, folks. I think we've seen enough. Why don't you head on outside. I'll be there in a minute."

The security guys hesitated.

The phone buzzed again.

"Guys, I really need some privacy here."

"Umm . . ." Ramos said.

The phone buzzed yet again, and Andrew said, "I'll be fine. I just need a minute. You can stand right outside and watch me through the glass."

Louise Landry left the building. Reluctantly, the security guys followed, leaving Andrew in the dark elevator lobby with nothing but his flashlight for illumination. The phone was in mid buzz when Andrew answered. "Please tell me you got him, Henry."

"Your voice sounds funny. I hear echoes. Where are you?"

"Inside one of the buildings in the Rutland Projects. Doing a quick tour."

After a brief pause, Henry said in a quiet voice, "I hate that place."

"I know." Andrew understood. One of Henry's friends, a former state police detective who had been something of a mentor to Henry—almost a father figure at times, before he'd retired with a full pension and become a private investigator—had been killed in one of these buildings years ago. Henry, who had been first on the scene, and—in Andrew's opinion—had never fully recovered from the loss of his close friend, was among those who couldn't wait for this place to be razed to the ground. "Tell me you were right about Rafferty, Henry. Tell me you've got him in cuffs."

"He's not our guy."

Andrew exhaled sharply. The words were a gut punch. Rafferty was their best lead—possibly their *only* lead. "So how the hell—"

He was interrupted by a vibration in his left pocket. The one in which he kept the mystery phone.

"He's calling again," Andrew said.

"The dickhead?"

"Yeah. I'll call you back, and we can fill each other in." He ended the call with Henry and took a breath before answering the other phone. "Yes?"

"That you, Governor Andy?" The same grating, monotone robotic voice from the first call.

"What do you want?"

"Have you found him yet?"

"Found who?" Andrew asked, playing dumb. Belatedly, he realized that maybe he *was* dumb, because he should be recording this call, as Henry had done the first time the guy had called. He quickly found the voice recorder app on his own phone, began recording, and held it as close as he could to the earpiece of the burner phone.

The caller, who had paused after Andrew's question, said, "Either you're being cagey, or you haven't found him yet. Either way, I might as well move on. Have you made your decision?"

Andrew took a steadying breath. "Yes. And I won't do what you're asking."

A brief pause on the line, then, "No? Not even if I could give you a video proving Tyler's innocence?"

A video exonerating Tyler? If they had that, this would all—

He shook his head. "I can't allow myself to be blackmailed. I can't let myself be forced to release a convicted felon before he's served his sentence."

"Prisoners are released early all the time."

"Because their cases make their way through the proper channels. Because their sentences have been reduced for good behavior, or when the parole board has carefully reviewed their specific situations and decided they should be granted early release. *Not* because someone murders an innocent woman and frames an innocent man for the crime, and tries to blackmail the state's governor—who has sworn to faithfully serve the people of Vermont—to force him to abuse his authority."

"Well, when you put it like that . . ."

"I take my oath seriously. I take the promises I made to the people of this state seriously. My answer is no. I will not release Gabriel Torrance for you. Or do anything else you want me to do. I urge you now to turn over to the authorities whatever evidence you have that you claim will exonerate my brother. I advise you to turn yourself in. But if you don't, we'll find you. And when we do, God help you for what you've done to my family."

Something scurried nearby in the blackness. Andrew whipped his flashlight around, and its beam caught a flash of dark movement disappearing through the open stairwell door near the elevators.

"Is that a threat?" the caller asked. "How nongubernatorial of you."

"I think we're done here."

"And that's your final answer?"

"It is. Don't call me again."

"Well, Governor Andy, you may be done, but I'm not. Far from it. And believe me, you're going to want me to call you again soon enough. You're going to be dying for my call. So I'd advise you to still keep that phone handy. Until then, remember that what happens next could have been avoided. *You* could have prevented it."

Silence screamed down the phone line. The caller was gone. Andrew stopped the recording on his phone.

He knew he should leave the building and join the others, but he had to call Henry back. He quickly filled his brother in, and Henry recounted his conversation with Rafferty.

"So where does this leave us?" Henry asked.

"In the dark."

Standing alone in that abandoned building, with things scurrying around him in the shadows, Andrew remembered the caller's last words and wondered if he'd just made a huge mistake.

CHAPTER TWENTY-TWO

The state police brought Tyler home the next day. Molly watched from a window as the cruiser waited for the small crowd standing on the sidewalk in front of the house to part so the vehicle could pull through the iron gate at the end of the driveway. Several of the people out there were reporters with their camera crews; others were merely curious onlookers hoping to catch a glimpse of a high-profile murder suspect.

When Tyler stepped out of the cruiser, he looked smaller and frail. His shoulders were hunched, as though he worried that one of the people who had gathered to watch his homecoming might throw something at him.

Molly hated everyone in the tiny crowd.

When the front door of the house opened, she greeted Tyler with a hug so fierce, he said, "Hey, you're squishing me." To their credit, the two troopers who had accompanied him home waited on the porch, giving them a moment. After several seconds, Molly released her hold on her twin brother and took a step back. As fragile as he seemed, it was clear he was trying to look brave and strong. It broke her heart.

"Look," he said as he tugged up the left leg of his jeans, exposing his bare ankle and the GPS bracelet encircling it—a bulky black device the size of a very small cell phone, held in place by a thick black band that they had attached before he left the jail. "It's uncomfortable."

"I bet it is," she said, the words catching slightly in her throat.

"I have to shower with it."

"I know. You'll get used to it, though. I promise."

One of the troopers cleared his throat, and Molly nodded and said, "Come on in."

The house was ready for Tyler. They needed a separate phone line in case there was ever an issue with the GPS signal and the monitoring company, WatchPro Solutions—to which the state outsourced monitoring functions—had to call. If they did, Tyler had better make it to the phone, or cops would be banging on the door within minutes. The line had to have a corded phone attached, with no added features like call waiting, voice mail, call forwarding, or the like. Fortunately, many years ago their father had installed a second line in his office for business use, and even though it had been unused for decades, no one had removed it. All Molly had to do was call the phone company to activate it again.

All systems seemed to be a go. Molly had filled out numerous forms, paid various fees, and arranged for the automatic electronic payment of the fifteen-dollar daily monitoring fee. The necessary equipment had already been installed and calibrated—a base system that would receive GPS signals from the ankle monitor and wirelessly transmit the information to the monitoring company. The troopers stood by while one of the two WatchPro employees who had accompanied them showed Molly and Tyler how it all worked. Most important for Tyler to remember—other than the fact that he couldn't leave the property— was that every day at 9:00 a.m. and again at 9:00 p.m., he was required to stand near the base so the monitoring equipment could register his presence and send that info to WatchPro. If the signal were ever lost, the phone would ring. If Tyler didn't come to the phone, he would violate the conditions of his bond, and he'd be taken back into custody to spend the rest of his pretrial time behind bars. If the ankle device or the monitoring unit were tampered with, same thing; Tyler would go back to jail. If he failed to check in at the designated times every day, back to jail. As the WatchPro rep explained all of this, the troopers stood nearby, nodding. Then they ran a test of the system, with a trooper and one of the WatchPro guys walking Tyler around the perimeter of the grounds while the other WatchPro employee stood inside, checking the monitoring base unit. The system worked perfectly.

A few minutes later, not soon enough for Molly, the troopers and the WatchPro guys were gone, and she was alone with her brother. She wanted to hug him again but knew he wouldn't want that. He surprised her, though, by putting his arms around her and leaning his head down until his forehead rested against hers. She closed her eyes and threatened her tears to stay the hell away. After a long moment, Tyler stepped back and announced that he was hungry, causing a small smile to creep onto her face.

Half an hour later, Molly was sitting at the kitchen table across from her brother, who was eating a grilled cheese sandwich Molly had made for him.

"You really do understand how important it is that you follow the rules, right?" she asked.

"Sure," he said as he stuffed a huge bite of sandwich into his mouth.

"You can't leave our property, not even for a single second. They'll know if you do."

"I know."

"If you do, they'll send you back to jail."

"I know."

"And you can't mess around with your ankle monitor."

"It's uncomfortable."

"I'm sure it is. But you have to leave it alone. Try not to even touch it. You can get in trouble if you do."

"I know. Those guys told me."

"And you can't—"

"Molly, I get it. I swear. I don't wanna go back to jail. I won't mess with the monitor. And I'm not gonna run away or anything. I need to have my trial and show everyone I didn't hurt that lady. So stop worrying about all this, and eat your sandwich."

"I don't have a sandwich."

"Well, you should make yourself one. Oh, and can you make me another one, too?"

He smiled. After a moment, she smiled back.

They were halfway through their sandwiches—Tyler's second, Molly's first—when the back door opened, and Julie Davenport stepped into the room. Her University of Vermont T-shirt and yoga pants told Molly she was coming home from the gym. Julie's eyes landed immediately on Tyler, and her face fell—a tiny slip—before she pasted on an uncomfortable smile. For a moment, it seemed as though she might head up to her au pair suite on the third floor without a word, but she said, "You're back, Tyler."

"Hi, Julie," he said around a mouthful of sandwich.

"Molly told me you might not be here until tomorrow."

"I'm glad I'm home. It's *so* much better than jail."

Julie's plastic smile stretched a little wider but never reached her eyes. And that was where Molly saw it: she was afraid of Tyler.

"Well," Julie said, "guess I'll head upstairs."

She left the room quickly and headed up the back stairs on her way to the third floor.

Molly watched her brother chew for a moment, then said, "I'll be right back."

She walked up two flights of steps and knocked on the door to Julie's suite.

"Who's there?"

"It's Molly . . . just Molly."

She heard the *clack* of the deadbolt disengaging. Julie opened the door but didn't invite her inside.

"How're you doing?" Molly asked.

Julie shrugged. "Okay, I guess. You?"

"I'm glad Tyler's home. I hated him being in jail."

Julie merely nodded. Neither said anything for a long, awkward moment. Finally, Molly said, "He's the same sweet guy you've known for two years, Julie."

Julie nodded and started to say something but stopped herself.

"He didn't do what they say he did," Molly added.

"Of course not," Julie said unconvincingly.

"You know him, Julie. You know how gentle he is. Have you ever even seen him angry?"

Julie said nothing.

"Ever seen him frustrated, even? Or impatient?"

She shook her head but still said nothing.

"He's a lamb and always has been. You know that."

Finally, Julie spoke. "I know. He's never . . . I mean, he's always been . . ."

"That's right."

"It's just that . . ." She trailed off.

And Molly knew. She just *knew*. "You can't leave, Julie. Please don't leave."

"I can't . . ."

"I need you. Tyler needs you."

"Molly . . ."

"This is a hard time for the family, for all of us, and Tyler needs everything to be as normal as possible."

"I understand that, but—"

"He loves you, Julie. You know that. He really needs you. And so do I."

It was true. Tyler loved her. He sometimes referred to her as his "other sister." And it was also true that he and Molly needed Julie in their lives. He didn't always exercise the best judgment, and Molly and her older brothers weren't comfortable with him being by himself for too long. He had burned himself twice, once using the stove and once using the microwave. One time he had started to run a bath, then got so wrapped up in a TV game show that he didn't remember he'd left the water on. That had been a $12,000 mistake.

And it was also true that as much as Tyler needed Julie, Molly did, too. They were friends. Moreover, they were both graduate students at the University of Vermont. If Molly were to have time to attend classes—or to have any semblance of a life outside the house—she needed someone to share the responsibility for keeping an eye on Tyler. He didn't require constant supervision, but a light monitoring was definitely in order. And she couldn't do it alone. She had tried during her first semester and found it too difficult. So she'd offered the au pair suite to a school friend, rent-free, in exchange for a second set of eyes to watch her brother a little. And for two years, it had worked out well. It couldn't last forever, of course. One day Julie was going to graduate. And one day she would move out. But Molly desperately didn't want that day to be today.

"Please don't go, Julie."

"I don't know . . ."

"Talk to him. For five minutes. If he doesn't seem like the same great guy you've always known, you can leave, no hard feelings."

After a long, long moment, Julie nodded.

For the next twenty minutes, Tyler ate—he'd finished his sandwich and was working through a bag of potato chips—and Molly and Julie sat at the table with him. Molly watched Julie as they talked, and as the minutes passed, she relaxed more and more. Tyler told them about how the food in jail wasn't nearly as good as the food at home. He showed Julie his ankle bracelet. He talked about the video games that Molly had bought him to replace a few that the police had taken. By the time Tyler had emptied the bag of chips, it looked to Molly as though Julie's doubts had been erased.

He stood, took his plate to the sink, and threw away the empty chip bag.

"I'm gonna go play a video game," he announced.

He was almost out the door when Julie said, "I'm glad you're home, Tyler." It sounded sincere.

He threw a grin over his shoulder and said, "Me, too."

Julie looked at Molly and, after a brief hesitation, nodded slightly. Molly gave her a small, grateful smile in return.

"Family dinner tonight to welcome him home," Molly said. "You're invited, of course, as always."

"Thanks, but you've all been through a lot. You should be alone with each other. Besides, I'm meeting friends. Next time, okay?"

There was going to be a next time, apparently.

Thank God.

CHAPTER TWENTY-THREE

Henry sat at the table in the kitchen where he and his siblings had watched their mother make thousands of meals. Molly sat across from him. They were watching Andrew and Rebecca prepare the evening's dinner. They all knew that Henry was a takeout kind of guy, and Molly was a mac-and-cheese-or-tacos-from-the-box kind of gal, so on those occasions when the family gathered for a home-cooked meal, Andrew and Rebecca did the cooking. They plainly enjoyed it, and even after fourteen years of marriage, they seemed to enjoy doing it together. Henry followed their movements around the room and wondered if they had been choreographed. The couple worked in harmony, each seeming to anticipate the other's moves, never bumping into the other, handing ingredients back and forth, taking away empty measuring cups and utensils. And they somehow kept their work area sparkling clean—counters wiped down, used prep tools in the dishwasher, pots and pans washed as soon as they had cooled enough—so that when dinner was ready, there was very little cleanup left to be done. Watching the finale of their cooking duet—when they carried the meal out of the kitchen—Henry knew he'd never have anything like that with anyone. He and Molly each grabbed two side dishes and followed the couple to the dining room.

"Where's Tyler?" Rebecca asked as she placed a basket of warm rosemary focaccia bread on the table, which was set for five. Staccato bursts of machine gun fire sounded from down the hall. "Oh," she said.

Molly headed for the doorway. "I'll get him."

Down the hall, the battle raged for another half a minute while Andrew filled the water glasses. By the time Molly returned with Tyler, the others were seated.

"Where's Julie?" Tyler asked. "At class?"

"She's got other dinner plans tonight," Molly said.

"Okay. What are we having?"

"Chicken," Andrew said.

"That's my favorite."

"That's why we made it."

"You guys are awesome. I had chicken in jail, but it was cold and tasted like rubber. And it didn't smell like *this*. It smelled . . . like rubber, I guess." His face brightened. "Hey, I used to have a rubber chicken. Remember? Henry gave it to me for Christmas one year. That's what the food tasted like. That rubber chicken." He chuckled, and everyone else smiled.

For the next forty-five minutes, they ate and talked and even laughed a little, and they didn't mention again the huge elephant in the room wearing striped prison garb. After wolfing down seconds of the chicken and three pieces of bread, Tyler stood and said, "I'm gonna go finish my game, okay?"

"Sure," Andrew said.

He started for the hallway, then stopped, turned, and said, "Thanks for dinner, guys," then hustled from the room. Before any of the others said a word, a huge explosion shook the walls, and a chorus of machine guns began barking.

"Sounds like he's taking heavy fire," Henry said.

"I'm sure he'll be all right," Rebecca said with a smile. Then she paused, and the smile slowly faded. They all paused, every one of them, and Henry figured they were all thinking the same thing: *I hope that's true.*

———

Because Andrew and Rebecca had done the cooking, it was left to Henry and Molly to clean up. And because the Fred and Ginger of the culinary world had left the kitchen looking as though they had ordered takeout instead of preparing a gourmet meal in there, the entire process would take very little time. Dishes, utensils, and glasses into the dishwasher. Napkins down the laundry chute. Easy. Which was why Henry didn't feel guilty saying to Molly, "You mind taking care of this? I want to talk to Tyler alone for a little while."

"Sure."

He followed the sounds of battle and found his younger brother in his favorite chair, his legs drawn up and a video game controller in his hands. Knowing he'd get nowhere with Tyler during a game, Henry took drastic action, stepping in front of the TV.

"Hey," Tyler said. "Jack Smiley's about to kill the bad guys' captain."

"Can you pause it, buddy? I want to talk for a minute."

Tyler looked like he wanted to protest, but instead he paused the game.

"Thanks." Henry sat down in another chair. "I need to ask you a few things, okay? Things you might have talked about with the detectives last Friday."

"I don't want to talk about that stuff."

"I know, but it would really help if you did. Okay?"

Tyler looked away from Henry, toward a dark window on the far wall. He shrugged.

"Did you know Sally Graham, Tyler?"

Tyler shrugged again.

"Listen," Henry said. "You can trust me, you know that."

"Rachel said I shouldn't talk to anyone about any of this stuff. Especially the police. And you're a policeman."

"Your lawyer's very smart. You should definitely listen to her. But I'm your brother before I'm a police detective. Always. I'm on your side in this. The detectives who interviewed you? They're on the other side. But not me. You can talk to me."

After a moment, Tyler nodded.

"Good. Great. So, did you know Sally Graham?"

Tyler hesitated, then nodded. "I met her last week. She came into the shelter. I showed her a puppy and two cats. She was really nice." He stopped talking.

"Then what?"

"A little while later, my hours were over, and I left . . . and she was in the parking lot, waiting. She asked if I wanted to go for a ride. So I did."

"Why did she want you to go for a ride?"

Tyler shrugged. "She didn't say. But she was really nice, so I went."

"And what happened?"

Tyler stared at the blackness out the window and said nothing for a long moment. "Nothing happened. We went for a ride. She brought me back to my bike a while later."

"Where did she take you?"

"I don't know. Around."

"You just drove around?"

"Yeah. Drove around and talked."

"That's it?"

Finally, Tyler looked Henry's way. "That's it," he said, his voice rising a little. "We drove around and talked. Okay? She was really nice, like I said."

He looked out the window again. Henry was on the verge of losing him.

"Did you see her after that?"

"What? No."

"She ever call you? Or did you call her?"

"She didn't give me her phone number, and I didn't give her mine. She didn't ask for it."

"How about her apartment? Did you go there?"

"What? Her . . . for what? Why would I go there? All we did was drive around, like I said."

He was getting agitated.

"I meant later," Henry said. "Did you go there later? After you drove around and she dropped you back at your bike."

"I don't even know where her house is, Henry. She could live in Florida, for all I know. Or Hawaii. Okay? Can I get back to my game now?"

Henry was unlikely to get anything more from him at that moment. "Sure, buddy."

A mortar round shook the room before Henry had even reached the doorway.

———

He found the others in the drawing room. Andrew and Rebecca were sitting side by side on the Victorian sofa, the one piece of furniture in the room that Henry found almost tolerable to sit on. Molly was in an upholstered side chair, and Henry was forced to sit, reluctantly, in an identical one on the other side of the cold fireplace.

"Are you sure we shouldn't sell this stuff," he said, "and buy some leather armchairs, maybe an electric reclining sofa with cup holders?"

"Mom wanted us to maintain the Victorian charm of the place," Andrew reminded him. "Remember?"

"Yeah, but she's been gone awhile. Maybe she changed her mind. Maybe she's up there wishing she had told her kids to be more comfortable and not worry about Victorian charm."

"What did Tyler have to say?" Andrew asked.

"Not much." He filled them in.

"Did you believe him?"

Molly glared at Andrew. "Why wouldn't he believe him?"

"He wasn't telling me everything," Henry said, "but I don't think he'd been to Sally Graham's apartment."

"Of course he hadn't," Molly said. "You guys sound like you're doubting him."

"Relax, Molly," Andrew said. "We all know he didn't kill Sally Graham. I'm just wondering what he might not be telling us."

"Me, too," Henry said, though what he was really still wondering was whether Sally Graham might have somehow let Tyler know that she sometimes did things for guys, special things in exchange for money. It didn't seem likely—not Tyler—but as innocent and even childlike as he often seemed, he was, after all, a twenty-nine-year-old man. And he had been alone in a car with a young woman who—

A soft *ding* came from Molly's direction. After throwing Henry a glare that convinced him she had been on the verge of unleashing a scolding, she checked her watch and said, "Almost nine o'clock. Time for Tyler to check in."

Saved by the bell, Henry thought. "He's not gonna be happy. I already interrupted his game."

"He's going to have to get used to it," she said.

She left the room, and Henry furtively checked out her chair to see if it looked more comfortable than his, even though it was the twin of the one on which he sat. It didn't. The walls abruptly stopped shaking as the sounds of battle disappeared. Tyler was checking in, his ankle brace-let telling the base device that he was home, right where he was supposed to be. Of course, if the system was working properly, and there was no reason to believe it wasn't, the folks at WatchPro already knew Tyler was home because he had never left the property. That would have sent an alarm to the company. So would tampering with the ankle monitor. But Tyler had to check in, so he did.

"This is terrible," Rebecca said into the sudden silence.

"At least he's home," Andrew replied.

After several moments, during which they sat, each in their own thoughts, Rebecca asked, "How are you boys doing?"

"You said it pretty well," Andrew replied. "This is terrible."

Henry added, "It sucks."

"I honestly do think he'll be all right," Rebecca said. "He didn't do anything wrong. I'm sure of it. Not Tyler. He couldn't have."

They fell into another silence until, moments later, the Vietnam War exploded out of the past again, straight back into the room down the hall. Seconds later, Molly returned.

"While you were gone, Rebecca asked how we're doing," Henry said. "Time for you to chime in on that."

"Me? I'm peachy. The past week has been great. Maybe the third best of my life."

Henry nodded. "I've had some great weeks, so this one doesn't crack my top five, but it's definitely in the top ten."

"I'm sorry, guys," Rebecca said. "I didn't mean to—"

"Ah, don't sweat it, Becks," Henry said. "We didn't mean anything by that."

"It wasn't directed at you," Molly added. "We're just stressed."

Rebecca nodded. Andrew reached over and squeezed her hand.

"So what's next?" Molly asked.

"The cops keep looking for evidence," Henry said.

"The state keeps building its case," Andrew added. "And our lawyer finds us an expert who, for a fee, will say the right things for Tyler's cause."

"And what are the right things?" Molly asked.

"Whatever Rachel Addison thinks they are. She's good."

Suddenly, Andrew stiffened. Rebecca looked over at him, frowning slightly. Henry saw him pat his left pants pocket and knew that the mystery phone had vibrated.

Andrew rose and said, "I'm getting a call. I'll be back in a minute."

Henry was sorely tempted to follow but figured it would look suspicious. They hadn't shared anything about their dickhead caller with Molly; and, to Henry's knowledge, Andrew hadn't done so with Rebecca, either. So he'd wait until he could steal a moment alone with his big brother.

When Andrew returned a few minutes later, he looked shaken. He sat beside Rebecca without a word.

"Everything okay?" she asked.

"State business," he replied—unconvincingly, in Henry's opinion.

Rebecca stared at him for maybe three seconds. "Bullshit," she said, surprising Henry.

"What?"

"You heard me."

Andrew sighed. He looked at Henry, who shrugged. *What the hell?*

Andrew frowned and seemed to be carrying on a debate in his mind. Finally, he began, "There are things I haven't shared with either of you. That Henry and I haven't shared with you."

Molly narrowed her eyes at Andrew, then turned Henry's way.

Thanks a lot, Andy, Henry thought.

"Spill it, guys," Molly said. "What things?"

Andrew took a deep breath, then started talking.

CHAPTER TWENTY-FOUR

With occasional help from Henry, Andrew told them almost everything. He started the story where it began, with Alexander Rafferty giving him a cell phone and a warning before disappearing. He talked about the caller admitting that he'd framed Tyler for Sally Graham's murder, and that he wanted Gabriel Torrance released. As he spoke, Andrew watched the emotions and reactions shuffling across the faces of his wife and sister—confusion, anger, shock, indignation, disbelief, even greater anger. When the narrative required Henry to jump in, Andrew was thrilled not to have the entire focus of the animosity in the room directed toward him. Molly and Rebecca were obviously beyond upset about what the blackmailer had done to Tyler, but they were also angry at having been kept in the dark about it. Henry filled them in on Torrance's details. They interrupted a few times—Molly, mostly—but Andrew asked them to hold their questions until he was finished.

"This isn't one of your press conferences, Andy," Molly said.

Andrew conceded that but said it would be easier if they allowed Henry and him to get through it all before the question-and-answer period began. For a moment, he worried that Molly might bound across the room and put him in some sort of dangerous chokehold she'd learned in the army, but she managed to control herself.

So they told their story, and they each played the recordings they had made on their phones of the calls with the blackmailer. When the women were fully up to speed, Molly took a long moment before finally saying, "So you knew that Tyler is innocent, and you didn't tell me?"

"Didn't think we had to, sis," Henry said.

"Low blow. And you know what I mean."

"Sorry, Molly," Andrew said. "You, too, Becca. But we wanted to learn all we could before sharing this."

"Well, we women sure do appreciate you sparing us all of that nasty stress," Molly said.

"That's not it. You know that. We just wanted answers so we could give them to you."

"Bullshit," Rebecca said. She'd said that earlier, too, and her language had surprised Andrew both times.

"We figured it would be best to—"

"Whatever," Molly said loudly, cutting him off. "It's over. It's done. Now we know. The question is what to do about it. And to me, there's no question at all."

"No?" Andrew asked.

"This guy Torrance? Give him his 'get out of jail free' card."

"Molly, Gabriel Torrance is—"

"Someone who has no record," Molly interrupted, "except the one offense. He panicked and left the scene of an accident, one he didn't even *cause*. And he has only *five months* to go on his sentence anyway? Who cares if he gets out a little early? What? You worried about him being a repeat offender? Worried that maybe he gets his rocks off by having other drivers smash into him so he can flee the scene?"

"It's not that simple," Andrew said.

"To me, it is. If there's a video that proves Tyler's innocent, we need it. And if Torrance isn't a threat, let him out. Who cares?"

"I do," Rebecca said, and all eyes landed on her. "I understand why Andrew doesn't want to give in to the blackmailer's demands. He's built his *entire career* on integrity. On staying clean in dirty professions. He's not like your . . ." She hesitated a moment, then said, "He's not like your average politician."

She'd been about to say, *He's not like your father.* Andrew was sure of it. And he was glad she hadn't. Because as he knew—and as he'd told his wife—the others didn't feel quite the same way about Patrick Kane as Andrew did. And there really was no need for them to.

She trudged on. "I remember Andrew coming home and talking about the crap other lawyers pulled, and how the judge in some case or other lacked the impartiality the law required of him. I remember Andrew resisting requests to run for governor. He was worried about even dipping his toes into those waters, yet he did. For the sake of the people of this state, he dove headfirst into the muck. And now they're even talking about him running for president one day. And if he wants to do that—"

"You plan to run for president?" Molly asked, mild surprise evident in her voice.

"Really, Andy?" Henry said. "I had no idea."

Andrew shook his head. "Hold on, I've never said I want to—"

Rebecca cut him off. "The point is, he cares about the people of this state, so he let them push him into this, hoping he could do some good, despite his initial misgivings. And through it all, somehow, he's remained clean. And he's made so much progress. He's cleaned up a lot of Barker's mess . . . he's cleaned up the state police . . . and I forget which government agencies, but there's more than one he's fixed. And through it all, he's maintained his integrity. It's what his campaign was founded on. It's everything he is. He can't do what that man wants. He can't free that prisoner. Not without betraying the people of Vermont . . . and himself."

Wow. She knew him so well. It was everything he'd been thinking.

"Don't hold back, Becks," Henry said. "Speak up and let us know how you feel."

"Henry . . ." Andrew said.

"I'm kidding. I get it."

"Well, I don't," Molly said. "No offense, Becca, but Tyler's not your brother."

"And that means I don't love him?" She seemed disgusted by the suggestion.

Molly shook her head. "It's not the same," she said unconvincingly.

"Bullshit."

That time, Andrew wasn't surprised at all about his wife's choice of words. He was a little surprised, though, that she and Molly were butting heads. Then again, emotions were running hot. "I see both sides of this," he said, stepping in. "I really do. For the record, Henry agrees with you, Molly."

"I haven't said that," Henry said.

"You don't have to. I can tell. But Rebecca sees the other side of this, which you refuse to see, Molly. And maybe you don't really, either, Henry. Of course I don't want to see Tyler on trial for a heinous crime he didn't commit. But I can't let myself be blackmailed. Where would it end? What if I did it, and word got out?"

"Your reputation means more to you than family does?" Molly asked.

"That's offensive. What I meant was that if word got out that I could be blackmailed, or bought like Barker, I'm finished. Maybe I could hang on for a while, but I wouldn't get any important work done. I'd have lost the trust of the people and everyone in my administration. And there's so much more I want to accomplish. Not for my legacy, but for Vermont. For the people. There are still pockets of corruption I need to address. There are civil rights laws to broaden. There's a bill we're drafting to toughen the laws against racketeering and the distribution of drugs. There's—"

"There's our brother facing a first-degree murder charge."

Andrew shook his head. "Damn it, Molly."

No one said anything for a few seconds. Andrew welcomed the silence. But there was more to say, he knew. They had told the women *almost* everything. There was one item left to cover.

"Listen, everyone. The call I received a little while ago? That was him."

"The blackmailer?" Rebecca asked.

"What did he say?" Henry asked.

"First, he made me confirm that I wasn't going to grant clemency to Gabriel Torrance."

"And then?"

"Then he said, and I quote, 'The plot thickens. The noose will tighten. And in case you wonder, which you will soon . . . the blood is definitely Sally Graham's and the DNA is indeed your brother's.' Then he hung up."

"What blood?" Molly asked. "What DNA?"

"He didn't say. But I think we're going to find out before long."

CHAPTER TWENTY-FIVE

Wyatt Pickman looked at the digital readout on the food scale on the kitchen counter. For a sandwich, each slice of whole wheat bread had to weigh between twenty-five and thirty grams. If he couldn't find two slices that fit the bill, he would have to eat something else. Fortunately, these slices were perfect, weighing in together at 58.6 grams.

He opened the jar of creamy peanut butter and, with a practiced hand, spread it on one of the pieces of bread. As always, not too thick a layer, not too thin. He weighed that slice. Perfect.

Next, with his usual precision, he spread raspberry jam on the other slice. Weighed it.

Finally, even though he knew that each slice of bread, covered with the appropriate spread, weighed the proper amount, he put the sandwich halves together and weighed the finished product, just to be certain. Perfect, as expected.

He measured exactly sixteen ounces of milk and poured it into a glass. Then he sat at the table and ate his sandwich in eight bites, four bites per half, with one sip of milk between them. He tried to make each sip as close to two ounces as possible, but he didn't measure them out. That would have been a bit obsessive. When he was finished, he washed his plate and glass, dried them, and returned them to their respective cabinets.

He left the kitchen, walked down a short hall, and entered the living room, which didn't contain a stick of furniture. Instead, taking up almost the entirety of the large space, resting on a twelve-by-sixteen-foot plywood surface supported by strategically placed sawhorses underneath, was a diorama Pickman had been constructing of the midday portion of the Battle of Antietam, the bloodiest battle in US history—in fact, the bloodiest day in the country's entire history. The product of fifteen months of painstaking work, the tableau was as magnificent and beautiful as it was historically correct. The ground was topographically accurate as of the date of the battle, with ground elevations, trees, structures, fence lines, bridges, and of course, troop placement. Each building had been painted to reflect photographs he had found through his research. Each stand of trees contained, to the best of his ability, the proper number of trees. And while he couldn't possibly populate his battlefield with all 127,300 soldiers had who fought that day, he allowed 3,244 of them—each just an eighth of an inch tall—to stand in for the rest.

Because 192 square feet of surface was too large to allow him access to sections toward the middle, he'd had to work on the project in four-by-four-foot sections before adding them to the project as a whole. That meant that once a section was complete, unless it was near one of the edges, he couldn't make any changes to it. Accordingly, he'd had to plan the entire battlefield out to the minutest detail ahead of time. That was fine with him, of course. That was the way he liked it. He had completed ten of the twelve four-by-four sections that way, and was halfway through the eleventh. After a year and a quarter of work, he expected to be finished in another three months at most. He allowed himself to feel a small surge of pride as he passed out of the living room again and over to the door under the stairs, which led down to the basement.

He entered his war room and sat at the desk, on which the black binder he thought of as his bible lay open to a tab titled "*Governor Call # 3 (if necessary)*." The call he'd made to the governor a little while ago had gone as he'd expected it would. If Kane had agreed to grant clemency to Torrance—which, honestly, would have been a surprise this early in the game—Pickman would have turned directly to Section G of the bible and proceeded from there. However, given Kane's fully anticipated refusal, he flipped to Section E and skimmed the pages there detailing the next phase of the plan. After reading his narrative summary, he studied the map he'd drawn months ago. He took note of the GPS coordinates of the location where he had to go. The "Items Required" part of Section E listed what he would need, all of which he kept in the closet at the end of the war room, along with the rest of the items Pickman would use to execute this beautiful but complicated plan. Some of the things were stored in cardboard file boxes, others in sealed Ziploc bags or airtight Tupperware containers, as needed. He opened the correct box and removed the plastic bag containing what he needed, then slipped it into his duffel bag. He put the bible in there, too, and the burner phone. He picked up the voice changer, chose a different setting, and spoke into it as a test.

"Hello, police?" he said, his voice sounding higher than his natural one, like that of a teenage boy. "I was jogging in the park, and I found something that you should see."

He nodded. The gears of his plan were turning with the precision of a Swiss timepiece. Everything was perfect. He was ready.

Unfortunately for the Kanes, they couldn't possibly be.

CHAPTER TWENTY-SIX

After leaving his siblings and sister-in-law, Henry made a quick trip to his office to grab a file, then headed to the town of Barre, the self-proclaimed Granite Center of the World due to its vast deposits of the stone, deposits that yielded granite famous for its even texture, fine grain, and exceptional resistance to weather. Henry's navigation system took him through a small neighborhood to a medium-size two-story house set on a small but well-maintained lot on a pleasant street. A big shade tree dominated the front yard, a rope swing with a plywood seat hanging from the lowest branch.

Henry pulled to a stop in front of the house. He left the file on his seat and headed up the front walk. He rang the doorbell, and a few seconds later, State Police Detective Thomas Egan answered the door wearing sweatpants and a navy New England Patriots sweatshirt.

Egan eyed Henry warily. "Yeah?"

"Detective Egan, I'm Henry Kane, Internal Affairs." He flashed his badge, which he'd had ready in his hand so as not to reach into his pocket and risk alarming a trained police detective.

"IA?" Egan said with evident distaste, but also with a look of poorly concealed unease. "What's this about?"

Henry heard a woman's voice inside, then a male teenager's muffled reply.

"Well, I think you may have some idea what this is about," he said, "but you'd be only half right. Wanna come outside and talk for a few minutes?"

Egan glanced over his shoulder into the house, then looked back at Henry, then over his shoulder again. "Tammy? Guy from work just showed up looking for my input on something. I'm going outside for a minute."

He stepped onto the porch. The second he'd closed the door behind him, he whirled around, the motion bringing him close to Henry. His face was hard. He radiated menace. He knew better than to touch a fellow law enforcement officer, though, especially an Internal Affairs detective.

"You came to my *home*?"

"Relax, Egan."

"My wife and kids are inside, asshole."

"I told you to relax. This isn't what you think. And it's time you stood down, or you'll be going back into your house through that window behind you."

Egan breathed heavily into Henry's face for a moment, then took half a step back. Just half.

"If this isn't what I think it is, then what is it?"

"Well, I'm not gonna lie; it's a little of what you think. I know what you've been doing. I have proof of it."

Egan considered that. He glanced at the window behind him. "Screw you. I've done nothing wrong. Now get off my porch."

He turned toward the door.

"You sure that's how you wanna play it?" Henry asked.

"I'm not playing at all. Trust me."

Henry ignored the implied threat. "Me, either. Wanna see my proof? It's right in my car."

Egan took another glance at the window, then started walking toward Henry's Taurus.

Eight minutes later, Egan, in the passenger seat, was shaking his head, looking both angry and defeated. He had the file in his lap and several eight-by-ten-inch photos in his hands. He hadn't even seen the video yet. Henry was behind the wheel, giving him time to process what he'd read and seen.

"Who else knows about this?" Egan asked.

"Nobody. Yet. There are suspicions—that's how I got involved—but nobody knows for sure. Except me. And your little buddy Simmons, of course, but only because, like an idiot, you brought him along a few times."

"Is he the one—"

"He had nothing to do with this. Leave him alone. He could be in trouble, too. Because of you."

Egan processed that. "This a shakedown? You looking for a cut?"

"I'm offended by the suggestion."

"Is that a no?"

"It's a no."

"Then what the hell do you want? This isn't exactly procedure, coming to me unofficially like this, so you obviously want something from me."

"You catch my name?"

Egan thought a moment. "Kane, right?" The light popped on. "You're the governor's brother. And your other brother . . ."

"Now we're getting there."

Henry could see it in Egan's eyes, the calculations he was running in his head. He didn't yet know what Henry wanted of him, but he was deciding that it must be important; therefore, he might have some leverage of which he hadn't been aware moments ago. The very beginning of a smirk began to grow at the corners of his mouth. Before it had the chance to fully bloom, Henry decided to yank it by its roots.

"Let me remind you that you haven't even seen the video yet, Egan. I could absolutely bury you. Your career dead. Public disgrace. A prison sentence. Probably followed by a divorce. I don't know anything about your relationship with your wife, I admit, but I've seen it happen in situations like this."

"Cheap shot," Egan said, dropping the photos into the file.

Henry shrugged. "I don't care."

Egan's gaze shifted to his house. Henry could see movement through the windows.

"What do you want from me, Kane?"

"Information about Tyler's case. I'm the accused's brother. I can't get it myself."

"What kind of information? I'm not gonna risk my career for—"

"You already risked your career, you dumbass. You flushed it away. I'm offering you a chance to fish it out of the sewer."

Egan said nothing for a moment. "What kind of info you looking for?"

"Nothing that would compromise the investigation. I just want to know what they have against my brother."

"You'll get that stuff when the state turns it over in discovery."

"That could be weeks. I'm not a patient guy."

Egan rubbed the back of his neck, thinking. "I'm not on your brother's case. That's the Major Crime Unit. I'm BCI," he added, referring to the Bureau of Criminal Investigations.

"Yeah, but I heard they're recruiting guys for legwork. You could be one of those guys."

"How?"

"Ask for the assignment."

"That would look fishy."

"Say you hate the governor, same as every other cop in Vermont, and you want to see justice done in this case. Whatever you have to say."

"I've got cases of my own to work."

"I do, too. Yours is one of them."

Egan blew out an exasperated breath. "And if they don't take me?"

"You might know guys on the case. You work out of headquarters, same as them. And if you aren't already pals with any of them, you could get to know a couple. Chat them up. Either way, get me what I want. Keep me in the loop."

"Or you'll bury me."

"In a heartbeat."

"You're a prick."

"Probably. I'm not asking for anything that the defense won't get eventually, though. I just wanna know what we're up against as soon as possible."

"And if I'm able to do this?"

"I'll bury that file you've got there instead of burying you. The video, too." Egan thought for a moment. "You have to stop taking bribes and payoffs, though," Henry added. "Big Brother is watching. I can say I couldn't substantiate the allegations at this time, but you're on the radar now. You keep doing it, it's just a matter of time before someone else catches you at it. Or one of the scumbags you're dealing with cuts a deal and rolls over on you."

Egan was looking down at the top photo in the stack. He looked up. "You're as dirty as I am, you know that? Abusing your position for personal gain."

"Shades of gray, Egan. Different motivations. Whatever. I don't care what you think of me. I just need you to do what I ask. And don't think about trying to set me up, because even if I go down in flames, you'll burn right along with me. Even if they grant you immunity, you think you'll ever get another promotion? My guess is they'll probably find some excuse to can your ass, but even if they don't, you'll spend the rest of your career in a dead-end assignment, looking over your shoulder, waiting for the ax to fall."

Egan nodded, thinking.

Henry continued. "Maybe you think I'm a bigger fish than you. That I'm wrong, and you could cut a good deal. Hell, maybe you'd be right. How much are you willing to bet on that, though? Everything you have?" He nodded toward Egan's house.

After a long moment, Egan shook his head.

"Okay then," Henry said. "For the record, I think you're making the right call."

"And for the record, I still think you're as bad as I am. Maybe worse."

Henry considered that a moment. "You're probably right."

CHAPTER TWENTY-SEVEN

For three and a half days, they waited for the caller's threat to materialize into something more. In the meantime, Andrew did his best to run the state's government while continuing to take searing heat from the media as local reporters and newscasters peddled baseless accusations to the public, accusing him of everything from failing to be sufficiently forthcoming about his brother's situation—which was true—to trying to use his power and influence to cover things up or even coerce the state attorney's office to drop the charges against Tyler—which was patently untrue.

Tyler, of course, remained at home, staying inside most of the time, playing video games and watching television. Nearly every day he complained about not being able to leave the property and ride his bike—which he was very distraught to learn had been seized by the police—but he seemed to truly understand how much trouble he would be in if he were to so much as step through their front gate.

Molly spent as much time as she could at home with Tyler, skipping class now and then when she thought she could afford to. Julie suddenly seemed to be a little busier with her schoolwork than usual, leaving Molly to hope that she wasn't still thinking about moving out. Either way, Molly felt the need to keep a watchful eye on her brother in these early days of house arrest. She wanted to make sure he followed the rules. More than once, she'd found him looking out the window—at the occasional reporter and camera crew taping a segment in front of the house, or merely at the people who either kept their eyes on the house as they slowed their steps walking past, or those who blatantly stood and stared, hoping to catch a glimpse of the now-famous house prisoner. One time he had suggested that he go out and see what they wanted. Molly had tried to explain that he shouldn't talk to anyone, especially anyone with a microphone and a video camera.

According to Rachel Addison, who spoke with Molly after spending a few hours with Tyler following his return home on house arrest, she was working hard on his defense. For an expert witness, she had lined up a respected psychologist who would meet with Tyler to assess his intellect in order to help determine in what ways his diminished capacity might bolster their defense. Also, Addison said she was close to obtaining from the prosecution a transcript of the verbal statement Tyler had given at the police station, along with the video recording of the meeting—which the state was calling an interview but which Addison considered an interrogation. And she had already drafted a motion seeking to have the statement and the video excluded from evidence on several grounds, including that the statement had been coerced, that some of Tyler's statements about wanting to go home—about which he had told her—amounted to his termination of the voluntary interview, and therefore should have resulted in his being driven home or being read his rights. Additionally, the motion argued that, given Tyler's intellectual limitations, the detectives shouldn't have interviewed him outside the presence of a guardian responsible for his welfare and interests. Addison also had hired experts in blood spatter and crime scene re-creation. Finally, she had a private detective who worked for her firm interviewing people in the neighborhood, hoping for an alibi, and people in the victim's neighborhood, hoping that one of them had seen someone other than Tyler emerge from Sally Graham's apartment covered in her blood. They were also hoping to find the anonymous caller who claimed to have seen Tyler leaving the scene, but the Kane family didn't share in that hope because they were dead certain the anonymous caller was actually their anonymous blackmailer.

For his part, Henry kept looking into Gabriel Torrance, digging deep, but he still couldn't see why someone would be willing to commit murder to get him out of prison five months early. There simply didn't seem to be anyone in his life who cared enough about him. Because he had no family, he'd had very few visitors during his nearly five years in prison; the only people who had come to see him were his attorney, who visited a few times shortly after his conviction, and again almost a year ago; and three friends—two of which, Henry learned through online research, had been college buddies, and one an old high school friend.

So the Kanes went about their days, always waiting for the other shoe to drop.

When it finally did, it landed hard.

Henry was at his desk, once again going over Gabriel Torrance's case file, the procurement of which hadn't seemed to have raised any red flags or set off warning bells, when his cell phone rang and the words *Blocked Number* appeared on its screen.

"Kane," Henry said into the phone.

"Kane, it's Egan."

"I'm listening."

"I'm in. I'm on the edges of the case doing crap work, but I'm in. And I have information. Just remember, though, I'm not gonna compromise the investigation or do anything illegal. I'm only gonna share what you'd get in discovery soon enough anyway."

"Whatever. I'm still listening."

"It ain't pretty for your brother." Henry could hear the smug satisfaction in his voice. "During the search of his house, they found a pair of your brother's sneakers in the garage with blood on them."

"And blood on an electric bike. I know about that. Is it Sally Graham's blood?"

"DNA results aren't back, but it's her type."

Henry was certain it would be her blood. Their caller would have planted it there.

"There's more," Egan said, and again Henry didn't like the pleasure he seemed to be taking delivering the news. "The other night they got an anonymous call from someone—sounded like a teenager, maybe. He was jogging when he saw some homeless guy pick up a small plastic shopping bag from under a bush. The homeless guy takes a peek inside, then drops the bag and runs away, like in a panic. The jogger goes over to the bag, looks inside, and sees a pair of latex gloves covered in blood and a bloody pair of women's underwear."

Henry said, "Let me guess. Sally Graham's blood type?"

"Bingo."

"Did they get prints off the insides of the gloves?"

"No, but you know that's not always easy with gloves. Besides, he could have worn two pairs and disposed of the inside pair somewhere else."

"That's their theory?"

"I have no idea. But if I just thought of it, you know they have, too."

Egan had no idea how right he was. Henry had no doubt that Sally Graham's real killer had done just that. "Let me take another guess," Henry said. "They think there's somebody else's DNA on the underwear?"

Egan fell silent a moment. A long moment. "How the hell did you know that?"

The mysterious caller's words came to Henry's mind. *The blood is definitely Sally Graham's, and the DNA is indeed your brother's.*

"Just a hunch," Henry said. "What is it? On the underwear."

"Probably semen. They're waiting on the DNA results for that, too."

To see if it matched the DNA sample they would have taken from Tyler. Which it would, of course. The dickhead caller would have seen to that. And if that were true . . . well, that would be extraordinarily bad. It would make Rachel Addison's job very difficult. He had no idea how she could explain that away, other than claiming the test was faulty and the results therefore unreliable, which was a weak and desperate argument.

He couldn't begin to fathom how their mysterious caller had obtained a sample of Tyler's semen.

Henry realized at that moment that, in his entire life, he had never wanted anything as badly as he wanted to find and kill the son of a bitch behind this.

"I'm not sure I should tell you this . . ." Egan said.

"What?"

"There's something they're holding back."

A common practice, Henry knew. Police often withheld from the public details of a crime to weed out false confessions and, perhaps more important, to help determine the guilt of suspects they arrested. If the suspect shared with the police knowledge of those details, there was a good chance he or she committed the crime, or at least knew who did. Even in the hands of the most inexperienced prosecutor, such information was powerfully persuasive evidence in court.

"What is it?" Henry asked.

"I probably shouldn't—"

"Don't make me threaten you again. It's getting old for both of us. Besides, it's gonna come out eventually. So what are we talking about here?"

Egan hesitated, then said, "The perp cut a smiley face into the vic's torso."

"A smiley face?"

"Yeah. Stab wounds above each breast—representing the eyes, they figure—and a slice across the stomach, curvy, like a smile. I saw the photos. It was messy."

"No doubt. But how does that implicate my brother?"

"A character in one of the video games they took from his house does the same thing."

A light bulb flared on in Henry's mind. "Those damn *Smilin' Jack* games," he said.

"Yeah, it's a Vietnam War game, and the hero's some kind of expert in hand-to-hand combat. When he kills an enemy, he stabs him twice in the chest to make eyes, then slices across the stomach for a smile."

The thought of Tyler, who seemed so young and innocent despite his twenty-nine years of age, spending so much time playing a game like that made Henry queasy. The memory of buying Tyler a *Smilin' Jack* game for Christmas last year made him even queasier. God, he was getting old. Whatever happened to games like Twister and Operation?

"The video game's got the investigative team pretty excited. One of the disks was actually in your brother's game console when they searched the house."

Henry rubbed his eyes. "Anything else?"

"Damn, Kane, isn't that enough for now?"

"Keep me posted."

"My pleasure."

The prick meant it, too. He was enjoying himself. Henry could hardly blame him. He'd blackmailed Egan into doing this. Nonetheless, Henry wanted to kill *him* now, too, along with the guy who had framed Tyler for Sally Graham's murder.

CHAPTER TWENTY-EIGHT

"I know this isn't something you wanna talk about, Tyler," Henry said, "but it's important."

They were on the front porch, sitting in wicker rocking chairs. Molly had told him how much time Tyler had been spending inside the house, so he decided to bring his brother out for some air. There had been no lookie-loos peering over the wrought-iron fence when they'd stepped out here, but a young woman pushing a baby stroller was slowing down now as she passed on the sidewalk. Henry's glare quickened her steps, and soon she was gone down the block.

"Yeah, I don't like talking about this stuff," Tyler said, squinting into the late-afternoon sun that had slid low enough in the sky to peek under the porch roof.

"I know, but like I said, it's important. I need to know something." Henry wasn't quite sure how to ask what he needed to ask, or whether Tyler would be any more inclined to answer questions than he had been the other night. "Did you and Sally Graham . . ." He started over. "Did she touch you someplace private?"

Tyler's eyes widened. Then he tried to recover. "I'm going back inside, okay?"

"No, buddy. Stay here. Talk to me."

Tyler shook his head.

"Listen," Henry said, "I already know that she did. I just need to hear it from you."

"Why?"

"It's important."

"You already said that."

"Because it is."

Tyler looked away. "It's sunny today."

Henry sighed. "Yeah, it's nice." He let his eyes wander. They fell on the big elm in the front yard, where a squirrel seemed to defy both death and gravity as it leaped from the safety of one branch to a distant one. He was about to give up on Tyler when his brother said, "She told me I was cute."

"She did?"

He nodded. "And that she liked me. She put her hand on my leg and . . . I felt something change. You probably know what I mean."

Henry nodded. He didn't want to speak and impede whatever momentum Tyler was building.

"She asked if she could touch me, and I told her she already was. And she said, no, she wanted to touch me . . . you know . . . *there.*"

Tyler paused, and Henry waited him out.

"I knew it was wrong because she wasn't my girlfriend or anything, but I told her she could. So she . . ."

"Yeah?"

"She took some girlie underwear out of her pocket. She said she was wearing it earlier. Then she . . . she put it on her hand, like a glove, and she . . . touched me with it. She made me . . . you know."

He knew. Sally Graham had given Tyler a hand job with her panties. And Henry knew why. Because the mystery dickhead told her to. Probably paid her to. She likely had no idea why he wanted it done—perhaps she thought it was a prank, or that he was Tyler's caring uncle who wanted to see his nephew lose his virginity, in a manner of speaking. She very likely wondered why it had to be done in that specific way. But Henry knew the answer to that. He also knew that the caller had intended to kill Sally Graham from the start, but not before using her to create the evidence that would help frame an innocent man for her own murder.

The caller was twisted and cruel. And very clever.

"I know it was wrong, Henry. I shouldn't have let her do that. You don't have to tell Molly, do you?"

The idea that what had very likely been Tyler's first sexual experience with another person had been twisted into such a perverted parody of intimacy made Henry immeasurably sad.

"Nah, Molly doesn't need to know," he said. Tyler looked the tiniest bit relieved. "It's not your fault anyway," he added. "You never had a chance."

"What do you mean?"

"I mean that sometimes it's really hard for guys to resist the things that women can do for them. And because you've never experienced it before—at least, I'm guessing you haven't—it'd be even harder for you. So don't feel bad about letting it happen, okay? Or ashamed. You're a good guy, Tyler. You're my brother."

Tyler nodded. To Henry, he looked like a kid again, maybe eight years old, instead of a man closing in on thirty. It had been years since Henry's heart had been this close to breaking.

"I have to go now, buddy," he said.

"Can I come with you?"

Henry sighed. "Tyler, I thought you understood—"

"Gotcha," he said with a small smile. "I was kidding. I know the rules. I promise."

Henry smiled back. He really loved his baby brother.

As he drove away from the house, he became painfully aware, yet again, of how monstrously he had failed Tyler. God knows he had done things in his life he wasn't proud of—things of which he was deeply ashamed, in fact. In order to survive, he had taught himself not to dwell on those things, to tamp down certain memories when they threatened to rise to the surface, but what he did to Tyler . . . he had never been able to push those thoughts far from his mind.

It was painfully clear that Tyler wouldn't be in this situation but for the tragic accident that had damaged his brain and forever limited his intellect. Were it not for that terrible moment on that terrible day, he might have achieved any number of wonderful things. He might have married, had a child or two. He might have moved across the country, or the world, to pursue dreams he never even got the chance to have because of his fall off the roof when he was seven. If not for that accident, everything in his life would have been different. And he almost certainly wouldn't have met Sally Graham.

And the accident that knocked Tyler's life completely off track had been Henry's fault.

No one in his family ever acknowledged that fact to Henry, not his siblings, not his parents—not even Tyler—but they couldn't fail to have been aware of it. It had been Henry, two years older than his younger brother, who had dared Tyler to take the sheet off his bed, climb onto the roof outside his room, and parachute to the ground. It was Henry who had stood on the roof, ignoring Molly's pleas to stop Tyler, and Henry who had encouraged his brother when he'd seen Tyler's resolve flagging. In his defense, he thought it could be done. He thought the parachute would work. And if it did, he was going to try it next. It was a lousy defense. He might have believed it would work, but he knew it was risky. Yet he let Tyler jump anyway—Tyler, who would have done anything Henry told him to do, anything to impress his older brother. The fact that Henry was just a kid at the time, too, was no excuse in his mind.

A horn blared, startling Henry, who realized he had drifted too far toward the middle of the street. He corrected quickly, and the oncoming car passed by with plenty of room to spare, though that didn't deter the other driver from giving Henry the finger. He didn't care. He deserved it. He had knocked Tyler's life off course more than two decades ago. He could never undo the damage he had done.

But he could sure as hell do everything in his power to protect his brother now, to keep him out of prison. And he would, no matter what it took.

CHAPTER TWENTY-NINE

"His semen is on a pair of Sally Graham's underwear?" Andrew said. "Along with her blood?"

"DNA results aren't back yet, but—"

"The caller told us about this ahead of time," Andrew finished for him, "that it would be her blood and his DNA."

"Yup."

Andrew was at his desk in his office on the fifth floor of the Pavilion, a red pen in hand, reviewing the draft of a bill his legislative team had written.

"How the hell did his semen . . . ?"

Henry told him, relating his entire conversation with Tyler.

"That bastard," Andrew said, trusting that Henry would know he wasn't referring to Tyler.

"I'm gonna ask around about Sally Graham, see if anyone saw her with anyone new lately, see if maybe she told anyone about having met our blackmailer."

"The cops have probably done all that."

"If they did, I doubt they worked it too hard. They focused on Tyler early. And now they have him. No reason to keep pursuing that angle."

Next, Henry shared with him information he'd gotten from Egan that the police hadn't made public, about a smiley face cut into Sally Graham's torso.

"A guy in Tyler's favorite video game does the same thing to his enemies," Henry said. "They found Tyler's games, of course, at the house."

"That's bad, Henry."

Andrew thought about the various efforts the caller had made to frame Tyler. The man was frighteningly creative and thorough. Then a thought struck him. "How did you get this information? It's not public, and there's no way the prosecution shared this with Rachel Addison so soon."

Henry shrugged. "I have contacts."

"I can't imagine anyone on the case would leak this to you."

Henry said nothing.

"If you accessed files you aren't authorized to—"

"I didn't do that."

"Then how?"

Henry hesitated. "You don't need to know."

Andrew knew his brother was protecting him. If Henry had done something illegal or unethical and Andrew knew about it, the political fallout, for Andrew at least, could be something on the level of Three Mile Island. And it wouldn't look good for Henry, either, especially given his Internal Affairs role.

"Henry, I don't want you doing anything against the law or—"

"Thanks, but I'm a big boy. I can make my own decisions."

"But you—"

"You're the lawyer," Henry said, cutting him off and changing directions. "Former prosecutor. How would you feel if you were trying this case?"

Andrew's thoughts stumbled momentarily, unready for the sudden shift in conversation. "Confident," he finally said. "Really confident."

"Yeah, that's my take on it, too. So I see only two options. First, we can let Addison do her thing building Tyler's defense, help her however we can, and hope for the best, trusting in a judicial process that we've both seen do its best but fall sadly short at times . . . hoping all the while that the mysterious dickhead is tapped out, that he won't anonymously call in more tips about additional evidence implicating Tyler."

"If we do that, we can still give the mystery phone to the detectives on the case," Andrew said. "As soon as the guy calls again, they'll know it's legit."

"They'll think it's a cheap, desperate tactic to create reasonable doubt. That we put someone up to it. Isn't that what you'd think?"

Instead of answering, Andrew said, "What are the odds that he's tapped out? That he has no more evidence linking Tyler to the murder?"

"Not good, I'd say. Which brings us to our second option." He paused, then said, "Getting the video that will clear Tyler."

"By granting Gabriel Torrance executive clemency," Andrew said, allowing a full dose of disgust to infuse his words. "Giving him a full pardon. Putting a convicted felon back on the street before he's paid his debt to society in full."

"A guy with no prior record who committed a stupid but totally unplanned crime, then panicked. A model prisoner with only five months to go on a sentence of less than five years."

Andrew sighed in frustration. He couldn't do what the caller was asking. Why didn't Henry understand that? There had to be another way. Unfortunately, he couldn't imagine what that would be.

"How do we know this guy would even keep his word and give us the video? Hell, how do we know such a video even exists?"

"We don't. But Tyler's innocent. He shouldn't go to prison. It's up to us to decide the best way to keep that from happening."

Andrew closed his eyes. His mind was suddenly a maelstrom of thoughts and questions, possibilities and ramifications. Finally, he said, "The guy might not even call again."

"For some reason," Henry said, "he wants Torrance out of prison. And soon. He'll call."

———

He called almost five hours later, while Andrew was brushing his teeth before bed. Andrew had left both cell phones—his own and the mystery phone—on his nightstand. With the water running and the toothbrush in his mouth, he didn't hear the latter's vibration against the wooden surface beneath it. He almost didn't hear Rebecca call from the next room, "Andy? The black phone is ringing."

He quickly spit and rinsed, then hurried into the bedroom. Rebecca was propped up by several pillows behind her back, a hardcover novel in her hands. Andrew picked up the mystery phone and headed toward the door to the hall.

"Stay here," Rebecca said. "I know about it now anyway."

Andrew hesitated. The phone vibrated in his hand. He started for the hallway, sneaking a glance over his shoulder at Rebecca. After thirteen years of marriage, they were good at reading each other's faces. At that moment, hers was registering disappointment. About precisely what, he wasn't quite certain. The phone vibrated again.

Out in the hall, he closed the door behind him. He'd forgotten his personal phone, so he wouldn't be recording this conversation, but he wasn't sure it mattered. If anyone was ever inclined to believe him, the two recordings they had already made would likely be enough. And if people chose instead to believe that the calls were fakes intended to create reasonable doubt, then a greater number of such recordings wasn't going to sway anyone.

The phone was vibrating yet again when Andrew answered with a curt "Yes?"

The familiar, grating, metallic voice intoned, "You know about the underwear yet?"

"Yeah."

"Good. Like I said, the DNA is your brother's. The blood is Sally's."

The phone felt fragile in his hand. He could have crushed it to plastic shards with ease. He *wanted* to crush it.

"Governor Andy? You still there?"

"You're sick."

"By some people's definitions, probably," the robotic voice said. "But let's not waste time with that kind of talk. It's not productive. I need you to understand that I have more evidence, Andy. A lot more. Enough to make sure your baby brother is locked away for the remainder of his days with the rest of society's most violent criminals."

"Listen, I can't do what you—"

"You're out of time. This is your last chance before I go nuclear and give everything I have to the police."

"There has to be another way. Something else you—"

"I need an answer. Right now."

"Please . . ."

"Don't make me start counting as if you're a naughty child. Make your choice. Does Gabriel Torrance go free soon, or does Tyler never go free again?"

"Give me a second here. This is—"

"Five . . . four . . . three . . . two—"

"I need proof," Andrew practically shouted.

After a moment, the caller said, "Proof of what?"

"I need to see the video you have showing that Tyler didn't do it. I need to see what I'll be getting if . . . if I agree to this." He almost hadn't been able to choke out the last few words.

The caller seemed to consider that. "If I send you the recording, then you'll have it and lose all incentive to do what I'm asking."

"We could meet. You could show it to me."

"Yes, and I'll trust that you'll be alone. That the cops won't be hidden behind every mailbox and shrub."

"Looks like we're at an impasse then. I can't do what you're asking without knowing whether you even have what you say you do."

They fell silent a moment. Finally, the caller said, "I'll be honest, Andy, I expected this. I planned for it. So here's what's going to happen: When we hang up, I'm going to text meeting instructions to the phone in your hand. You show up where and when I say, or send someone on your behalf, for all I care. I'll have a representative of my own there who will show you or your guy the video. Then you can decide if what I have is worth trading for. Aaaaaand . . . for a limited time only, if you act soon, I'll throw in the rest of the evidence against Tyler absolutely free."

The creepy robotic voice imitating the chipper style of a late-night infomercial pitchman was beyond unnerving.

"Am I correct in assuming that you won't want to agree to my demands during a phone call?" the caller asked. "Which I could be secretly recording?"

"Do you think I'm stupid?"

"No, I do not. So tomorrow, send someone authorized to close the deal for you. And don't do anything dumb like sending the cops instead, or following my representative after the meeting. That will only make me assume you have no intention of coming to, or keeping, an agreement, and I'll have no choice but to pull the pins on all my grenades. I don't care who you send, as long as it's not a cop. And that includes Detective Henry. Understand?"

Andrew said nothing.

"I'll take that as a yes. Don't worry, Andy. If all goes well, both Gabriel Torrance and your brother will be free men soon."

The caller disconnected. Andrew suddenly felt the need for a shower. Instead, he returned to the bedroom and slipped under the covers beside his wife, who had turned off the lamp on her nightstand but was still sitting up, wide awake.

"Well?" she said. "Are you going to do what he wants?"

Earlier in the evening, Andrew had shared with her the news about the victim's bloody, DNA-covered underwear. She knew how strong the case against Tyler was growing.

"I don't know."

"Andrew?"

He hesitated. "I sure as hell won't do it without proof he can exonerate my brother." He paused again, then said, "I've told him I need to see he has that."

"And if he does?"

"I don't know, Becca."

But that wasn't true. He knew it, and she did, too. If the blackmailer had what he said he had . . .

She rolled onto her side, facing away from him, without giving him the peck on the cheek she'd given him every night they had ever shared a bed. A moment later, though, she reached behind her, took his hand, and placed it on her hip. It wasn't a kiss, but it was something, at least.

He reached up and turned off his bedside lamp, plunging them into darkness.

CHAPTER THIRTY

"I don't like this," Andrew said.

"I'm not wild about it, either," Henry added.

Molly loved her brothers and knew they were only looking out for her, but they were being stupid—which didn't surprise her. This certainly wasn't the first time they'd been stupid about trying to protect her. How many boys had they scared away from her in high school? How hard had Andy tried to convince her not to join the army, which had turned out to be one of the most rewarding experiences of her life?

"I'm the only option, guys. You two can't go. Who else is there? Rebecca? No offense, Andy, but unless she did two tours in the Middle East like I did that I'm not aware of, I'm the only logical choice. And what's there to worry about? We have no idea who this guy is, what he looks like. If he wanted to try to hurt me, he could do it anytime he felt like it, right on the street, or even in our house. He wouldn't have to get me alone in a deserted parking lot at night. Besides, you sexist pigs, since when haven't I been able to take care of myself? I'm battle-tested, remember? How many people have you had to kill, Andy?"

"None," he admitted.

"Henry? Ever killed anyone?"

"Uh . . ."

"That's a no for you, too, then," she said.

The two brothers shrugged and mumbled a bit. Eventually, Andrew made clear that he was folding when he asked, "Should she be wearing a wire, Henry? So we can record the meeting for evidence?"

Henry shook his head. "Again, they'd just say we set it all up to create reasonable doubt. It's no better than giving them the phone and a fairy tale about the boogeyman who gave it to you. Besides, whoever he sends to the meet may check Molly for a wire, and if we piss our guy off, he may say to hell with it and give all the evidence against Tyler to the cops and destroy the recording proving his innocence."

"Look, this is simple," Molly said. "I check out whatever evidence he has to show me. If it looks legit . . ." She glanced at Andrew.

He hesitated, then said, "If it looks legit, tell him I'll agree to his demand."

No one said anything for a moment. Molly and Henry exchanged glances. Then they looked at Andrew. He took a long, slow breath, then nodded.

"Okay then," Molly said. "Time for me to go."

———

Molly eased her car to a stop at the edge of the parking lot of the Burr and Burton Academy—a secondary school founded almost 200 years ago—where the meeting was to take place. At 10:53 p.m., the lot was deserted, and the nearby buildings looked dark and lifeless. The moon was bright tonight, though. Molly raised a pair of binoculars and looked out through the windshield, her army training kicking in as she coolly scanned the area for threats—the parking lot, the buildings, the tree line at the north end of the lot. She snuck a glance at her watch: 10:59.

A minute later, a solitary figure appeared at the far end of the lot. A man. She wasn't concerned. She could handle herself. She considered retrieving the slim, sleek Glock 43 she kept in the glove compartment, but after assessing the situation decided against it. She truly believed she wouldn't need it, in which case its presence could make a tense situation far more tense . . . and dangerous. Besides, she could handle herself without a gun.

She stepped from her Land Rover and was about to start walking toward him, to meet him in the middle, when she thought, *Why the hell should I do the walking?* She leaned against the front of her SUV and watched him approach. She hoped he saw her easy confidence. Finally, he came close enough that she could see him reasonably well in the dark. He carried what looked like a cell phone in one hand and something long and thin—maybe a weapon—in the other. He was Hispanic. Late twenties. Medium height. Big tattoo on his neck. Wiry but muscular.

When he was ten feet away, Molly said, "That's far enough for now."

He stopped. She noticed earbuds hanging around his neck and could hear faint music emanating from them. Their cord trailed into the front pocket of his jeans, where she could see a rectangular, smartphone-size bulge.

"Just so you know," she said, "I'm a trained killer. Army. I could end you in five seconds. If that's a weapon of some kind you've got there, it might take me ten."

"Damn," the guy said, smiling. "That was pretty cool. Like a line from a movie. Is it true?"

"Trust me, you don't want to find out."

The guy was still smiling. "Damn."

She nodded toward the long, skinny thing in his hand. "What's that?"

"Something he gave me to see if you're wired. I'm supposed to wave it over your body."

She didn't like the way he said the word *body*.

She pushed off the vehicle, stepped forward, and raised her arms. "Get it over with."

He took his time, looking her over while he scanned. When he briefly met her eyes and caught the threat there, he stepped back and announced, "You're clean."

"I know."

"I didn't see a cell phone in any of your pockets, either."

"I was told not to have one. So who are you?"

"Nobody."

"How do you know him?"

"Who?"

"The guy who sent you."

"I don't. He gave me four hundred bucks and this detector. Told me if it made any noise when I waved it over you, I should walk away. Also gave me this phone, which I'm supposed to show you if the wand didn't beep."

She eyed the phone. If there was a recording that would prove Tyler innocent on it, all she had to do was take it from the guy. She could do that. No problem at all.

The guy nodded knowingly. "He said you'd be thinking about trying to take the phone from me, so I'm supposed to tell you the video's not on it. But you'll see it there."

"What does that mean?"

"That's all he said about it."

"You know his name?" she asked.

"Nope."

"What's he look like?"

"He looked like a guy in a ski mask. Pulled up next to me and offered me a quick hundred bucks. I thought he was looking for a blow job or something, and I was trying to decide whether to just walk away, or to pull him out of his car and beat him bloody and *then* walk away. Then he upped it to four hundred and told me what he wanted me to do. He talked with one of those things that made his voice sound weird. Like a robot's."

Well, just in case Molly had harbored any doubt that she was at the right meeting . . .

"Show me what he wants you to show me," she said.

"I gotta wait for it to ring."

"How long do we have to wait for that?"

He shrugged. "Wanna have some fun while we wait?"

"Wanna piss through a special tube for the rest of your life?"

He smiled appreciatively. "Damn."

They stood in awkward silence for another minute or so until the phone rang. The guy turned the screen toward her. Then, with his other hand, he slipped the earbuds into his ears, one by one. "Doing as I was told," he said. "Can't hear a thing now."

The phone rang again.

"It's a video call," the guy said a little too loudly in the deserted parking lot, to be heard over the music pounding in his ears. "For your eyes only. Press the 'Answer' button."

She did, and an image appeared on the screen. An image of another screen. She realized that the camera on his end was facing a computer monitor. She could see nothing else in the frame, just the monitor, on which she saw a frozen scene. Looked like an apartment. There was someone in the center of the frame, across a dimly lit room.

"Are you there?" a harsh robotic voice said from somewhere off-screen. It sounded like metal scraping against metal. It was the first time Molly had heard it herself.

"I'm here," she said.

"I can't see you, of course. A woman, though. Is that Molly Kane, the governor's sweet little sister?"

"Not that little. Definitely not sweet."

"I guess your brothers have let you in on this. Welcome."

"I hope you know that if I ever find you, I'll do terrible things to you. I learned a lot of terrible things in the Middle East." Without waiting for him to reply, she said, "Now show me what I'm here to see."

The camera shook slightly; then the image on the screen unfroze, and the person across the room in the video moved.

Smart, showing her the video in a way that made it impossible for her to steal it by grabbing the device playing it . . . which she had totally been planning to do if she got the chance. The recording she needed wasn't on the phone in front of her. It was somewhere else. It could have been anywhere—two blocks away or in Paris.

On-screen, the person—a woman, Molly was now able to discern—was doing something with her hand. Ah, she was drinking from a glass. She put the glass down and stood motionless for a moment, staring in the direction of the camera. Then she took a tentative step forward, followed by another. Suddenly, a figure stepped into frame, apparently from behind the camera. It walked toward the woman . . . toward Sally Graham, she realized. This must have been her apartment. The figure kept getting closer to her. A man, by its size. In fact, a man several inches taller than Tyler. And heavier, too, by at least forty pounds. But that was all she could tell about him, because everywhere she should have seen skin was covered by white fabric of some kind, like a chemical protective suit she'd seen others wear in the army, only his was white instead of olive or camo. The suit had a hood, and dark goggles covered the man's eyes. Over the white suit, he wore regular clothes that were quite obviously a few sizes too small for him: a long-sleeved Pac-Man T-shirt, blue jeans, sneakers. He looked like a white mannequin wearing ill-fitting garments. The clothes were—

Tyler's. She was nearly positive. She'd bought him that T-shirt last fall.

The man stepped up to the woman, and she . . . didn't do anything. She didn't run. She didn't scream. Why didn't she run or scream?

He reached out and put his hand over her mouth, then he stepped behind her and . . .

He stabbed her in the chest. She grunted.

Molly almost cried out.

He stabbed her in the chest again, the knife making a wet thudding sound. She grunted again.

Molly had seen death. She'd seen people die. She'd seen them killed by other people. She'd killed enemy soldiers herself in conflicts. But the cold, methodical way the man on-screen stabbed the woman—*then slowly sliced her stomach open*—was the most disturbing thing she'd ever witnessed. His actions were so mechanical and precise that she wondered for an irrational moment whether he truly *was* a robot.

The man lowered the woman's body to the carpet, almost gently, and hovered over her, touching her . . . no, not just touching her. He was *positioning* her—straightening a leg a little, arranging her hair. What the hell?

Finally, mercifully, the image froze again.

"Do you understand, Molly?" the robot asked.

He was questioning whether she could see why this video would clear Tyler. And she could. The man was undoubtedly too big to be her brother. Also, she realized, the level of planning evident in the video was likely beyond Tyler's capabilities. He was innocent. She had believed it in her heart. She'd believed what her brothers had told her. But now she'd *seen* it.

"If I'm ever in the same room with you," she said, "I'm going to kill you."

"Your tough talk is getting boring, Molly. Now, there's a little more for you to see."

The camera turned away from the computer monitor and panned across several items of clothing laid out on a big, otherwise empty surface, perhaps a dining room table. Men's clothes. Tyler's clothes, she realized again. Several shirts and pairs of pants.

"I took these from the hamper in Tyler's room. They undoubtedly have his DNA on them. I could use them in any number of ways to dig his hole a lot deeper. But if Governor Andy does what I ask, I'll give these to you guys along with the recording."

The camera swung back to the computer monitor and the frozen image of the killer, wearing Tyler's clothes, standing over Sally Graham's bloody corpse.

Molly took a moment just to breathe. It was something she'd learned in the army. Before you momentarily expose yourself to return fire; or begin your sprint across open, deadly terrain; or step through a doorway without knowing whether there was someone on the other side waiting to kill you . . . just breathe. Finally, she said, "How do I know you'll give us the recording?"

"I don't care about your brother," the caller said, his robotic voice still offscreen. "I care only about Gabriel Torrance. There's no way to know from the video who really killed Sally Graham, so I'm not at risk of suspicion. So I'm better off giving you guys the video and hoping you'll be content to leave me alone than I am screwing you guys over and ensuring you'll never stop trying to prove Tyler's innocence and, at the same time, looking for me. Sound reasonable?"

She mulled that over. It made sense. Besides, what choice did they have? Tyler was their brother.

"I'll tell Andrew you're legit."

"Did he authorize you to make a deal?"

"Yeah."

"And?"

"He'll do it."

"In exchange for the video you saw and the rest of the evidence I have against your brother Tyler, he'll grant clemency to Gabriel Torrance, get him out of prison?"

"He will."

"No halfway house, either. Totally free."

"He knows that," Molly said.

"When will it happen?"

"When you give us the video and the evidence."

A burst of something like static erupted from the phone's speaker, but Molly realized it was the caller laughing, a hideous metallic cackle. "I don't think so," he said. "First, Gabriel goes free; then I'll send the stuff wherever you want. How about your house? I know where you live."

Molly ignored the implied threat. "Give us the stuff first."

That horrible cackle again. "No. We'll do it my way. I'll send the evidence to your house as soon as Gabriel walks out of prison." Without waiting for a reply, he said. "Now, how soon will that be?"

She took a deep breath. "I don't know. As soon as he can, I guess. He told me it could take a little while."

"He has one week."

"The timing's up to him."

"That's fine. Tell him to take his time. But in exactly one week from this moment, if Torrance still hasn't joined the rest of free society, I'll start—"

"Yeah, yeah. Threat received. I'll pass it along. And while we're at it, I have one for you. If you screw us over and I ever come face-to-face with you, I'm gonna kill you really, really hard. You can count on it."

"You already said that, but I appreciate the warning."

"It's not a warning. It's a threat. Bye, asshole."

She punched the "Disconnect" button on the phone, then tugged a bud from one of the ears of the guy holding it and said, "Bye, asshole" to him, too.

She was behind the wheel again, pulling out of the lot, when an image of Sally Graham being stabbed rose in her mind like a wraith. She turned on the radio to drown out Sally's pained whispers and the slippery sounds of the killer's knife.

CHAPTER THIRTY-ONE

Andrew pushed the speakerphone button on the cordless handset sitting in the middle of the kitchen table, ending the call with Molly. He looked across the table at Henry, who nodded almost imperceptibly, then across the room at Rebecca, who was leaning against the granite counter, a mug of hot tea in her hand. As soon as his gaze met hers, she dropped her eyes. Andrew shifted his eyes quickly back to Henry's, wondering if he'd seen that. He had. Andrew could see it on his face.

Henry stood up from the table. "It's late. I'm gonna head home."

Andrew stood, too. "I'll walk you to the door."

He followed Henry out of the kitchen and down the hall to the front door, where his brother turned and said, "You're gonna do it?"

He didn't want to. Almost every instinct warned him not to. And he was certainly aware of the distinct possibility that, like many blackmailers, this one wouldn't let him go even after he'd done what the man asked. Still, Andrew shrugged. "I have to, right? For Tyler." He thought about his youngest brother, asleep in his room upstairs, completely unaware of the machinations taking place all around him.

"I know this isn't easy for you," Henry said, "but people do way worse than this all the time and somehow find a way to live with themselves."

Despite knowing Henry since the day his brother was born, something in his brother's eyes made Andrew wonder for a brief moment if Henry might be one of those people.

"It may not be easy, Andy. It may be damn hard. But they manage. You will, too. That probably doesn't help you very much right now, but it's true."

Henry was right. It didn't help much . . . not when Andrew was discovering that he wasn't quite the man he'd thought he was. Not long ago, he never would have imagined he'd be for sale. It turned out, though, that it had been largely a question of price.

"Listen, Henry," he said, "we have to keep tabs on Torrance. We have to have him watched, and the minute it looks like he's going to hurt someone, he has to be stopped. Otherwise, I can't let him out and Tyler will very likely go down for murder."

"Nothing in Torrance's history suggests violence. Nothing. I don't think this is about anything like that. More likely it's about stolen goods. Maybe drugs. Anyway, he's gonna have eyes on him around the clock. I'll take care of that. We can afford it. He won't get the chance to hurt anyone, if that's even his intention, which I highly doubt."

Andrew nodded, mostly to himself.

"And I'm gonna keep working this, Andy, until I find the guy behind this, which I *don't* doubt at all."

"Any chance you'll find him in the next couple of days, before I irrevocably compromise my integrity?"

"Ummm . . ."

"Good night, Henry."

———

Andrew and Rebecca waited at the house until Molly came home safe and sound, then left, with Andrew's ever-present security detail in the black SUV behind them. He spent his first ten minutes behind the wheel wondering whether he should break the awkward, stifling silence that had followed them from the house. He wondered whether he even wanted to. What was there to say?

The black cell phone vibrated in his pocket, rendering the question moot. Driving as he was, he didn't bother trying to record the conversation with his personal phone.

By way of answering the call, he asked, "What do you want now?"

"It sounds like you're in a car," the harsh metallic voice said. "Are you driving, Governor? If so, and I'm not on speakerphone, you're committing a moving violation. You could get in trouble."

"I'll ask again: What do you want?"

"I just wanted to thank you for your cooperation. It's been a pleasure doing business with you."

Andrew was well aware that the caller could be recording this conversation. In every call so far, he had agreed to nothing. But there was something he needed to know.

"When will . . . this be over?" he asked carefully.

"When will you have what you want? When *I* have what *I* want. That's when. Oh, and when Gabriel's out, I don't want you guys watching him. No following him around. You leave him alone."

"That wasn't part of the deal, damn it," Andrew said, forgetting to be circumspect.

"It was always part of the deal, Andy. You just didn't know it."

Andrew snapped the flip phone shut, ending the call.

Rebecca stared out at the road, giving him a few moments, then asked, "How soon will you do it?"

"As soon as I can. The guy on the phone wants him out in a week. That will be damn difficult. I'll have to put pressure on some people to make that happen. But I want this to be over for Tyler. I don't want more evidence piling up against him, evidence that would just make it harder for people to accept his innocence, even in the face of a video proving it."

She fell silent. Two miles later, he said, "I know you're disappointed in me." He paused, very briefly, in case she wanted to give him a surprise and contradict him. She didn't, so he went on. "I'm disappointed in me, too, Becca. Believe me. But I don't feel like I have a choice."

"Of course you have a choice," she said, suddenly animated. "You can choose to trust the system you were part of for years."

She was wrong. He couldn't do that. He wished he could, but he couldn't. "He's my brother."

She looked out at the darkness beyond the passenger window for a few minutes, then turned toward him, the sadness in her eyes plain to see in the dim blue light of the dashboard.

"You've always been the most honest man I've ever known. No matter what you were doing, or with whom you were dealing, you floated above everyone. Your integrity has always been your defining trait. It's hard to see you . . ." She trailed off.

"Without it?" he finished for her.

She looked out the window again.

She wasn't being mean. She didn't intend to hurt him. But her words bit deep, hitting bone. He understood, though. He wasn't exactly the man she thought she'd married. He was pretty close but not quite the same. He was having trouble accepting that about himself, so why shouldn't he expect her to have the same difficulty?

"I'm not all that different than I was, Becca," he said. "I still have the same heart. And it's breaking for my brother." *And over the way this is making you look at me,* he almost added. "And I know for a fact that I still have the same conscience, because it's torturing me over this."

"I know."

"I'm also still the governor, still in position to do a lot of good. And once this is all behind us, I can focus on everything I want to accomplish for the people of Vermont. And I'll do so with the integrity you expect of me. And that I expect of myself."

She nodded, then said, "What if he hurts someone when he gets out?"

"He won't," he said with just a bit more confidence than he felt. "Like Henry said, he was never a violent man. And besides, we're gonna have him watched 24–7, at least until we figure out what he's up to."

She nodded again but said nothing.

"Still love me?" he asked.

She turned to him, and the look in her eyes erased any doubt he might have been having about that. There were many unseen weights pressing on his shoulders, but one of them disappeared in a blink. "Don't be an idiot." She took his right hand off the steering wheel and held it tight between hers. "I know he's your brother, Andy, and you know how much I love him, but to allow this . . . to let yourself be . . ."

"He's my little brother, Becca. He's family. I'd do anything for him. And Molly and Henry, too. You may not understand this, but . . . it's a blood thing."

Her grip on his hand loosened slightly. "And what about me? I'm not *blood*?"

"I'd do anything for you, too. You know that."

"What if I asked you not to do this, to just let the court system do its job?"

"Are you asking that of me?"

She hesitated. "No."

"Good." He was glad she didn't press him to answer her hypothetical question, because she wouldn't have liked his response. "It's a blood thing," he repeated. "That's all there is to it."

But that wasn't really all. That was a great deal of it, absolutely. But there was more. And it was finally time he told his wife about it, though it was something he'd never said out loud to anyone.

"Tyler is the way he is because of me," he said quietly.

"What?"

"The accident that made him who he is . . . was my fault."

"How?"

He took a breath, said a silent prayer that Rebecca truly loved him as much as she seemed to, then began. "Tyler and Molly were seven at the time, and Henry was nine. I was twelve. Dad was at work, and we were home with my mom, only she had to run to the store for milk. Mrs. Gallagher was off that day. I'll always remember that it was milk she needed. Anyway, she left me in charge. She was gone less than an hour." He was quiet a moment, remembering. Rebecca waited in patient silence. "I had a friend. Danny Hatcher. Lived two streets over. He knocked on my door and said he'd just seen my mom leave. He opened his jacket and showed me something he'd brought with him, a *Playboy* he'd found in his dad's nightstand. I'd never seen anything like it before. It was . . . exhilarating. So I told the other kids not to get into trouble and left them playing a game. Hungry Hungry Hippos. I'll always remember that, too."

He slid into silence and let a mile of road play out behind them. He kept his eyes on the road. He had to.

"Danny and I snuck off to the basement to look at naked ladies. The next thing I know, I heard footsteps pounding through the house above us, and Molly yelling for me. I ran up the stairs and followed her out the back door and found Tyler in the yard, near the house, lying in a heap. He had a bedsheet twisted around him."

"Oh, Andy . . ." Rebecca said.

"Molly told me he had parachuted off the roof. Henry was suddenly behind me asking if Tyler was dead. And I thought he might have been. He wasn't moving. I ran inside and called 911, then told Henry and Molly to wait on the front porch and bring the paramedics around back when they arrived while I stayed with Tyler. I didn't think they needed to keep looking at him just lying there." He paused. "The ambulance got there at the same time my mom came home. I remember her racing around the side of the house, ahead of the EMTs. I can still see her face when she looked at Tyler . . . then at me." He took a deep breath. "Another thing I'll always remember."

Rebecca sniffed. Andrew wondered if she was crying. He didn't want to look, though. He didn't want to know.

"He woke up three days later," he said. "When he did, he wasn't the same. And he never will be."

Rebecca's voice was soft. "You were just a kid."

"I was almost a teenager. I had a responsibility, and I knew it. But I chose to look at a girlie magazine."

"I'm sure Tyler doesn't blame you."

"Of course he doesn't. He doesn't even remember how it happened. And even if he did, he probably wouldn't blame me, because he's the best person I know. But everyone else in the family did."

"They told you that?"

"No, they never said it to me."

"You overheard them talking to each other, blaming you?"

"I didn't have to."

"So you never actually heard them blaming you? Any of them? Not your brothers or your sister? Not even your parents?"

"No," he said, "but how could they not? It was obviously my fault."

She squeezed his hand tight. "Oh, Andy. You've been carrying this around since you were twelve years old? Hon, I'm betting nobody ever blamed you. If your mother blamed anyone, it was probably herself for leaving the four of you alone in the house that day. Your dad probably blamed her, too. And Molly and the boys? They know you were all just kids. Nobody ever thought it was your fault. I promise you."

He stared out through the windshield for a long moment. What she said had never occurred to him. None of it. "It doesn't matter either way, I guess, because I blame myself. And that's enough. Tyler's my responsibility."

"Andy—"

"And anyway, like I told you before, it's more than that. A lot more. He's my blood, Becca, and his life is on the line here. It's like someone has a gun to his head and is telling me he'll pull the trigger if I don't let some guy out of prison. Can you picture that, Becca? Can you try to see it that way for a second? Let someone out of prison, or I blow you brother's brains out. Wouldn't I have to free that prisoner in those circumstances?"

"This isn't like that."

"It's close enough. If I don't do what he wants, Tyler's life is over. End of story. I won't let that happen."

Rebecca fell silent. Finally, he looked over at her.

"I'll do whatever I can to protect him, Becks. And Molly and Henry, too. I don't think I ever realized how strongly I felt about that until this happened. Until just now, in fact. You understand, don't you?"

She shrugged and gently let go of his hand. "Sure. It's a blood thing," she said, echoing his words.

The rest of their ride home passed in silence.

CHAPTER THIRTY-TWO

The following day, Andrew sat at his desk on the fifth floor of the Pavilion, reading through the file he'd asked his assistant to retrieve for him. It was full of pardon and clemency petitions submitted to his office since the beginning of the calendar year. There were a couple of dozen or so, each stamped with the date on which it had been received. He read through a few. Prisoners who believed they had been rehabilitated even though the parole board disagreed. Prisoners who simply thought they had served enough time. Prisoners who didn't claim innocence but who opined that their sentences had been too harsh. Andrew had probably seen each one of these letters when they had first crossed his desk, probably even read them, but he couldn't remember a single one, which ignited a tiny spark of guilt.

Historically, in a country with so many registered voters wanting their government to be tough on crime, the decision to pardon prisoners was not popular with almost anyone other than the pardoned prisoners and their immediate families. That was why so many chief executives waited until the twilight of their terms in office to grant pardons. Without giving it much thought, Andrew had always believed that when his time as governor was drawing to a close, he would do the same. Now that he was being forced to consider the subject, he wondered why he should wait. If a petition had merit, it had merit, and whether the voting public would be displeased shouldn't factor into the calculus. He resolved to go through this folder again carefully and with an open mind when all of this was over.

He looked at the elegant Waterford crystal clock on the corner of his desk, a parting gift from his colleagues when he left the state attorney's office—a time when he could never have imagined crossing an ethical line—then picked up the phone and dialed. Henry answered on the second ring. "Hey."

"What have you got?" Andrew asked.

"Nothing. I've been checking out the people who visited Torrance during his time in prison. There were only four, remember? Including his public defender."

"And there's nothing there?"

"Nothing I can see. His PD's name is Wesley Jurgens. He visited a few times in the months after he lost Torrance's case—presumably to talk about an appeal. Next up were a couple of old college friends." Andrew heard papers rustling over the phone. "Samuel Ordway and Scott Figgis. They each paid him a visit in the first year, separately, and Figgis came back once in the second. Next up was Derek Closterman, an old high school classmate, who also visited in the second year. Then no one until almost a year ago, when Jurgens went to see him again. Probably to talk about an appeal again. Or maybe clemency."

"Probably. Whatever it was, it's privileged," Andrew said, referring to the confidential nature of communications between an attorney and his client.

"Yeah, that's what Jurgens told me when I called him."

"I'm not surprised. You tell him why you were calling?"

"No."

"He tell you anything else?"

"Nothing useful. I caught him between appearances in court, so he was a bit abrupt, but he was willing to tell me what a fine guy Torrance

189

is, how he got screwed on the sentence, blah, blah, blah. Said he hadn't seen him in at least a year."

"Which we knew."

"Right."

"And you said you looked into those three school friends?"

"As deep as I could," Henry said. "And I spoke with them each by phone. Kept my reason for the calls vague."

"And nothing?"

"Nothing. I just don't see any reason someone would want him out of prison so badly."

"Damn it."

"Don't forget the good news, though."

"Which is?"

"We've also found no reason to worry about the guy when he gets out. He was clean as a whistle before his accident and a model prisoner after. No reason to think he's gonna do bad things. That's not much comfort, but it's something, isn't it?"

Andrew sighed. He was right. It wasn't much comfort.

He ended the call, then glanced at his desktop computer before reaching into a desk drawer for his laptop. After powering it up, he opened a word processing program and typed a letter to himself from Southern State Correctional Facility prisoner Gabriel Torrance, seeking executive clemency. Writing as Torrance, he expressed deep regret for the accident that resulted in the injury to Craig Whitworth, the other driver—though Andrew knew that at least one witness had blamed the accident on Whitworth. He wrote that he regretted leaving the scene. He promised to never touch another drop of alcohol. He dated the letter seven months ago and sent it to the printer in the corner of his office.

He sat for a moment with the printed letter facedown on his desk, unwilling for a moment to turn it over, to see what he had created. Instead, he studied Torrance's signature on a copy of a form Torrance had signed when he was first sent to prison, which Henry had procured from his file. Andrew practiced signing Torrance's name several times on a scratch pad, then flipped the letter over and, quickly, before he could stop himself, forged Torrance's signature. Then he deleted the document from his laptop.

Next, he held the forged letter roughly in his hands, forcing the paper to bend back and forth. He even folded over the upper right corner, creating a tiny crease. He thought the document now looked older than five minutes. He was appalled to realize he was better at this kind of deception than he wanted to be.

Using the intercom, he asked his assistant to come into his office. A moment later, there was a small knock as the door opened.

"Sir?" Peter said.

He kept his eyes on the letter in his hands so he wouldn't have to meet the younger man's gaze. "I was going through these petitions for clemency, and I noticed that this one doesn't have a date stamp like the others."

"I'm so sorry, Governor," Peter said, sounding abashed. It was his job to stamp every piece of mail that made it into the governor's in-box. "I can't imagine how—"

Andrew held up a hand and, filled with shame, said, "Don't worry about it. It's not a big deal. It's just that this one interests me. I'm considering it." He looked up and caught the mild surprise on Peter's face. "But I don't think I should act on it if we don't have all our *i*'s dotted and *t*'s crossed."

"I'm not sure what . . . I mean, what would you . . ."

"Can you just backdate it? Can you change the date on your stamp and go back seven months? Date the stamp a few days after the date on the letter?"

Peter hesitated.

"Is that something you could do for me, Peter?"

"Uh . . . sure, I could do that, sir. Absolutely."

"Thanks so much."

He handed the letter to Peter and dropped his eyes quickly to the open file on his desk. It was one thing to cross an ethical line; it was quite another to drag someone across with you.

Peter returned a minute later with the backdated document. Andrew knew he didn't need to ask his assistant to keep this incident to himself. Such discretion was part of his job.

Soon, various offices, agencies, and individuals would be notified of the pardon, including, among others, the office of the Secretary of State, the commissioner of the Department of Corrections, the parole board, the judge who originally had sentenced Torrance, and of course, Torrance himself. Andrew would meet resistance, he knew, given how unorthodox it would be to rush the process, but he'd never pardoned anyone before and had never asked anything of the officials involved, so he believed that with some coaxing—and, where necessary, a hint of reciprocal cooperation down the road, should it be needed—Gabriel Torrance would soon be a free man.

Having sold his soul to a blackmailer, however, Andrew had to wonder whether *he* would ever be free again.

CHAPTER THIRTY-THREE

Five days later, a little after 11:00 a.m., Henry sat in a rented green Jeep in the parking lot of Southern State Correctional Facility, watching Gabriel Torrance walk out through the prison's front doors wearing a cheap suit and carrying a plastic bag. Mindful of the blackmailer's admonition against keeping an eye on Torrance, he had rented the Jeep, thinking it looked very little like something a cop would be driving. Across the lot, Torrance looked lost as he squinted into the sun and scanned the parking lot. Henry knew that at this distance, and with the glare off the Jeep's windshield, he would be virtually invisible inside the car. A moment later, a four-door silver sedan pulled out of a spot and stopped in front of Torrance. A Toyota Camry, Henry noted as he jotted down the plate number. The driver's window rolled down. Henry was too far away to hear any words exchanged, but Torrance didn't react with recognition, though he got into the back seat, both of which likely meant he wasn't being picked up by a friend. Probably a car service.

The prison was close to the middle of nowhere, surrounded by trees, like a lot of Vermont was. That was a great deal of its charm— Vermont's, not the prison's. More than three-quarters of the state was covered by forest. But the remoteness made it more difficult to follow the silver car without appearing to be doing so. The last thing he wanted was for Torrance to report back to the blackmailer that Henry had broken the no-follow rule. That would be bad for Tyler. But he had to follow. Torrance was their best lead. The caller had been careful so far, but at some point they had to meet up, right? Otherwise, what was the point of all this?

In just a few minutes, they drove into the nearby town of Springfield. Henry kept as far behind the Camry as he could without risking losing it. Before long, the car pulled in to the lot of a Holiday Inn, and Torrance got out carrying a canvas bag by its strap, a bag he hadn't been carrying when he'd walked out of Southern State Correctional. Must have been given to him by the livery driver. Henry would find the guy later and have a chat with him. He found a spot quickly and hurried over to a window near the front doors, where he peeked into the lobby and saw Torrance standing near the front desk, talking on a cell phone.

If a cell phone had been among the possessions the state had kindly held for him for almost five years until his release, it couldn't possibly have held a charge all this time. That meant either he had charged the phone in the car or it had been in the bag given to him by the driver, no doubt per the blackmailer's instructions. Henry was betting on the latter.

He watched Torrance slip his phone into his pocket and step up to the reception desk, where a woman gave him a professional smile. They spoke for a moment, then the woman handed him a key card. He didn't sign anything or produce a credit card—which most decent hotels required these days even when guests planned to pay in cash—so Henry assumed that Torrance's room had already been paid for.

Henry's smartphone rang in his pocket. He looked at the screen and saw that the caller had blocked his number.

"Henry Kane here."

"Henry?" the caller said in his familiar metallic tone. "It's me."

Wyatt Pickman sat at the desk in his war room, leaning back in his chair. Through the voice changer, into the burner phone, he said, "Henry, Henry, Henry . . ." as though addressing an ill-behaved child.

"How did you get this number?"

"I've had it for months."

"I'm glad you called. When do we get the evidence you promised?"

"I was just about to send it when I learned that you aren't playing by the rules. You broke our agreement."

"Rules? What rules?"

"My rules. You're not supposed to follow Gabriel Torrance."

The slightest hesitation. "I'm not following him. I just pulled out of the lot at headquarters."

"That's not true, Henry. We both know that. See, Gabriel called and told me that you're following him."

Pickman smiled, imagining Kane wondering when Torrance had spotted him. There was no way the cop could know he was bluffing. Pickman actually had no idea whether Kane or anyone else was following Torrance. But he figured someone would be, and the logical choice was Lieutenant Henry Kane. When Torrance had used his phone, he hadn't called Pickman about a tail. He'd simply followed the instructions in the note inside the bag the driver had given him, dialing a certain number when he reached the Holiday Inn. Pickman hadn't even answered. But he knew that Kane, if he was watching Torrance, would have seen him on the phone.

For his part, the livery driver, a man named Larry Aronson, had done well. When he'd arrived at the quiet street corner where he'd been told his passenger would be waiting, there was no one there. He couldn't have seen Pickman watching around a corner two short blocks away. But Pickman had been given Aronson's phone number by the owner of the car company, and when he texted the driver and told him that if he wanted to make some good, easy money without doing anything illegal, he should look underneath the nearby park bench for a bag with an envelope taped to it, Aronson hesitated only long enough to make sure no cops were in sight. Pickman watched him read the letter inside the envelope, then surreptitiously pocket the five crisp $100 bills that accompanied it.

It's nothing illegal, the note had reassured him. *Just wait at the prison for a certain man about to be released, have this bag ready for him, and drive him to the Holiday Inn in Springfield. There, he will give you another $500.* Of course, that money was already in the bag. *I have your contact information. I will know if you disappear with that money. Trust me, it wouldn't be worth it.* The pickup had been paid for using one of numerous credit cards Pickman had associated with one of several false IDs he had created years ago and still maintained. He'd thought Aronson might have questions, or concerns that the bag contained drugs and he was being recruited to act as a courier, but Pickman was wrong. Not good old Larry Aronson. At the sight of the first $500, he'd jumped right on board. And, as expected, everything had gone perfectly.

"I'm not following him," Kane repeated in an obvious lie, though he'd delivered it fairly convincingly.

"Yes, you are, but I should tell you that if you were hoping to catch me meeting with him at the Holiday Inn in Springfield, you're destined for disappointment. I'm not there."

As he spoke, Pickman allowed his eyes to drift slowly across the mosaic filling the wall opposite him, as he often did when in this room. The colors and connections. The angles and patterns. A seamless web, the labor of a year of his life. It could have been hanging in a museum of modern art, more beautiful by far than anything painted by Jackson Pollock. But where the appeal of Pollock's work grew from what Pickman perceived to be a chaos barely contained by the edges of the canvas, the beauty of his own masterpiece lay in the fact that the colors and connections and patterns and angles represented order, rigid precision, and efficiency—a study in complex yet flawless perfection. It was stunning in both form and function. It was, by far, his greatest work.

"Listen," Kane said, "Your guy is wrong. I'm not—"

"You've breached our agreement, and you'll have to pay the penalty for that."

"Wait a second, we held up our end. Now you have to—"

"I'm going to release more evidence, Lieutenant Henry. In a very short while. Maybe it won't matter in the long run. Maybe when you finally stop following Gabriel around so I can send you the recording and other evidence, the authorities will realize that Tyler has been innocent all along. But maybe . . . just maybe . . . another piece of damning evidence coming to light will make it difficult for everyone to jump on the bandwagon and proclaim your brother's innocence. Maybe some folks might require more convincing, and the case against Tyler might move forward despite the video, and—"

"I'm tired of this. We had an agreement."

"Which you broke. So you suffer the consequences. You don't get the video or the rest of the evidence yet. And another piece of evidence will come to light. But I'm feeling sporting, Henry. I'll give you a head start. I'll tell you exactly where I planted the next evidence to be discovered, and I'll give you a chance to get there first. From the moment we end this call, you will have one hour before I call the local police anonymously and report finding a white plastic bag with several pieces of jewelry in it wrapped up in a blue Pac-Man T-shirt. The jewelry, of course, belonged to Sally Graham. And, of course, it's covered with her blood. The shirt . . ."

Was Tyler's, Henry knew. He'd seen his brother wearing his Pac-Man shirt several times. "Listen, dickhead—"

"It's in a parking lot just off Main Street, in Rutland." He provided the address. "It's hidden behind a stack of wooden pallets."

"I'm not gonna—"

"On your mark . . . get set . . ."

"You son of a—"

"*Go.*"

He pushed the "End call" button, then went upstairs to microwave some popcorn. After it finished popping, he took it to the kitchen table, then placed two empty bowls beside it. He sat down and, piece by piece, checked the popcorn to ensure that each kernel had popped fully. He put those that had into the first bowl, while those that hadn't went into the second, which he would dump into the trash when he was finished sorting. It took some time to get through the entire bag, but that was okay with him. He had almost an hour to kill.

———

Henry had a decision to make. If he left for Rutland, Torrance could walk out of the Holiday Inn and into the wind. Henry might never see him again, which would be bad because he was their best lead to finding the blackmailer. Also, if their dickhead caller had wanted Torrance released so he could do something illegal, losing him wasn't a good way to stop that thing from happening.

But if he stayed here and waited for Torrance to show his face again, the cops in Rutland would find the evidence the caller had planted—more evidence linking Tyler to Sally Graham's murder.

He could call Molly and send her to Rutland, but the cops would get there long before she did. He made a quick call to the PI firm with whom he had contracted to watch Torrance round the clock, but he was reminded that he had wanted to take the first shift to get a feel for the situation, and, unfortunately, none of the PIs was free on a moment's notice.

He hurried to his rented Jeep. As soon as he was under way, he called Detective Tom Egan.

"Kane? What do you want?"

"I need you to watch someone for me."

"I'm off today."

"Now you're on."

"I was going fly-fishing."

"Then I'm doing you a favor, because fly-fishing is boring. I tried it once and couldn't stand it. Anything's more fun than that, including sitting in a Holiday Inn parking lot, watching to see if a certain person comes out, and following him if he does."

"That wouldn't be more fun."

"Well, after today you'll have done both, so you'll be able to tell me definitively."

"I said I'd get you some information, but I'm not your errand boy."

"You're whatever I need you to be for now."

"Damn it, Kane."

Henry softened his tone. No reason to make this harder on Egan than it had to be. "I just need your help for a little while. Then this will all be over, and you'll never hear from me again."

Egan said nothing.

"Listen," Henry said, "just watch this guy for a few hours, okay? Someone will take over later, and you won't have to do it again. You can go back to police work and keeping me informed on developments in my brother's case."

Egan was quiet for a moment; then he sighed into the phone. "Man, it's beautiful outside. Would have been such a great day for fly-fishing."

"It's never a good day for fly-fishing," Henry replied. "When we hang up, I'll text you a picture and details on the guy you're watching. If he leaves and you have to tail him, don't get made."

"He won't spot me. And thanks for the vote of confidence."

"You'll need to hurry because I had to leave a few minutes ago."

"It'll take me a while to get there. What if he's already gone when I do?"

"The guy just got out of prison. I'm betting he'll take a little while to relax on a nice hotel bed."

"But how will I know he's still there?"

"For God's sake, Egan, use your head. Show your badge at the desk. Tell 'em all you need to know is whether the guy's still in the hotel. Get tough. Or be their best friend. Whatever works. You seriously need me to walk you through this? How long have you been a cop?"

"All right, Kane. Shut up. I'll figure it out."

"And I know what you're thinking."

"What's that?"

"You're thinking that you can head out to the river with your fishing rod and call me on the way, tell me he was already gone. Don't do that, Egan."

"I won't."

"I'm serious."

"I *won't.*"

It took Henry fifty-three minutes to get to the address the caller had provided in Rutland. If the blackmailing prick was true to his word, Henry had seven minutes to find whatever evidence had been planted before local police would be called, and then, depending on how credible they believed the tip to be, anywhere from three to fifteen additional minutes before the cops actually rolled up. Should be enough time, if only barely.

He reached the address, a nail salon called Elegant Nails. To the right was a strip of asphalt running between the salon and the Chinese restaurant next to it, leading to a shared parking lot in back. According to the caller, that was where Henry needed to look.

He drove past the salon and pulled in to a spot on the street a block away. He checked his watch; fifty-six minutes had elapsed since his call with the blackmailer had ended. He was cutting it close. He'd thought it all through on the drive here from Springfield. How would the police or a jury view evidence found here in Rutland? Tyler never ventured anywhere close to this far on his electric bike. Then again, he knew how to take a taxi. In the end, jewelry covered with Sally Graham's blood and wrapped in Tyler's T-shirt would be damning no matter where it was found.

He walked down the block—as quickly as he could while still appearing casual—past the nail salon and turned into the lot. To his left, against the back wall of the salon, he saw a loose pile of wooden pallets. He scanned the backs of both buildings abutting the lot and saw no security cameras, so he knelt down next to the pallets, reached into the space behind them, and felt around, hoping he wouldn't encounter something with fur or, worse, teeth. He also hoped that the local cops wouldn't show up right then and find him digging around where a bag of evidence tied to his brother's murder case was supposed to be stashed. That wouldn't have looked good at all. A moment later, his fingers found a plastic bag, which he lifted out. Peering inside, he saw a blue T-shirt balled up. He didn't bother taking it out of the bag to see what was wrapped inside it.

He left the lot and walked back to the Jeep, employing his semi-casual speed walk again, which wasn't easy with his heart racing as it was. He wondered what to do with the bag. His first inclination was to dump the jewelry in the nearby reservoir and burn Tyler's shirt, but destroying evidence was serious business. It was irreversible. He'd have to give it some thought.

As he pulled away from the curb, he glanced in his rearview mirror and saw a police cruiser turn into the lot.

That had been close.

———

Snacking on popcorn, Pickman had watched the whole thing on his computer monitor. Just a few hours ago, he had hidden a battery-powered video camera among a pile of milk crates behind the Chinese restaurant and streamed the video over the nail salon's Wi-Fi. He'd had to get a pedicure a few weeks ago to obtain the password, but his toes still looked pretty good and the calf massage had felt great. He'd tested the system at that time but didn't leave the camera, of course. Instead, he'd taken it with him to keep until it was time to hide it again this morning.

He played the recording he had made of the video. He watched Henry Kane enter the lot, head slightly down, and Pickman worried that he wouldn't be easily recognizable. But then he had been kind enough to raise his head and look up at the buildings, presumably searching for security cameras, making his face plainly visible. Pickman fast-forwarded to the part where Kane lifted the bag out from behind the pallets, looked inside, and left the parking lot with it. Just over two minutes later, two uniformed Rutland police officers entered the lot. One searched behind the stack of pallets. The other moved over to a row of three withered plants in large black pots along the back of the Chinese restaurant. Of course, the one looking around the pallets came up empty while the one by the plants waved his partner over. He'd found something, which came as no surprise to Pickman, because he'd hidden it there and told them where to look.

CHAPTER THIRTY-FOUR

Tyler looked around the dinner table at Molly, Henry, Andy, and his sister-in-law, Rebecca, and was happy they were having dinner together again—second time in two weeks. They used to do it almost every Sunday, but that was a long time ago. Then Molly went away to the army for a bunch of years, and they did it less. And when she got back, Andy became governor, which was a really important job, and they did it even less. But here they were, together again after not too long, which he liked. He knew it was probably only happening because he'd gotten into trouble, but still, it was nice to have everybody eating together. The only person missing was Julie, who hadn't been around as much as usual lately. When Tyler asked Molly why, she said Julie was really busy with college stuff, which made Tyler glad he wasn't in college.

Even though it was great to have the whole family together, Tyler could tell that Andy wasn't in a very good mood. It sounded like he was worried that he'd done the wrong thing at work, which surprised Tyler because Andy never did anything wrong. But they were talking about some reporter named Angela asking him questions about a guy Andy let out of prison. Andy said she was a dog with a bone, which made Tyler smile.

"I don't know why she's focusing on this," Rebecca said. "No one else is paying attention to this story. Governors pardon people all the time. A few years back, one of your predecessors pardoned almost two hundred people at once."

Andrew said, "They'd been convicted of marijuana-related offenses that are no longer even criminal in many states. And none of them had been convicted of felonies. Gabriel Torrance is different. He's a felon. His crime is still on the books in this state, and every other, I assume. His pardon has the appearance of being arbitrary on my part without much to support my decision."

"I'll tell you why Baskin is focusing on this," Molly said, looking at Andy. "Because she hates you and has had it in for you from the start."

Tyler didn't believe that. Everybody liked Andy. That was why they made him the governor, which was the biggest job in Vermont.

Molly added, "This is barely news. Like Rebecca said, no one else seems to care. You pardoned one guy near the end of his sentence. What's the big deal?"

They talked about boring stuff for a while, and Tyler found himself drifting in and out, listening at times, and thinking about other things at times—things like video games and TV shows and how much he missed riding his motorcycle and how weird it was not to be able to leave their property, not even for five seconds. He couldn't wait to go to trial and prove that he would never, ever kill anyone no matter what, so that everything could go back to normal, and his family wouldn't worry, and he could get this stupid, uncomfortable bracelet off his ankle, and he'd be free again to ride around town and volunteer at the shelter and see the animals.

Thinking about Sally Graham made him remember the thing she had done to him and the way it had felt. He knew his cheeks were getting red, and he hoped no one would notice. No one did, though, because they were focused on their long and boring conversation. They spoke to him now and then—they weren't the kind of people who left him out of conversations for long, like a lot of people did—but most of the time, he didn't care what they were saying.

When he heard his name, though, he listened more closely, but he still didn't follow along very well. Henry said something about DNA, which Tyler had heard about on TV but wasn't sure what it was. Whatever it was, though, it made everyone look worried. They talked about Sally Graham's blood, too, which kept them looking worried.

"When is he going to give us the recording and whatever else he has in the way of evidence?" Molly asked.

"Soon, I guess," Andy said. "He said he'd do it once Torrance is out."

Henry cleared his throat and looked like he didn't feel well. "I screwed up," he said.

"How?" Andy asked.

"He caught me following Torrance from Southern State. I don't know how, but he did."

"Are you sure?"

Henry told a story that Tyler didn't listen closely to, something about a shirt and some jewelry. "He says he's punishing us for breaking the rules. He's not giving us anything yet, not until we stop following Torrance around."

"Are you kidding?" Andy asked. He sounded both surprised and upset. "You *took* the bag? Do you know how serious that is? That's obstruction. If you got caught, your career could be over."

Tyler almost asked what *obstruction* was, but he didn't really care.

"I know what it is," Henry replied. He looked angry but not as angry as Andy looked. "I know what I did. But I didn't have a choice. I couldn't let the cops find it."

Andy sighed really loudly and shook his head.

"What did you do with it?" Molly asked, looking at Henry.

"Nothing. Yet."

Tyler asked Rebecca to pass him the crescent rolls and the butter.

"So he's screwing us over?" Molly asked. Now *she* sounded angry, too.

"For now, I guess," Henry said.

"He'll call again," Rebecca said. She hadn't said much so far, Tyler noticed. "We'll find out then when we'll get it all. He keeps calling, so I'm sure he'll call again."

"When he does," Molly said, "he'd better be ready to hold up his end."

"And if he doesn't?" Andy asked.

They sat silent a moment, and Tyler, who hadn't been listening closely, wondered what had happened to make everyone look so weird all of a sudden.

"I gotta find this guy," Henry said.

"When you do, I'd like a shot at him," Molly said, and Tyler was glad they were talking again because that silence had been uncomfortable.

"If Rebecca's right and that son of a bitch calls back," Henry said, turning toward Andy, "you tell him that if he doesn't hold up his end of the bargain, we'll find Torrance and put him away for another five years."

"For what?" Andy asked.

"For whatever I decide to pin on him. I'll figure something out, and I'll make it stick."

"Henry, you can't talk like that."

"Don't listen to him, Henry," Molly said. "You go ahead and cowboy up if you need to."

Andrew shook his head. "Damn it, Molly."

Tyler sighed. Everyone was getting mad again.

"I think Rebecca's right," Molly said. "He'll call back."

"I think you're both right," Andy said. "At least, I hope you are. And when he calls, I'll deal with him."

"I hope I'm right, too," Rebecca said.

"Me, too," Molly said.

"Me, too," Tyler added because he wanted everyone to think he'd been listening, and it seemed like the right thing to say.

CHAPTER THIRTY-FIVE

Andrew sat with Molly and Henry on the front porch, drinks in their hands—merlot for Molly and Andrew, a bottle of Corona for Henry. Tyler was inside, down the hall, watching TV, something with a laugh track they could hear through the open windows. Rebecca was watching whatever it was with him. She always enjoyed spending time with Tyler, but Andrew suspected that she was doing so now because she felt the three older Kane siblings could use a few minutes alone. And, Andrew had to admit, despite the circumstances, it was almost nice. He hadn't sat like this with Molly and Henry . . . just sat and relaxed . . . in a long time.

"Who's watching Torrance right now?" he asked.

They had all agreed that there was no way they could let Torrance out of their sight, despite the caller's orders. They just had to be careful. But he was their only real link to the blackmailer, and therefore their best chance of proving Tyler's innocence and, hopefully, catching Sally Graham's killer.

"I had a buddy on the force do it earlier," Henry said, "when I had to leave quickly to . . ." He trailed off. They didn't need to discuss Henry's decision to conceal evidence again. "Anyway, don't worry; he doesn't know anything. And now I've got private detectives keeping an eye on him around the clock."

None of them mentioned how much that might be costing. None of them even gave it a thought.

"They can't let themselves be discovered," Andrew said. "If he catches them surveilling him—"

"Don't worry about it. These guys are good. Better than I am. I hired Dave's old firm. His son, Dave Junior, is giving us a discount . . . even though I told him we didn't want one."

Andrew nodded. He understood why Henry would have tried to refuse a discount. Dave was Dave Bingham, a Vermont state police detective who had become something of a mentor to Henry when he'd made detective. When he could retire with a full pension, Dave pulled the pin and spent a year lying in a hammock and watching the grass in his yard grow until he couldn't take it any longer and got himself a private investigator's license. Business was solid enough that he brought in his son—Dave Junior, as everyone always knew him—and later hired a few other ex-cops. According to what Henry had told him, the elder Dave was good at what he did, really good, and he was respected enough that guys still on the job, both state and local, helped him out now and then with access and information. Everything was going well for him—right up until he got himself killed one night eight years ago in Rutland, in the projects there. Bled out after being shot in the neck. Henry, whom Bingham had asked to meet him there, had been the one to find the body. He'd also tracked down and arrested the killer before the man could leave the area. It had been a dark time for Henry, who understandably never wanted to talk about the night he lost his friend.

To Andrew, something seemed to have changed in his brother that night. Maybe it was a loss of idealism, or a too-close glimpse of mortality, or maybe he thought he somehow could have saved Dave. Whatever it was, not long after, saying he needed a change, he put in for a transfer out of the Bureau of Criminal Investigations and into Internal Affairs, which came through a few months later when the detective in the position retired. And after Dave's death, Dave Junior took over the PI firm. After all that the elder Dave had meant to Henry, Andrew figured his brother probably felt an obligation to hire them. And if Henry said they were good, Andrew believed him.

"They'll keep tabs on Torrance," Henry said. "Report in regularly."

Andrew nodded. Henry suddenly looked tired to him. They probably all did, he thought as he took a sip of merlot.

"What the hell is Torrance up to?" Molly wondered aloud. "Him *and* the jerk on the phone?"

No one had an answer for that, so they all took another sip. Henry pointed with his beer bottle toward the state police cruiser parked on the street in front of the house, the silhouette of a trooper visible behind the wheel. "You ever get tired of those guys following you around everywhere?"

"I'm used to it. I barely notice anymore. If I ever need them, though, I'll be glad they're close by."

"It would annoy me."

"Everything annoys you," Molly said.

"Did you talk to the driver who picked Torrance up at the prison?" Andrew asked.

"Yeah, a few hours ago. Not helpful. Said he showed up to pick up a fare and found a bag waiting for him with five hundred dollars in cash and a note with instructions to pick up a guy at Southern State and give him the bag."

"That's it?"

"That's it. Whoever left the bag texted him, and he gave me the number, which I'll run, of course, but it's probably a dead end. Our guy's too careful for that."

"So we're nowhere then?"

"At the moment."

"Until he calls again," Molly said.

Henry let out a low growl of frustration and rubbed the back of his neck with one hand. "How's Tyler handling all this, Molly? He seems okay, but how's he really doing?"

She shrugged. "Honestly, he seems fine. If he were still in jail, I don't think that would be the case, but here at home, he seems all right. He doesn't really talk about any of it. Believes that everything will come out okay. He says he didn't hurt Sally Graham, and when he tells everyone that in court, they'll believe him and this will all be over."

"If only it worked like that," Andrew said.

"I'm gonna go in and talk to him for a bit," Henry said. "Just chat a little. Haven't really done that for a while, at least not about . . . normal stuff."

"Good luck with that," Molly said. "He and Rebecca are watching TV together, remember?"

Henry chuckled. "I'll just sit with them for a few minutes then."

Henry was apparently feeling the need to spend a little extra time with Tyler. Andrew understood that. Though they didn't speak of it often, they all knew there was a chance that their time with their youngest brother might be limited one day soon. Andrew was struggling with that notion as much as any of them. He watched Henry head back into the house, leaving him alone with Molly. He took a sip of wine and looked out into the night.

"You okay?" she asked.

"Me?"

"Yeah, you. I know that having to . . . do what you did was hard for you."

He shrugged. "I'm not sure Henry really understands why this wasn't easy for me. I'm not very proud of myself."

"You should be. You've done so many good things as governor, accomplished so much. And this situation with Tyler . . . well, you're taking care of the family, like Dad used to do."

Andrew shook his head and said, almost under his breath, "Dad."

He kept his eyes on the street but could feel Molly looking at him. "Whenever anyone mentions Dad, you get quiet. I didn't notice that until a few years ago."

He finished his glass of wine and placed it on the wooden porch floor beside his chair. "He was mostly okay, I guess. We never saw him mistreat Mom. He worked hard, left a lot of money behind when he died. He was certainly a towering figure in the Vermont legal community, and they seemed to like him well enough in Washington. Wasn't the warmest guy I've ever met, but I didn't need him to cuddle with me. The rest of you were closer with him, but that didn't really bother me."

Molly never spoke badly about their father. Whatever her reason for that, Andrew had chosen long ago to respect it, which was why he didn't bring up any of the things about Patrick Kane that he didn't care for, things Molly might not have known, things Andrew had learned later in life by doing a little research and asking around. Like the man's cutthroat legal tactics—respected by some, despised by others. And like his voting record in the Senate that suggested—to some, at least—that he might have been too good a friend to big businesses . . . businesses with a lot of money to throw around to make sure things went their way on Capitol Hill. And like the rumors of the special relationships he had with at least two of the secretaries in his old law firm. But those things were supposition, gossip, without hard evidence to support them. No, Andrew never talked about any of those things with Molly or his brothers . . . just as he never, *ever*—

"There's more, though, isn't there?" Molly asked. "I can see it on your face . . . you *know* there's more."

He wasn't sure how she could see it. He was facing the street, giving her his profile, not wanting to meet her eyes. Finally, he sensed her turn away and look out toward the street as well.

"He never touched me, Andy," she said softly.

They had never spoken of this before. Not in all these years. He'd figured they never would, and that would have been fine with him.

She said, "It's true that he came to my room now and then after Mom was asleep, but he never touched me."

Andrew said nothing.

"You knew that, didn't you? That he came to my room at night sometimes."

He nodded but just barely.

"All he did was talk, Andy."

"It went on for months," he said. "I'd hear him walk past my room. You weren't even ten years old."

"He just sat at the end of my bed and talked. That's all. About things he said he couldn't talk to Mom about."

"Like what?"

"Like how hard he was working for the family. How difficult it had been to step down as senator at Mom's request and return to his legal practice. The pressure he felt carrying on the Kane name. How Mom didn't really understand him."

"I'm getting teary."

"I never wanted him to visit me. I was always . . . a bit nervous, I guess. And I was definitely relieved when he stopped coming. But he never touched me, Andy. I swear."

"I know."

"What?"

"I know he didn't touch you."

She paused. "How could you know that?"

"Because I stayed up as late as I could, listening for him."

"When?"

"The first night I heard him, I followed him and sat outside in the hall, listening at the door. I couldn't hear what you two were saying, but I could hear your tones of voice, both of you, and you sounded okay. After that, at night, I'd stay up late, listening for him going down to your room. If he did, I followed. And listened. And you were always talking. If I'd ever heard you stop talking, I'd have . . . wondered what was going on. But all you did was talk—mostly Dad, but you, too."

"You stayed up late?" He sensed her turn toward him, but he kept his eyes forward, on the darkness. "Every night?"

"Until he stopped going to your room."

She looked at him a long moment. He looked at the night. Finally, she said, "I never really worried that he was going to . . . do anything he shouldn't."

"He shouldn't have been going to your room after Mom fell asleep."

"You know what I mean. I think he was just . . . lonely. He and Mom weren't as close as they should have been. I'm not sure if you knew that, but he told me."

"I knew." He didn't think it had always been like that, at least not if the photographs of his parents' early life together were any indication. But somewhere through the years, maybe sometime after the kids came along, things apparently changed.

"So he came to my room and talked," Molly said. "I never knew why he eventually stopped."

"I do." He finally turned to her. "I let him see me. Usually, when I heard him start to leave, I'd run back to my room. One night, though, I decided it had to stop. So I just sat there. He opened the door, and there I was. Neither of us said anything. He just stood there for a second, looking down at me, and I looked up at him." Andrew could still see his face—first surprise, then shame. "Then he went back to his room. For the next couple of weeks, I didn't hear him in the hall, and I realized he'd stopped for good." And for the next couple of weeks Andrew couldn't even look at his father.

"You stayed up late listening for him every single night, sitting outside my door when he was in there with me? For all those months?"

She looked directly into his eyes, a gaze strong and steady but still soft, and though he wanted to look away, he found he couldn't. Instead, he gave a small shrug.

"Andy, what would you have done if . . . if you heard . . ."

"Whatever I had to," he said. He didn't tell her that after that first night, whenever he listened at his sister's door, he brought his Little League baseball bat with him. She didn't need to know about that. But their father knew. He'd seen his son holding it that final night—the night Andrew finally found the courage to let their father see him—and the old man had never gone back. Andrew didn't imagine that his father had been afraid of a fourteen-year-old kid, even if the kid was armed with a Louisville Slugger, but something about his son sitting outside his sister's door had been enough to put an end to the nighttime visits.

"You're a good man, Andy," she said. "You always have been. You may be having your doubts about that right now, but no one else in this family is."

She reached over, gave his hand an affectionate squeeze, and headed inside. He considered what she'd just said. Was she right about him? Or was it too early to tell? Was the jury still out? He closed his eyes and let the soft night breeze roll gently across him. He was tired. He hadn't been sleeping well lately. He was certain that none of them had. He thought he might have been able to fall asleep then and there, though . . .

Then the peaceful moment was shattered by the vibration of the black cell phone.

CHAPTER THIRTY-SIX

Wyatt Pickman's eyes were closed. With one ear, he was listening to the ringing of the burner phone while his other ear was attuned to the contrapuntally complex *The Art of Fugue* by Johann Sebastian Bach, playing at background-level volume through the top-of-the-line Klipsch sound system in his war room. He loved *The Art of Fugue* because it was considered by many music scholars to be a nearly perfect musical composition. It had even been opined that the mathematical architecture of the piece suggested that Bach had been inspired by the Fibonacci sequence—a pattern of numbers that appeared in such an astonishing variety of arenas as mathematics, science, art, and nature. Pickman knew next to nothing about music, but he'd read about Bach's compositions in general, and *The Art of Fugue* in particular. How could he, of all people, not love a piece founded on math and science? He listened to it every day. In fact, long ago he had disposed of all other music in his home. To listen to anything else would have been to subject himself to something . . . *less*. Interestingly, Bach never finished the piece. Yet it was somehow perfect nonetheless. Incredible.

The phone at his ear rang a fourth time before he finally heard the governor's voice on the line. "I'm here," he said. "Where the hell's the evidence you owe us?"

Speaking into his voice changer, Pickman said, "Your brother broke the rules. He breached our contract. The deal's off."

"Are you serious?" Governor Andy sounded really upset. "How the hell—"

"Whoa there, pardner," he said, and the quaint phrase sounded particularly odd coming through the voice changer, even to his own ears. "Don't worry. I have a new deal for you."

"You son of a bitch. No new deal. I did what you asked. Now it's your turn to—"

Pickman snapped the phone closed, ending the call. He closed his eyes again and listened to the music as a harpsichord, an organ, and other instruments he couldn't identify plinked and trilled and thrummed in patterns he could barely follow, sounding harmonious and melodious at times and dissonant and clashing at others, as if they weren't certain whether their relationships with one another were based on love or hate. The burner phone rang—the governor trying reach him—and he ignored it. A few minutes later, it rang again, and, mostly because the instrumental was nearing its end, he ignored it a second time. When the last strains of the music faded away, he called the governor back.

"You do not want me to hang up again," Pickman said when Governor Andy answered. "I might not call back. I might call the police instead. And trust me, you do not want that. Now, are you ready to listen?"

"I'm not cutting a new deal with you."

"If you give me a minute, I think you will. So I'll ask again: Are you ready to listen?"

"Say what you have to say."

"First, let me play you a recording." He held the phone near one of his computer's external speakers and pressed the "Play" button on the keyboard, starting the audio file he had downloaded from where he had paused it. The speakers were good quality, and the sounds through them were perfectly clear.

"*I'll tell Andrew you're legit.*" There was no doubt that was Molly Kane's voice.

"*Did he authorize you to make a deal?*" Pickman found that hearing his own voice on the recording, distorted into a harsh metallic monotone, was interesting.

"*Yeah.*"

"*And?*"

"*He'll do it.*"

"*In exchange for the video you saw and the rest of the evidence I have against your brother Tyler, he'll grant clemency to Gabriel Torrance, get him out of prison?*"

"*He will.*"

"*No halfway house, either. Totally free.*"

"*He knows that.*"

"*When will it happen?*"

"*When you give us the video and the evidence.*"

Pickman smiled. He wished he could have seen Governor Andy's face at that moment, the moment he realized that Pickman not only held all the cards, he had created the game and was setting all the rules.

———

This is devastating, Andrew thought.

"Did you hear that clearly?" the caller asked through the speaker on the black cell phone. After the blackmailer hung up on him initially, Andrew had called the others, except for Tyler, into the drawing room so they could listen together when the bastard called back. And there they were, standing in a tight circle, listening to the phone in Andrew's hand. He'd left it to Henry to record the conversation on his phone.

"I did," he said, seething.

"In case you're wondering, my guy checked her for a wire, but she never checked him."

"You won't release that recording."

"I won't? Why not?"

"Because it exonerates Tyler. It shows he didn't do it. And that someone out there has the evidence to prove it."

"You weren't listening closely, Andy," the caller said. "Nothing in what I just played you exonerates your brother. Nothing identifies the party Molly is speaking to. It could be a cop on the take. It could be anyone with access to evidence against Tyler. The only thing that is clear from the recording is that Molly was saying that you would let Torrance out of prison in exchange for evidence against Tyler."

Andrew realized he was right.

Molly looked stricken. "I'm so stupid," she whispered.

"Who was that?" the caller asked abruptly. "Was that Molly? Am I on speakerphone?"

Andrew sighed. "Yes."

"Is Detective Henry there, too?"

"I'm here, you twisted—"

"Hold on there, Henry. Before you say anything you might regret, I have something for you, too. I can't send it to you, but I can describe what I'm watching. Are you ready?"

"What the hell?"

"Give me a sec," the caller said. "Okay, here we go. So there you are entering a parking lot . . . You're looking around . . . up at the buildings. I think you're looking for cameras."

Andrew turned toward Henry, who looked equal parts surprised, furious, and embarrassed.

"It's too bad you didn't look in the big stack of empty milk crates to your right. Now there you are . . . kneeling down . . . feeling behind the wooden pallets . . . ooh, it looks like you found something. How exciting." The juxtaposition of the caller's upbeat content and robotic monotone made for bizarre listening.

"That's enough," Henry said.

"What's that you found, Henry?" the caller said, ignoring him. "A white plastic bag? You're looking inside the bag now. What do you see? What's in the bag?"

"Knock it off."

"Well, whatever it is, you decided to keep it when you left the parking lot . . . Now I'm seeing nothing but empty lot. Here, let me fast-forward two minutes and thirteen seconds."

Henry said, "You don't need to—"

"Hang on . . . almost there . . . ah, here we go. Two minutes and thirteen seconds after you left the parking lot, two of Rutland's finest boys in blue showed up. I told you they would, Henry. I told you I'd give you an hour's head start, and I did. You got there ahead of them. But look at them now . . . one of them searching behind the pallets for the bag I reported in my anonymous tip, a bag containing a T-shirt and bloody jewelry. But it's not there, is it, Henry?"

Henry mumbled a bunch of curse words very far under his breath, name-calling of the most offensive kind, and Andrew wasn't certain whether Henry was directing the slurs at the blackmailer or himself.

"All right," Andrew said, his voice carrying more weight and authority than it had moments ago. "We get it."

"I don't think you do yet. Not completely, anyway. Because the other cop is looking where I told him to, behind the dying plants in the big pots, looking for the second bag of evidence I planted. Did I forget to mention that one, Henry? My bad."

The look on Henry's face made it plain that he hadn't searched behind the pots, or anyplace else where evidence might have been hidden. He'd looked only behind the wooden pallets, as the blackmailer had wanted.

"What's in the second bag?" Henry asked.

"A pair of blue jeans belonging to Tyler, most likely with his DNA on them. They also have Sally Graham's blood on them—and a lot of it—because I was wearing them when I killed her. *Now* do you get it?"

"Yes," Andrew said, "we do."

He sure as hell did, at least. Henry had been caught on video obstructing justice in a high-profile murder case in which the accused was his brother, as well as the brother of the sitting governor. Molly had been secretly recorded negotiating on the governor's behalf, brokering a deal involving the pardoning of a prisoner in exchange for evidence against Tyler. Andrew wasn't thinking as clearly as he would have liked, so he didn't know in that moment whether Molly had broken any laws, but this certainly wouldn't look good on a state police job application. And Andrew? If the media got wind of any of this, he'd be flayed alive. He could only imagine the fire he would take from Angela Baskin alone. And in a blink, the public would turn on him and tear him to pieces. He was looking at an ignominious end to his time in office, and possibly even prison. His wife, Rebecca, innocent in all this, would face public scorn, as well. And Tyler? This sure as hell wouldn't help his legal defense any. These recordings were a catastrophe for the entire family. A sudden pain shot down into Andrew's lower jaw, back by his molars, telling him that he'd been clenching his teeth far too hard.

"There's a problem with your plan, though," he said with a confidence he didn't feel.

"I doubt that."

"Tyler rarely leaves Manchester. He wouldn't go all the way to Rutland to—"

The caller cut him off. "Now you're just fibbing, Andy. Of course he leaves Manchester sometimes. I've followed him around many times as he rode his adorable electric bicycle from town to town. He likes to explore."

Damn it. "Look, no one's going to believe he rode all over Vermont on his e-bike hiding incriminating evidence. It just doesn't make sense. Why wouldn't he just throw it out?"

"No offense, Governor, but a man of Tyler's . . . uh . . . limited intelligence and stunted emotional maturity, faced with a stressful and frightening situation, couldn't necessarily be expected to handle things the way other people without his particular challenges would. But if you're willing to believe that the authorities—and, more important, a jury—won't find the evidence that has come to light so far to be persuasive . . . if you think he'll be acquitted without the benefit of the video recording I have of me in Tyler's clothes killing Sally Graham . . . then you're more of a gambler with your brother's freedom than I would be in your shoes."

Andrew wasn't certain what was worse: the thought of the caller following Tyler around for God only knew how long, or the fact that what the man had just said, sadly, made sense.

"So," the man said in his robotic monotone, "are you ready to hear the new deal?"

Furious and frustrated beyond measure, Andrew said nothing.

"I'll take your silence to mean that you're willing to listen. First of all, thanks for letting Gabriel Torrance out of prison. However, it's time to come clean: I don't give a damn about Gabriel Torrance. He's nothing to me. He's just a prisoner whose felony was minor and whose time left to be served brief enough to compel you, Governor Andy, to compromise your famous integrity the tiniest bit. Gabriel Torrance was nothing more than a lever I used to pry the door open farther."

"What door?"

"The door to Southern State Correctional Facility."

Andrew suddenly felt light-headed. He saw where this was going. He'd known where it was going all along. He had wanted to be wrong, but he'd known.

"See, I need another prisoner pardoned. Start the paperwork tomorrow. He has to walk out of Southern State in less than a week."

Andrew said, "I can't do—"

"Of course you can," the caller said. "You already have. I just need you to do it again. Just one more time. Cross my heart."

Henry stepped back into the conversation. "Why the hell should we trust you? We're still waiting for you to turn over the video you showed Molly, and whatever additional evidence you manufactured against Tyler."

"Oh, Henry . . . you poor fool. This isn't just about Tyler any longer. This is about you keeping your job and staying out of prison. And your esteemed brother not facing the greatest scandal a governor of this state has ever faced. And Molly? Didn't I read in some article about Andy that you're planning to follow in big brother Henry's footsteps and become a state trooper? What are the odds of that coming to pass after this recording is made public?"

Andrew closed his eyes and tried *not* to imagine the further damage this man could do to their family. He didn't want to contemplate it.

Molly said, "I don't care about—"

"Molly," the caller said, "can you imagine the scandal? Can you fathom how this would rock Andy's administration? Can you imagine the venerated Kane family name dragged through the mud? What would your father, the senator, say if he were alive today? Or your grandfather? He was also a senator, I believe. Or great-granddaddy Kane, author of several legal treatises and one of the most respected judges ever to sit on the Second Circuit? Or the one who came before him and made all the money you Kanes have been living off of for generations? Or take a moment to picture the glee of Andy's political adversaries, and of all the neighbors jealous of your family's wealth and status for years, and of the cops who were disciplined and even fired because of Henry's Internal Affairs investigations. How they would all rejoice to see the Kanes brought low."

"I'm not agreeing to anything," Andrew said, unable now to keep a defeated tone from his voice, "but who's the prisoner this time?"

"His name is Kyle Lewis. And I'm afraid you'll find he's not quite the choirboy Gabriel Torrance is."

Andrew took a long, deep breath. "I'll call you back at this number in a day or two."

"Take your time, Governor Andy. Just know that the clock won't stop ticking. Lewis has to be out within a week, or the entire Kane family burns."

The line went dead.

No one spoke for a long moment. Both Molly and Henry looked like whipped pups. Andrew thought he probably looked the same. Finally, he said, "Henry, you know what to do. Look into this Kyle Lewis as quick as you can. Everything you can find out, like you did with Torrance. You have two days."

"This guy could just keep jerking your chain over and over, Andy," Molly said. "You could give him what he wants again, and he could just turn around and ask for another prisoner's release, then another's, then another's."

"I *know* that, damn it," Andrew said. "I said that to Henry at the beginning. So I knew the risk. We all did. But I didn't have any choice, did I? Not if there was any chance that Tyler . . ." He paused. Took a deep breath. "Look, I doubt his endgame is to see me empty Vermont's prisons. I suspect this has all been about getting this Lewis guy out. I'm guessing his record is such that the caller knew I wouldn't agree to pardon him unless I had absolutely no choice. With Tyler's situation, and yours," he said, looking at Molly, "and now Henry's . . . and my own, too, having pardoned Gabriel Torrance in response to blackmail, well . . ." He trailed off.

Molly nodded but said nothing.

"So you're going to release him?" Rebecca asked.

He thought about Henry's career being over, about his possibly going to jail; and about Molly's own career in law enforcement ending before it even began; and his own time in office coming to a scandalous close. And, of course, he thought about Tyler spending the rest of his life in prison.

"I don't know yet. But I may not have much of a choice."

CHAPTER THIRTY-SEVEN

Two days later, after Henry had learned all he could about Kyle Lewis, there was one thing he knew for certain: the man was never going to be nominated for a humanitarian award. He was thirty-seven years old and over the course of three separate incarcerations had spent fourteen of his nineteen adult years behind bars. He had been convicted of heroin possession and distribution, second-degree arson, assault, resisting arrest, aggravated assault on a police officer, manslaughter, and other less serious but related offenses.

Henry was about to head into the Pavilion to meet with Andrew to fill him in on all of this when his cell phone rang.

"Henry Kane," he said upon answering.

"Kane, it's me. Egan."

Henry had been expecting this call. He was glad Egan was being a good little mole. "What have you got?" he asked, though he already knew.

"Somebody called in an anonymous tip."

"Isn't it funny how they're all anonymous?"

"You know how it is; they're getting more anonymous all the time. Nobody wants to get involved, nobody wants to testify, everybody's afraid of retribution from the bad guys, nobody trusts us good guys."

"Nobody wants to be tied to his own bullshit story," Henry added.

"Hey, we take them with a grain of salt, Kane, you know that. But we're not gonna ignore them. So you want to hear what I have to tell you or not?"

"I'm listening."

"They found a bag containing a pair of jeans covered in blood."

"I assume DNA results aren't back yet, but they typed the blood and it's the same as Sally Graham's."

"Yup."

"And they think the jeans are Tyler's."

"Yup. And there were hairs on the pants, which they also sent off for DNA analysis, and they think those belonged to your brother and/or Sally Graham."

Damn. Though he hadn't known about that second bag, the one containing the bloody jeans, he'd been just a few feet away from the thing in that parking lot behind the nail salon. It had been *right there*. "Okay," he said. "Anything else right now?"

"Nope."

Henry ended the call, then texted Andy to tell him he'd arrived, albeit a few minutes late. He entered the Pavilion through the side entrance on Governor Davis Avenue, and though the security guards in the lobby knew him on sight, he still had to dump his weapon, badge, cell phone, and the rest of the contents of his pockets into a little plastic bin and pass through a metal detector. They also made him wear a visitor badge. As he was returning his belongings to the various pockets and holsters in which they belonged, Andrew replied to his text, telling him to meet outside one of the conference rooms. Henry asked a security guard for directions, and when he arrived, Andy was waiting outside a closed wooden door.

"I don't have a lot of time," Andrew said in a hushed tone. He told Henry that on the other side of the door sat the director of Policy Development and Legislative Affairs, waiting to meet with him to review the latest draft of their new and dramatically tougher antiracketeering bill.

"What do you have on Lewis?" Andrew asked.

Henry gave him the rundown of the man's criminal history. Andrew looked horrified. "What's he in for right now?"

"At the moment, he's in for the aggravated assault and resisting."

"But not the manslaughter?"

"Nope. He did seven years for that. Eight months after he got out, he went back in for aggravated assault on a police officer."

"Well, that's something, at least," Andrew said. Henry knew it would have been harder for Andrew to justify pardoning Lewis if he were presently serving time for killing someone. The victim's family would have been understandably upset and would have—again, understandably—been vocal about its displeasure. "How much time does he have left on his current sentence?"

Henry hesitated.

"Let me have it," Andrew said.

"Seven years left on a fourteen-year sentence."

Andrew winced. "Seriously? That much? This is bad."

"It's not good," Henry conceded.

"Our blackmailer was clever."

Henry thought he knew what his brother was thinking. Andrew never would have considered pardoning Lewis if he hadn't been coerced into releasing Torrance first, thereby giving the blackmailer significant leverage.

"He's a smart dickhead," Henry said. "I'll give him that."

Two staffers turned a corner and headed in their direction, causing them to pause their conversation. The staffers nodded deferentially to Andrew as they passed, and Andrew nodded back politely. When they were around a corner and out of earshot, Andrew looked at his watch. "Damn, I'm twenty minutes late for this meeting. What else do we know about Lewis?"

Henry handed him a copy of a mug shot. On seeing Lewis's face, Andrew asked, "Why am I not surprised?"

In the photo, Kyle Lewis looked as though he wanted to break the neck of whoever had taken his mug shot. His eyes were dark and cold. Below the left one was a tattoo of a black teardrop, often meant to symbolize that the tattooed person had killed someone. A three-inch scar left a white line through the beard stubble on his right jawline. Across his throat at the level of his Adam's apple, the phrase *No Regrets* was tattooed in shaky cursive script. Both tats had almost certainly been the work of a jailhouse tattoo artist.

"He also has *EWMN* on the knuckles of both hands," Henry said.

"The true classics never die, do they?"

Given their collective experience with the criminal justice system, they both knew *EWMN* was a common tattoo among a certain element, standing for *Evil, Wicked, Mean, and Nasty*. Located on the knuckles meant it would be the last thing a victim would see as he was beaten unconscious.

The conference room door opened, and a fresh-faced, uptight-looking aide in a necktie that seemed to be cinched far too tight poked his head out, saw Andrew, and quickly withdrew.

"He wants to tell you to hurry your ass up," Henry said, "but he probably thinks that would be a bad career move."

"Come on, Henry, give me the rest."

"Tons of priors, as you know. A long history of violence, including some ugly altercations behind bars early in his long career as a prisoner. However, on the plus side . . ."

"There's actually a plus side?"

"There is. He's only killed one person that we know of, and that was years ago and, quite possibly, mostly unintentional."

"Quite possibly? That's not a huge help here."

"It was an altercation in a bar that got out of control. One witness said Lewis wasn't the aggressor. Still, he got hit with a manslaughter charge, and the prosecution made it stick."

"Probably wasn't too hard. How's he been behaving in prison?"

"According to his prison record, he's not exactly a model prisoner."

"How bad?"

"Worse than most, but not as bad as the worst."

Andrew sighed.

"The thing is, I've been looking hard into him," Henry said, "and I can't imagine how he could have pulled all this off. Like Gabriel Torrance, he doesn't seem to have anyone on the outside. No family. And with him pissing away most of his life behind bars, he never spent long enough on the outside to make any friends."

"Well, someone wants him out. Former criminal associate, maybe?"

"Always been a loner. When he dealt drugs, he was low-level and didn't have ties to anyone. Never had partners in any of the trouble he got himself into."

"Visitors in prison?"

"That's where it gets interesting. Only two. The poor schlub of a public defender who drew his dog of a case originally—and lost, of course—and another lawyer who visited just once, a little over a year ago. The lawyer's name? Wesley Jurgens."

"Jurgens?" Andrew said, frowning. "He's Gabriel Torrance's lawyer, right?"

"Yup."

"But he didn't originally represent Lewis? Only hooked up with him a year ago?"

"Looks like. Hell of a coincidence."

"Sure is. I assume you tried talking to Jurgens again."

"Left nine messages over the last two days till he finally called me back this morning."

"Let me guess . . . he asserted privilege again."

"That was way too obvious to call that a guess."

"The mere fact that he's representing both Torrance and Lewis isn't privileged," Andrew said, "but whatever he talked about with them

228

would be. And if our mysterious caller hired him to represent them both—"

"Then all three of them would be clients and arguably entitled to attorney-client privilege. Hypothetically, of course. That's what he told me."

"Wait, he admitted that he was hired by someone to represent them both?"

"Of course not," Henry said. "He just said that, hypothetically, in that situation, all three such people would be clients."

"And he wouldn't be able to talk to you about his communications with them."

The conference room door opened again, and again the kid in the tight necktie leaned his head out.

"All right, Joel," Andrew said with a looser grip on his patience than he'd had the first time Joel peeked out. "Tell them I'll be right in."

The aide drew his head back in quickly and pulled the door shut.

"Is that kid the boss of you?" Henry asked.

"Let's wrap this up, Henry. Kyle Lewis is obviously a horrible person."

"*But* . . . it's been years since he's killed anyone, or even assaulted anyone that we know of other than a cop who might have even deserved it—if he was anything like some of the cops I know—and possibly a few fellow inmates."

"He's a violent criminal," Andrew said grimly. "And if I don't start the pardon process within the next few hours, he'll never get out in five days." Which was the blackmailer's deadline, of course. "As it is, I'm pushing it."

"So you're gonna do it?"

"Given his criminal record and bad behavior behind bars, he sounds largely immune to rehabilitation, which makes him a lousy candidate for a pardon." Andrew shook his head. "More important, he's a danger-ous man. If I pardon him, and he does something . . ."

"If it makes you feel any better, we've had round-the-clock surveillance on Gabriel Torrance, and he's been doing a whole lot of nothing. Taking long, meandering walks, eating fast food. He went to the movies once. But he hasn't caused any trouble and doesn't look like he's planning to."

"Torrance is Mother Teresa next to Lewis. And if the blackmailer is to be believed, he was never part of the plan anyway, other than to get me to pardon Lewis. But if I let Lewis out, and he hurts someone . . ."

"But if you don't let him out . . ."

"I know . . . Tyler."

Not to mention me, Henry thought, *and Molly, and even you, Andy.* But he didn't say any of that. "We'll keep eyes on him 24–7," Henry said instead. "I'll have Dave Junior put guys on him round the clock. If he's part of some plan—"

"*Of course* he's part of some plan. That's the blackmailer's whole game, isn't it? We just don't know what that plan is. Because you—" He cut himself off.

Henry frowned. "Because I'm the cop, and I haven't found the bad guy yet?"

"I wasn't going to say that."

"It doesn't matter," Henry said, unconvinced. "Listen, if Lewis *is* part of some plan, Dave Junior's guys will catch him at it. They're good, Andy. Most of them were cops. They know what they're doing. They'll figure out what this guy is up to as soon as he gets up to it. And they'll stop him if they have to. I promise."

Andrew shook his head in frustration. "Damn it, why didn't I turn this all over to the state police at the beginning?"

"Because I talked you out of it," Henry said, shaking his head and feeling his stomach twist.

"No, you simply advised me," Andrew said, and he sounded sincere. "It was my call. And I think I made the wrong one."

"But you can't come clean now, Andy. I know you. There's a little voice in your head telling you to. But you know you can't, right? Whether you come forward or that asshole does it, it would be equally bad for all of us. And either way, if that happens, you wouldn't be able to pardon Lewis, which would mean the blackmailer disappears with the evidence we need to clear Tyler."

He felt like the proverbial devil sitting on his brother's shoulder, whispering dark things into his ear, urging him yet again to do bad things. But even though they may have been bad, under the circumstances, Henry knew they were the right things to do.

Andrew looked thoughtful a moment; then, to Henry's relief, he nodded. "You think we'll ever see that evidence even if I do what he wants?" he asked.

"We'll get that evidence. I'll find him. We just need to keep playing his game and minimizing the damage he does until I do."

"Are you remotely close to finding him?"

"Not yet," Henry admitted. "But I'll find him. I swear I will."

"And you won't let Lewis hurt anyone? Dave Junior's guys are good?"

"The best. All ex-cops, like I said."

Andrew took a deep breath, then slowly exhaled. "Okay. I'll start the pardon process."

To Henry, in that brief moment, his brother's voice suddenly sounded like that of an older man. He was surprised to realize that it sounded more than a little like their father's voice. He saw tiny wrinkles creasing the corners of Andrew's eyes. Had those been there a month ago?

"It sucks that you have to do this," Henry said, and he meant it. Andrew merely nodded in response, and Henry handed him a copy of the file he'd put together. "Everything I have on Lewis is in there."

Andrew nodded. "Henry . . ."

"Yeah?"

"I'm serious. We can't let Lewis hurt anyone. I think I could probably live with almost anything else, but not that. If it comes to that, he needs to be stopped before he gets the chance."

"Even if it means that Tyler . . ." He trailed off.

Andrew hesitated a moment. "Yeah, even if it means that."

Henry didn't say anything. He wasn't certain he agreed. He'd have to think about it. So he merely nodded.

CHAPTER THIRTY-EIGHT

Immediately after the meeting with his legislative staff, Andrew returned to his office and asked Peter to reschedule his lunch with the insurance commissioner, pushing it to later in the week, and to set up a meeting this afternoon with Jim Garbose, his press secretary. Garbose could use a heads-up about his pardoning another prisoner, especially given Kyle Lewis's record. There were going to be questions from the press and the public, lots of them. They'd need to be ready with their answers. The problem was, Andrew didn't have good answers, either for them or for Garbose.

"Would you also bring me the pardon request file again, please?" Andrew asked his assistant before heading into his office and closing the door behind him. As soon as he was alone, he dropped heavily into his chair, put his elbows on the desk, and rested his head in his hands. He was still in that position when, minutes later, a soft knock sounded on his door. He raised his head.

"Come in."

Peter entered with the pardon file. Andrew thanked him and, as soon as the door was closed again, took the black cell phone from his pocket and dialed the now-familiar number.

"Hi, Andy," the blackmailer said in his monotone robot voice.

"I'm going to pardon Lewis," Andrew said. "It will take a few days."

"Terrific. You're making the right decision for your family."

"First, I want everything you have—the video clearing Tyler, the recordings of Molly and Henry, and anything else."

"Don't be silly. If I give all that to you now, I'll have no leverage. No, you leave Lewis alone for two weeks, and then you'll have it all. Pinky swear."

Andrew said nothing. He certainly hadn't expected his demand to be met.

"Governor," the caller said, and Andrew could hear a suddenly more serious tone in that one word, even with the voice changer, "I honestly don't give a damn about your family. I don't care if Tyler rots in prison or goes back to whatever the hell he did before all of this. I don't care if Henry stays a cop or if Molly becomes one. And I don't care if you continue doing whatever the hell you're doing in office. This isn't about all of you. It's about Kyle Lewis and me. So in two weeks, when everything is over and done with, I'll give you everything I promised."

"When *what* is over and done with?"

"Whatever it is that I want Lewis for."

Andrew drew in a long breath. "Is he going to hurt anyone?"

"Lewis? What makes you think he'll hurt anyone?"

"History. *His* history."

"I promise you, Andy, if he hurts someone, it won't be because I told him to. That's not part of the plan. My hand to God."

Andrew had no idea if the man was lying, but because he had no other choice, he said, "And I get what you promised exactly two weeks after Lewis gets out?"

"Two weeks."

Andrew closed the phone, making a mental note to discuss the two-week deadline with Henry. There was no way for him to know whether that time frame truly had meaning or whether it was intended to send them down a false avenue of investigation, but they would have to consider the possibility that something important would happen within two weeks, something for which the blackmailer needed Kyle Lewis.

Andrew opened the pardon file but didn't bother looking through it. Instead, as he had done not long ago for Torrance, he powered up his laptop and forged a letter to himself from Southern State Correctional Facility inmate Kyle Lewis, requesting a pardon. Referring now and then to the file Henry had given him on Lewis, he trumped up reasons for the request, trying to make the prisoner sound as remorseful as possible. He dated the letter eight months ago, then printed it. He studied Lewis's signature from documents in the file Henry had given him, then forged it on the letter. Not terrible. It would survive most scrutiny.

It was even easier the second time. It shouldn't have been, but it was. And that was damn depressing.

After deleting any trace of the document on his laptop, he took a breath, then called Peter into his office. This part wasn't going to be any easier this time, though.

"I have a favor to ask," he said to his assistant.

"Of course, sir. Anything."

Andrew paused a moment. "Remember when I asked you to backdate that letter recently? The one from the pardon file?"

"Yes."

"Well, I need you to do it again."

Andrew held out the forged Lewis letter. A tiny part of him hoped Peter would resist. That he would question his boss. Maybe even boldly ask what the hell he thought he was doing. Instead, after a brief hesitation, Peter took the letter without a word.

"You understand what I'm asking, Peter?"

"I think so."

"I can count on you?"

After the briefest of moments, Peter said, "Of course, sir. Always."

When he left, Andrew sat with his eyes closed until Peter returned with the letter, neatly backdated eight months. Andrew met his eyes squarely—which wasn't easy—thanked him, then said, "Would you please get the warden of Southern State Correctional on the phone, if you can?"

"Right away."

A moment later, Andrew was on the phone with Warden Robert Mannheim.

"Hello, Governor Kane," Mannheim said. "This is an honor. What can I do for you?"

"You have a prisoner there named Kyle Lewis."

"That wouldn't surprise me."

"I'm told he hasn't exactly been a model prisoner."

"That wouldn't surprise me, either. Give me a second to look him up."

Andrew heard typing.

"Got him. You heard right, Governor. He's given us some trouble over the years. Every time he's been a guest here, in fact."

"I see."

Andrew said nothing for a moment. This was the hard part, made even harder because he wasn't used to doing anything remotely like this.

"Warden, I'm thinking of pardoning Kyle Lewis."

Andrew was certain Mannheim suddenly had a dozen questions he wanted to ask, chief among them no doubt was, *Why the hell would you do that?* But he said only, "Okay."

"And, well, his record in prison would make that . . . more difficult for me than I'd like."

"I could certainly see that being the case."

"And I'm wondering . . ."

He trailed off. A moment later, the warden picked up the thread. "You know, it's possible that some of the things Lewis has been accused of while he's been here have been a little blown out of proportion, Governor."

"It is?"

"Sure. Inmates get into it, tattle on each other like schoolkids. And the guards? Sometimes they could stand to be a little more patient."

"Is that so?"

"Absolutely, Governor. Someone like Lewis, who already had a bit of a reputation from earlier stays with us, probably never got the benefit of the doubt in any of these . . . incidents. It could be that we were a bit hard on him. Sadly, those things made it into his file." The warden paused a moment. "But, see, the file could be corrected. I could handle it myself, actually. I couldn't excuse away every single mishap in it, but I have no doubt that it could be revised to look . . . as it should."

"You could do that, Warden?"

"I could. Wouldn't take more than half an hour."

"Well, I'd appreciate that," Andrew said. "When you're finished with that, would you mind emailing me his records? I could use those."

"Of course."

Andrew recited his email address, then took a deep breath and added, "And you know, while I have you on the phone, I should mention that I've been thinking about increasing your facility's operating budget. I bet you've got a few things that could stand to be upgraded. You'll see it reflected in the next state budget."

For a terrible moment, he had a vision of Jackpot Barker sitting in this very office making countless calls just like this one.

"That would be terrific, Governor. We could definitely use it."

"Okay then. Consider it done."

After an awkward pause, Mannheim said, "Well, I'll get right on that thing. You'll have it shortly. It's been an honor speaking with you, Governor."

Andrew ended the call, wishing Mannheim hadn't used the word *honor*, then spent the next few moments hoping he wouldn't vomit into the trash can behind his desk. After that, as he'd done for Gabriel Torrance, he completed the paperwork and made the phone calls necessary to put Kyle Lewis's pardon into motion. He faced resistance from a few officials—even more than when he had pardoned Torrance—who balked at the compressed time frame. The commissioner of the Department of Corrections was opposed to such extreme expedition of the process in general, and especially opposed to it in Kyle Lewis's case. But Andrew leaned on each of them with the full weight of his authority—loathing himself for it—and, one by one, they collapsed beneath it and agreed to cooperate. The rest of the process was in their hands now, but he felt confident that he had successfully, and despicably, bullied them into meeting his deadline.

With a little while before he had to meet with his press secretary, he sat back with Lewis's mug shot in his hands and stared at the hard face. Cold, dark eyes stared back at him. The tattoo across his throat—*No Regrets*—told Andrew and the rest of the world all it needed to know about the man's feelings on his life of crime.

Andrew was certain he'd never get a *No Regrets* tattoo of his own.

"Whatever you're planning to do," Andrew said softly, "please don't hurt anyone."

He looked at the Waterford clock on his desk. Garbose would be arriving soon. Good thing, too, because they needed to get a handle quickly on what they planned to say about the pardon. Releasing Gabriel Torrance, a relatively low-level felon, without much in the way of justification was one thing, but pardoning Lewis, with his sordid personal history, would be another thing entirely. Andrew and Garbose had to get on the same page fast.

Because word would get out soon.

And so would Kyle Lewis.

CHAPTER THIRTY-NINE

Over the next several days, Henry pored over the same facts again and again, hoping to see something he'd overlooked the first few dozen times, hoping to discover what, if anything, Lewis and the blackmailer could be planning to do in the next two weeks. Andrew and he had put their heads together and come up with nothing—no important figures due to visit Vermont who could be the targets of kidnapping or assassination; no high-profile, expensive items passing through worth going to such lengths to steal; no reason Henry could see why there would be a two-week deadline. He'd even contacted a few confidential informants he'd used many years ago to see if they'd heard anything on the street, but that got him nowhere, too.

At one point, he received a call from Detective Egan, who told him that the first round of DNA results were back—thanks to a rush job urged by the prosecution—and that, as expected, the blood on Tyler's e-bike was indeed Sally Graham's, as was the blood on Tyler's sneakers, which the police had found behind some garden tools in the garage. It was too early still for results relating to the bloody blue jeans the Rutland police had found behind the nail salon in Rutland, but the prosecution had little doubt that the pants were Tyler's and the blood was Sally Graham's.

From time to time, Henry checked in with his siblings. Andy was spending the five days before the blackmailer's deadline doing his job—taking meetings, reviewing draft legislation, making public appearances—and dodging Angela Baskin's questions about his pardoning of Gabriel Torrance, questions which, after several days, seemed to be petering out just in time for a new storm of controversy to blow into town, which Andy knew would happen as soon as news of his impending pardon of Kyle Lewis came to light. If Henry knew his brother, and he did, Andy was knee-deep in guilt and self-loathing. Henry understood what he was going through better than Andy realized, but it wouldn't do either of them much good to talk about it, so by unspoken agreement, they didn't.

For her part, Molly said she was passing the time going to class, studying, and exercising. Though she and Tyler had always been close, she was also spending a little more time with him lately than she'd done in the months before his arrest. She admitted that she couldn't keep from wondering how much time they would have left to just sit and talk or watch television together or eat sandwiches at the same table. It was entirely possible, she said, that in the near future, their only contact would be during prison visiting hours. Henry did his best to reassure her with words that he only half believed.

Tyler hadn't felt like talking on the phone when Henry called, but according to Molly, he was spending his time as expected—watching TV and playing video games—though at her urging he'd spent a little while with a middle-grade novel about wizards and dragons. She'd suspected the book was slightly beyond his reading level and he was turning the pages without actually reading them, but he would never have admitted that, and she hadn't asked him.

Henry knew that, with the exception of Tyler, they were all anxiously awaiting Kyle Lewis's release.

It occurred a little before 5:00 p.m. on the fifth day. Lewis walked out of Southern State Correctional Facility a free man. Because he had been given a full pardon, he had no need to report to a halfway house or check in with a parole officer going forward. He was unconditionally free, a point Angela Baskin drove home during her story on the news that evening.

A brief lead-in was followed by footage of Lewis exiting the prison with a plastic bag under one arm. Rather than a state-issued suit, he wore torn jeans and a T-shirt from which the sleeves had been cut— probably the same clothes he'd been wearing upon his arrest more than seven years before. The camera moved toward him quickly, and he gave it a malignant glare as he kept walking.

"Mr. Lewis," came Baskin's voice from off-camera, "how does it feel to be a free man?"

"Kind of a dumb question," Lewis responded.

Undeterred, Baskin asked, "Were you surprised that Governor Kane granted your pardon request?"

Lewis's black eyes developed a slight twinkle, and he smirked as he said, "Can't tell you how surprised I was."

Baskin and her camera crew moved smoothly along with him. "Do you have any idea why he granted it?" she asked.

He slowed his steps for a moment, apparently thinking. "Didn't want to see someone in prison who doesn't deserve to be there, I guess."

"What do you mean by that?" she called as Lewis resumed walking across the parking lot, his eyes appearing to be searching for something or someone. "Are you saying you didn't deserve to be in prison?"

"That's all I got to say," Lewis said. "Now stay the hell away from me."

With that, he approached a dark-blue sedan. Not a silver Camry, like the car that had picked up Gabriel Torrance. The passenger window rolled down, and Lewis appeared to say something to the driver, who handed him a small black duffel bag through the open window. As Angela Baskin stepped into the foreground of the frame again, microphone in hand, in the background, Lewis slipped into the rear seat and pulled the door shut behind him. As the car pulled away, he smiled and raised a middle finger to the camera.

"And there goes the second former prisoner pardoned by Governor Kane this month," Baskin said, "after he had granted no pardons during his first three years in office. Here's what the governor had to say about that when I caught up with him earlier today."

The scene cut to footage of Andrew Kane as he walked out of the Pavilion surrounded by aides and security personnel. Baskin's voice called from outside the frame. "Governor Kane, can you tell us why you're pardoning Kyle Lewis, despite his long record of violent criminal behavior?"

Andrew kept walking, and the camera followed. To Henry, watching the story on television, his brother looked a little too much like the guilty subject of an exposé who had just been ambushed by the investigative reporter who broke the story: the upstanding landlord who turned out to be little more than a slumlord, or the respected investment advisor who had swindled dozens of retirees out of their life savings.

"Governor Kane," Baskin continued, "this is your second pardon this month after never granting one before. Is it possible that you're looking at prisoners in a different light now that your brother is facing first-degree murder charges?"

Andrew's steps slowed for a moment before resuming their brisk pace. Over his shoulder, he said, "My press secretary has already released a statement. Please refer to that. Thank you."

"Governor, do you—"

The governor slipped into the back seat of a black SUV and pulled the door shut behind him, the vehicle's dark-tinted windows causing him to disappear completely from view. As the SUV pulled away, the footage cut back to a static shot of Baskin standing in front of Southern State Correctional, microphone in hand.

"Though the press release the governor referred to is sparse on justification, it is apparently the only official word the public will receive on the pardon of Kyle Lewis. Reporting from Southern State Correctional Facility, this is Angela—"

Using his remote control, Henry changed the channel, landing on another news station, where the florid, doughy face of ex–Vermont Governor Jackpot Barker suddenly filled the screen, clearly in mid pontification. "Worse than anything I ever did, I can tell you that. I never pardoned anyone like Kyle Lewis. The man's a violent career criminal. And this right after pardoning the first guy not long ago, whatever his name was. It's like pardoning prisoners is our governor's new hobby. Or is it a side job? A source of a little extra income, maybe? What could Governor Kane be thinking?"

The dislike Henry had always had for Barker suddenly blossomed into disgust and hatred.

"And please notice," Barker blathered on, "that I'm not even bringing up the governor's brother, the one who killed that girl. That young man isn't right in the head, and maybe that's why he killed her, but I'm not going to bring that up. That's not what we're talking about right now."

How had this man ever been elected governor?

"No, we're talking about the current governor's injudicious use of his pardon power. And did I read that he's going after our guns now? He's drafting legislation to go after our guns? For the love of God, what won't that man do?" With a smile, he added, "I bet you folks are missing old John Barker right about now, am I right?"

When Barker winked at the camera, Henry turned off the TV and reached for his cell phone. He almost dialed Andy's number, but he'd already spoken with his older brother twice today and there was nothing new to discuss. Andy was having a rough day, and there wasn't anything Henry could say to change that. It was after 10:30 p.m.; by now, he'd be home with Rebecca, who could do far more than Henry could to take his mind off things—assuming everything was okay between them. There was an obvious strain there lately, though it seemed minor enough that Henry wasn't worried for his brother . . . not about his marriage, at least.

Instead, Henry called Dave Junior, which he never really liked to do because the man sounded so much like his late father. Henry apologized for calling late and asked how the day's surveillance of Kyle Lewis was going.

"As you requested, I've got my four best guys assigned to Lewis, in two-man shifts, each with their own vehicles. Also as requested, I've still got two guys on Torrance. Those guys are a little greener, but they're good."

"Anything happening?" Henry asked.

"My guys reported in less than two hours ago, right on schedule. Lewis had a pizza delivered to the motel where he's staying."

"Did your guys figure out how he paid for his room?"

"Cash. It's not the kind of place where you need a credit card."

No card to trace then.

"What about the driver of the car that picked him up?" Henry asked.

"It was a livery service."

"I don't suppose the driver was named Larry Aronson."

"Aronson? Who's he?"

"He's the one who picked Torrance up from prison."

"No, this was someone named Pawlik Mazur." He spelled it out.

"I assume you guys talked to him."

"Of course." Then he told Henry essentially the same story that Henry had gotten from Aronson about showing up to pick up a fare and instead finding a bag, and $500, and a note promising $500 more if he picked up a prisoner being released from Southern State Correctional and drove him where the note instructed.

Henry thought he knew the answer to the question he was about to ask, but he asked it anyway. "He tell you what was in the bag he gave Lewis?"

"Besides the envelope—which he said was thick enough to contain some decent cash—there was a cell phone and some clothes. That's it."

As expected. "So he's done nothing but order a pizza so far?"

"So far. He was behind bars for a few years, so I'm guessing he's also ordered porn by now on the motel TV, but we can't confirm that. We don't even want to."

"What about Torrance?"

"He spent the day the same way he's been spending all his days— just wandering around. He's aimless. Eats in restaurants sometimes, orders in other times. My guy got excited this morning when he took a cab to Brattleboro, but he did the same thing there. Wandered the streets, ate at McDonald's, sat on a bench for a while before taking a cab back to the Holiday Inn in Springfield. The guys watching him want hazard pay, say they're gonna be bored to death."

"Stay on him. Lewis and him both. And tell whoever's on Lewis tomorrow that if they see someone they don't recognize tailing him not to get excited, because it'll be me. Give them my description. In fact, give me your guys' cell numbers, and I'll talk to them myself. I want to be able to check in with them directly from time to time anyway."

Dave Junior read off the phone numbers, which Henry wrote down.

"Thanks," he said. "I'll call them in the morning. Everyone has to stay sharp. We expect Lewis to do something within the next two weeks."

"Yeah? What's he gonna do?"

"No idea. Thanks, Dave."

He ended the call, then went to bed, where he stared at the ceiling for hours before finally falling asleep shortly before dawn.

CHAPTER FORTY

Shortly before noon on the fourth day after Kyle Lewis walked out of Southern State Correctional, Wyatt Pickman stared into the soldier's face and knew something was terribly wrong. He was supposed to have blue eyes—he was sure of it—but this soldier's eyes were brown. How could that have happened?

These days, only about 17 percent of people born in the United States had blue eyes, but during the American Civil War about half did. Pickman knew this because he'd researched it. So of the 3,244 model soldiers on the expansive battlefield in Pickman's living room, 1,622 should have blue eyes.

He'd planned it all out ahead of time, of course. He always planned everything out. Before placing his first soldier on the battlefield more than a year ago, he'd painted all 3,244 of them, making certain to maintain the proper percentages of blue uniforms to gray uniforms, brown to blond to red hair, brown eyes to blue eyes—all according to statistics and historical records.

And *this* soldier's eyes should have been blue. He closed his eyes a moment and concentrated, just to be certain . . . and yes, the Confederate soldier kneeling at the end of the split-rail fence was supposed to have blue eyes. That had been his plan. But this soldier's eyes were brown. They were . . . wrong.

While biding his time as the Kane job glided along without a hitch, Pickman had allowed himself several days of solid distraction from his work, time during which he could focus on his hobby. For four days, he'd become almost completely lost in time, transported back to September 17, 1862, and he'd been enjoying himself.

Until *this*. How the hell had this happened?

While he was pondering that question, his cell phone dinged, signaling that a notification had arrived. He had set several alerts on his personal smartphone, which would notify him when certain names or phrases were mentioned on the Internet.

He looked at the phone's screen and saw a link to an online local news article about Vermont Superior Court Judge Morgan Jeffers, the subject of one of Pickman's alerts. He frowned and clinked on the link, which brought him to the article. Skimming, he read that Jeffers, a widower who was retiring after almost forty years on the bench, was not stepping down so he could live out his remaining days fishing for trout on Golden Pond or wherever, as everyone had thought, but because he was suffering from stomach cancer that had been discovered far too late. The article closed by paying lip service to everything the people of Vermont owed to the good judge for his decades of public service.

Pickman clenched his teeth, the muscles in his jaw bunching.

Stomach cancer? How the hell could he have foreseen that?

Who knew how long the old judge had left now?

Weeks? Days? Hours?

Pickman's mind sped through the intricacies of his grand plan— events, reactions, cause, effect, timing . . .

He hurried from the living room and down the basement stairs into his war room. He stared at the mosaic on the wall. An article about Jeffers over there. A string . . . another string . . . Tyler Kane . . . Kyle Lewis . . .

He dropped into his desk chair and pulled his bible in front of him. He scanned the tabs, flipped to Part VI, Section H, Subsection 2 and began to skim, turning the first page quickly, then the second, then flipping back again. Then he sat back and tried to take calming breaths.

A fly in the ointment.

A wrench in the gears.

Whatever the phrase, Jeffers's stomach cancer was a real headache to Pickman. It didn't *change* the plan exactly. No, it fell short of that, thank God, because Pickman was loath to change his plans once they were finalized and put into motion.

But it required revision of a sort . . . not a change, but a *revision*. And not of the plan itself, but of the timeline. Things had to speed up. Because Jeffers had a part to play, and he couldn't be allowed to die before he played it. And because he could die any day now, apparently, the plan had to be accelerated.

Pickman was unhappy about this, but at least the plan remained intact. He didn't know what he would have done otherwise.

He closed his bible, and his eyes fell on a small object on the desk beside it. The brown-eyed Confederate soldier whose eyes should have been blue. He must have brought it down with him without thinking.

He carried the soldier back up to the living room and surveyed the battlefield he had so faithfully re-created. He looked down at the defective soldier in his hand. Then back up at the soldiers dotting the landscape, each painted almost a year ago before a single shrub, tree, or structure had been added, using tiny brushes, sometimes the tips of toothpicks for the most delicate work, like the eyes. And he had carefully counted how many he would paint of each soldier—1,914 for the Union, representing the 59 percent of soldiers who had fought for the North in the battle that day, and 1,330 for the Confederacy, making up the remaining 41 percent. He'd painted the correct percentage with the historically correct color of hair and eyes . . . or at least he thought he had.

But now this . . .

What to do? He could repaint this one soldier's eyes, of course, but if *his* eyes were wrong, then how many others could be, as well? He never seriously considered ignoring the problem, of course, despite how minuscule the pinpricks of color representing eyes on the one-eighth-inch-tall soldier's face were. He couldn't possibly do that. They were wrong, and he'd always know that.

His own eyes swept across the vast battlefield, almost 90 percent complete, the work of countless hours over the past year and a quarter, a project that had filled nearly every hour he hadn't spent sleeping, eating, or planning and executing the Kane job. Notebooks full of research. Thousands of soldiers. Thousands of tiny eyes. How many eyes were wrong? How many didn't conform to his plan? And if a soldier's eyes were wrong, could one of the uniforms be wrong, too? Or could there be an extra man on horseback? Or too many men near the Dunker Church? One too few crossing the stone bridge over Antietam Creek? Not enough wagons? Too many wagons?

His mind was awhirl.

First, Jeffers's stomach cancer. Now this catastrophe.

He couldn't possibly re-count the eye colors of all the soldiers now. The battlefield was too large; he couldn't see the faces of the tiny figures near the center of the board.

But he couldn't live with the possibility that the scene was historically inaccurate. That he'd failed to execute his plan properly.

He took a deep breath, then another. Then a third. He closed his eyes and gathered his thoughts. Then he opened his eyes, reached out, and flipped the nearest four-by-four-foot section of the diorama into the air, watching it crash against the wall, scattering the figures that hadn't yet been glued into place. Soldiers, horses, and trees clattered to the hardwood and slid across the floor.

Pickman moved to the section to his left—which he had completed but not yet secured to the sawhorse foundation—gripped it by its edges, lifted it, and sent it spinning like an oversize square Frisbee across the diorama, where it plowed through the battlefield like the hand of God—or perhaps the scythe of Death—mowing down soldiers and horses, felling trees, and razing buildings. In ten seconds, he had destroyed a third of the project, nearly half a year's work. Over the next few minutes, he destroyed the rest. In the morning, he would use a circular saw to dismantle the boards and their foundation. He would fill trash bags with thousands and thousands of pieces of set decoration.

But he would retain his binders full of notes, his painstaking research. Because soon he would start the same project all over again. From the very beginning. And next time, he'd get it right. Next time, he'd be sure to follow his plan more carefully.

But at this point, he knew, all of that would have to wait. Because Judge Jeffers's goddamn cancer had forced him to start the final phase of the plan immediately.

It was almost over. The job was nearly finished. Yet, at the same time, there was so much left to be done to bring things to a close.

Without a glance at the destruction he had wrought in his living room, he headed back down to his war room to start the beginning of the end.

CHAPTER FORTY-ONE

In the four days since Kyle Lewis had walked out of prison with a full governor's pardon, Andrew had tried to dodge questions and controversy and focus on his job. It wasn't easy. The press sliced away at him. Jackpot Barker took every opportunity to step in front of a camera and rub salt in the wounds. In his interactions with everyone from individuals to the media, Andrew's opinions and motives seemed to be questioned in numerous subtle ways—sidelong glances and veiled comments—and he knew his popularity and power were eroding fast, like the face of a hill in a California mudslide.

Still, he carried out his duties as well and as faithfully as he could and waited . . . waited for Kyle Lewis to do whatever the hell he was planning to do.

The blackmailer wasn't answering Andrew's calls lately. He'd made it clear that he had no intention of meeting his end of the bargain until the two-week period he had insisted on expired—if even then. Andrew had no choice but to continue waiting . . . and hoping that whatever Lewis was going to do, it didn't involve hurting or, God forbid, killing anyone. Andrew could handle it if this was about money, or even drugs, but not if it came down to murder. Henry's detectives were following Lewis night and day. They were good men who'd all once been good cops. They'd been instructed not to let Lewis hurt anyone. So if it looked like Lewis was even thinking of crossing that line, they'd know when, and exactly how, to step in to stop him.

At least that was what Andrew told himself every night as he tried to fall asleep.

If Lewis had evil on his mind, though, he was taking his time getting around to it. According to Henry, he hadn't broken a single law. The private detectives following him hadn't witnessed any evidence of it; nor had Henry during the sporadic hours he'd joined the surveillance team.

That wasn't to say that Lewis hadn't visited some of Vermont's seedier locations. Henry had related that the ex-con had visited a bar in Winooski yesterday that had a back room known to both law enforcement personnel and the criminal set as the place to go if you wanted the best untraceable firearms in Vermont. And the day before, he had eaten at Greenland Terrace, a restaurant in Burlington owned by Stanley Bolton, a guy with an arrest record as long as Lewis's but with the money to afford a better lawyer. He'd served two and a half years for fraud twenty years ago and, despite several arrests since, had never spent another day behind bars. He was thought to be the brains and bankroll behind numerous crimes—relatively small jobs, perpetrated by others who would give a hefty percentage to Bolton if successful—but the authorities had never gotten anything close to reliable evidence against him. He wasn't a major player, though, so nobody got too worked up about the fact that no one could pin anything on him. And there didn't seem to be a previous connection between Lewis and him—and Henry assured Andrew that he had looked hard for one—so there was no reason to suspect that Bolton had engineered Lewis's pardon. But still, Lewis's eating in Bolton's establishment was interesting.

Either that, or it was a red herring. Something to distract. It was impossible to tell.

The fact that Lewis hadn't done anything illegal seemed to be making Henry nuts. And, Andrew had to admit, it was driving *him* a little insane, too . . . as was Henry and his twice daily phone calls to report next to nothing. Molly claimed to be going a bit crazy, too, just waiting. Only Tyler, confident that his day in court would end with a declaration of his innocence, seemed not to be too tense.

Angela Baskin's relentlessness certainly wasn't helping Andrew's state of mind, either. She had taken to questioning everything he did, everything he said, everywhere he went, and every decision he had made during his entire time in office—and she had the ear of every Vermonter, it seemed.

When did everyone go back to relying on local TV reporters to catch up on the day's events? he wondered. *Didn't anyone get the news from anonymous journalists on the Internet anymore?*

The buzzing of a cell phone interrupted his thoughts, and it took him a moment to realize that it wasn't his personal device.

After four days, the black cell phone was ringing.

"Yes?" Andrew said into the phone. He knew he sounded hostile. He had good reason.

"Good afternoon, Andy," the caller said in his annoying robotic voice. "I feel like I can stop using your title, by the way. We've known each other awhile now."

"It's ten days until the deadline you imposed on yourself to give us your evidence. Any chance you're calling to tell me you're turning it over early?"

"Sorry, but no. In fact . . . well, you're not going to like this."

The back of Andrew's neck began to itch.

"You'd better not be thinking about—"

"Andy, I'm afraid you've done it again."

"Done what?"

"Broken our agreement."

"Like hell I have."

"I'm not saying you did it personally."

"I don't know what—"

"You haven't left Kyle Lewis alone, as we agreed. You're having him followed."

Andrew hesitated only a split second before saying, "No, I'm not."

"Don't be a fibber, Andy. Lewis caught them. Said they stuck out like sore thumbs."

"What the hell did you honestly expect?" Andrew snapped. "That we would just—"

"Aha, I knew it," the caller said triumphantly. "Honestly, Lewis wasn't certain, but I decided to bluff, and it worked. You just tipped your hand."

Damn it. Andrew took a steadying breath. "Listen to me very carefully—"

"No, Governor, you listen to me. I warned you to stay away from Lewis. And you haven't. Now there will be repercussions."

The phone went dead at Andrew's ear. He snapped it closed hard enough that he thought for a moment he'd cracked it.

Andrew had never felt so helpless in his life. He was purportedly the most powerful man in Vermont, yet some faceless figure, a voice on the phone, was pulling his strings, making him dance like a marionette to a tune Andrew couldn't even hear. His every action had been controlled, from his first choreographed act, the pardon of a low-level prisoner, to the action for which it paved the way—the release from prison of a violent career criminal who, it seemed, was part of a plan that would come to fruition sometime in the next ten days.

God only knew what that plan was.

There could be no doubt that, despite having spent much of his adult life in public service, Andrew had chosen his family's welfare—especially poor, innocent Tyler's—over that of the public at large. He could only pray that whatever Lewis and the blackmailer were doing, it didn't involve physical harm to anyone—and if it did, that the detectives Henry had hired would prevent that from occurring.

He prayed also that whatever "repercussions" the caller had in mind weren't too devastating to whomever they were directed at.

He glanced at the desk clock. He was already several minutes late to yet another meeting with his press secretary to discuss how to minimize the damage his pardons had done to his approval rating over the past few days. Poor Jim Garbose was doing his best to deflect and spin and recharacterize, but Andrew knew that the man was having as much difficulty as everyone else trying to understand the governor's rationale behind the unusual pardons.

Andrew hated to keep him waiting any longer, but he had calls to make. His siblings and his wife had to be alerted to the possibility that a bombshell would be dropping soon.

With any luck, they'd all be near their phones.

CHAPTER FORTY-TWO

Henry slipped his cell phone back into his pocket and tried to make sense of the latest update that Dave Junior had just given him—namely, the still-somewhat-surprising news that Kyle Lewis had spent his first four days of freedom not doing much of anything, certainly nothing worth committing murder and blackmail to spring him for. He'd merely wandered around in almost aimless fashion, only now and then visiting a questionable part of town, or stopping by a questionable place of business, or speaking with a person of unquestionably bad reputation. But he hadn't done anything illegal yet. The detectives' theory, one Henry deemed reasonable, was that he was killing time before a scheduled meeting with someone—perhaps the blackmailer himself, though Henry didn't share that piece with Dave Junior's guys. But the thinking was that Lewis probably had some special knowledge needed to pull off a job or heist of some kind—maybe he had a desired familiarity with a specific location, or perhaps he possessed a much-needed skill of which Henry wasn't aware. Maybe he had contacts that someone needed. Whatever the case, for now, he wasn't doing much. And, for that matter, neither was Gabriel Torrance, who still seemed to be meandering without purpose through the streets of several Vermont towns, though that had become old news by now.

Henry needed a pick-me-up. He grabbed his coffee mug and was in the process of locking his office door behind him on his way to the break room when he heard a familiar voice. "Hello, Henry."

He turned to find Commissioner of Public Safety Warren Haddonfield walking down the hall toward him. Haddonfield was a big honcho. In addition to being in charge of the Department of Public Safety, as his title implied, he also oversaw other areas, including the state's forensics lab and crime information center. Additionally, he was in charge of the Vermont State Police. Although Henry was a lieutenant and there were higher ranks in the VSP, he reported directly to Haddonfield to help preserve the integrity of his Internal Affairs role. Otherwise, he might not be free to investigate his superiors, if needed, without fear of facing adverse employment actions.

Henry almost said, *Hey, boss*, the way he often greeted Haddonfield, but something in the man's demeanor made him change his mind. "Hello, Commissioner," he said, and because Haddonfield's steps were slowing as he approached, he added. "Looking for me, sir?"

"Got a sec?"

"Of course." He started to unlock his office door.

"Let's head to my office," Haddonfield said, and the first warning bell sounded faintly in Henry's head.

The phone in his pocket vibrated, causing another warning bell to ring, but he didn't dare sneak a peek.

"Lead the way, sir."

They passed the elevators and headed left to the commissioner's office. Henry had been there many times before. It was far bigger and more nicely appointed than Henry's office. It paid to be the commissioner of public safety.

Haddonfield took a seat behind his desk and pointed to the straight-backed chairs in front of it. Henry took a seat in one. Haddonfield looked troubled, and Henry's mind flashed back to the time he'd been sent to the principal's office in the eighth grade after having been caught by a teacher's aide with his hand up Tina Herlihy's shirt in the science section of the school library.

"What can I do for you, sir?" he asked as the vibration of the phone in his pocket told him that the caller had left a message.

"Got an incident of trooper misconduct."

Henry relaxed a little. This wasn't the typical way an investigation found its way to him—usually, he received a written complaint dictated to a trooper on duty when a member of the public called or stopped in with a complaint, or perhaps a supervisor gave him a call about some matter that warranted his attention. Never before had Haddonfield himself come to Henry directly and personally. But in and of itself, that wasn't cause for alarm.

"Okay," Henry said, pulling a pen and small notebook from his pocket.

"No need to write anything down, Henry. Got something here I need you to see, though." He angled his computer monitor so that both he and Henry could see it. "An email came in a little while ago, with a video attached, and it was routed to me. I'm told it was also sent to all the local news outlets."

Another bell clanged in Henry's head, and it was louder this time. Much louder.

Haddonfield nudged his computer mouse, and his screen, which had been dark, crackled to life. In black and white video, Henry saw a parking lot he recognized at once, though he'd seen it from a different angle. It was the lot behind the nail salon. He saw himself looking up at the buildings for security cameras. He watched as he knelt beside the wooden pallets and removed the white plastic bag, which he now knew had contained jewelry covered with dried blood that no doubt had once belonged to Sally Graham, wrapped in a Pac-Man T-shirt that belonged to Tyler, though Haddonfield couldn't have known those things.

"Sir," he began, but Haddonfield cut him off with an upraised hand.

Henry then watched as he carried the bag out of the parking lot. Then nothing happened for several long moments. Haddonfield didn't fast forward, though Henry knew what they would see if he did. It didn't matter, though; they'd see it soon enough. Until then, for two minutes and thirteen seconds, Haddonfield was content to wait in silence. Henry again opened his mouth to speak, but Haddonfield silenced him with only a glare this time, and they sat quietly for several more moments that lasted an eternity to Henry. Eventually, two Rutland Police officers entered the lot. One searched behind the pallets without success while the other found a white plastic bag behind some large planters. Finally, Haddonfield stopped the recording.

"Sir?" Henry began, and this time Haddonfield let him speak. The problem was that he had nothing to say.

"How did you know that bag would be there, Henry?"

"I got an anonymous tip."

"I see. Did you suspect the bag contained evidence relating to your brother's case?"

"Of course not," he lied. "I was just told there was a bag of evidence there, something we should see."

"You didn't think to call it in?"

"I thought it might be a prank."

"I want that bag, Henry, and whatever was inside."

"I can't give it to you, sir," Henry said truthfully, given that the bag was at the bottom of the Chittenden Reservoir. "I don't have it anymore. There was nothing in it but empty snack bags and wrappers. Potato chips. Hostess cupcakes. I threw it all out. Figured it had definitely been a prank."

Haddonfield gave him a hard stare. "Why did you take it with you then? Why not put it back where it was?"

"All due respect, sir," Henry said, "and I'm not trying to sound like a smart-ass here, believe me, but that would have been littering."

Haddonfield took a deep breath. Below his boss's sight line, Henry wiped his palms on his pant legs, palms that had grown damp.

"We have reason to believe that bag contained evidence related to your brother's murder case."

"No, sir. Just trash."

"Because the other bag? The one the locals found? That did, in fact, contain evidence we strongly believe relates to your brother's case."

"Well, that's good then. Because Tyler's innocent. And if it really does, then I think the anonymous caller was just messing with me, sir. Wanted to get me into trouble. Probably found the real bag of evidence and added a second bag full of snack wrappers to screw with me."

"Who would want to do that, Lieutenant?"

He wanted to say, *The guy who framed Tyler and is blackmailing and threatening our entire family.* Instead, he said, "Oh, let's see . . . dozens of cops I've investigated over the years. Anyone I've ever arrested. Any member of the public who doesn't like my brother, the governor, or my other brother, the murder suspect, or God knows who else."

Haddonfield sighed heavily. "There's going to be a full investigation. You know how it goes."

"Yes, sir."

"That's usually your job, but I'll ask the FBI office in Burlington to help us out with this."

"I understand."

"What's on your plate right now?"

Henry knew what he was asking. "Nothing pressing, sir. Nothing major. Run-of-the-mill investigations."

"Nothing that won't keep for a little while?"

"No, sir."

"If I knew for an absolute fact that the bag you took contained evidence in a case, rather than having to rely on the word of an anonymous caller, you'd already have been arrested. As it is, consider yourself suspended without pay until this matter is resolved one way or another. And I expect you'll cooperate fully when asked to do so."

"Of course."

Haddonfield nodded. In a different, less officious tone, he said, "You're going to lose your job, Henry. Hell, you may go to prison."

"Yes, sir."

"I can't help you. Not with this going so public. And besides . . . I wouldn't want to. Not with something like this."

Henry understood. He'd breached a trust . . . hell, several trusts—the public's, the VSP's, and Haddonfield's—in profound fashion.

"I understand, Commissioner."

"Please collect your things, lock up your office, and give your keys to Sergeant Yasovich. Along with your badge and gun, of course. He's waiting outside."

Which meant that Sergeant Yasovich was going to escort Henry to his office, oversee the gathering of his things and the locking up of his office, then walk Henry out of the building. Henry didn't blame Haddonfield. The man didn't have a choice. Nor would he blame Yasovich, though he could imagine the feeling of schadenfreude the good sergeant would experience upon facilitating the expulsion of the head of Internal Affairs from the building under a cloud of suspicion.

"Understood, sir," Henry said.

He rose and headed for the door.

"And Henry?" Haddonfield said, not without sympathy. "Get yourself a really good lawyer. You're going to need one."

CHAPTER FORTY-THREE

As soon as the video of Henry in the nail salon parking lot hit the news outlets, it began to spread rapidly, like blood in water, and it wasn't long before the sharks were circling. A day later, Andrew stood at a podium in the press briefing room of the Pavilion facing a huge school of them, members of the news media in a standing-room-only crowd. Dozens of video cameras pointed at him. Hundreds of eyes watching him; thousands more would see him on the news or the Internet later. The questions came at him hard and fast with barely enough time between them for him to try to answer.

"Were you aware that your brother Henry was planning to destroy evidence in Tyler's case?"

"Why did you pardon both Gabriel Torrance and Kyle Lewis within a matter of weeks?"

"Have you tried to use your position to influence Tyler's murder investigation?"

"Do you feel as though you have a conflict of interest in trying to run the state while charges are pending, or soon will be, against *both* of your brothers?"

"Given the serious allegations against two of your family members, are you going to issue a public apology to former Governor Barker for your many insinuations about corruption in his administration?"

"Are you going to try to convince the state attorney not to file obstruction charges against Lieutenant Kane?"

"Are you considering resigning from office?"

Andrew did his best to answer, and Jim Garbose stepped in now and then to referee the bloodbath, slow the questions down, and give each reporter a chance to hurl a dagger at him. And through it all, Angela Baskin sat in the front row, the look on her face convincing Andrew that she was content to take it all in, to let the rest of the pack bring him down.

When it was finally over, when Garbose finally called the match—a TKO for the reporters—Andrew left the podium feeling battered and bruised. What he didn't feel was wronged. He deserved this. He wasn't guilty of most of what they were accusing him of, but he was guilty nonetheless. Guilty of a lot of things. Of putting his family's welfare over that of the people of Vermont. Of not turning the black cell phone over to the authorities immediately after receiving it. Of allowing Henry to convince him that he needed to keep his options open in case—just in case—he wanted to negotiate with the blackmailer. Of pardoning Gabriel Torrance. Of being foolish enough to hope that the caller would do as he promised in return. And, finally, of pardoning Kyle Lewis.

Yes, he was guilty of so many things. And what was worse . . . he knew, even now, that if this all led to Tyler's freedom, he could live with it. Just a few short weeks ago, he couldn't have imagined compromising himself in the first place, much less justifying it to himself. Those were things his father might have done, that Jackpot Barker definitely did, but not Andrew Kane. Yet he realized that as long as Tyler was acquitted, and as long as Lewis didn't hurt any—

"Andrew?" Garbose said. "You okay?"

Andrew blinked. The open elevator doors in front of him were starting to close with them still inside the car. Garbose shot a hand out and held them open.

"Sir?"

Andrew hadn't even realized he was on the elevator. He'd been lost in thought as his press secretary led him up to his offices on the fifth floor. He stepped out of the elevator car, and Garbose followed.

"I'm fine, Jim. Thanks for your help."

"Not sure how much help I was down there today."

"I meant thanks for your help all along. Today, before today, and everything you'll be doing to help me going forward. I'm afraid you'll be earning your salary in the days ahead."

"I guess it's about time," Garbose said.

Andrew smiled wanly. "This is all really bad, Jim."

"It's not good, but you'll get through it. You're certainly not as bad as Barker."

"But I wasn't supposed to just be 'not as bad as Barker.' I was supposed to be much better."

"You are. And they'll remember that soon enough."

Andrew merely nodded—there wasn't much he could say—then turned and headed toward his office.

As he passed Peter's desk, his assistant said, "Governor Barker left a message for you, sir."

"Sympathy or gloating?"

"If I had to guess, gloating."

"If he calls back, tell him to go to hell."

"Will do," Peter responded, though they both knew he couldn't do that.

Henry was waiting in Andrew's office, staring out the big window at the gold dome of the State House. He turned when Andrew entered.

"Sorry, big brother," he said. "I screwed up bad."

"You were trying to protect Tyler, same as I've been doing. And you messed up, same as I've been doing."

"I think I may be going to prison, Andy."

Andrew, a former prosecutor, nodded. Henry was right. That was a real possibility, which was a terrible thing. Still, he said, "This is one mistake after a lot of good years. They'll keep that in mind."

"You could always pardon me, of course."

He might have been joking. But maybe not. Andrew had crossed the line for his other brother. For Tyler, he had pardoned not one but two prisoners. Surely he would do it for Henry, too, right? The thing was, this was different. Tyler was innocent. He didn't kill Sally Graham. Henry, on the other hand, had done exactly what he was accused of doing. But then, who was Andrew to judge? If it came to it, he honestly didn't know what he would do if Henry were convicted of obstruction. He didn't even want to think about that. So he said, "Haddonfield asked for the bag you took, I assume. Did you give it to him?"

Henry hesitated, no doubt noticing Andrew's dodge, then said, "I can't."

"It's nothing worse than they already have on Tyler. Just more of the same. If we ever find the son of a bitch behind all this and turn his recording over to the authorities, it won't matter. So why not just cooperate and give it to them?"

Henry hesitated. "Because I'm not a scuba diver."

Andrew dropped into the chair behind his desk and sighed. "You can't tell me things like that, Henry. I'm the governor."

"Sorry. You asked."

Silence settled on the room like a fog. Henry turned back to the window, and Andrew placed his elbows on his desk, rested his head in his hands, and tried not to think about anything at all. A few long moments later, Henry said, "I'm not sure I'll remember how not to be a cop."

Andrew paused before answering. "Hopefully, you won't have to, Henry. You should hire a lawyer, though. Call Rachel Addison. She won't be able to represent you—it would be a conflict—but I'm sure she can give you the name of someone good."

Henry held his gaze for a moment, then nodded, and Andrew wondered if his brother felt abandoned in that moment.

Then, with false jocularity, Henry said, "Whoever it is had better be *damn* good. I'm too pretty to go to prison."

"That's debatable," Andrew said with a rueful smile, "but try to stop thinking like that."

"Easy for you to say. Listen, Molly called a little while ago. She thinks we should be together for dinner again tonight. You in?"

"I'll be there. I'll see if Rebecca wants to come, too." He figured that was a fifty-fifty proposition given the way she'd been feeling about everything lately. But they'd be okay in time, he knew. Probably not even too much time. "How about you? See you there?"

"I'm not gonna turn down a home-cooked meal," Henry said. "Who knows how many I have left? Soon it could be nothing but prison chow for me."

Andrew could manage only a forced, half-hearted chuckle before hanging up.

CHAPTER FORTY-FOUR

Wyatt Pickman sat at his kitchen table finishing an early dinner of exactly one-third of a pound of Prince spaghetti with precisely one-quarter cup of jarred Prego tomato and basil spaghetti sauce. It had to be Prince, of course, and it had to be Prego tomato and basil.

The small television on the counter was tuned to an early evening news program. He smiled as he watched recorded footage from Andrew Kane's afternoon press conference. The governor looked beleaguered. The poor man wasn't yet aware of the trials and tribulations he still had to face. But he would be. And soon. Very soon.

Pickman pushed his empty plate to the side and pulled his bible in front of him, opening it to the first tab of the index, labeled *Contacts*, where he found the number of the burner phone he'd had the second livery driver deliver to Kyle Lewis on the day he'd walked out of prison. He and Lewis had spoken only twice. During the first call, shortly after Lewis was released, he'd made sure that Lewis had received the cash Pickman had sent and had read the letter accompanying it. He had wanted to make sure Lewis understood his instructions. At the time, it had taken a few minutes for Pickman to convince the man that he had no intention of revealing his identity; nor was he ready to share with Lewis the reason he had facilitated the pardon.

"I don't get it, man," Lewis had said. "Do we even know each other?"

"We've never met," Pickman had said into his voice changer. "But I need you for a job."

"Not that I'm complaining, not one bit, but why me? You had to get me pardoned. Wasn't there nobody else who could do the job?"

"Not like you," Pickman had said. "It has to be you."

"And you can't tell me what the job is?"

"Soon. Until then, follow your instructions to the letter. I'll call you when I need you."

"And there's five G's in it for me, like you said?"

"That's right."

"Is it dangerous? 'Cuz if it's dangerous, maybe I should get more money. Like, a bonus."

"I got you out of prison seven years early," Pickman had said. "Consider that your bonus."

During their second conversation, the night before last, he'd called to make sure Lewis was still following his instructions, which the man promised he was.

It was time for the third and final phone call. He turned off the television with a remote control, then dialed Lewis's number. The man answered curtly. From the style of music playing on the TV in the background, along with the urgent grunting of at least two people, perhaps more, Pickman could guess what Lewis was watching.

"The time has come," Pickman said into his voice changer.

"Damn, man, I'm still not used to the creepy voice."

"As soon as we end our call, change into the black pants and black shirt that were in the bag I had delivered to you. Then find a taxi—it's easy in that part of town—and take it to a restaurant called Porta Bella's. It's not far from you. Once inside, move quickly because there are at least two people following you, and you absolutely must lose them."

"How do I do that?"

"Go immediately to the restroom and climb out through the window. That will put you in an alley. There's a fire escape ladder on the side of the next building over. Climb to the roof—it's only two stories—and hurry across and climb down the ladder into the alley on the other side . . . Are you getting all this?"

"Bathroom, fire escape, cross the roof, next alley. Got it, man."

"In that next alley, enter the back door of a bar called Moonshine Eddie's. They never lock it during business hours. That will bring you into the bar, back by the restrooms. Go through the bar and leave by the front door, then stand in the doorway of the stationery shop to your left. The doorway will be dark, so you will be in shadow. The entire procedure should take you no more than four and a half minutes. I'll be watching the door to Moonshine Eddie's. When I see you, I'll pull up in a four-door sedan and roll the back window down as a signal; then you'll hurry into the back seat. Do you understand?"

"Sure, boss."

"Are you certain? You'll have four and a half minutes. You have to lose the men following you."

"Back door of Moonshine Eddie's, out through the front, wait in the doorway to the left for you to pull up and roll down your window. Easy as pie."

To Pickman's surprise, Lewis did indeed seem to understand his instructions.

"Okay then," he said. "I'll see you shortly."

He ended the call and, still using his voice changer, placed another. Gabriel Torrance answered on the third ring.

"Hello?"

"Checking your progress," Pickman said. "We're running out of time, like I told you."

"I've been doing nothing but search this place the last couple of days, like you told me to. I'm searching as we speak."

"And you still haven't found it?"

"Not yet. But I will tonight. There's only one building left. I checked all the others carefully. This is the last one left. It has to be here. If I'm right, I'll have it before morning. Hopefully, long before morning."

If Torrance was right, the job would be over tonight. If not, Pickman would resort to his contingency plan for the final task. He didn't want to do it that way. His client had felt strongly that it should be done as planned, but if Torrance couldn't find what he was searching for, there would be no choice.

"Keep looking," he said. "Call me when you find it."

He snapped his burner phone shut and turned his attention to his bible again. Under Part VIII, Section A, Subsection 1, he found the summary of the action that would take place shortly, though it had originally been scheduled for a week from tonight. At least today was Tuesday. It would have been more difficult if it had been another day. He read through the summary, studied his diagrams and sketches, and committed every fact and image to memory. Then he washed his plate, utensils, and drinking glass by hand, dried them, and put them into their respective cupboards and drawers. After that, he changed into dark pants and a dark shirt, then slipped his bible into a small black duffel bag, which contained everything else he would need for his encounter with Lewis. Then he retrieved a much larger duffel, which contained items he would need even later, and carried it all out to the car he had rented under a false name, using a fake ID and a credit card issued to that identity.

Twenty-four minutes later, he was parked two doors down from Moonshine Eddie's when Lewis exited the bar, looked both ways, then slipped into the shadows of the doorway to his left. Pickman scanned the street, saw no sign of a tail, and pulled up in front of the stationery store, lowering the rear window as he did. Lewis hurried into the back seat. Pickman calmly pulled away from the curb and headed down the street. Still no sign of a tail.

It had gone perfectly, of course.

"You the boss?" Lewis asked from the rear seat. "Or hired help like me?"

"I'm the boss," Pickman said.

"Thought you might have one of those boxes in your throat, you know? Like, a permanent one. But you talk normal."

"Thank you."

"Where are we headed?"

"A private residence."

A glance in the rearview mirror. Still no one following.

"To do what? Steal something?"

"Possibly."

"We gonna hurt someone?"

"Possibly."

Lewis paused. "I don't wanna kill no one, man. It ain't that I'm against it on principle, you know? But it's riskier. I just got out. I don't wanna go back in. But if I do gotta go back in, it ain't gonna be for murder, you know?"

"I promise you won't have to kill anyone," Pickman said. "And if you want out, I'll pull over right now. You won't get the five thousand dollars, of course."

"That'd be fair, I guess."

Pickman checked for a tail again and saw none. "And, of course, seeing as I got you out of prison specifically for this job, if you don't want to do it, I guess you'll have to go back in."

"Wait . . . what? You can do that?"

"I got you out, didn't I? That was hard. Getting you back in would be easy."

A sigh sounded from the back seat. "Okay, man, I'm game for whatever. I hope we're not killing anyone, though. Like I said, it ain't like I haven't done it before, and I'll do it again if I have to, but it's better to avoid it if you can."

"Words to live by," Pickman said.

They rode for another ten minutes before Lewis got chatty. At first, he tried asking more questions about the job they were heading to—"whatever the hell it is," he added more than once—and when he eventually realized that he wasn't going to learn anything more, he shifted the conversation into idle talk. Prison life. How much better the food was on the outside. How many girls he was going to lay once this job was over. How hard it had been not picking up a prostitute as soon as he got out, but he'd remembered the instructions in the letter he'd been given, instructions forbidding him from breaking even the most minor law.

Pickman tried to tune him out and let him talk himself dry, but he was apparently on something of a prison-release high and didn't seem on the verge of slowing down anytime soon, so Pickman interrupted him midsentence, saying, "Ever heard of Bach?"

"The songwriter?"

"Sure, we'll call him that. So, you've heard of him then?"

"Yeah."

"This one's my favorite," he said, turning on the in-dash CD player. *The Art of Fugue*, which was always set to repeat, began to play. The perfection of the music soothed him, and he didn't hear another word from Lewis over the remaining twelve minutes of the ride to the town of Woodstock, if indeed the man even spoke again.

Eventually, Pickman turned off the music and slowed down slightly as he passed a white clapboard-and-brick center-entrance Colonial. No lights were on in the house, as expected. Judge Jeffers attended a meeting of the local Rotary Club every Tuesday at 7:00 p.m.

At the end of the block, he turned right and eased the car to a stop in a prechosen spot he had scouted months ago, one largely untouched by the light from the nearest streetlamp.

He led Lewis through the shadows of big shade trees, along the rear edge of a spacious backyard, and onto Jeffers's property. From one of his numerous reconnaissance trips, he knew the house had no home security system. One of the benefits—at least from the perspective of people up to no good—of living in a bucolic state like Vermont: folks could be conveniently, albeit naively, trusting.

Pickman moved quickly to Jeffers's back door, with Lewis right behind him. He reached into his duffel bag and removed a set of lock picks, with which he made short work of the lock in the doorknob. Then he slipped on a pair of black leather gloves.

Once inside, he moved confidently through the dark house, remembering its layout from a prior visit. Also, less than two hours ago he had used the sketch he had made that night to refamiliarize himself with the floor plan.

"Slow down," Lewis whispered. "What, you can see in the dark, man?"

"There's no need to whisper. No one's home."

"Then why don't we turn on a light so I can see where the hell I'm going?"

Pickman ignored the question. They entered the living room. "See that sofa over there?" he asked.

"Barely. Can we at least open the curtains, let a little moonlight in?"

"No. Have a seat on the sofa."

"Why?"

"Because that's your job at the moment. Have a seat."

"That's it? Just sit on my ass?"

"For now."

"I don't get any of this. You get me out of Southern State, then have me wander around for days doing nothing. You have me pop into a few places, but don't tell me to do anything there."

"You did plenty," Pickman said, thinking about what a good decoy Lewis had been, giving the Kanes someone to follow, something to worry about, when all along his only contribution to all of this was to be here tonight. Pickman could almost hear the Kanes frantically asking each other, *Why did Lewis have to be out in two weeks? What's going to happen in two weeks?* He smiled to himself. He liked thinking about the people he controlled chasing their tails.

"I just don't get why I'm here, man," Lewis said.

"In case I need you."

Lewis stood in the dark and said nothing for a moment. Pickman imagined he could hear rusty gears turning in the man's head.

"Oh," Lewis finally said, "I'm the muscle, right? In case things go south, like, the guy comes home or something."

"Sure," Pickman said. "But no one's home right now, so have a seat."

"Gotcha, man. Easy money."

"I have to go upstairs for a minute. Wait here."

Pickman entered the front hall, which was right off the living room, and ascended the stairs. In a nightstand drawer in the master bedroom, he found the judge's .38 Special right where he'd first seen it. He checked to make sure the gun was loaded, then slipped it into his pocket.

Back in the living room, he settled into a surprisingly comfortable upholstered side chair.

"Now what?" Lewis asked.

"We wait." Pickman glanced at his watch. "We have less than twenty minutes, thirty at the most. Just relax. Close your eyes if you want."

"We're waiting for the guy to come home? We *want* him to come home? What the hell?"

Pickman didn't bother to respond. A moment later, Lewis said, "Oh, I get it. He's got info we need, like the combination to a safe or something, right?"

"Sure."

"Won't he see our faces, though? I ain't going back to prison."

Pickman sighed, opened his duffel, and removed a black ski mask, which he tossed across the room. Lewis caught it. "Oh, good, man. That makes more sense. Where's yours?"

"I'll put it on when the time comes."

Half an hour later, tires crunched on the pea gravel in the driveway out front. The muffled rumble of a garage door followed, first opening, then closing. Soon Pickman heard the sound of someone entering the house through the door between the garage and the kitchen.

In the dark living room, he stood up. From his right pocket, he pulled the judge's .38. From his left, he took an untraceable throwaway handgun, one of several he owned for occasions like this.

"Ready?" he whispered to Lewis, who got to his feet on the far side of the room.

Down the short hall, a light switched on in the kitchen.

"What about your mask?" Lewis whispered.

He turned to look at Lewis standing in front of the fireplace, near the left end of the mantel. "Move a few feet to your right," he ordered, still whispering.

"What? Why?"

"Move to your right about four feet. It's important."

"I don't get this—"

"Do it *now. Move.*"

Lewis shrugged and moved a few feet to his right. Pickman noted his location and nodded. Then he turned back toward the dimly lit hallway. Behind him, almost under his breath, Lewis said, "What the hell . . . ?"

Turning again, Pickman saw the man looking at several framed photographs on the mantel above the fireplace. Pickman had seen them on a previous visit. The one on the left was of a younger, tuxedo-clad Morgan Jeffers, smiling widely on the day he married the woman who would make him a widower thirty-eight years later. The one in the middle was of a middle-aged Jeffers standing beside a lake with his middle-aged wife, squinting in the bright sun and smiling more widely than on their wedding day. The final photo was of an elderly Jeffers in his black judge's robes, standing between two other similarly attired judges, each of them brandishing a gavel like a caveman holding aloft a club. Good times.

"I know this guy," Lewis said quietly. "He's . . . hold on . . . oh, shit, that's the judge who put me away for manslaughter."

"Is it? What a coincidence."

"I shouldn't be here," Lewis whispered harshly. "This is crazy."

"You have to be here," Pickman whispered back. "It's part of the plan."

Just then, a light snapped on right behind him, and Judge Morgan Jeffers appeared in the hallway, heading for the stairs. He was flipping through a small stack of mail as he walked. When he reached the bottom of the steps, Pickman said, "Good evening, Judge."

Jeffers turned, and when he saw Pickman standing in the middle of the living room, he dropped his letters. With the gun in his left hand, the throwaway gun, Pickman gestured toward the closed front door, eight feet to Jeffers's left. "Please step over to the door, Your Honor."

"What is this?" Jeffers said. "Who the hell are you?"

"Move over to the door, Judge, or I'll shoot you where you stand."

Perhaps Jeffers was wondering whether to comply, whether it mattered if he was shot tonight or died from cancer in a few weeks. But there must have been a few folks he hadn't yet had the chance to bid farewell to before shuffling off his mortal coil, because he moved eight feet to his left until he was in front of the door.

"Perfect," Pickman said.

Behind him, Lewis said, "Listen, man, this is just crazy. I'm outta—" but that was as far as he got before Pickman turned, took careful aim, and shot him twice in the chest with the gun in his right hand, the judge's gun.

Pickman turned back toward Jeffers. "Nice shot, Your Honor."

"Huh?" Jeffers said, evidently too shocked to register the horror of the moment. "I didn't—"

Using the throwaway in his left hand, Pickman again took a moment to aim before shooting the judge in the neck, precisely where, months ago, he had planned to. The old man fell against the front door and slid to the ground.

Stepping carefully to avoid any blood on the hardwood floor, Pickman verified that both men were dead, or would be within moments. Then he placed the throwaway gun in Lewis's hand and squeezed off a shot toward the hallway, one that the state police's Crime Scene Search Team should conclude had been an errant shot before his second bullet found its mark in Jeffers's neck. Revenge for sending him to prison fifteen years ago. Lewis now had gunshot residue on his hand and shirt cuff. Pickman ran through the same routine with the judge, putting the man's own pistol into his dead hand and firing a shot toward the fireplace, the bullet shattering one of the picture frames—the one in the middle, holding the photo of Judge Morgan Jeffers and his beloved wife enjoying a long-ago sunny day by a lake.

Properties in the neighborhood were large, as much as an acre and a half each, so the nearest houses were fairly far away, but sound tended to carry at night, and it was very possible that neighbors had heard the gunshots. So Pickman had to move quickly. Still, he took a moment to survey the scene carefully, ensuring that every detail matched the narrative he had written far ahead of time and the sketches of the scene he had made. He closed his eyes, ignored the ticking of the clock in his head, and visualized the drawing he had made of Lewis's body. It had fallen almost exactly where and how he had anticipated, though its legs were splayed more than he had expected, and its left arm was across its stomach instead of at its side, as Pickman had sketched it. He figured he could adjust the body to match his drawing without leaving behind forensic evidence of his actions. Then he moved back to the judge's body and ran through the same visualization. The man had fallen against the door, as Pickman had planned, and . . . yes, it looked almost exactly as he had drawn it.

He grabbed his duffel bag and hurried through the house, out the back door, through the shadows of the next-door neighbor's yard—noting that there seemed to be no sense of alarm in the house—and returned to his rented car.

In a few short minutes, he was miles away from Woodstock, Vermont, and the bodies of the Honorable Judge Morgan Jeffers, as well as the far-less-honorable Kyle Lewis, the violent career criminal Jeffers had sent to prison years ago for manslaughter, and whom Governor Andrew Kane had pardoned just five days ago.

CHAPTER FORTY-FIVE

Dinner hadn't been much fun tonight. Everyone had been kind of quiet, and Tyler wasn't exactly sure why. Julie probably thought the same thing, because the second she finished eating, she went upstairs to study instead of hanging out for a while after like she sometimes did. As soon as she left the table, everybody got a little more talkative, but it still seemed like they were all in bad moods. It sounded like Henry and Andy hadn't had good days—especially Henry, who'd gotten into some trouble at work. Still, good old Henry tried to lighten things up by saying a few funny things, but nobody laughed except Tyler, and he wasn't even sure why he was laughing because he hadn't really understood the jokes. Andy had said he wasn't in the mood for "gallows humor," whatever that was. But even Henry stopped trying to make everyone feel better when he got a phone call from someone named Dave Junior. After hanging up, he'd looked at everyone at the table and said, "They lost Kyle Lewis," which made everyone real upset—except for Tyler, who didn't know who Kyle Lewis was, though he sort of remembered hearing the name. Andy was the maddest, though. He and Henry argued, and nobody wanted dessert—again, except for Tyler, but he didn't ask for it because everyone was in bad moods.

And now they were all quiet again. To Tyler, they looked tired. Andy and Henry still looked angry, of course, but also tired. Molly, too. Rebecca hadn't come to dinner tonight for some reason, but Tyler thought she had also looked tired the last time he'd seen her. Now that he thought about it, everyone had looked tired for days, maybe even weeks.

And he knew why. He'd been thinking about it. It was because of *him*. Nobody looked this tired before he got into trouble and got arrested and went to court and had to wear this thing on his ankle. Nobody argued with each other before that. This was all his fault. It had to be.

"I'm sorry," he said.

One by one, they looked at him. It almost seemed like they'd forgotten he was even there.

"Sorry for what, Tyler?" Andy asked.

He shrugged. "I don't know. For everything, I guess. For getting arrested. For what happened to . . . to Sally. For whatever happened to you and Henry today. For you guys fighting. I'm just sorry."

Suddenly, they were all talking at the same time, telling him that nothing was his fault, that he didn't have anything to be sorry for, that they were the ones who should be apologizing to him for making him feel this way. He didn't believe them, though. They just loved him and didn't want him to feel bad for making such a mess of things. He loved them even more for that and wished none of this had ever happened. He'd give anything to make this go away for them. But he didn't know how to do that.

———

Henry was pissed off. He knew he'd let Andrew down. He'd let them all down. Even though it was Dave Junior's guys who'd lost track of Kyle Lewis, Henry still felt somehow responsible. He'd promised that Lewis would be watched 24–7. He'd sworn that Dave Junior's guys were the best. And now . . .

"What are we going to do about Lewis?" Molly asked. "Knowing what we know, we can't let him just walk around free."

For some reason Henry couldn't fathom, they were sitting in the drawing room, on the least comfortable furniture in the house. Except for Tyler. He was eating ice cream in front of the TV down the hall.

"There's not much we can do," Andrew said. "We don't know where he is. Besides, it's not like we can call the police and tell them that the guy I pardoned five days ago *might* be thinking of doing something illegal. He's a free man now, and he hasn't committed a crime since he's been out of prison."

"Yet," Molly said.

"The plan was to watch him closely," Henry said, "and stop him if he looked like he was gonna hurt anyone. Hopefully, Dave Junior's guys find him again before he does anything like that."

"You agree with Andy that we can't call the police about him?" Molly asked.

"I do. And hey, Dave Junior's guys weren't even sure Lewis gave them the slip on purpose. It might just have been bad luck. A timing thing where someone looked the wrong way at the wrong time. They'll find him again."

"Hopefully before it's too late," Molly said.

"Amen to that." Henry rose from the side chair he'd been suffering in, stretched his back, and added, "I'm gonna head home. I may be suspended, but that doesn't mean I can't keep working this. In the morning, I'll try talking with Wesley Jurgens again."

"The lawyer?" Molly asked. "Will he tell you anything?"

"No," Andrew said, answering for Henry.

Henry scoffed. "He hasn't met me face-to-face yet, Andy. He doesn't know how persuasive I can be."

"Henry . . ." Andrew said.

"Relax. I'm not stupid. But maybe I can convince him to share more than he's been willing to so far. Or maybe I can bluff him into thinking we have something on him, some sort of conspiracy evidence."

"He won't fall for that," Andrew said. "He's a lawyer himself. And anyway, you're suspended, remember?"

"I still have friends on the force, though."

"You do?" Molly asked, looking as though she were only half joking.

"Okay, not many, no. But *he* doesn't know that." Then he shrugged as if to say, *Besides, what else do I have to work with?* "I'm gonna go say good night to Tyler, then head out."

Molly stood, too. "I won't be far behind you. Got my study group tonight. Talk to you tomorrow, Andy."

Henry nodded good night to Andrew, who nodded back. In the car a little while later, Henry thought about Dave Junior's report tonight. About his guys losing Kyle Lewis. And about something he hadn't mentioned to the others, something that wouldn't have meant much to them. Gabriel Torrance had spent the last three days walking through the projects in Rutland. At first, Dave Junior's guys figured he had gone there looking to score drugs, but almost three days later, they believed it had to be something else. The thing was, they couldn't follow him closely. He'd see them if they did. Instead, they waited outside the buildings for Torrance to come out, which he did after spending several hours in each one. He'd stop only long enough to go for food before returning to the projects. Apparently, he'd even spent the last two nights inside the buildings, a dangerous thing to do these days. The investigators concluded that he was searching for something, but they didn't know what. Henry concluded the same and wondered what connection Torrance could possibly have to the projects where Dave Bingham had died eight years ago. He could have asked for Dave Junior's opinion, but he doubted the man wanted to focus on the Rutland projects any more than Henry did. Most likely Dave Junior, like him, had spent the past eight years trying *not* to think about that place, or what had happened there.

But what the hell *was* Torrance doing there?

———

For the entire twenty minutes he'd been in the car heading toward home and his wife, with his ubiquitous security detail following behind, Andrew couldn't help but think about poor Tyler blaming himself for everything. If anyone were to blame, other than the man who had orchestrated all of this, it was Andrew. And though he'd gotten angry with Henry about Kyle Lewis slipping away from the private investigators Henry had hired to follow him, Andrew was actually angry at himself, and he knew it. He never should have pardoned Lewis. He never should have pardoned Gabriel Torrance. He should have found another way. He should have—

The phone in his pocket vibrated.

That phone.

Andrew considered not answering it, not giving the bastard the satisfaction of gloating or twisting the knife, but he couldn't stop himself.

"Listen, you son of a bitch—"

The caller's familiar, grating metallic monotone cut him off. "No, Governor, I don't want to listen. And you can't make me. Because I'm done."

That stopped Andrew. "Done? With . . . ?"

"With everything. It's all over. I'm finished with you. With all of you. You and Henry and Molly and poor Tyler. I'm done. I'm walking away. After I hang up, you'll never hear from me again."

Panic surged through Andrew. If that were true—

"What about Tyler?" he asked, unable to keep a tremor out of his voice.

"Very sweet, Andy. With everything crashing down around you, you still worry about your little brother first."

"What about the video you have?"

"I destroyed it."

"*What?*"

"Part of you must have known all along that I would, Andy. But still, you did what you did, hoping against hope for Tyler's sake. You're a good brother, Andy. A terrible, dishonest governor in the end, but a good brother."

Andrew couldn't find it in himself to protest. The caller was right.

"And I'm afraid your decisions are going to be called further into question when they find out what happened tonight."

"What do you mean?"

"I mean that there's been a home invasion, Andy, and two men are dead."

Andrew felt numb. He suddenly couldn't feel his hands.

"One is a respected judge. Did you know Judge Jeffers, Andy? I bet you did. The other . . . well, here's where things get tough for you. The other is Kyle Lewis. It appears that Lewis broke into Jeffers's house, the good judge had a gun for protection, and they shot each other."

"You lying bastard. You killed them both."

"I never said that's what *happened*. I said it *appears* to be what happened. Because that's how I staged it. As though Lewis killed Jeffers in revenge for sending him to prison for manslaughter all those years ago."

"But . . . why?"

"All part of the plan."

"*What* plan? Nothing you've done from the start has made any sense."

"Not to you, maybe. But that doesn't matter. My job is now done. It's time for me to disappear."

"You can't just—"

But the line was dead. He tried to call the man back but got no answer. The caller was gone. Maybe for good.

And with him, any realistic chance of proving Tyler's innocence.

CHAPTER FORTY-SIX

Pickman closed his burner phone, turned the device off completely, and dropped it into the large black duffel bag at his feet. He wondered if the governor had believed him when he'd said he was finished. It sounded like he had. If so, Andy was in for a big surprise.

Standing in the moon shadow of a big elm, he regarded the back of the Kane house through the goggles he wore over the mask that was part of the white full bodysuit he donned when things were going to get messy. The rambling, stately Victorian looked peaceful and quiet, with warm light spilling from several windows even though only two people were home—Tyler, who couldn't legally leave, and Julie Davenport, the graduate student living on the third floor who had been home all evening, as she had been on every single one of the fourteen Tuesday nights Pickman had surveilled the house since he'd taken this job.

Over the past twenty minutes, he had watched from the shadows as the Kanes left one by one. First was Henry. Then Molly followed not far behind with a light backpack over her shoulder, the one she took to the late-night study group she had attended nearly every Tuesday during this entire school year. Andrew had been the last to leave.

Pickman picked up the duffel bag—the larger of the two he had brought with him this evening—and walked to the back door. His bible was inside the bag, of course, and after finishing with Judge Jeffers and Kyle Lewis, he had pulled over in a Pizza Hut parking lot and studied Part VII, Section E, Subsection 1, taking great pains to memorize every detail of the relevant pages, because this time he wouldn't have the luxury of lingering over the scene to ensure that he had made everything as perfect as he needed it to be. He would have to get it right the first time, adhering rigidly to his plan.

Using his lock picks, he made quick work of the lock in the knob on the Kanes' back door, then opened the door slowly and stepped into the kitchen. He tried to be as quiet as possible out of habit, though a great deal of stealth wasn't necessary at that moment given the racket coming from down the hall.

Even over the gunfire erupting from his video game assault rifle, Tyler heard the beep of the timer Molly had set and placed on the table right beside his chair: 8:55 p.m. He'd told her he didn't need a timer. He would remember. He knew how important this was.

Still, he sighed as he paused his game, then walked across the room to stand near the stupid thing so it could talk to his stupid ankle monitor and tell whoever was paying attention to it that he was home, like he was supposed to be.

The sudden silence in the house after so much noise was always weird to him, every time he stopped playing one of his games.

He stood next to the machine, looking at the little screen. Finally, the words *Reading Device* appeared. A few seconds later, he was free to go back to his *Smilin' Jack* game and continue shooting his way through that Vietnamese jungle.

He picked up the game controller and was about to sit again when he heard a sound come from somewhere in the otherwise quiet house, a sound different from the usual ones. He didn't know what it was, but something about it made him want to find out. He snuck a look at the game paused on the screen. Jack Smiley would be there waiting for him when he got back.

He walked down the hall, toward the front of the house. No one in the rooms there. Back down the hall again, past the sitting room on his left, his TV room on his right, the dining room on his left. No one there, either. He walked into the kitchen.

No one.

He was about to give up and get back to his game when he heard another sound, definitely coming from upstairs. He called up the back staircase—loudly, because Julie was all the way on the third floor. "Julie!"

No answer.

He called again.

No answer.

With a longing look down the hall toward the doorway to the TV room, he started up the steps. There were a lot of them. His room was on the second floor, so when he wanted to go to bed, he only had to go up one flight of stairs, but Julie had to go up *two* flights. Every time. If he was her, he'd ask them to put in an elevator to take her up and down. No, even better: an elevator to take her up and a really long fireman's pole to take her down. That would be fun.

Now *he* wanted a fireman's pole from his room to the first floor. Molly would say no because they'd have to cut a hole in his floor or something, but he decided to ask for one anyway.

When he reached the top of the steps, he saw that the door to Julie's rooms was a little bit open.

"Julie?"

She didn't answer, so he pushed open the door.

"Hello?" he said a little louder.

He walked slowly through her sitting area, then her kitchenette, and stopped outside her partially open bedroom door.

"Julie?" he said, more quietly this time.

He heard a sound inside the room and gave the door a nudge. It opened slowly.

Inside the room, Julie lay on the bed, on her back. She wasn't wearing pants, only girlie underwear, and her T-shirt was pulled up, exposing her bra. Seeing her almost naked like that embarrassed Tyler. But he couldn't look away. It wasn't the undergarments that were making him stare, though, but the stab wounds on her chest, one a few inches above each lace-covered bra cup, and the long, bloody slice across her stomach, curving up on the ends like a grin. The wounds looked like those that Jack Smiley left on the enemies he killed in hand-to-hand combat in Tyler's favorite video games. Only this wasn't a game. It was real. That was really Julie lying there, bloody, maybe even dead. He blinked back tears. He liked Julie a lot.

He should probably run, he realized. But that wouldn't be brave. Cowards ran. Brave people didn't, not unless they were chasing bad people. Besides, Julie might still be alive. She might need his help. He stepped over to the bed on legs that were a bit wobbly, then stared down at her, wondering what to do. He'd seen things like this on TV. He should put his fingers on the side of her neck. They did that on TV. But he didn't want to, because what if she was dead? He didn't want to touch her if she was dead. The problem was that he didn't *know* if she was dead, and if she wasn't, she needed his help. He reached toward her, leaning on the bed for support. The comforter under his hand was wet with blood, and Tyler almost turned and ran again, but he stayed brave. He put his fingers on her neck. Then he leaned down and put his ear near her mouth. He had to put both hands on the bloody comforter this time, which felt squishy and gross, but he leaned close. He figured he was checking for breath or something. While he was waiting to see if she was still alive, but figuring that she probably wasn't, he heard a small whisper.

She *was* alive! *Holy cow.*

"Don't worry, Julie. I'll get help."

"*Tyler . . .*" she whispered right into his ear.

"Yes?" he whispered back.

"*Run . . .*"

The door behind him closed suddenly, and he turned to see someone standing in front of it, only he was like no one Tyler had ever seen before. He was bigger than Tyler. He was wearing goggles and had a white mask that covered his whole head. In fact, he was wearing a white suit that covered his whole entire body under clothes that looked too small for him. He held a knife in one white-gloved hand, and there was blood on both of his gloves and on his clothes. The man's bloody T-shirt, stretched tight over the white suit and across his chest, had the cover of a Beatles album on it. *Abbey Road.* Tyler used to have a shirt just like that. He hadn't seen it in months.

"You hurt Julie," he said in a voice he fought to keep steady and strong, even though he was close to crying.

"I think I did more than that," the man in white said, and it was a little hard to understand him through his mask. "I think I killed her."

Tyler took a quick look at Julie, and though her eyes were still open, they looked different now. Like the eyes of a doll. Or a dead person on TV. He was really sad, really suddenly. Julie was always so nice.

"Are you gonna kill me, too?" His voice wasn't very brave that time. His knees weren't very brave, either. They were shaking badly.

"No, Tyler. But I think you're going to be in a lot of trouble."

"*Me?* Why?"

"Because everyone is going to think *you* killed Julie."

"I didn't do it. You did."

"Yes, but they'll think you did. They already think you killed Sally Graham, right?"

Tyler nodded, and as he watched the man slip a pair of rubber gloves over his bloody white gloves, a thought came to him. "You killed her, too, didn't you? Sally Graham. You're the reason everyone thinks I'm a murderer."

"Look, I'm sorry about that, Tyler. But it's too late to do anything about it now. At this point, you need to think about Julie's murder. They already suspect you of stabbing one woman to death, so of course they'll think it was you who did the same to another woman right in your own house, when no one else was home."

"I'll tell them about you. That you did it. And you killed Sally Graham, too."

"Really, Tyler? You'll tell them to pretty please believe that you're not a killer, and the real killer is some guy wearing a white suit, dressed in *your* clothes? You think they'll believe that? Or will they think it's just some ridiculous story you're telling to try to get yourself out of trouble?"

He was right, Tyler realized. No one would believe him. They'd think he killed Sally Graham *and* Julie. He'd be in twice as much trouble. He'd never be able to prove his innocence at trial now. Not after this. He wasn't sure, but he thought he felt a tear running down his cheek.

"Here, take these," the man said as he handed two items to Tyler, who was too surprised to refuse them. In one hand, he now held a bloody knife. In the other, he held a white plastic bag.

"I don't want them," he said, dropping them on the floor. He blew out a shaky breath, closed his eyes, and lowered his chin to his chest. "What do I do?" he asked softly.

He wasn't really expecting an answer, just asking the question out loud, but the man in the white suit responded. "You run." Tyler looked up. "Run away, Tyler."

Run. It was the same thing Julie had told him to do right before she died. "I wouldn't know where to go," he said, shaking his head. "I ride my motorcycle around, visit other towns sometimes, but I never go too far away. Most of the time it's just to the animal shelter or the high school. I wouldn't have any money to buy food or anything. And I don't even have my motorcycle, anyway. The police took it."

"That's a tough break. But you know what? I could help you. I could give you a place to stay."

"You could?"

"Sure. For a while, anyway. Until you figured out where you want to be in the long run."

"I wanna be here. At home."

"Of course you do, Tyler. But you're not a dumb person, no matter what some people think, right? You're smart enough to see that you can't stay here. Everyone is going to find out about Julie soon. The police. Your brothers. Molly. They'll all think you killed her. Maybe your family thought you were innocent with Sally Graham, but they'll never believe you now. Not with *two* dead people you seem guilty of killing. No, you can't stay here."

More tears formed in Tyler's eyes. He couldn't stop them.

"You see that, don't you, Tyler?"

He nodded and sniffed. "You'd give me a place to stay for a while?"

"I would."

Tyler had never been so confused in his life. This guy had killed Sally and Julie, so he was a terrible person. But he sounded calm and normal when he talked. He was even being kind of nice to Tyler, offering to help him. And what he was saying made a lot of sense.

What should he do? What was the right thing? Never before had he wished so hard that he was smarter. Then something occurred to him. "I can't leave. There's a thing on my ankle. They know where I am all the time."

"I can take care of that. I have something with me I could use to cut it off. But when I do, you'll have to be ready to move very fast, because as soon as it comes off, the cops will be on their way here. And we need to be long gone before they get here."

Tyler nodded. His head hurt. It was all happening too fast. Everything was changing. Could he leave his home, his family, forever?

"I know you're sad, Tyler, and I don't want to make you feel worse, but have you considered the idea that Molly and Henry and Andy might be better off if you left?"

"Wait . . . what? That's not true. We're family. They love me." The man was wrong. He *had* to be wrong.

"I'm not saying they don't love you, Tyler. But think about it: Right now they have to worry about you. They have to deal with a trial. That's going to cost them a lot of money. Plus they're probably embarrassed about all of this. I know for a fact that Andy is having to do a lot of explaining to people about you. Don't you think it would be a lot easier on them if you just disappeared?"

Tyler was crying freely now. He didn't bother trying to stop. The man in white was right. Tyler hadn't wanted to admit it, but he'd seen evidence of it just a little while ago at dinner, when he realized that everyone looked tired and cranky lately, which had only started after he got arrested. And he heard about how people were mad at Andy, and that Henry got into trouble at work, and that too had happened after his arrest. *Everything* seemed to be going wrong since then. It was true, he realized with a terrible, achy feeling in his stomach. They'd all be better off without him. He had to leave.

"You can get this thing off my ankle?"

"I can."

Tyler thought for a moment longer, then said, "Okay."

He didn't like relying on the man for help, and he sure didn't want to live with him, even for a short time, but he couldn't think of any options.

"Do I have time to pack some things?"

"We won't cut your ankle monitor off until the very last possible moment, so that we'll have more time before the police get here. And Molly won't be home from school for at least another hour. We have a little time. Just give me a second to finish packing up my things," he said as he picked up the white plastic bag, which Tyler saw had blood on it from where he had held it with his bloody hands. He couldn't imagine why the man wanted it. He put it into a black canvas bag along with another white plastic bag. There was other stuff in the black bag, too, but Tyler couldn't see what it was.

"Okay, Tyler," the man said as he zipped the bag closed. "Are you with me?"

Tyler sniffed. "I guess."

CHAPTER FORTY-SEVEN

On the drive back to his apartment building, Henry wondered when someone affiliated with the state police would remember that he had been issued a state-owned vehicle, and more important, when that person would ask for it back. It wasn't as though he couldn't afford to buy a car of his own, but after turning in his badge, gun, and office keys, the Taurus was the last part of the job he had with him, and he wasn't looking forward to giving it up. He also wondered briefly whether he should head straight home for the night or if he felt like trying to drown his troubles in beer at one of the dive bars he preferred, either Timberland Tom's or the Village Tap. He realized quickly, though, that he wasn't in the mood to run into anyone who knew him, and there was a good chance that *everyone* would know him if they'd watched the local news over the past day and a half. He had just decided to drive straight home when his cell phone rang.

"I just got off the phone with our mystery caller," Andrew said without preamble.

"Again? Doesn't that guy have anyone *else* to call? Somebody else he's blackmailing? What did he say?"

"Remember Judge Morgan Jeffers?"

The name more than rang a bell. "Sure. Testified in his court two or three times." He didn't bother to add that he would have testified before the judge another time years ago in the trial of the man charged with the murder of Dave Bingham, if the accused hadn't confessed before trial. "Why?"

"Jeffers is dead. Our caller killed him and pinned it on Kyle Lewis, a revenge thing, then turned around and killed Lewis, too. Made it look like they'd shot each other."

"Holy shit."

"This is exactly what I feared when I pardoned him, Henry. That someone would get hurt or killed."

Actually, Andrew had been worried that *Lewis* would kill or hurt someone, but Henry didn't think this was the time to point out the distinction. Besides, it didn't matter. The fact was that a respected judge had been murdered, and he probably wouldn't have been had Andrew not pardoned Lewis . . . because framing Lewis for murder had apparently been the caller's plan for him all along.

And the public would blame Andrew for the judge's death.

"From everything I ever heard, Jeffers was a good man," Henry said. "Damn that asshole." He trusted Andrew to know that he was referring to the blackmailer.

"He was," Andrew said. After a pause, he added. "And it gets worse."

"How?"

"He said that it's over."

"What is?"

"Everything. He's done. This whole thing is over."

"That's it?" Henry asked, surprised. "Just like that? It's all over?"

"That's what he says."

That seemed implausible to Henry. Though he already knew the answer, he asked, "What about the recording that would clear Tyler? Any chance he's gonna give us that like he promised?"

"He says he destroyed it."

"I knew it. That son of a bitch."

"So," Andrew said, his voice tired and flat, "all of this . . . everything . . . was for nothing. Judge Jeffers is dead. Tyler will get a life sentence. You're looking at termination and possibly prosecution. And my reputation has been destroyed. He's ruined us all. And for what? So he could frame Kyle Lewis for the murder of the man who sent him to prison fifteen years ago?"

Henry thought about that for a moment.

That was his endgame all along?

It didn't feel right.

Gabriel Torrance poking around the Rutland projects . . .

The murder of Judge Jeffers . . .

What did these things have in common? The only thing Henry could think of—the thing that clawed itself into his mind—was that Dave Bingham had died in the projects, and Jeffers would have presided over the resulting murder trial had there been one. But that was eight long years ago. What could Torrance's connection be to that? He hadn't been there that night. And neither had Kyle Lewis, whom the blackmailer had framed for killing Jeffers. So why kill Lewis, then set him up for that murder? Did the blackmailer have some specific grudge against him?

"I have to go," Andrew said, derailing his train of thought. "I have to bother Jim Garbose at home and tell him about the firestorm we're going to face from the media in the morning. I don't see how we recover from this, Henry. I really don't. He's destroyed us all, with the possible exception of Molly. Doesn't seem like he plans to release the audio of her negotiating Torrance's release. So at least there's that. I'll call you tomorrow."

They disconnected, and Henry slid his phone into his jacket pocket.

. . . with the possible exception of Molly . . .

He drove with his eyes on the road, his hands on the wheel, and his mind on recent events—turning them over in his head, examining them from all angles.

Let's see, he thought . . .

Judge Jeffers is dead.

Kyle Lewis is dead, though that's not a huge loss.

Tyler goes to prison.

Andrew's career is ruined.

I lose my job and will probably go to prison myself, but . . .

If the blackmailer can be taken at his word—not a great bet, of course—Molly gets off without her life ruined, other than the sadness she'll probably feel watching her brothers suffer.

Why?

Could the blackmailer's endgame really have been to frame Lewis for Judge Jeffers's murder?

Why such a complex plot to achieve a relatively simple result? Why destroy the lives of so many people—

Unless that was the point. Maybe this had always been about destroying certain people. Maybe the rest of it was smoke and mirrors.

The blackmailer had wanted them to think this was all about Kyle Lewis and something he was supposedly needed for in the next two weeks. But that was all misdirection. Despite how their caller had wanted this to look, it had never been about that.

In less than a minute, he arrived at his apartment building, but rather than pull in to his assigned parking space, he left the Taurus on the street while he ran up to his apartment, grabbed what he needed, and hurried back to the car.

He felt certain he was onto something.

Maybe this had been personal all along.

CHAPTER FORTY-EIGHT

Everything had gone according to plan, as Pickman had anticipated. He had trained himself to be an astute judge of human nature, first by reading sixteen books on the subject, and then by applying their lessons during his interactions with people. To be confident that he knew what to expect of someone of Tyler's limited intelligence, over the past few months he'd read three more textbooks that dealt specifically with the minds of both children and the mentally impaired. And Tyler had behaved as Pickman had expected he would.

He glanced at Julie Davenport's body on the bed. To the best of his powerful memory, it looked precisely like the sketch he'd made four months ago, a sketch that was in the three-ring binder in his duffel bag, encased in a plastic sleeve. Also in the bag was the knife he'd used to kill both Julie Davenport and Sally Graham, a small nick taken from the end of its blade, the blade itself twisted ever so slightly so as to leave wounds on both bodies as distinct as the bloody fingerprints Tyler had left on the knife's handle when Pickman had handed it to him. Tyler had also left prints on the metal doorknob as he'd opened the bedroom door.

Pickman followed Tyler down the steps, watching the young man touch the bannister and the wall, leaving behind more fingerprints in

Julie Davenport's blood. They were leaving no bloody footprints as they walked because Pickman had taken care not to let blood get on the floor. He knew they would both be walking around, and he didn't want two sets of bloody footprints trailing around the house.

On the second floor, Tyler walked to his room, his head down.

"You have a suitcase or something?" Pickman asked.

"I have a backpack I can use."

"Okay. Only take what you really need. You'll want to travel light. A few sets of clothes."

"I have to bring my toothbrush. Molly would want me to do that."

"Of course. I'll wait out here."

Tyler left the door open, so Pickman was able to watch him packing his small bag, touching numerous surfaces, leaving behind irrefutable evidence of his guilt. As he waited, Pickman carefully stripped out of the bloody clothes he had stolen from Tyler and worn while he murdered Julie Davenport and stuffed them into a plastic garbage bag. He would keep them in case they should come in handy later. Then he took off the white suit—he didn't want to get blood in his car, of course—balled it up, and jammed it into a second garbage bag. Then he crammed both bags into his large duffel bag.

Whenever Tyler finished packing and returned to the hall, he would find Pickman waiting for him wearing his own clothes—as well as a new pair of latex gloves, which he doubted Tyler would even notice. He had originally considered wearing a ski mask, too, but realized that it didn't matter whether Tyler saw his face, because he didn't have long to live anyway. Once Pickman cut off his ankle monitor and drove off with him, leading everyone—including his sister and brothers—to believe he'd escaped after killing Julie Davenport, Pickman would simply kill Tyler and dispose of his body where it would never be found. He would have served his purpose. With him missing, everyone would assume he was still on the run.

And as long as he was believed to be on the run, he could be framed for anything.

"We should probably hurry this up a bit, Tyler. We don't have all night."

———

Henry broke all sorts of motor vehicle laws on his way to VSP headquarters. He hoped like hell he wouldn't be pulled over on the way, because he didn't have time to spare, and he doubted that his status as a disgraced and soon-to-be-former Internal Affairs investigator was going to get him any sympathy from the cop making the stop. Fortunately, the gods of the road were on his side.

He'd called Detective Egan's cell phone as soon as he'd left his apartment a short while ago, expecting he'd be home, but Egan said he was catching up on some paperwork at his desk.

"I'm coming to see you," Henry had said.

"Like hell you are," Egan had replied. "You don't worry me anymore, Kane. You've been declawed."

"I still have my file on you. Still have pictures and video of you taking payments from a local drug dealer. Doesn't matter if I go down, Egan. Pictures don't lie. Video lies even less."

After a long pause, Egan exhaled into the phone. "Don't you dare come into headquarters. Call me when you're here, and I'll come down."

"See you soon."

When he was two minutes from VSP headquarters, he called Egan again. The man was waiting for him outside when he pulled up. Egan slid into the passenger seat.

"Now what the hell do—"

Henry handed him a thick envelope.

"What's this?" Egan asked.

"My case against you. That's everything."

"Everything?"

"Everything. My notes, records of who you met with and when. Photos. Video. That's all of it. There's nothing on my computer at work. Once I decided to . . . let's say, once I decided to work with you, I took everything off it. There's no trace of my investigation into you in there," he added, nodding toward the building.

"This is just a copy, right?"

"Nope."

"Why're you giving it to me?"

"Because I think it's all coming to an end very soon, and I need your help. I need the best you've got right now, and I'll get better from you if you willingly hop on board than if I have to drag you along."

"And I should just hop on board because . . ."

"Because it's actually the right thing to do here. Helping me is the right thing, even though you probably won't believe me."

Egan looked inside the envelope.

"If you give this to me, I have no incentive to help you anymore, no reason to keep feeding you info on your brother's case."

"Except, like I said, you'll be doing the right thing."

"And I'm supposed to take your word on that."

"My brother's innocent, Egan," Henry said. "You won't believe that, either, but it's true. I'll prove it eventually, with or without your help. But all I've been getting from you is information we would've gotten eventually anyway. So fine. You can stop. I release you from that obligation."

"Terrific. Have a good night."

He reached for the door handle.

"Just do one more thing for me. It's not illegal. Not even a little. But I need you to go upstairs and do it right now."

"Now?"

"It's important."

Egan thought a moment. He looked into the envelope again, must have realized it held his career inside it, and Henry had just given it to him.

"What do you need?"

"Search the databases up there, every one you can think of, for cases involving the following names . . . you gonna write this down?"

"Why don't you do the research yourself?"

"At the moment, I don't have the access you do."

Egan nodded and pulled a small notebook from his pocket, clicked a ballpoint pen.

Henry said, "Andrew Kane, Henry Kane, Judge Morgan Jeffers, Kyle Lewis." He spelled out *Lewis* for Egan. "I want anything that comes up with those names in it. Anything at all. A case, a news story, whatever."

He left Tyler off the list because he was convinced that this had never, not for a single moment, been about Tyler. His youngest brother had been nothing more than a tool the blackmailer had used to get to Andrew, whose career he would ruin. And to get to Henry, whose career he would also ruin, and whose freedom he would try to take. He also left Molly off the list, having decided that this wasn't about her, either, in large part because the blackmailer didn't seem to care about destroying her. As for Jeffers, it was possible that his murder could have been nothing more than a means to an end, merely another way to ensure that Andrew was destroyed, but that seemed like a complicated way to pile on Andrew when the public was already calling for his head. No, it was more likely that Jeffers was a target, too.

But not Kyle Lewis, who didn't seem to fit the profile—men in public service, men who . . .

Did what, to whom, and when?

"Judge Jeffers?" Egan said. "We got a call a little while ago. Jeffers was murdered."

"I know. And I know who they're supposed to think did it, because he's dead at the scene, too. But he didn't do it."

"How the hell do you know that?"

"Because I know who did. And I'm trying to find the guy."

"If you know anything about Jeffers's murder, Kane, you have to—"

"I don't know the killer's identity. That's what I'm trying to find out. And the longer we sit here talking about it, the longer it will take for me to do that."

Egan regarded him a moment.

"If I come up empty," Henry said, "I'll come totally clean with you guys. But for now, this is the way it has to be. And if I figure it out, I'll give it to you, okay, Egan? You'll get to bring the guy in. You'll probably get a promotion and a raise. You won't have to take payoffs from drug dealers anymore."

"Screw off, Kane."

"Come on, Egan. Are you in?"

"Okay," Egan said, "we'll do it your way for now. But tomorrow, if—"

Henry cut him off, saying, "Terrific. You might also need to run the names a second time, do the same searches, but leaving out Lewis." He gave that instruction in case he was correct that Lewis was nothing more than a pawn in the game. "So, you in, Egan?"

"This could take a little while."

"Try not to let it. It's important."

Finally, Egan nodded. He opened the door and stepped out of the car, the thick envelope in his hand. Before he closed the door, he looked back in at Henry.

"This really the only copy?"

"As far as you know."

Egan shook his head. "You're an asshole, Kane."

"Hurry up, Egan."

The detective shut the door, leaving Henry with nothing to do but wait.

CHAPTER FORTY-NINE

Tyler fought back tears as he walked for a final time through the house he'd lived in his entire life. He walked down the stairs, remembering the way he'd flown down them every Christmas morning when he was a kid. He moved down the hall, past the dining room where his family used to eat together on most nights, their parents on either end of the table, past the rooms in which his mother read to him and where he played games with Molly and Henry and Andy. They had a dog named Sugar when he was young. A boxer. His dad said it stood for Sugar Ray, but they called her only Sugar because she was a girl. Her bed used to be right there, in the drawing room.

He opened the front door.

"Whoa, Tyler," the man said from behind him. "Are you allowed to go outside? With your ankle monitor, I mean."

"Yeah. I'm just not supposed to leave the yard."

He looked out through the front door. It was dark outside. The closest streetlights were pretty far away, so the very front of the property was darker than other parts of their yard. He reached for the light switch just inside the door, but the man put his hand on Tyler's arm, stopping him from turning on the porch light.

"Better if it's dark, right?" the man said. "People won't see us leave then."

Tyler nodded and stepped out onto the porch, then walked down the stairs. He was leaving the only home he'd ever known . . . the only life he'd ever known. Which was really scary. He heard the front door close behind him.

"My car's over there, on the street right outside the fence. You'll need to ride in the trunk so no one sees you."

Tyler looked at the car not far away. "I don't want to ride in the trunk."

"Just until we get to my house," the man said. "It's safer that way. I'm sure you're smart enough to see that."

Tyler thought about it. He guessed it made sense. The guy seemed to think he was smart, or at least not stupid, which Tyler liked. He had to remind himself that this man had killed two women.

The guy pointed a small remote control at the car and clicked a button with his thumb. On the street, the car's trunk rose.

The man knelt down and pulled from his bag a metal tool with two handles, almost like a big pair of scissors. "As soon as I cut your ankle monitor off," the man said, "we need to move fast. They may try calling your house first to see if you're home, but they might just show up here with lights flashing and guns drawn, understand? So as soon as this thing comes off, we need to run right to the car. You jump into the trunk, and I'll close it before anyone sees you. Are you ready?"

Tyler stared at the open trunk. He looked back at the man. His face was mostly normal—probably about as average a face as Tyler had ever seen, actually—but there was something about it Tyler didn't like. Something in his eyes. Suddenly, things Molly used to tell him about strangers came to his mind, almost like she was standing right next to him in the dark, whispering in his ear. He thought his mother might have said those things a long time ago, too, but it was Molly's voice in his head just then.

"Tyler?" the man said, looking around. "We need to get going before someone sees us."

The man was starting to look nervous. Tyler understood that, though. He'd just killed Julie, and he was helping Tyler escape. But . . .

"Come on, Tyler . . ."

He kept hearing Molly's voice, her warnings. This man was a stranger, which Tyler shouldn't trust. Not only that, he was a murderer, which was way worse.

"Tyler, we're running out of time. Molly will be home soon. She'll find Julie and think you did it. Then your chance to get away will be gone. And remember, your family will be better off without you here, right?"

Even though the man was a murderer, he was right about a few things. Everyone would think Tyler had killed Julie, just like they thought he'd killed Sally Graham. Even his own family would probably think that. And the man was also right that they would all be better off without Tyler.

"Tyler," the man said, starting to sound angry.

"I'm ready."

The man let out a loud breath. He lifted Tyler's pant leg, exposing the ankle monitor, and held the metal tool to it. "Remember," he said, "as soon as I cut this, we have to run as fast as we can to my car. You get in the trunk, I'll close it, and we'll be long gone by the time the police get here. Got it?"

"Got it."

"Okay, here we go."

———

Pickman brought the handles of the bolt cutter together, and the jaws snapped shut on the strap securing the monitor to Tyler's ankle. With a pop, the jaws bit through, and the monitor fell to the ground.

"Let's go," he said, grabbing his duffel from the ground and trotting toward his car. Tyler ran with him at his side. They had only thirty yards to go in all, but Tyler began to fall behind.

"Catch up," Pickman called quietly over his shoulder as he neared the gate, where his car waited only another ten yards away. But Tyler's footsteps behind him were growing fainter. Pickman risked a glance over his shoulder and saw Tyler sprinting in the opposite direction across the front yard, his backpack bouncing on his shoulder.

Tyler was running away from him.

Damn it.

How had he not foreseen this?

How the hell had that brain-damaged idiot tricked him?

Why had he not behaved as Pickman had predicted? As the psychology and human behavior books had led him to believe he would?

He dropped his duffel and started off across the yard in pursuit. He'd made it only a third of the way before Tyler reached the gate on the far side of the lawn, threw it open, and ran through. By the time Pickman got there, Tyler had disappeared. Surely, he'd raced across another property on the street and disappeared behind one of the other houses, but which one? He probably knew the area like the back of his goddamn hand.

Should Pickman chase him?

But his car was on the street on the other side of the property with its trunk lid wide open. Worse, his duffel bag lay on the lawn, with everything inside it to incriminate him: his bloody white suit filled with his own DNA; the clothes he'd worn over the suit when he'd killed Julie Davenport; the murder weapon; and his bible, which contained his entire plan on which he'd worked for over a year.

Obviously, he couldn't risk being caught. There was simply no way he would allow himself to go to prison. There was nothing on earth he feared more. Loss of his freedom. His schedule dictated by others. His need to surround himself with perfection left to the whims of those around him. The potential for beatings and sexual abuse. No Bach in prison. Doubtful they served Prince spaghetti in there, either. Probably even made their own sauce. Sure as hell wouldn't be Prego tomato and basil.

No, he could *not* be caught.

His course was clear. He had to grab the duffel bag and drive away before the authorities arrived. With any luck he'd catch sight of the freak and be able to subdue him or kill him quickly.

He was in his car three blocks away when he heard the first siren.

His hands were shaking.

Was he in shock?

How had this happened?

How could something have gone *wrong*?

He always, *always* knew what would happen before it did. He knew what people would do as events unfolded before they knew it themselves. He had spent *a year* carefully planning this, everything, down to the last detail. He was as meticulous as ever this time—no, even *more* meticulous. Nothing had ever gone wrong before, on any of his jobs. *Ever.*

Unthinkably, things were unraveling. First, there was that goddamn model soldier's eyes that were the wrong color, then Judge Jeffers's damn stomach cancer, now *this*.

As he drove, mindful of the speed limit, listening to the sirens fade away behind him, he reflected on his plan. He desperately wanted to pull over and consult his bible, but he couldn't risk it. Instead, he forced his mind to flip through the binder and study its pages, to consider all the contingency plans he had created, to picture the tiniest detail of the mosaic of photos and summaries and sticky notes and arrows and lengths of fine, colorful yarn on the wall in his war room.

He needed to see it. In person. Could he still perform the final tasks? Could he complete the job? The answers were in his mosaic. He had to see it. Seeing it would calm him. Refocus him. He needed to sit and gaze upon his creation, at the thousands of words and dozens of photographs and countless bits of information that, together, made up his beautiful plan. He needed to rethink it all because . . .

Doubt had set in. He hadn't experienced it in so long, he almost didn't recognize it. But, he realized with something close to horror, if he had made one mistake, perhaps he could make another. Perhaps more things could go wrong.

It was unheard of.

Unprecedented.

But . . . possible.

He risked giving the car a little more gas. He wasn't certain he'd be able to breathe properly until he got home and into his war room.

CHAPTER FIFTY

Egan had been gone for more than an hour, and Henry had begun to consider the possibility that the guy had strung him along, that he had no intention of looking for a connection among the names Henry had given him. Then there was a knock on the passenger window, followed by Egan opening the door and sliding into the passenger seat.

"I thought maybe you were screwing me over," Henry said.

"I considered it. You deserve it. But before I could, I found something."

Henry's pulse quickened.

"I tried all four names first," Egan said, "and when I kept coming up with nothing, I took out Lewis, like you told me to, and finally got a single hit, from eight years ago. A guy named Kevin Austin. Ring a bell? It should."

It did. A clanging, deafening bell.

"Austin was convicted of the murder of one of our guys," Egan said, "a former state police detective named Dave Bingham. They found Bingham in Rutland, in one of the abandoned buildings in the projects everyone's been fighting over for the past year. Bingham had retired, become a PI. Everybody liked him. Records list you as the arresting officer on the case. Remember that?"

Henry nodded almost mechanically.

"It was a big story, murder of an ex-cop. Your brother was an assistant state attorney at the time, held a bunch of press conferences about it, made a lot of noise about assigning the top prosecutor they had to it. Made a lot of headlines, both the case and your brother. I pulled the file. Seems there had been rumors that Austin had an accomplice, the son of Clifton Barnes. I assume you know that name, too."

He nodded again. Part of him wanted Egan to shut the hell up. It had taken years for Henry to train himself not to think about that night, the last night of Dave Bingham's life. In visits to a therapist mandated by his captain at the time, Henry had learned special mental techniques to help him compartmentalize his thoughts and feelings about it. But he didn't employ them now. Egan kept talking, and Henry had to listen; if they were going to stop all of this, whatever it was, he needed to hear what the man had to say.

"Barnes owns several commercial properties in Vermont and nearby states—New Hampshire, Massachusetts, Maine. Everyone pretty much assumes he's connected with organized crime, as you probably know, but nobody's proven it. Anyway, you remember who the judge was on Austin's trial?"

"Jeffers," Henry said quietly.

"Bingo. The same Judge Jeffers who was killed earlier tonight by another person he'd sent to prison."

"And Kevin Austin—"

"Died in prison two years ago. Beaten to death by some homophobic skinhead."

Henry took a long breath. He'd known Austin had died in prison, but he hadn't known the details. "Homophobic? Was Austin gay or just in a jailhouse relationship?"

"Supposedly, he was gay. I guess someone took offense to that, instead of him just doing things out of physical necessity—you know, being in prison and all."

Henry tried to focus . . .

Jeffers was the judge on the trial, Andrew was the assistant state attorney pledging to assign their office's best and brightest prosecutor to the case . . . and Henry had been the arresting officer and potential star witness.

Tumblers began falling into place. "If I remember right, Austin didn't have much of a family."

"Being the hotshot detective that I am," Egan said, "I figured you'd ask me that. According to his obituary, he was survived by his father. Nobody else. Guess his mother wasn't in the picture, or she'd died before him. No brothers or sisters."

"I remember that now."

Just a grieving father, he thought, *one who might go to great lengths to exact revenge on those who took his only child away from him.*

"And the father . . . ?"

"No criminal record. Not even a speeding ticket. Served in the navy, according to the son's obituary."

"Is he local?" Henry asked.

"Yeah, not that far away actually. Less than a half hour."

"Any chance you'll give me the address?"

"You gonna do something stupid?"

"Got a badge and gun on you?"

"Of course. Why?"

"Because I don't."

With that, he cranked the engine, threw the car into drive, and screeched away from headquarters before Egan could utter a word of protest.

"Buckle up," Henry said.

"What the hell, Kane?"

"Sorry, but I need you. So where are we going?"

Egan looked like he was considering his options: perhaps grabbing for the steering wheel, or throwing open his door and rolling out of the car, or drawing his gun. Finally, he said, "Are we on our way to find whoever you think killed Judge Jeffers?"

"I think so."

"And I'm the only one in this car with a gun?"

"As far as you know."

"I'm serious, Kane."

"Cross my heart."

Egan gave him the address.

CHAPTER FIFTY-ONE

When Andrew had left the house earlier, he had planned to go straight home, but before he'd made it there, the blackmailer had called, informing him that he'd killed Judge Morgan Jeffers and pinned it on Kyle Lewis; that he had destroyed the recording that could have cleared Tyler of murder charges; and that everything was over now and he intended to just disappear. After that call, Andrew couldn't imagine going home, couldn't imagine facing his wife, knowing that he was guilty of so many things, including, to a large degree, playing a significant role in the murder of Judge Jeffers. And it didn't matter to him that Jeffers had very little time left to live because of his cancer; he had lost precious days on this planet in no small part because of Andrew. And everything . . . all of it . . . had been for nothing. He hadn't helped Tyler. And now he and Henry were ruined.

No, he wasn't prepared to face Rebecca right now. He wasn't proud of himself. He hadn't been for some time.

Instead of going home, he headed toward his office, hoping he might be able to lose himself in his job for a bit. Maybe it would help take his mind off everything else, at least for a little while. He could use some of that. He had draft legislation he could review, remarks to write, letters to compose, and the like. In his rearview mirror, he saw the lights of his security detail's vehicle following not far behind.

At that time of night, the Pavilion was quiet. He went in through the back entrance, as always, then headed up to his offices on the fifth floor. Not surprisingly, everyone else had gone home hours before.

He sat wearily in his office chair and reached for a pile of mail that Peter had opened and date-stamped before leaving in the in-box on the corner of his desk. He read a few letters, his eyes glazing over every minute or so. He was tired. And despite his plan to fill his mind with work for a few hours, he was also distracted by the recent tragic events and his part in them.

Morgan Jeffers, a good public servant and an even better man, was dead because Andrew had pardoned Kyle Lewis. Even if Lewis hadn't actually killed the judge, his pardon had led to it.

Andrew vowed never to look at the pardon file again.

Then he remembered the promise he had made himself not long ago: when this was over, he planned to review the file and give serious consideration to worthy pardon requests—because the recent trouble hadn't been caused by pardons in general, but a very specific pardon requested by a bad person, on behalf of another bad person . . . and granted by a morally questionable governor. But it was possible, perhaps even probable, that there were those whose requests truly warranted consideration. And if that were true, it was cowardly for Andrew to wait until he was about to leave office to consider them solely because he wanted to avoid the enmity of registered voters. It didn't have to be done tonight, of course, but if he was determined to get some work done anyway, why not? With the recent abuses of his pardon power, perhaps he could atone—even if only a little—by using that power the way it was meant to be used.

He walked down a hall to a small room where, during his first month in office, he'd had Peter relocate numerous files, including pardon requests. The door was locked. The file cabinets inside would no doubt be locked, too. On a hunch, he walked back to Peter's desk, opened the top drawer, and found a key on a ring labeled *File Room*. On the ring was another, smaller key that no doubt opened the cabinets themselves. He'd have to speak with Peter about file cabinet security.

He located the pardon request folders, of which there were several, and without bothering to check the dates of the requests within them, he grabbed several thick folders and headed for his office. Before he'd gone ten steps, his cell phone rang.

Caller ID told him that Molly was calling. It was late, but he remembered that she had been planning to attend her regular study group tonight after they'd parted ways. Perhaps she was on her way home.

He sighed, knowing he would have to tell her about the murder of Judge Jeffers. And of Kyle Lewis, too.

"Hey, Molly," he said. "I'm glad you—"

"Tyler's gone, Andy."

"What?"

"Tyler's gone, and Julie's dead."

"Hold on. Julie? Davenport? She's dead?"

"Someone killed her. I overheard them say it was the same way Sally Graham was killed."

Julie . . . dead? That couldn't . . . Julie was . . . she was a friend of the entire family. Tyler loved her. She couldn't be dead.

"They think *Tyler* murdered her and ran off," Molly said, her voice tight.

"Who thinks that? Slow down, Molly."

"The police. They're here at the house. They're everywhere. And Tyler's gone."

"I don't understand. How the hell can he be gone?"

"They found his ankle monitor in the front yard. He left."

Tyler's gone?

It didn't cross Andrew's mind for a fraction of an instant that his brother had killed Julie—he knew their blackmailer had certainly murdered her, as he had Sally Graham—but if Tyler had discovered the body, he almost certainly would have panicked. Panicked and run. Unless . . .

Unless for some reason the blackmailer had taken him.

"Did you try calling Tyler's phone?" Andrew asked.

"Yeah. A cop inside the house answered. Tyler must have left it behind."

"Where are you?"

"Standing in the yard. They won't let me inside. What do we do, Andy? He's out there all alone with almost every cop in the state looking for him, convinced he's killed two women."

Molly—battle-tested, combat-hardened, levelheaded Molly— sounded close to breaking in two.

"I'm on my way," he said.

Rather than spend time returning the pardon files to their cabinet, Andrew tucked them under one arm and hurried back downstairs and out to his car.

Tyler was gone.

———

Pickman ignored the ringing. He stood in the middle of his war room, staring at the mosaic taking up the entire wall above his desk, from corner to corner, five feet high and fifteen feet long. Seventy-five square feet of graphical representation of a year-long plan. It was beautiful. It was creative. It was impeccably detailed. It was *perfect* . . .

Until Judge Jeffers's cancer and Tyler Kane's disappearing act.

Pickman's plan had been sailing along smoothly, every puzzle piece falling neatly into place according to his grand design, until Jeffers went public with his stomach cancer, necessitating his murder earlier than originally planned. Couldn't have him dying of natural causes. *That* wasn't the plan. No, he had to die in a way that looked as though Lewis had killed him after being pardoned by Andrew Kane. And once it had been executed, *that* part of the plan had gone well. But then . . .

Tyler Kane had done the unexpected, the unanticipated, and run away from Pickman. That was definitely *not* part of the plan. Now . . .

The phone kept ringing. Pickman tuned it out.

Things had to change. The mosaic was no longer perfect. It no longer reflected events as they would need to unfold. And it was supposed to. It *needed* to.

But he hadn't determined how to fix things yet. Tyler Kane should have come home with him. Tyler Kane was supposed to be dead before morning, with the entire world—including his family—convinced that he was on the run.

That was what was supposed to happen.

That was the *plan.*

Now Pickman was going to have to revise the plan for the second time in one night, something he'd never had to do even once before. He was going to have to . . . *improvise.*

He hated the word. The very sound of it in his head was harsh and ugly.

He wanted the phone to stop ringing. Surely, it was the governor calling, but Pickman didn't trust himself to speak yet. He needed to be cool when he talked to Andrew Kane, to speak with authority and make certain the governor knew who was in charge, but he was too upset at the moment to do that, too unsure of himself.

So this was what self-doubt felt like. He didn't care for it.

The phone wouldn't stop its damn ringing. He could shut it off, but he didn't want to take his eyes from the wall for even a split second. He didn't want to diminish his focus any further as he stood rooted in the center of the room, his eyes on the mosaic, his mind on his bible.

His plan could stay largely intact, he believed, but he had to review his bible to be sure. He had to think it through. He would likely be forced to make at least a few hopefully minor revisions.

And his wall . . . despite its beauty, despite how perfect it was exactly as it now appeared, he'd have to tweak a few things.

Damn Tyler Kane.

Damn the phone that wouldn't stop *ringing*.

He took a deep breath, then another, then walked over to the desk, picked up the voice changer, and punched the "Talk" button on the burner phone with his thumb.

"Yes?" he said.

"You'd better hope I never get my hands on you."

"Well, good evening to you, too, Governor."

"My brother's gone, you son of a bitch."

"I know. Believe me, that wasn't part of the plan."

"I did everything you asked."

Pickman's eyes traveled ruefully over his masterpiece on the wall. "I disagree. You followed Lewis after he was released, counter to my instructions. But that doesn't matter now. He's played his part. No harm, no foul."

"I was a fool to think you'd hold up your end of the bargain."

"To be honest, Andy, I agree. But don't beat yourself up. Hindsight is twenty-twenty, as they say. And you shouldn't dwell on the past right now. Your brother is out there somewhere. Who knows what trouble he might get into?"

A long pause followed.

"You don't have him, do you?" the governor finally said. "I thought you might, but you don't. He got away from you."

Pickman hesitated. "That's not what I meant. What I said was . . . I mean, he's not . . ."

"Don't bother," Kane said. "I know now that he got away from you."

Damn it. Pickman wasn't sure whether he had just lost a tactical advantage he hadn't even considered. He needed to get back to thinking things through. *This* was why he didn't like to improvise. *This* was why he planned so meticulously. This had happened only because Tyler Kane had run from him instead of getting into his car trunk as expected.

And now Pickman was going off script, talking about things he wasn't ready to talk about, things he hadn't thought through, hadn't outlined ahead of time.

"I'm going to find you," Kane said.

He was tired of this conversation, tired of thinking about what to say, how to respond, trying to maintain the upper hand when all he wanted to do was *think*, damn it, get the plan back on track. He never should have answered Kane's call in this frame of mind.

He hung up on the governor, switched the phone off so it wouldn't distract him by ringing again, and stared at the wall.

He saw the big picture first, as clear as always. Then his eyes began to pick out the details. Most of them were fine, but . . .

That red piece of yarn running from the photo of the Kane family house to the note containing the GPS coordinates of the location where he had intended to bury Tyler's body . . . that had to be changed. And that blue yarn, that was wrong now, too. And that list of bullet points, that had to be moved.

His hands were shaking again.

He leaned forward and pulled the thumbtack holding one end of the red yarn. When he removed it, the other end slipped from the tack securing it to the wall.

Damn it.

He tried to tack that other end in place again, but a photograph of Molly Kane walking across the University of Vermont campus slipped from under a piece of tape and began to fall. Pickman shot his hand out to stop it but missed, accidentally tearing two pieces of paper and a length of purple yarn from the wall. He watched the yarn drop and the photo and papers flutter to the floor.

Damn it all.

This section of the mosaic was a mess now. And the one next to it . . . that was wrong now, too. There should be yellow yarn from the picture of Andrew's house to . . . wait, should it go to the prison or the courthouse? He suddenly couldn't remember.

And was the photo of Henry supposed to be there next to the list of phone numbers? Sure, that made sense before, but with things as they were now . . .

Nothing looked right to him any longer.

He could feel his pulse in his head.

Too many things were different. They had to be changed. He had to adjust them. He had to fix it all. He couldn't stand for anything to be wrong.

But as he worked, his hands shook. His fingers were clumsy. He tore one photograph by accident and had to tape it back together. For everything he tacked or taped into place, something else fell. When he tried to put those items back, he couldn't remember where they were supposed to be.

This red yarn doesn't go here. In fact, it doesn't even belong any longer. He tore it from the wall.

And this picture? He suddenly couldn't even remember adding it in the first place. He crumpled it into a ball and tossed it behind him.

That list? It goes there . . . no, wait . . . there. No . . .

He ripped it in two.

He grabbed two fistfuls of colorful yarn and gave them a sharp yank, sending thumbtacks flying.

With fingers like claws, he swiped at the photos . . .

and the lists . . .

and the news clippings . . .

and the sticky notes . . .

and the summaries . . .

until nothing was left on the wall but torn corners of paper held by tape, and thumbtacks securing nothing.

He dropped into his desk chair and let his head fall to his chest. As he did, his eye fell on a torn photograph on the floor, one he'd copied off the Internet. There were only two goals left to accomplish. Gabriel Torrance was working on one. The person in that photograph was the other. It could still be done.

He closed his eyes and thought . . .

. . . and realized that if he acted before Tyler Kane was captured by the police, he could accomplish this penultimate objective. He had to move quickly, though, because Tyler would certainly be caught, and before too much time passed. He wasn't smart enough to remain at large for long. And when he was captured, he would, of course, spout a thoroughly unbelievable and self-serving story about a mysterious killer dressed all in white who'd killed Julie Davenport tonight, and even killed Sally Graham weeks ago. Meanwhile, Tyler's hands were covered in Davenport's blood, and his prints were all over the house. Moreover, he'd packed a bag, cut off his ankle monitor, and gone on the run, something an innocent man would be unlikely to do. No one would believe his story but for his siblings, and it was far, far too late for them to credibly corroborate his story. They'd all come off as liars.

But nonetheless, the plan required that Tyler remain at large long enough for Pickman to complete this nearly final task.

So it would be a race against time. Suddenly, to his surprise, he found the uncertainty he was facing just a little bit thrilling. A little exciting.

With renewed drive, he turned to his computer, opened his email program, then composed a message titled, "It ends tonight." When the email was ready, he jabbed the "Send" button, then sprang from the chair and quickly packed everything he would need into his large duffel bag. He left his bible on his desk and hustled out of his war room, ready for the final assault.

CHAPTER FIFTY-TWO

Henry was making good time getting to the home of Grady Austin, Kevin's father. On the way, he finally revealed to Egan most of what he'd been holding back—not everything, of course, no way, but damn near most of it: the black cell phone, the threats, Tyler being framed for Sally Graham's murder, the pardon of Gabriel Torrance, the circumstances leading up to Henry taking the bag of evidence from the parking lot behind the nail salon, and the pardon of Kyle Lewis. He left out Molly's part in the negotiation of Torrance's release, though. He didn't see the need to drag her into the story.

For his part, Egan looked skeptical as hell, but he also seemed to realize that Henry's behavior, and that of the governor, seemed to support the story. Still, he wasn't yet anywhere close to believing it.

They had almost reached Austin's house when Andrew called with the tragic news that Julie was dead and Tyler was gone. Both were like mule kicks to Henry's chest.

Damn it. That son of a bitch.

Julie was so young . . . and always so good to Tyler . . .

And Tyler? *Missing?* His little brother out there, by himself, trying to stay—

"We have to find him before the cops do, Henry," Andrew said, cutting through his tangle of thoughts. "He might do something desperate, make the wrong move, which could be dangerous for him with the cops thinking they're dealing with a double murderer."

Henry desperately wanted to change course and look for his little brother, but he couldn't. Not now.

"I'm following a lead," Henry said. "I could be wrong, Andy, but I may know who's behind all of this. If I'm right, hopefully we can end this before Tyler gets hurt. I'll call you soon."

He slipped his phone back into his pocket and, reluctantly, told Egan about Tyler's disappearance.

"He was in the house alone with this Julie Davenport?" Egan said. "Now the woman is dead, and Tyler is gone?"

"I know how it sounds, Egan, but it fits with everything I told you. The anonymous voice on the phone is behind all this. The question now is whether that voice belongs to Grady Austin."

Henry could see that, in Egan's mind, there were plenty more questions, but he kept them to himself.

Five minutes later, they arrived at Grady Austin's house, a small ranch squatting on a lawn that, even in the dim moonlight, Henry could see was more dandelion than grass. A battered old Chevy Malibu sat parked in an uneven, cracked driveway. Despite it being close to midnight, there were lights on somewhere in the house; their glow was visible through the windows of the dark rooms at the front. The fact that Austin lived alone—if Egan was correct about that—likely meant either that he had left lights burning when he'd gone out to commit mayhem, or he was still home. The latter possibility, if it turned out to be the case, would be problematic for Henry's theory. But if it was the former, perhaps they would find something that would lead them to Austin, wherever he was, and stop him from doing any more harm. They might even find evidence that would clear Tyler, though the blackmailer had said he'd destroyed the video. Still, they might get lucky.

Of course, for that to happen they'd have to figure a way to get inside and look around that wouldn't betray their having done so; otherwise, they would risk seeing everything that would be found in a later search being thrown out as illegally obtained without a search warrant. Henry worried that Egan would balk at illegal entry. Then again, the guy wasn't above taking bribes, so maybe it wouldn't be too tough a sell.

"I have to report in," Egan said. "Tell them where I am."

When Egan was finished, Henry reached under his seat, removed a metal box, and unlocked it with a key on his key ring. Inside was an unregistered .45 he'd taken off a guy he'd busted years ago. Henry had thought the gun might come in handy one day, and the guy, being a convicted felon, had been more than happy to trade the weapon for Henry's willingness to pretend the ex-con hadn't been carrying it, which would have added time to whatever sentence he was facing for the car theft. Henry had a very small collection of guns he'd acquired in the same manner over the years. When he'd started in Internal Affairs, he'd decided he should probably get rid of them, but for some reason, he'd never quite gotten around to it.

"No way, Kane," Egan said when he saw the gun.

"If Grady Austin is what I think he is, you're gonna want the guy who's watching your back to be armed."

Egan sighed in resignation and got out of the car.

Quickly and quietly, they made their way through the weed-choked lawn, up to one of the dark windows, through which a little light from inside was bleeding out into the night. They took positions on either side, Henry on the left, Egan on the right. Slowly, they leaned over and looked into a dark, empty living room.

"If he's there, he's toward the back," Egan whispered. "Why don't you go around and watch the rear of the house while I knock on the front door?"

Henry was too quick. He walked up to the front door. "*You* go around back," he said quietly. "Hurry, or you might miss him."

"Damn it, Kane."

It wouldn't take long for Egan to run around the building, so before the man could argue, Henry rang the bell, then banged on the door and called, "Mr. Austin, it's the police. Please open the door. We have officers at every exit." *Or we will if Egan moves his ass.* Henry watched him sprint around the corner of the house.

He waited. Nothing. He banged his fist on the door again.

"Mr. Austin? It's the police. If you don't open this door in five seconds, we're going to break it down."

That wasn't true, of course, but Austin wouldn't know that.

He was about to bang on the door again when he heard movement on the other side. He quickly moved back to the window to watch Austin walk to the front door. A moment later, a light clicked on in the small foyer, and a moment after that a man appeared, walking toward the front door. Henry's heart sank. Grady Austin wasn't their blackmailer.

Henry moved back to the front door as it was opening. Standing in the foyer, leaning on a cane on which Henry had seen him rely heavily during his trek through the house, was Grady Austin. When he saw Henry, his eyes registered mild surprise, followed by resignation. Henry was reminded of the way Alex Rafferty had greeted him at his door, as though he'd hoped the cops wouldn't come knocking but wasn't surprised when they did.

Before Henry could utter a word, Austin said, "You weren't supposed to find me, Lieutenant Kane. You weren't supposed to connect any of this to me. But I knew you would eventually." He sighed. "You might as well come in. Or should I just go with you?"

A moment ago, on seeing Austin's profound limp—which Henry was sure he didn't have eight years ago—Henry had felt defeated, certain that they had the wrong guy. But now, maybe . . .

"Egan," he called loudly enough to be heard on the other side of the small house, "get back here and come inside."

He followed Austin into the house and left the door open for his temporary partner, whom he had coerced into helping—hell, whom he had arguably kidnapped. If by some miracle this all came out okay, he owed the man a beer.

Austin led him through the foyer, down a dimly lit hall, and into a kitchen with avocado-colored appliances and a mustard-colored linoleum floor. As they sat at the table and waited for Egan to join them, Henry studied Austin, on whom he hadn't laid eyes since the man's son went to prison for Dave Bingham's murder. Egan had said Austin was sixty-eight now, but he looked fifteen years older, his face deeply lined and the wispy, grizzled hair he had left poking out from his head in a variety of directions. He wasn't quite rail-thin, but he wasn't much thicker. With his limp, and how hard he had apparently aged, he looked broken.

Which wasn't surprising, considering that Henry had utterly destroyed the man's life years ago.

CHAPTER FIFTY-THREE

When Andrew arrived at the Kane family house, the place was a hive of activity. In the driveway was a van belonging to the Vermont State Police Crime Scene Search Team. On the street out front were two Manchester Police cruisers and a black sedan that most likely belonged to VSP detectives. Parked behind the sedan was Molly's Land Rover.

Rather than enter the driveway as he always did when coming here, Andrew parked his car behind one of the cruisers. The SUV containing the trooper assigned to his security detail tonight pulled up behind Andrew's vehicle. Andrew walked over to the driver's side of the SUV as the trooper at the wheel was starting to get out.

"Just hang here, okay, Mike?" he said.

"Yes, sir."

Andrew turned toward the house and wondered where Molly was. Had they let her inside? It seemed unlikely. It was a crime scene. He heard Molly call his name and turned to see her standing with a man holding a small notebook. A detective, no doubt. Andrew walked quickly over to them across the low-cut grass of the lawn.

"I'm Andrew Kane," he said to the man, extending his hand out of habit. The man shook it and introduced himself as Detective Ramsey.

"Ramsey," Andrew repeated. "You're the detective who arrested Tyler, right?"

"One of them, sir. And I hope you know I was just doing my job." Andrew nodded.

"Just like I have to do tonight," Ramsey said.

"Of course. Any sign of Tyler yet?"

"Not yet."

Andrew's heart sank. He had hoped that by the time he arrived here, they would have found Tyler and brought him in unharmed. Instead . . . who knew where the hell he was?

"I'm sorry about all this, though," Ramsey added. "About your brother. About . . . well, the things that happened here tonight. It can't be easy for any of you."

He actually seemed sincere, which was unusual given that an event like this, one that seemed to cement his suspect's guilt, was good news for the investigating detective, even though it was bad news for the suspect and his loved ones.

"I was just asking Ms. Kane here a few questions. We're about finished, and if you're gonna be around for a little while, sir, I'd like to ask you some, too."

"That'd be fine."

"I just have to check in with my partner inside for a minute, if that's all right."

Andrew nodded.

Ramsey said to Molly, "Ms. Kane, I think that's it for now. There will be more questions, of course. A lot more, I'm afraid. But not at the moment. Let me repeat what I told you just before your . . . uh, before the governor showed up, so you can both hear it together. If you think of anything that can help us find Tyler, let us know right away. It's dangerous for him to be out there. Cops get anxious when a suspected murderer is running around."

Molly said, "He's not—"

Ramsey held up a hand, silencing her. "And if either of you hears from him, please tell him to turn himself in. No one wants to see him get hurt."

"No," Molly said, "you just want to lock him away for the rest of his life."

"Thanks for your cooperation," Ramsey said as he turned to walk away. He stopped, though, when Molly said, "Tyler's innocent, Detective."

He took a moment before answering. "I don't want to be rude, Ms. Kane, because despite what your brother Henry probably thinks of me, I know this is a tough time for you and your family, so I'll just say that I respect your loyalty to Tyler."

He walked off toward the house, leaving Andrew alone with Molly. The second he was gone, Molly reached out a hand and rested it on Andrew's shoulder, which spoke volumes about the toll this was taking on her. She looked vulnerable and fragile, something he wasn't used to from her. Despite his paternalistic and usually misguided instinct to protect her, he'd long ago come to believe that she was the toughest of them all. Over the years, he had watched her care for Tyler more deeply than anyone ever had, including even, in Andrew's estimation, their mother, who had loved them all dearly. But Molly's bond with Tyler was special. She had been his twin and his best friend their entire lives, and after their mother passed away, she was a maternal figure to him, too. And now he was gone, and neither she nor Andrew knew where he was, or how scared he might be, or if he was safe for the moment wherever he was. To be honest, they couldn't be sure he was even still alive, a fact Andrew refused to contemplate. He didn't want to imagine, for even a moment, a world without his baby brother in it.

He reached up, put his hand on top of Molly's, and gave it a quick squeeze, then said, "Hang on," before hurrying off after Ramsey.

"Detective," he called.

Ramsey had almost made it to the front door. He stopped and turned.

"Yes, Governor?"

"You said something about my brother Henry not thinking much of you. But the truth is, he told me that he asked around about you, back when all of this started."

"I guess I'm not surprised."

"And he'd probably shoot me for telling you this, but he said that everyone told him the same thing about you: that you're good at your job." If Ramsey was surprised to hear that Henry had said *that*, he didn't show it. "The word he kept hearing was *solid*."

"I appreciate your letting me know that, sir."

"Henry also told me the way he thinks it probably went down with the search warrant, the way you got Tyler to say just enough to get what you needed. And he understood it. As do I. Henry said he did it like that himself once or twice back in the day. And as a former prosecutor, I've defended the tactic a few times."

Ramsey didn't seem to know what to say, so he just nodded, waiting for more.

And he waited a bit longer.

The problem was, Andrew wasn't sure how to proceed. Finally, he said, "I know you're confident that Tyler's guilty, and I can even see why you'd feel that way."

"There are bloody fingerprints all over the house, Governor. I'd bet my pension they're Tyler's."

"I hear you, but—"

Perhaps forgetting momentarily to whom he was speaking, Ramsey interrupted. "The prints are all over dresser drawers, which were pulled out, clothes in disarray, like he dug through them quickly, grabbing what he needed before he ran."

"I'm not saying he didn't run," Andrew said. "Just that he didn't kill Julie Davenport. Or Sally Graham."

Ramsey seemed to be deciding how best to respond. Finally, he said, "I'm sure you understand that we can't take your word for it, Governor."

"I'm not asking you to. I guess I'm just asking . . ."

He trailed off. Ramsey waited.

"I'm asking for you to keep an open mind. It's not easy, I know, but try. And if you find him—"

"*When* we find him," he said, interrupting the governor a second time.

"Okay, *when* you find him . . . please take him in as easy as you can. He won't fight you. He's not the type, no matter what you believe. He's a good young man, Detective, I promise you. And when this is all over, you'll see that. I swear to God."

Ramsey met his eyes for a moment. "I can only promise to keep an open mind, sir. And that whatever cops bring him in will act professionally and use the appropriate amount of force and no more."

Andrew could only hope that was true. "Of course. Thank you."

Ramsey nodded. "As I said, I have to check in with my partner. You'll be available to answer a few questions when I come back out?"

"I'll be here. I want Tyler brought back safely, same as you, Detective. If there's anything I can tell you that will help with that, I'll be glad to share it."

Ramsey nodded, then turned and headed for the house.

Molly stepped close and leaned her head against Andrew's shoulder. Neither said a word. They didn't have to. They were thinking the same thing . . .

Wherever Tyler was, they hoped he was okay.

CHAPTER FIFTY-FOUR

Henry hated to think about it. He had spent countless hours over the past eight years trying *not* to think about it. Some days he was even marginally successful. Other days . . . not so much. Those days he was unable to forget, even for a moment, that he had killed Dave Bingham.

It was an accident. A terrible accident.

And it was a long story with a lot of players and a lot of moving parts, a story he didn't have time to think about now even if he had wanted to, which he never did. Still, even when he wasn't thinking about it, he could never quite clear his mind of the story's lowlights . . . of the fact that he accidentally shot Dave and let a local junkie—Kevin Austin—take the fall for it. He hadn't meant to do either, not really, but to his horror, both things just sort of happened, and after a while, there was nothing he could do about either. Especially not after all these years. All he could do now . . . the important thing now . . . was to focus on helping Tyler. It wouldn't be easy under the circumstances, but for Tyler, he'd do what he had to do.

Grady Austin offered Henry and Egan something to drink, and though it was after midnight, Henry had asked for coffee just so he could observe the man limping around the kitchen, performing the task of serving them, while Henry tried to determine whether it was possible for him to have killed Sally Graham. And watching him fuss with the coffee maker, take cups and saucers from the cabinets, and put sugar and creamer on the table, Henry determined that it wasn't. Molly hadn't mentioned the man she saw in the video walking with a limp, and it was hard to believe that someone with this profound a physical handicap could do what their mysterious caller had been doing. Austin could have hired someone, of course, but to engage the services of a person to accomplish something that required as much planning and effort to execute as what their blackmailer had been doing would no doubt be expensive. And judging by the appearance of Austin's house and the way he lived, the guy wasn't exactly rolling in money. But the look on his face when he'd first seen Henry at his door, and heard his name, and the fact that he'd said that Henry "wasn't supposed" to find him, left no doubt that he was deeply involved in all of this.

Ever mindful of the clock, and the fact that Tyler was out there somewhere—on the run, alone, scared, and in danger—Henry continued his questioning, which had begun the moment Egan had joined them in the kitchen. The detective just sat and listened, content to let Henry take the lead even though he wasn't exactly on the VSP payroll at the moment. But Egan knew enough to realize that he didn't know nearly enough to ask the right questions.

"If you don't mind, Mr. Austin," Henry said, "can you tell me how you hurt your leg?"

"Car accident a few years ago."

Henry nodded and considered how best to phrase the next question so as to appear to know more than he did while still eliciting a substantive response.

"You seemed surprised to see me at your door," he said as he added sugar to his coffee. "Surprised that we connected you to all of this, is the way I think you said it."

"Yeah," Austin said, lowering himself into a kitchen chair with a bit of effort because of his leg. "He said you wouldn't."

"Who said that? The man you hired?"

Austin nodded very slightly, confirming Henry's theory.

"Is that who's been calling us, Mr. Austin? Or was it you?"

"Wasn't me."

Henry believed him. "So who is he?"

Austin said nothing.

"Mr. Austin?"

Austin looked away. Shook his head.

"Mr. Austin, the man doing all of this, the man you hired, he's hurt a lot of people."

Still no response.

"Ruined a lot of lives," Henry added.

"That was the *point*," Austin finally snapped. "He was *supposed* to destroy lives. The way my Kevin's was. And mine."

Henry sat back hard in his chair, as though shoved in the chest by the raw emotion in the man's voice. He took a breath. "I don't want to hear about how your life was destroyed, Mr. Austin. Or your son's."

It was true. He really didn't. Because it was Henry who had destroyed them. They didn't know that, of course . . . no one but Henry did.

He glanced at Egan, who looked surprised at Austin's near confession. The man was starting to make Henry's story about Tyler's innocence a bit easier to believe.

"Your son, Kevin, killed a man, Mr. Austin," Egan said, joining the conversation.

"No, he didn't. He was framed. By the person who really killed Dave Bingham."

Almost unconsciously, Henry sat forward, his pulse kicking up a tick. *The person who really killed Dave Bingham?*

"And who was that?" Egan asked patiently.

"Zachary Barnes," Austin said, and Henry sat back again, his pulse slowing a fraction. "His old man's in the mob, they say. Connected somehow, anyway." And once Austin started talking, he barely paused to take a breath. "Kevin was there that night, it's true, in the Rutland Projects. That place . . . that hellhole . . . no one goes there for a good reason, not since they closed it all up, sent the residents off to look for someplace else to live. Nothing but drug dealers and gangbangers and hookers ever since. Thank God they're tearing those goddamn buildings down. My Kevin, yeah, he was there that night. He went for drugs sometimes. I'm not proud of that, but there it is. Anyway, somehow he got mixed up with something."

"And what was that?" Egan asked.

Henry sat and listened, a captive audience, as Austin filled in holes in the story Henry had been reluctantly retelling in his head over and over for years.

Austin shook his head. "Kevin wouldn't tell me exactly. But he and the Barnes kid knew each other. All my boy told me later was that he didn't kill anyone, said it was really important that I believed him. They built a case against him, even without the goddamn murder weapon. Didn't bother looking for anyone else," he said with a glare at Henry. It was all Henry could do to keep from dropping his eyes. "Kevin pleaded not guilty and was all set for trial, but then his lawyer gave him a message from Clifton Barnes. Said if Kevin tried to hang it on his son, Zachary, then . . ."

"Then what, Mr. Austin?" Egan asked. "Let me guess: He'd have someone kill Kevin in jail? Before it even got to trial?"

Austin shook his head. "No. He'd have someone kill me. But if Kevin kept his mouth shut, played along and took the fall, he'd . . ."

"He'd what?"

"Barnes would take good care of . . . of me."

"Of you?" Egan asked.

"He'd send me money."

"Your son told you about this alleged threat?"

"Nothing alleged about it."

Egan said, "So you're saying that Clifton Barnes knew his son killed Dave Bingham, and he threatened you and your son, and offered to pay you off, to keep his kid out of trouble?"

"That's what I'm saying."

"And Kevin did what he asked? To protect you?"

"He did."

Henry closed his eyes again. He hadn't known any of this. It came as a shock. They had all been wrong about who had killed Dave Bingham, of course, but it said a lot about local junkie Kevin Austin that he would take the rap for a murder he didn't commit in order to protect his father. This new piece of information caused Henry to feel a familiar stab of guilt and shame. If such wounds were physical, he'd have been a giant mass of scar tissue.

Austin continued. "The next day, Kevin changed his story and pleaded guilty. Confessed to killing that ex-cop, even though he didn't do it. And his damn lawyer, the bastard, knew it wasn't true because he's the one who delivered Barnes's message to Kevin. He just let it happen. Probably got paid a lot for that. I wasn't too torn up to hear he drowned a year later when his fishing boat sank, I'll tell you that. And for the record," he added, looking at Henry, "your brother let it happen, too. Sure, he was the prosecutor, and it was his job, but he should've known something was wrong. He should've known it from the start. My boy was innocent, and your brother cared more about TV press conferences and sending Kevin to prison than knowing what really happened. I could say the same about you, too, Lieutenant Kane. And you know I'm right. I can see the guilt all over your face."

Henry said nothing. What was there to say? So he kept his mouth shut and sat there burning with shame. He had to endure this. He had to understand everything that was going on if he wanted to help Tyler.

"Judge Jeffers was no better, either," Austin said. "He didn't care about the truth. Just wanted to get the trial over with and start the next one." His voice had gotten shaky. He stopped, took a deep breath, and said, "So Kevin did what Barnes wanted, changed his plea to guilty and let them sentence him to twenty-five years in prison, just so I wouldn't get hurt. So I'd be taken care of. And Zachary Barnes got off scot-free, paid for by his daddy's threats and his daddy's money and my son's freedom . . . and, later, his life. Someone killed my boy in prison. Beat him to death like an animal because they didn't like the way he was."

Henry listened stoically, the only person in the room who knew what he'd done, who knew how grievous his sins were. He'd learned a while back that Kevin Austin had died in prison, but he hadn't known how until Egan told him. How many times had he thought about turning himself in? About confessing? But every time he did, he came up with a reason not to. That was something he had to live with.

"And he went to prison for me," Austin said. "I didn't want that, but I couldn't stop him. He confessed, and I couldn't stop him. No one would listen to me. His lawyer wouldn't meet with me. Your brother," he said, looking Henry's way again, "only cared about the publicity. Didn't want to listen to what I had to say. The state attorney's office got its confession, your brother held his final press conference, and that was that. End of story. I called your brother's office and sent letters telling him that they got the wrong man, that they needed to look into the Barnes kid, but he ignored me. And Kevin went to prison. A month later, I got a cashier's check in the mail. Twenty-five thousand dollars. And every six months, I got another one, fifty grand a year, all the way up until Kevin died. Never spent a dime of the money on myself, though. Just saved it up until . . ."

He trailed off. Egan finished for the older man, "Until you used it to hire whoever is behind all of this."

Henry had to step in. He had no choice. Egan simply didn't know enough of the facts. "Wesley Jurgens was your messenger, I'm guessing," he said. He had represented Torrance from the start, last visiting him a year ago—around the same time he'd visited Lewis for the first time.

"Not *my* messenger."

"The guy you hired then," Henry said. "He had Jurgens communicate with Torrance and Lewis, get them on board?"

"Wasn't hard to convince Gabriel. He's the one that got me thinking about all this in the first place. After Kevin died, Gabriel contacted me and told me he thought he might be able to find the gun with Zachary Barnes's fingerprints."

Henry stiffened. The gun? In the confusion of that night, the struggle that led to his accidentally shooting Dave, the tangle of emotions he'd felt immediately afterward, Henry hadn't realized until much later that he'd lost the unregistered gun he'd been carrying, the one that had killed his friend. After months passed, then years, he'd thought it lost for good.

"You all right?" Egan asked.

Henry realized both men were looking at him.

"I'm fine." He looked at Austin and tried to keep his voice steady as he asked, "What about the gun?"

"Kevin had told Gabriel generally where he'd hidden it in those projects. He made Gabriel promise never to tell me, but after Kevin was killed, well . . . Gabriel wanted to set things straight. For Kevin."

"Why the hell did Torrance care so much?" Egan asked.

Austin raised his chin, almost defiantly. "He and Kevin were close in prison."

"They were lovers?"

"More than that. Kevin told me they were *in* love. When Kevin was killed, Gabriel was devastated. He knew Kevin wouldn't have wanted Zachary Barnes brought into this, that he wanted to protect me, but after Kevin was gone and Gabriel told me about the gun, I didn't give a thought about me. I wanted revenge, same as Gabriel did. The problem was that those projects are coming down soon."

"And you guys were worried that the gun would be lost forever," Henry said, "so Torrance had to get out earlier."

"Like I said, he wouldn't tell me where to look for it. *He* wanted to be the one to find it. That was real important to him. He insisted on being the one to avenge Kevin by destroying Zachary."

"Along with everyone you hold responsible for what happened to your son," Egan said.

"Not Kevin's lawyer," Austin said, "the son of a bitch. He was already dead."

For a moment, Henry couldn't catch his breath. It was all his fault. It started with his accidentally killing Dave Bingham, and his arresting Kevin Austin for the crime—though he hadn't planned that . . . it just happened. Then Kevin dying in prison, and Grady Austin's father hiring someone to exact his revenge. Henry was responsible for it all. Sally Graham and Julie Davenport. *Everything* was his fault.

Austin was still talking. "But all the others?" he said. He glared at Henry. "You. The damn judge. Your brother—"

Wait a second. Henry cut him off. "What the hell did Tyler have to do with any of this?"

Austin shook his head. "Not that brother. Your other one."

"I repeat: what did Tyler have to do with this? Me, my brother Andrew, Judge Jeffers . . . I can almost understand. But Tyler?"

Austin looked away.

"How about Sally Graham, Mr. Austin?" Henry asked. "And Julie Davenport?" He knew that, of all people, he had no claim to the moral high ground here. But Tyler? He was innocent in every sense of the word. And not one but two blameless women?

Austin turned toward him, confusion in his eyes.

"Did you know he killed Julie tonight?" Henry asked. "Had you ever even heard of her? Her only crime was living in the house with my brother Tyler. Helping to take care of him. Yet the man you hired killed her tonight."

Austin looked away again.

"Kane," Egan said softly to Henry. "Maybe it's time to read him his—"

"Too soon," Henry replied quietly. He felt they were getting somewhere now. Austin was showing signs of weakening. "It's just the three of us here right now, Egan. No need for Miranda yet."

"I don't want this going tits up because—"

"We'll do it, just not yet. Not when we're getting close." He lowered his voice even more. Austin could probably still hear him, but the man was focusing on the black night beyond the window. "If it ever comes to it, it'll be his word against ours as to when he heard his rights."

Egan shook his head. "Man, for an IA cop, you play fast and loose with the rules."

Henry turned toward Austin again. If he wanted answers, he had to continue to push the man despite his own culpability. "How about them, Mr. Austin? My brother Tyler? Sally Graham? Julie Davenport?"

"I didn't know his plans for Tyler. Didn't know he'd even be involved. And I didn't know he was going to . . . you know, kill Sally Graham. Or the last one you mentioned, Julie . . ."

"Davenport."

"I didn't know about any of them. I just told him who I wanted to see punished. I left it to him to decide how to do it. He said there might be collateral damage, but . . ."

"Collateral damage?"

"I wanted you all punished. But I didn't want you killed. *Not you.* Not the ones who did what you did to Kevin. No, I wanted you all alive, alive but miserable. I wanted you to lose what mattered most to you. I wanted your lives ruined like ours were. But I left it to him to decide how to do all that."

"Okay, so he's destroying Andrew's career and mine. But he *killed* Judge Jeffers, Mr. Austin. What about that?"

Austin shrugged. "I read yesterday that he's dying of cancer, and dying soon. Maybe the only way to punish him was to kill him sooner.

Like I said, I left all that up to him. I never knew any of the details. Just wired him all the money Clifton Barnes ever sent me, every penny of it. Three hundred twenty-five thousand dollars. Waited for almost a year. I thought maybe I'd been ripped off. But then a few weeks ago . . . things started happening."

"You keep talking about the guy you hired," Henry said, getting to the meat of it now, what he needed to know for Tyler's sake. "Who is he? How do we find him?"

"You can't. He's just someone I found on the Internet. I did a lot of research on the computer. I wasn't any good at it at first, but I got better. Eventually, I found a thing called a darknet or something. You can hire people to do anything. Everything's in some sort of code. We emailed back and forth, but nothing's traceable. I couldn't tell you who he is if I wanted to."

Henry knew what Austin was talking about, the kinds of websites where almost anything illegal could be bought and sold, all communications were encrypted, and payment was often made in bitcoin. Online retail sites where the likes of drug dealers, human traffickers, arms dealers, and hit men sold their goods and services. If that was how Austin had hired the man behind everything, it was a devastating blow to their chances of finding him, especially if he was true to his word and considered the job finished. If he was ready to disappear, he had a very good chance of doing so successfully.

"Who's next on your hit list?" Egan asked. "Where's he going next?"

Austin closed his eyes and said nothing. Egan didn't know what Henry knew, that their mystery caller had said he was ready to ride off into the sunset.

"It's only gonna get worse for you, Mr. Austin," Egan said, "if someone else gets hurt. If there's another name on your list."

Austin said nothing.

"Or what about someone who's not even on your list getting hurt or killed?" Egan pressed. "You really wanna see another innocent person end up dead as collateral damage?"

Austin merely shrugged, indifferent to the deaths he had paid for, as well as the ones the killer had thrown in for free.

Henry almost—*almost*—wished he could be as indifferent to the death of Dave Bingham, which *Henry* had caused. It would have saved him from countless hours of mental torture and a thousand sleepless nights.

Then again, he knew he didn't deserve to be spared that.

CHAPTER FIFTY-FIVE

Pickman truly hated the thought of improvisation. Hated to consider deviating from his well-laid plans. But it wasn't like he hadn't already had to make sacrifices tonight. And the opportunity presenting itself at that moment . . . well, it was so tempting.

He weighed his options. He could forge ahead as planned, or he could do this one thing first, then get right back on track.

And this one thing could be very helpful. He doubted anyone would believe Tyler Kane when they caught him, but he couldn't ignore the fact that the idiot had seen Pickman's face. If there was even the smallest chance Tyler could get someone to listen to him, and he could describe Pickman, then, hell . . . maybe Pickman could actually be in danger. Unlikely, yes, but conceivable.

The solution? Make sure Tyler wasn't arrested. If he was found, better he be killed than brought in. There was no way Pickman could guarantee that, but it was possible to make it a smidge more likely, to make Tyler seem even more dangerous than he was already considered to be. And Pickman could accomplish that while also making him reviled by law enforcement personnel. With any luck, some cowboy cop would decide to spare the state the expense of a trial.

His mind made up, Pickman turned right at the next the corner, pulled to a stop at the curb, and hurried on foot back to where he'd passed a cop car parked in the mouth of an alley, the cruiser facing out into the street, the officer behind the wheel, drinking coffee.

Pickman's eyes quickly scanned the street in both directions. It was quiet, as so many Vermont streets were at that time of night. Not a soul in sight when he approached the alley and walked in—staggered, really, as though drunk—right past the cruiser, even bumping into it clumsily as he passed. Deeper in the shadows, a few feet behind the car, he stumbled to his left until he hit a brick wall, where he remained leaning, as though collecting himself. If the cop was watching, which Pickman was certain he would be, he would think Pickman was either drunk or injured.

As expected, he heard the car door open.

"You okay?" the cop asked. He had the voice of a young man.

Footsteps approached less warily than Pickman considered wise under the circumstances.

He turned his head and saw the cop getting closer. Young and clean, new to the uniform. Probably had a pretty wife at home, maybe a baby, too.

In his pocket, Pickman gripped the knife he'd used to frame Tyler Kane—the one with the notched tip and the slightly twisted blade— and, when the cop was close enough, he spun and jabbed the weapon into the man's chest, toward the upper right. The cop went down, and Pickman landed on top of him, pinning his arms with his knees.

"What's your call sign?" Pickman asked.

The cop groaned through gritted teeth.

"You reach for your gun, I'll cut your throat," Pickman said. "Now give me your call sign. I won't ask again."

The cop told him, then Pickman stabbed him again in the chest, toward the upper left this time. Then, without a word, he got up onto one knee, jammed the knife into the cop's belly, and drew it from one side to the other in a curving slice.

"Smile," he whispered as the cop bled out.

Pickman looked down at the clothes he was wearing. Blood. Damn. Well, what had he expected? Some would transfer to the interior of the car he was driving, too, but of course, he'd rented it under a false identity, and it was unlikely it could be traced back to him. He had a change of clothes in the trunk, but he would save them until after he finished what he'd set out from his house to do.

He left the cop lying in a spreading pool of blood and hurried back to the cruiser. He radioed in, gave the call sign that had been the cop's final utterance, and said in a voice a little higher than his own, more like the cop's, "Just saw a man enter an alley on Logan Street, near the Dunkin' Donuts. Fits Tyler Kane's description."

Without waiting for a response, he hurried from the alley and down to the corner half a block away, then trotted to his car. Within seconds, he was under way and back on course.

He felt energized. He had deviated from the plan and found it exciting. His heart thundered. Though there had been no one on the street when he'd entered the alley, it had been possible that someone could have driven by, seen activity in the shadows, and decided to investigate. He'd had no idea whether he would be discovered right in the middle of committing murder. Yet he'd followed his instincts, let his gut lead him despite the uncertainty, despite the lack of planning. He had acted spontaneously, a spur-of-the-moment decision to kill, and had pulled it off. And in so doing, he may have lessened Tyler Kane's chances of being taken in alive.

When this was all over, when this job was complete, Pickman might have to consider allowing himself a little room for improvisation on future assignments. This little detour had been exhilarating.

He had settled in behind the wheel, driving well within the speed limit to avoid unwanted attention, when his cell phone rang. He glanced at the caller ID, and his heart quickened. It had to be good news. After their conversation a few hours ago, Gabriel Torrance would have no other reason to call him.

"Yes?" Pickman said into the voice changer.

"I found it," Torrance said.

Pickman chuckled . . . laughed, actually, something he hadn't done for weeks, probably, maybe as long as a month. He couldn't help it. Despite a small bump in the road earlier, things were going his way again. He'd allowed himself to kill that cop minutes ago, an act that was both useful to his plan and a revelation with respect to the way it made him feel, and now this . . . the last piece of the puzzle but for what had just become the final task, which Pickman was on his way now to complete. He had hoped that Torrance would have been successful before now, but he'd understood that it would take time. He wouldn't have been surprised if the man had taken another week, actually. Or, quite possibly, failed entirely.

"I did nothing but search the projects for the past three days," Torrance said, "like you told me to do, but there was a lot of ground to cover."

Apparently, Kevin Austin hadn't wanted anyone to go looking for the gun and put his father in danger, so almost in passing, he'd given Torrance only a very general description of the weapon's hiding place.

"You can tell me now," Pickman said. "Where was it?"

"Kevin said he hid it in a wall behind a recessed radiator."

"If you knew that, why did it take so long to find it?"

"He said he was pretty high when he hid it. He'd gone to the projects looking for drugs, and he found them. So he was high to start with when he saw Zachary Barnes, a guy he knew, head into one of the buildings. He followed. The next thing he knew, someone was dead and Barnes was running away, so Kevin ran, too. Ran and hid. When he thought the coast was clear, he came out again. That's when he found the gun. He panicked and ran into one of the buildings with it, ran up some stairs, and hid the gun in an abandoned apartment. He never knew which building it was, though, just that it wasn't the one the guy was killed in. Couldn't remember the apartment number. Or even exactly what floor it was on. All he knew was that it was on the second or third floor."

Pickman quickly did the math. Two possible floors, sixteen apartments to a floor, made thirty-two apartments per building to search, and six possible buildings—after subtracting the one where the murder took place—made 192 apartments to explore. Several rooms in each apartment. Maybe even more than one radiator per room. That left a whole lot of searching to be done.

It didn't matter, though. What mattered was that they had the weapon now, which would be tied to the murder of Dave Bingham, and which likely still held Zachary Barnes's fingerprints on it. The gun should be enough to land Barnes in prison, which was part of what Kevin Austin's father had paid Pickman to make happen. But if the gun itself wasn't enough to put Barnes away, Pickman had a contingency plan, as always, to ensure that result—a plan in the form of additional evidence he had manufactured and would make sure came to light at the proper moment. But he doubted that would be necessary.

There was just one thing left for Pickman to do then before he would consider the job he'd been paid to perform to be complete. Though deviations had uncharacteristically been required, he had executed his plan nearly—*very* nearly—flawlessly.

As expected.

CHAPTER FIFTY-SIX

Andrew and Molly had moved to a cast-iron verdigris bench in the shadow of an ancient oak tree. Their mother had sat there in the early evenings decades ago and read stories to her children, not far away from the house from which a dead body had been removed tonight. Molly appeared lost in thought. Moments ago, Andrew called Rebecca to give her a quick update; she had wanted to meet him here, but he'd asked her to stay home in case Tyler showed up there. Now he sat in silence, waiting for Detective Ramsey to return, praying that Henry would call soon to tell him that his lead had been solid, that he had found the man behind all of this.

Beside him, Molly said in a quiet voice, "I shouldn't have talked her into staying."

"It's not your fault, Molly."

"She wanted to leave. I know she did. And I wouldn't let her. She stayed because she trusted me."

"No, she stayed because she trusted Tyler. She believed in his innocence and knew he'd never hurt her. And she was right. He never would have. The blackmailer . . . the murderer . . . killed her. Her death isn't on you."

Before she could reply, her cell phone rang. She dug it out of her back pocket, looked at the caller ID, and frowned.

"Hello?"

A second later, her eyes grew wide. She glanced quickly toward the house, toward the members of law enforcement buzzing around it, and said into the phone, quietly, "Tyler? Are you okay? Where are you?"

Andrew's eyes widened. *Tyler?*

She listened for a moment, then said, "That was really smart, Tyler, but listen to me. You need to come home . . . I know you didn't . . . We all know you didn't . . . Well, no, the cops don't know that, but if you come home we can—"

Andrew was growing anxious listening only to Molly's half of the conversation.

"What happened?" she asked. "Oh, that's horrible . . . A white suit? . . . No, Tyler, don't hang up . . . You *have* to come home. It's dangerous for you out there . . . *What?* God, Tyler, that's not true. Why would you think that? . . . It's just not true, I swear it . . . Please, Tyler, you have to—"

Andrew saw a tear in her eye. She slipped her phone into her pocket, saying, "He hung up."

"Where is he? What did he say?"

"He borrowed someone's cell phone outside a bar."

"What bar?" Andrew asked.

"He wouldn't say. He was leaving there anyway."

"I hope like hell he wasn't recognized."

"Me, too. He said he didn't kill Julie. A man in a white suit did."

"Same as in the video you saw."

"And the bastard told him that everyone already thought he was a murderer, and now they'd be sure of it, so he should just run away. Even told him the family would be better off without him."

"That *son of a bitch*."

"He told Tyler to come with him, that he'd give him a place to stay."

"Thank God Tyler was too smart for that. He's lucky as hell he got away. He wouldn't say where he is? Where he plans to go?"

"No, just that he's going somewhere he'll be safe."

"He say anything else that can help us find him? Anything at all?"

"Just that he thinks the killer was right, that we'd be better off without him, so he's not coming home. I'm supposed to tell you and Henry, and Rebecca, too, that he loves us, because he's not going to call again. He sounded really scared. *I'm* scared, Andy."

"Me, too. If only we had some idea . . ." He trailed off, seeing the faraway look that had suddenly taken hold of his sister's eyes. "Molly?"

"Shh. I'm thinking." As difficult as it was, he remained quiet until she turned to him abruptly, her eyes diamond bright, and said, "I know where he is. Or where he's going, if he's not there yet."

"You do?"

"And there's a bar not far from there. Pete's Place or something. If he ran through the woods, it wouldn't take him long to get where I think he's headed."

"And where's that?"

She told him.

"I think you're right, Molly."

"I'm gonna go to him. Right now. I'll talk him into coming back with me."

"Whoa, hang on. Shouldn't we just tell Ramsey where to find him?"

"Absolutely not. He could panic. He must be scared out of his mind. What if he sees them coming and runs? They could shoot him, Andy. No, I have to get to him first."

He thought a moment. She was right, of course. "When you find him, tell him that the man who killed Julie is wrong. That we never wanted him to leave. That we aren't better off without him. That he has to come back with you and—"

"I know what to tell him, Andy. And I think he'll listen to me. He usually does."

Andrew nodded. "Hurry up then, before Ramsey comes back. And be careful, Molly."

She looked at the policemen standing at the end of her driveway. "Will they let me leave?"

"I don't know." He paused, thinking. "Sneak out the side gate, and go to the black SUV behind my car. My security guy's in there. I'll text him and tell him to take you wherever you want to go."

"He's a state trooper, right? What if Tyler sees him and gets scared off? If I lose him, who knows if we'll find him again. And we have to find him before the police do."

"I'll tell Mike to hang back. Now go."

Molly nodded, then slipped off through the shadows. Andrew sent his text to Mike, and a few moments later, he heard an engine start and saw the lights of the black SUV snap on. The vehicle pulled away, Mike giving a wave out his open window to the cop at the end of the driveway as he passed. The tinted rear windows were closed.

Andrew sat back down on the bench feeling utterly impotent. Henry was off following whatever lead he thought he had on this. Molly was racing off to find Tyler before the cops did. And Andrew just sat there waiting for Ramsey . . . who was suddenly striding across the lawn, his body language screaming bloody murder.

"Governor Kane," he said, his anger almost a physical thing. "I just got word that your brother killed someone else a few minutes ago. A Bennington Police officer, less than a year on the job. Carved him up the same way he did the others."

Oh, God . . .

"That wasn't Tyler, Detective."

"Bullshit. All your talk about how good a guy he is, how innocent he is. Nothing but bullshit. *Sir.*" He looked puzzled for a moment. "Where's Ms. Kane?"

Andrew thought quickly. "You said you were done with her, Detective. She went to stay with a friend."

Ramsey cut his eyes toward the street. "Isn't that her Land Rover?"

"She's understandably upset, so I had my security guy drive her."

"I need her back here . . . sir."

"I'll call her and tell them to come back."

Ramsey nodded. Then he stood there waiting.

"I'll do it this very moment then."

He dialed Molly's cell number. When she answered, he said, "Molly, listen to me. Detective Ramsey just told me that they think Tyler has killed someone else, a police officer this time. Same MO as Julie and Sally Graham. So it's really important that he's found, you understand? Tyler has to be found before anyone else gets hurt, including him."

"What are you saying, Andy?" Molly asked.

"I'm saying that the detective here wants you to turn around and come back here."

Ramsey, listening to Andrew's half of the conversation, nodded slightly.

"I'm not coming back without Tyler," Molly said.

"Perfect," Andrew said. "See you soon." He slipped his phone back into his pocket.

Ramsey took out a pen and small notepad and said, "I need you to talk to me, Governor. Anything you can tell me to bring your brother in is in everyone's best interests, especially Tyler's. Do you have any idea at all where he might be? Is there anything you can tell me to help us?"

Andrew sat on the bench and hung his head. Ramsey gave him a moment.

The blackmailer had killed again. And as before, he'd done so in a way that was certain to cast blame on Tyler. Why, exactly, Andrew wasn't sure, but he knew one thing for certain: it was time to come clean—past time, actually. It was the best thing for Tyler at this point. He had to tell Ramsey everything. Everything he'd done. Everything . . . he'd become. He took a deep breath. This was going to hurt. It was going to leave a mark. He looked at the little pad of paper in Ramsey's hand and said, "You're going to need a bigger notebook, Detective."

Over the next several minutes, he told it all—everything—to the stunned detective, who, as he listened, seemed to vacillate between outright disbelief and strong skepticism. Andrew showed Ramsey the black burner phone, as if its very existence were confirmation of his story. He also played the recording he'd made of one of the blackmailer's first calls. There were questions throughout, of course, and Andrew did his best to answer.

"Why didn't you turn this phone in right away, Governor?"

"At first, I thought it might have been a prank. After that, I kept it in case . . . in case the caller had framed Tyler so well that he looked guilty, like his being acquitted looked unlikely, and I . . . had to do what the caller asked me to do."

"In order to help your brother."

"I'm not proud of that. But, Detective, my brother is innocent."

"And so you pardoned this . . . Gabriel Torrance?"

"He wasn't a danger to anyone," he found himself rationalizing, "wasn't a violent man, and his sentence was nearly up anyway."

"And what about Kyle Lewis? He wasn't a danger, either? You pardoned him, and he killed Judge Jeffers tonight."

"No, he didn't," Andrew replied, growing frustrated. "The man who framed Tyler did, then framed Lewis for it. Haven't you been listening? Check your notes."

"Why would whoever you claim framed your brother turn around and frame Lewis for a different murder?"

"To make me look bad. I already told you that, Detective."

"So this is all about *you* then? All these bodies piling up?"

Andrew shook his head. "Not just me, no, but I'm . . . not really sure of anything anymore. Other than that Tyler didn't kill anyone."

Andrew kept talking, and Ramsey at least appeared to be listening, though Andrew couldn't tell whether the detective believed a word he said.

CHAPTER FIFTY-SEVEN

Henry watched in silence as Egan continued to question Grady Austin, who seemed to have resigned himself to explaining everything. Perhaps he just wanted to get it off his chest, something Henry had never been able to bring himself to do. Austin definitely seemed to display at least a little regret for the "collateral damage" suffered during the events he had set into motion. The problem was that, though he was spilling his guts in great volume now, nothing he was saying would help them find the man he'd hired, at least not anytime soon. And Tyler was out there somewhere. And, though it had to be a secondary consideration at the moment, there was still the matter of Torrance searching the projects for the gun with which Henry had killed Dave Bingham.

"Well, Austin," Egan said, "are you really gonna let someone else die tonight? Or will you tell us if there's another name on your list, another person you paid to see punished?"

Something shifted in Austin's eyes. Suddenly, he looked less forthcoming, cagier. He shifted in his seat. Averted his eyes.

And Henry knew that there was at least one more name on the list. "Who's left, Austin?" he asked, interrupting Egan in the middle of a question.

"I don't know what you mean."

"Sure you do. Tyler? Collateral damage. Sally Graham and Julie Davenport? More collateral damage. But Judge Jeffers had to be punished, right? He sentenced your son to twenty-five years. So Jeffers is dead now. And Kevin's lawyer, you said he drowned years ago, so he was beyond your reach. But there was my brother Andrew, the ASA who pledged to put your son away and wouldn't listen to your claims of Kevin's innocence. Andrew had to be punished, so you destroyed his reputation, one of the things that mattered the most to him. He'll probably have to resign. And me. I arrested Kevin, would have been called to testify against him in court," which, as far as Austin knew, was the extent of Henry's involvement. "So my days as a cop are almost certainly over now, and I may be facing prison time. But who else?"

"I don't know what you're talking about."

"Yeah, you do. There's someone else I'm not seeing, someone you think shares the blame. The warden at Southern State Correctional? One of the guards? How about the inmate who beat your son to death?"

Austin gave Henry a level gaze. "That murdering son of a bitch died of lung cancer a year and a half ago."

"Then who?"

"Shouldn't you read me my rights?"

"We already did that," Egan said. "I remember it. How about you, Lieutenant Kane?"

Henry was glad to see that Egan had his back after all Henry had put him through.

"I remember, too."

"But you still insisted on singing like a bird," Egan added. "We couldn't stop you, could barely keep up with you, in fact."

Austin's mouth was set in a hard line.

"Austin," Henry began, "when we talked about Sally Graham and Julie Davenport . . . hell, even when we talked about Tyler . . . I could see that you never intended to hurt them. I could see it in your eyes. So why don't we end all of this? Why don't you tell us who's left on your list before another innocent person gets hurt?"

The line of Austin's mouth turned into a sneer. "Because he's *not* innocent," he said, then sat back and crossed his arms.

Bingo. Henry was right. "Let's just beat it out of him," he said.

"That isn't helping," Egan replied.

"I'm semi-serious. Someone's gonna get hurt, Egan. Maybe killed."

"We aren't assaulting him. End of story."

Henry shifted his eyes over to Austin, who was starting to look smug. "Why is this asshole not wearing cuffs yet?"

"I usually do that when I Mirandize them," Egan said, then quickly added, "which I did a while ago, of course. Guess I forgot the cuffs."

Egan removed handcuffs from his belt and secured Austin's hands behind his back where he sat, which left him leaning forward awkwardly.

"You're going to prison, you know that, right?" Henry asked.

The man shrugged.

"Another dead body on your doorstep's not gonna make things easier on you."

"Won't make it much harder on me at this point, either, though, wouldn't you say?"

He was right. Which meant he wasn't going to talk. But he had *been* talking, which meant . . . what?

That he had nothing to lose? Probably.

That everything was over now, or would be soon?

Yes. That was it. There was one more name on his list, and it didn't matter if he admitted that because it would all be over soon. Tonight, possibly any minute now, the last person he considered responsible for what happened to his son would have been punished . . . possibly murdered.

"You lied to us," Henry said. "You've been in communication with whoever you hired all along, haven't you?"

Austin seemed to be done talking now.

Henry stood. "I'm gonna find his computer, check his email."

"Like hell you are," Egan said as he rose to his feet. "You being here's gonna be enough of a problem. I'm gonna have to figure out how to spin that to keep it from biting us in the ass later. Last thing I need is you poking around, screwing things up, getting everything there is to find excluded from evidence."

Henry dropped back into his chair. "Then *you* check his email. We have a confession. And another potential victim out there. That's exigent circumstances. Turn the place upside down. But start with his email, because this son of a bitch is lying."

"Okay, you babysit our boy here, and I'll take a look. Where's your computer, dirtbag?"

Austin was still done talking.

"I'll find it. And I'll call this in while I'm looking. Get someone to haul this trash away, get a few more bodies here to help search the place. In the meantime, after I check the computer, I'll keep looking for whatever this guy's not telling us."

"Yeah, whatever. I have a call to make, too."

Egan disappeared through a doorway leading out of the kitchen. Over his shoulder, he said, "I'm serious, Kane. Don't touch that guy."

Henry glared at Austin for a long moment, and Austin glared back . . . and it was Henry who dropped his eyes first. He took out his cell phone.

———

Andrew had finished his story and was responding to Ramsey's incredulous follow-up questions when his personal cell phone rang.

"Excuse me, Detective," he said, then took Henry's call while Ramsey stood waiting. "Hey," he said to his brother, "any chance you found our man?"

"Not quite, but almost. Got the guy who hired our man. He's sitting right in front of us, and he's told us almost everything."

"Who's *us*?"

"Another VSP detective. I'll explain later. Anyway, we're with the father of a man named Kevin Austin."

"The name rings a bell."

Ramsey was watching with undisguised impatience.

Henry said, "You were all ready to prosecute him for Dave Bingham's murder eight years ago when he suddenly pled guilty."

Very quickly, Henry filled him in on the story of Kevin Austin, his being killed in prison, and Grady Austin's desire to ruin everyone he deemed complicit in his son's tragic fate.

"He pleaded guilty," Andrew said, remembering. "I didn't see a reason not to let him. Neither did the judge. But wait . . . if he's after everyone involved in the case, how does Tyler fit in? And Julie and the Graham woman?"

"Collateral damage, apparently."

"My God. And he confessed to everything?"

"*Almost* everything. There's something he's not telling us. Hey, Andy, hang on. The cop I'm here with found something."

Andrew heard Henry's voice and that of another man talking back and forth on the other end of the line; then Henry was back on.

"Egan found an email from the other guy, the guy who's been calling us. Came in about ninety minutes ago. It'd been encrypted originally but was decrypted to allow Austin here to read it. Turns out there's another target, and they're going after him tonight."

"Who?"

"The email doesn't say, just that the final target will be hit tonight. Austin won't say, either. And Egan won't let me break one of his legs."

"Be sure to thank Egan for me. Listen, Henry, a Bennington cop was murdered tonight, staged to look like Tyler did it." He ignored

Ramsey's derisive snort. "Young guy, less than a year on the job. Any chance that's the last name on the list?"

"Less than a year? That's almost seven years after Kevin Austin was sent to prison, a year after he was killed there. Sounds to me like the cop is more collateral damage."

"I hate to interrupt, Governor," Ramsey said. "But I've got a job to do here, and we aren't finished yet."

"Can you think of anyone else involved with the case, Andy?" Henry said. "Anyone else the father might blame for . . ." Henry paused a moment. "For his son dying in prison?"

Andrew ignored Ramsey's glare, closed his eyes, and thought a moment. And a moment after that. Then he said to Henry, "You know what? Maybe I do. Did you say there's a VSP detective with you who heard your guy's confession? He knows Tyler is innocent?"

"Yeah, he's right in the next room."

"Put him on; have him talk to Detective Ramsey here. In the meantime, I have to check something. I'll be right back."

He shoved his phone into Ramsey's hands and rushed to his car. Inside were the pardon files he had inadvertently taken from the Pavilion during his rush to get here tonight. The files contained several years' worth of pardon requests, dating back many years before Andrew took office.

He flipped through the file folders, locating the one that would contain requests from eight years ago, and began thumbing through the papers. Nothing from or about Kevin Austin. He did the same with the file from seven years ago and, before long, came across a letter from Grady Austin. Andrew skimmed it and saw that Austin was requesting a full pardon for his son, Kevin, who the father claimed was innocent. Andrew quickly flipped through the rest of the file, then the next two folders. In all, he found four letters from Grady Austin; each was addressed to Governor John Barker.

He wondered if there were any letters in later folders, letters Grady Austin had written to *Andrew*, begging for his son's release, letters he'd barely glanced at when they'd crossed his desk.

With the letters addressed to Barker clenched in his fist, he ran back across the lawn to Ramsey in time to hear him say into Andrew's phone, "And you're sure about all this, Detective Egan? Absolutely sure? You heard all of this yourself? Directly? Not through Henry Kane?" He listened a long moment. "Okay, thank you, Detective." He handed the phone back to Andrew and said, "Okay, Governor, I'm listening. I mean, I'm *really* listening now."

With his eyes locked on Ramsey's, without knowing whether it was his brother or the other detective on the other end of the line, he said into the phone, "I think he's going after John Barker."

"*Governor* John Barker?" Ramsey asked.

"And I doubt we have much time."

CHAPTER FIFTY-EIGHT

"We're almost there," Molly said to Mike, Andrew's security guy. "Can you go any faster?" There she was, counting on the trooper to get her to Tyler before something terrible could happen to him, and she didn't even know the man's last name.

They were roaring along an otherwise quiet, winding, wooded stretch of road, the SUV's engine growling, its tires fighting to keep their grip on the pavement through the tighter turns.

"This is as fast as we want to go along this stretch, ma'am," he said over his shoulder to Molly, who was still in the back seat, leaning forward, digging her fingernails into the passenger seat headrest. They couldn't get to the animal shelter where Tyler volunteered quickly enough for her. When Tyler had said that he was going somewhere he would feel safe, she realized where that was. There were only two places, he'd once told her—home and the animal shelter—where people didn't treat him like he was stupid. Where he could be himself. Where he felt okay. She figured that also meant he felt *safe* there.

"Thank God it's late, and we're the only vehicle on the road," Mike said, "or we couldn't risk going as fast as we are."

Two minutes later, they reached the final bend in the road—the shelter was just around the corner—and Molly saw immediately that something was wrong. The trees ahead were lighting up with alternating flashes of blue and white, and for a moment, Molly couldn't breathe.

"Mike . . ."

"I see it."

They rounded the bend, and just up ahead was the animal shelter, an isolated building set back twenty yards from the road. In front of it was a Manchester Police cruiser with the lights on its roof rack flashing, parked broadside, its passenger side facing the building. A patrolman in uniform squatted behind the vehicle, talking into his radio.

As Mike pulled in to the parking lot, the SUV's headlights swept across the cop, and his head whipped around while his hand flew to the grip on his still-holstered weapon.

Mike, who was already waving his badge out the open window, called, "Officer, I'm a state trooper. Mike Burrows."

"Stay back, sir," the cop yelled.

"I'm a state trooper," Mike said again, opening his car door and stepping out slowly with his hands up and empty but for his badge. "Please stay here, ma'am," he said to Molly.

Molly lowered her window, her eyes on the Manchester Police officer, who had his eyes on Mike. He seemed to register Mike's uniform; then he nodded.

Staying low, Mike made his way over to the cop, then dropped to one knee beside him. "What's the situation, Officer?" he asked.

"Think we got Tyler Kane in there."

"Yeah?"

"Yeah. He cut off his ankle monitor and ran, after killing a woman who lived at his house with him. He used to work at this shelter, so they thought he might come here, told us to check on it every hour. When I rolled up, I saw movement inside. Called his name, and he opened a window in front and responded, said yeah, it was him, and I'd better not come in because he has a gun."

"He doesn't have a gun," Molly called from the SUV. She got out and hurried over to them. Unlike the others, she didn't bother to squat behind the police car.

"Ms. Kane," Mike said, "please go back to—"

"Please listen to me. He does *not* have a gun."

"After he killed that woman," the cop said, "he went and murdered a Bennington cop. Heard it on the radio just a little while ago."

"He didn't kill anyone," she said desperately. "He was framed."

He ignored her and said to Mike, "I just called for backup. Should be here in less than ten." He looked up at Molly. "This might be a good time for you to get back in your truck, ma'am, and keep your head down."

She remained standing. "He doesn't have a gun, Officer," she insisted.

"If he says he does, then as far as I'm concerned, he does until I find out different for sure. Now go find some cover, please."

Instead, as calmly as she could, which wasn't very calmly, she called out, "Tyler, it's me. It's Molly. I'm here, buddy. Listen, you need to tell them you don't have a gun. You need to come out of there with your hands up before you get hurt."

A moment later, a shadow appeared in front of the open window. A silhouette against the slightly lighter dark behind him.

"Molly?" Tyler called. "Is that really you?"

Hearing his voice broke her heart.

"It's really me. Please come out, Tyler. *Please* tell them you don't have a gun."

"I do have a gun. So that policeman should leave me alone."

"I know you don't have a gun. Listen, more policemen are on the way. This is only going to get worse." She was pleading now. "*Please* come out."

"I do have a gun. And I'm not coming out. And nobody better come in, or I'll shoot them."

The radio in the police car crackled, and someone announced that two more units were en route.

"Almost got him now," the cop said, and Molly didn't like what she heard in his voice. Maybe he wanted revenge against an accused cop killer. Maybe he wanted to be a hero. But there was violence in that voice. Molly had heard the same thing in Afghanistan, guys amped up and ready—no, *hungry*—for action. Whatever it was, she knew the man desperately wanted to be the one to take Tyler down, one way or another.

———

Tyler crouched beneath the window in the dark building, his legs aching from the long run—through several neighborhoods and two different woods—from his house, then to that bar where he borrowed that guy's phone, then here to the animal shelter. He was really tired. And still really sad about everything. About Julie being killed, and about having to run away forever and never see his family again.

Still, he was feeling pretty clever. If he hadn't told that cop out there that he had a gun, the guy would have just walked right in and arrested him. But if they thought he might shoot them if they tried, they couldn't do that.

He had a problem, though. They weren't going to just leave now that they knew he was there. His clever trick about the gun kept them from coming in, but they weren't going to just give up and drive away. So he'd have to be the one to get away instead. And Molly said that more police were coming, which would only make it harder to escape. So he had to do it soon.

The shelter had a back door. He used to take dogs for walks out back now and then, in the small grassy area between the building and the trees behind it. It wasn't that far to the trees. He could run to them. Then, even though he'd never been more tired in his whole life, he could keep running—through the woods, just keep going until he got someplace where they wouldn't find him next time.

Yes, he decided. That's what he'd do. And right away.

Well, as soon as he refilled the water in one of the kennels. When he'd snuck in before, the French bulldog puppy had gone crazy, jumping around and barking, and he'd knocked over his water bowl. Tyler couldn't leave him without water all night.

He unlocked the puppy's crate and grabbed the bowl, refilled it at the sink, and returned it to the crate. He gave the dog a scratch behind the ears and a quick belly rub, too. At the same time, he ignored the cop yelling at him from outside. And though it was harder, he ignored Molly calling to him, too. He didn't like doing that, but she kept telling him to give himself up, and he wasn't going to do that. He knew it would be better for everyone if he just went away and never came back.

The puppy had his water now, so it was time to go.

As soon as he gave fresh water to the other dogs. There were six of them, all in different cages, and they were all looking at him like they also wanted fresh water.

Then he had to give fresh water to the cats, too, of course.

After that, it would definitely be time to go.

———

Wyatt Pickman wasn't terribly surprised but was nonetheless pleased to see that John "Jackpot" Barker hadn't installed a home security system in the six weeks since Pickman's last clandestine visit to the ex-governor's house. But there was no reason he should have, as Pickman had left behind no trace that he'd been there. He'd merely had a look around, snapping photographs of the interior, taking measurements for the detailed floor plan he'd sketched the following day, and generally checking out Barker's things. There were no family pictures on the walls or shelves. The man had no family to speak of; according to reports, he'd enjoyed his decades of bachelorhood too much, considering himself a playboy, so there was no wife, and he had no children he would admit to having fathered. Where others might place framed family photos, Barker kept pictures of himself looking self-important: taking the oath of office, giving speeches, shaking hands with minor celebrities and athletes.

As he had done at Judge Jeffers's house, Pickman walked through rooms lit only by moonlight spilling in through the windows. He wore the same bloody clothes he'd worn when he'd killed the cop in the alley a little while ago. He also wore latex gloves. When he was finished here, he'd wash up, change into the spare set of clothes he'd brought, and take the bloody clothes and gloves with him to destroy later. He didn't need to plant any more evidence implicating Tyler Kane. At this point in the game, the victim's cause of death—the grisly smiley face carved into his torso—would be more than sufficient as a signature.

As Pickman moved down the dark hall toward the front of the house, he heard low sounds and saw dim light flickering. The television was on in Barker's media room, which likely meant that Barker was watching TV at that moment instead of sleeping upstairs where he was supposed to be.

No matter. He could die as well in front of the TV as he could in bed.

Pickman was unexpectedly pleased with himself. Not long ago—just hours ago—he might have become enraged at even the most minor deviation from his plan. After all, not one time in his six late-night visits to this house—the two times he'd been inside or the other times when he'd merely watched from the shadows of the yard outside—had Barker stayed up this late. And when he did, he was up in his bedroom with the light on, not down here watching television. And yet, though Barker's corpse wouldn't closely resemble the sketch Pickman had made of it months ago—lying on its back in bed, sheets twisted around it, blood pooling beneath it—he didn't care. So the grisly scene wouldn't match the drawing in his bible . . . who cared? He hadn't even bothered to *bring* his bible tonight.

No, all that mattered was that Barker would die in the same manner as Sally Graham, Julie Davenport, and that cop in the alley tonight, killed with the same blade as the others, the one with the notched tip and the slightly twisted blade.

Tyler Kane's last victim.

Another nail in Andrew Kane's political coffin.

And when that was done, Pickman's work would be done, too. After more than a year of planning and weeks of active execution, the job would be complete. The plan would *not* have been executed to the letter, but it would be complete nonetheless, each of his objectives accomplished . . . which, in a sense, made it a perfectly performed job.

Of course.

At the end of the hall, he peered around the corner into a room with a huge flat-screen TV on one wall and two plush sofas in front of it, one of which had the sleeping, snoring, pudgy form of Jackpot Barker sprawled across it.

CHAPTER FIFTY-NINE

Tyler had given water to all the animals and was standing at the back door, ready to run. What would happen if they saw him, though, and could see that he didn't have a gun in his hand? He'd told them he had one. His eyes had adjusted to the darkness in the room, and looking around, he spotted a black stapler on the desk. If he held that, it might look like a gun. It might fool them. He picked it up and again felt clever.

He took a deep breath, unlocked the back door, then pushed it open and started to run. He'd pushed it way too hard, though, because it banged against the back wall of the shelter, then slammed closed again. Tyler's legs were already feeling heavy as he ran. He heard shouts from the front of the building.

They'd heard him leave.

They'd be following him.

He wasn't running fast enough, not with his legs so heavy.

Now the shouts were getting closer, coming around the building, which wasn't far behind him. He wouldn't make it to the woods before they got there, even though the trees were just ahead.

The cop yelled for him to stop. Then Molly did, too. And because he knew they'd just catch him anyway, because his legs were so tired, he stopped running.

And he started to turn around.

And because he thought that now would be a good time to tell them that he didn't really have a gun, he raised the stapler to show it to them.

———

Andrew stood on the front lawn of the house in which he'd grown up and watched Detective Ramsey alternate between talking into his cell phone and barking orders to the officers and techs around him. As he stood watching, Andrew had his own phone to his ear, listening to the ringing, praying Molly would pick up.

———

As Molly ran, ignoring her phone buzzing in her back pocket, she experienced the surreal slowing of time depicted in books and movies, and which she had personally experienced in the chaos of combat. Things happened lightning fast, but the brain miraculously slowed them down and registered them each very clearly, frame by frame, instant by instant.

Not far in front of them, Tyler stopped, turned, and raised his right hand, which had something in it, something black and gun-size.

The cop, who had started running before Molly and was now half a dozen steps ahead of her, yelled, *"Gun!"* as he skidded to a stop and drew his weapon.

Tyler extended the hand with the black thing in it toward them, as though pointing it at them.

The cop, in a firing stance now, had a two-handed grip on his gun. He was about to pull the trigger. Molly recognized the body language instantly, having seen it countless times.

"I'm sorry," Tyler said.

Though the cop had stopped running, Molly hadn't. She covered the last twelve feet between them at a dead sprint, launching herself at the last second. She slammed into him from behind, and the gun discharged. As her momentum carried her to the ground, from the corner of her eye she saw Tyler go down.

———

Pickman looked at the high-end audio-visual equipment filling the built-in shelves next to the television and smiled. Recalling that there was a CD player in the master bedroom, where Pickman had expected to find the ex-governor tonight, Pickman had brought the Bach CD from his car. That Barker had instead fallen asleep in his media room, though, with its top-of-the-line sound system was perfect. Killing Barker was the finale of his beautiful plan. How better to bring down the curtain on this entire drama than by adding a soundtrack . . . *The Art of Fugue*?

Pickman saw a big, complicated-looking universal remote control on the sofa near Barker's hand. He picked it up and studied it as he walked to the bank of entertainment equipment.

Within a few seconds, he had it figured out. He slipped the Bach disk from his back pocket, inserted it into the CD player, and used the remote to switch audio sources. The sounds of the film ended abruptly, though the movie continued to play on the screen.

On the sofa, Barker stirred.

Through the speakers, clear as crystal, came the first of Bach's perfectly chosen notes—played on an organ in this arrangement. A few beats later, a second melodic theme—also an organ—began to weave through the first. As the third theme began, low notes thrumming through the room, Barker's eyes fluttered open, blinked stupidly, then shot wide when they landed on Pickman walking toward him, just three steps away now, knife in hand.

Bach filled the room. This was *exactly* how this was supposed to end. This was *perfect* . . .

. . . until he noticed a sound in the music that didn't belong. A high sound, shrill. Quiet at the moment but slowly growing in volume. What instrument was this? How had he never noticed it before? He didn't understand. He had listened to this piece literally thousands of times.

And then he *did* understand. It wasn't a musical instrument. It was sirens. Not far away. Getting closer.

Damn it.

A thousand thoughts ricocheted through his mind. He knew he should turn and run, through the house and out the back door. The cops would crash in at any moment. If he ran, he'd escape. He knew that. There was no way that they could know his identity, even though they had obviously known he would be coming after Barker. They'd probably found Grady Austin. He'd probably told them about Barker. But there was still time to get away, if only just barely.

He should leave.

But if he left now . . .

He wouldn't be able to finish the job. Maybe ever. Barker would be on his guard from now on. He'd get a security system, hire bodyguards, whatever.

Pickman might never get another shot at him.

The job would be incomplete.

Could he stand that? Would he be able to live with himself if he didn't finish the job?

Earlier, he'd been so proud of himself for having evolved, yet he stood now on a knife's edge, with everything hanging in the balance, everything telling him to run . . .

And he couldn't do it.

He couldn't leave the job unfinished. No matter the cost.

The strains of Bach clashed discordantly with the wailing sirens, which had almost reached the house.

Barker finally spoke, his voice quavering. "Who the hell are you?" he asked as he retreated into the corner of the sofa.

"I'm Tyler Kane."

Barker's eyes squinted in confusion. "No, you aren't."

"Well, I won't tell anyone if you won't."

Sirens screamed just outside. Pickman was barely aware of them now. What he heard was *The Art of Fugue* . . . the soundtrack of his life.

He strode forward and drove his knife into Barker's chest, just under his left shoulder.

Blue and white flashing lights lit up the room through the window above the sofa on which Barker now lay moaning and bleeding.

Tires screeched in the driveway. Pickman barely registered their sound. The organs were building to a crescendo.

He pulled the blade from Barker's body, and the man's animal cries of pain and fear were strangely melodic, blending perfectly with the music. Pickman didn't remember percussion in this part of the piece, but there it was, timpani drums . . . or maybe it was a sudden pounding on the front door.

Pickman plunged the blade into Barker's chest again, below his right shoulder.

Ah, yes, not drums. Pounding on the door. Louder now. And there were voices, too, Pickman realized. Cops yelling warnings.

Barker screamed for help at the top of his lungs.

Pickman yanked the blade from the ex-governor's chest.

The music grew louder, the pounding on the door more furious, the warnings more urgent.

Time to lower the curtain. "Smile," Pickman said as he gripped the knife in both hands, ready to drive it into Barker's belly.

Then he felt a punch to his chest as thunder bellowed and shards of glass filled the air. He staggered back a few steps. Through the window, awash in flashing blue and white, stood a uniformed policeman, his arms raised, a gun pointing at Pickman.

Pickman dropped the knife. Not because he wanted to, but because he couldn't make his fingers hold it any longer.

He waited for the cop to fire again, but the shot didn't come.

The front door crashed open as Pickman fell to his knees. He looked down at the hole in his chest, just below his left shoulder, the same spot where he had always first struck when killing people whose murders he would pin on Tyler Kane.

The room flooded with cops. He didn't want to go to prison. He didn't know if he could live like that. He saw the bloody knife lying on the carpet three feet to his left. If he could just get to it, they'd have to shoot him. They'd kill him. He tried to reach for it, but his left arm wouldn't move.

He felt weak.

And stupid. How had he let this happen?

Why hadn't he run when he should have?

But he knew the answer to that . . .

He couldn't.

Had someone turned off the music?

He looked down at the wound in his shoulder again and willed it to bleed more profusely. The last thing he wanted was to be taken alive. There was no greater hell on earth for Wyatt Pickman than a prison cell. There was no way he could live like that.

But the blood flow seemed to be slowing . . .

And sadly, tragically, he didn't seem to be dying . . .

CHAPTER SIXTY

When Molly had seen Tyler go down after the cop fired, she'd known he was dead. And she'd known that it might have been her fault. Maybe the cop had merely been firing a warning shot, though she was almost certain he hadn't been. Maybe he would have missed. But Molly had tackled him, and he'd shot Tyler and—

"Ow," Tyler said.

Molly was on the ground, in a tangle with the cop. She freed herself and felt his hand graze her back as she leaped to her feet too quickly for him to get hold of her. She sprinted over to where her brother lay on his back. Beside his right hand was a stapler. The outer part of his left thigh was bleeding. It was a flesh wound, at most. The tidal wave of relief she felt drove her to her knees beside him and left tears in her eyes. She wiped them away and smiled down at him.

"It hurts," Tyler said.

"I know. But you're going to be fine."

"That's good. You know, you can't tell in video games how much it hurts people when they get shot."

"Yeah."

"I'm not sure I wanna play those games anymore. There's a race car game that looks pretty good."

She smiled again.

Somewhere, a phone rang.

Molly sensed someone standing behind her. She turned and saw the cop looking down at them, his eyes hard, his gun still in his hand. Then his eyes drifted to the stapler on the ground, and something in those eyes changed. They softened at the edges.

"I have to arrest you both, ma'am," he said, though not in the hard-ass way he'd spoken before.

She nodded and stood.

From a few feet away, Mike said, "You can bring Tyler in, Officer, but I don't think he's going to prison."

"He's not?" the cop said.

"I just got off the phone with a Detective Ramsey of the state police. Said they think Tyler might have been framed. So yeah, do your duty and take him in until they get this all sorted out. Just don't expect him to stay long."

If Molly were more of a crier, she would have cried then. Instead, she said, "You hear that, Tyler? You're not in trouble anymore."

He smiled.

"I'm afraid I still have to arrest you, ma'am. Obstruction, assaulting a police officer. What you did was dangerous as hell."

"I understand."

As sirens sounded in the near distance, Mike said, "Officer, it seems to me that this woman just prevented you from shooting and possibly killing an unarmed man. That kind of thing is frowned upon. It can put a big dark stain on your record."

"Yeah, but—"

"The way it *looks*, though, is like fine police work on your part. Suspect turned, you thought he might have had a gun but you weren't sure, so you dropped him with a well-placed shot in the leg. Impressive."

"Okay, but . . ."

The sirens ended as the sound of cars screeching into the parking lot in front of the building carried to them.

"And, Officer?" Mike said. "You really want your buddies to know you were taken down by a woman?"

Cops were shouting nearby.

The officer thought a moment, then said to Molly, "You never touched me."

"No, sir," she said.

He spoke into the radio on his shoulder. "This is Officer Lichtman. We're behind the building. The situation is under control. The suspect is down but injured. We could use an ambulance."

Molly gave Mike a nod of thanks and he nodded back and smiled. He had a nice smile. She turned and knelt beside her brother again and stroked his hair, the way she used to do when they were kids and he woke up from a bad dream.

The nightmare is over, she used to say. *You're safe.*

CHAPTER SIXTY-ONE

Over the next several days, more and more of the story became clear to Andrew . . . and, more important, to the rest of the world.

In a room in Wyatt Pickman's basement, stunned authorities found an absolute treasure trove of evidence, neatly organized and labeled, filed in file cabinets or stored in boxes—evidence pertaining to the recent events involving the Kane family, as well as numerous other cases, some of which had gone unsolved, others of which had been solved incorrectly. So far, Pickman's records indicated eighteen murders and dozens of other crimes committed in furtherance of elaborately designed plots, which authorities who were tasked with reviewing the material deemed far more complex than necessary to accomplish Pickman's goals. Privately, they started referring to him as Rube Goldberg, a cartoonist and inventor famous for creating ridiculously overcomplicated machines to perform the simplest of tasks. As a former assistant state attorney, Andrew could well imagine the excitement the abundance of evidence provided the police and prosecutors alike.

Wyatt Pickman was in jail, of course, recovering from a gunshot wound and facing a lengthy list of charges pertaining to his recent activities. Other charges were expected to pour in from other cases involving other victims, both in Vermont and nearby states. Andrew knew it would take a lot of time, cops, and lawyers to sort everything out, but unfortunately for Pickman, as well as for everyone who had ever hired him to either kill someone or destroy another person's life, he kept those voluminous records. Every case relating to his past crimes would almost certainly be reopened and reinvestigated, and unless the statutes of limitations had run—which they never would on murder—some guilty people who thought they'd gotten away with their crimes were going to be in scalding hot water very soon. And fortunately, some innocent people framed by Pickman would eventually be freed. As for Pickman himself, there wasn't the slightest chance he would ever spend another night outside of a cell.

Neither would Grady Austin, who was in jail awaiting trial on numerous charges relating to his having hired Wyatt Pickman to commit numerous crimes, including murder. Austin was going to die in prison one day, as his son did . . . though, unlike his son, the elder Austin deserved to end his days there.

With respect to Tyler's case, authorities found hundreds of papers, notes, and photographs littering the floor, where they had evidently come to rest after being torn from the wall. They found dozens of related files in one of the file cabinets. They found the video of Pickman murdering Sally Graham while wearing Tyler's clothes. And they found a thick binder Pickman had created, outlining in extraordinary detail his plan for executing the job Grady Austin had hired him to do—that was, ruining the lives of everyone Austin blamed for the conviction, incarceration, and eventual death in prison of his son years ago. All charges against Tyler were dropped, of course, even though he'd technically violated the terms of his bail by leaving his property. All things considered, the prosecutor's decision to dump the case entirely was an easy call. It was doubtful there had ever been a more sympathetic defendant in the state's history.

The funeral and burial of Judge Morgan Jeffers was attended by the greatest number of mourners Andrew had ever seen. It seemed as though everyone involved in the Vermont criminal justice system was there. The courtroom over which he had presided for more than three decades was renamed the Honorable Morgan Jeffers Courtroom.

A somber funeral service, only slightly smaller than the judge's, was held in a packed church for Officer Gregory Blake, the last person killed by Wyatt Pickman. Andrew paid his respects from the back of the church.

Julie Davenport's body was flown to Illinois and laid to rest in a quiet cemetery in her hometown of Naperville. The entire Kane family attended, with the Davenport family's blessing. Molly served as a pallbearer. The day after the funeral, Andrew established a college scholarship in Julie's name at her old high school.

Sally Graham, the first of Pickman's recent victims, had been buried weeks ago, days after her murder, following a sparsely attended service. At Molly's suggestion, the Kanes commissioned an elegant yet tasteful granite headstone to replace the plain cement marker originally placed over her grave.

Andrew was told that Kyle Lewis's body had been cremated with no fanfare and no one in attendance but the crematory technician.

Ex-governor John Barker survived his attack and within hours of his release from the hospital had announced that he was considering running for governor again, which didn't surprise Andrew in the least. Barker talked a lot about karma, irony, and not throwing stones if you live in a glass house.

Detectives Ramsey, Novak, and Egan were commended for their roles in the Pickman-Austin case, and Andrew took no issue with that.

Even though all charges against Tyler were dropped when Wyatt Pickman and Grady Austin's involvement became clear, Rachel Addison claimed it as a victory, putting the case in her "win" column—a designation reflected in the size of her final bill, which the Kanes paid without a second thought.

By contrast, for his role in Pickman's scheme, public defender Wesley Jurgens was facing disbarment and, very possibly, a prison sentence.

Gabriel Torrance, who had broken no laws after his release, remained a free, fully pardoned man. He turned the gun he found in the Rutland Projects over to the authorities, informing them that, according to Kevin Austin, it was the weapon they'd never been able to find, the gun that killed Dave Bingham eight years ago, on which should be the fingerprints of Zachary Barnes, son of Clifton Barnes. Ballistics testing and fingerprinting of the gun began soon after receipt of the evidence.

Among the evidence collected at Pickman's house was the audio recording of Molly acting as Andrew's negotiator with respect to the pardon of Gabriel Torrance. There would be no charges against her, though, and she was assured by almost anyone whom she asked that, under the extraordinary circumstances, this was unlikely to negatively impact her chances of becoming a state police officer once she completed her graduate courses and earned her master's degree in criminal justice. In short, no one seemed to place blame on her for her role. Which Andrew found to be a relief and totally appropriate.

The nail salon's security footage of Henry finding the alleged bag of evidence hidden by Pickman—which Henry said contained nothing but trash, and which he claimed to have disposed of—proved to be a bit more problematic. The problem for the authorities was that they couldn't be certain the bag had actually contained evidence because Henry had gotten rid of it. Pickman's records indicated that it had, and those records had generally proven to be both detailed and accurate, but on this specific issue, they were contradicted by the statement of a veteran state police detective with a spotless record—namely, Henry. Possibly because of that—but more probably, Andrew thought, because most of the cops and FBI agents who reviewed the matter wondered whether they would have done the same thing in his shoes—Henry was reinstated, and no charges were filed against him. His career in Internal Affairs was over, though. His supervisor, Warren Haddonfield, hadn't yet decided where to put him.

Of the Kanes, it would apparently be Andrew who would suffer the worst. His reputation was in tatters. His famous integrity was, in the eyes of nearly everyone in the state, nothing but fiction. He'd lost the respect of everyone outside the family. And because the story had gone national, his had become yet another face that would spring to the minds of people everywhere when they heard the word *corruption*. Whereas Henry and Molly essentially had been given passes because of the circumstances surrounding their actions, Andrew's breach of the public trust was apparently deemed a far greater sin. He couldn't disagree.

He looked at the others sitting around the dinner table—Rebecca, Molly, Henry, and Tyler—and said, "I have an announcement, everyone. I've decided not to run for president."

After a brief moment of confused looks, Henry chuckled and Molly laughed. A second later, shaking her head, Rebecca smiled. Only Tyler looked disappointed.

"And I'm resigning from office this week," Andrew added.

Objections filled the room, but no one's heart seemed to be behind any of them. They had expected it. The outcome had seemed a foregone conclusion—to Andrew, at least, and he suspected to the others—the moment he'd confessed everything to Ramsey.

"They're calling for my head," Andrew said. "Everyone. So I'm going to step down before they kick me out." He glanced at Rebecca, who gave him a small nod of support, which he appreciated. She hadn't been thrilled with his decision when he had shared it with her this morning, but she'd understood.

"Like Nixon," Henry said.

"Well done, Henry," Molly said. "Politicians just love being compared to Richard Nixon."

Henry shrugged. No smart comeback, which Andrew found a bit odd.

Tyler said, "I don't think you should quit your job, Andy. They made you governor because everyone likes you. They want you to be governor."

"Well, things have changed, buddy." He looked at each of their faces. "Honestly, I couldn't stay in office even if they let me. I don't deserve it. Not after everything I did, the way I abused my position and failed those who had placed their faith and trust in me."

Molly objected, less half-heartedly than the last time. Henry, though, said nothing.

"First, I'm going to pardon Kevin Austin posthumously. Then I'll go through the pardon file and see if anyone else in there truly deserves one. I'll have to work fast before the villagers show up with torches and pitchforks."

"What villagers?" Tyler asked.

"It's just an expression, Tyler," Andrew said. "After I start the pardons rolling, I'll resign. Lynne Kasparian's great," he said, referring to his lieutenant governor, who would assume office when he stepped down. "A terrific person. She'll do a wonderful job. Better than I did."

"But what happens at the next election, in a year?" Molly asked. "We get Jackpot Barker again?"

"He's not really going to run. He's just saying that because he likes the publicity. If he became governor again, he'd have to be scrupulously honest because everyone would be watching him a lot more closely next time, and he'd never want that. We don't have to worry about Jack. It'll either be Lynne again, or someone new."

"Either way, gotta be better than Jackpot," Henry said, though the remark didn't have his usual snap to it. They'd all been through a lot.

After dinner was finished and all the dishes were in the dishwasher and the pots had been cleaned and dried, Tyler announced that he was going to go for a ride on his motorcycle.

"It's dark," Molly said.

"I have a light on my motorcycle, remember? And besides, I wasn't able to do it for a while, and now I'm allowed to again."

"Come on, Molly," Andrew said. "Let him go."

She relented, and Andrew listened to his footsteps pound through the house and out the back door. A moment later, they heard the whine of his electric bike's motor as he sped past the kitchen windows. Within seconds, the sound faded away.

With the kitchen clean, they went out to the front porch and sat side by side in wicker rockers. They didn't say much for a while, just sat and rocked and looked at the night. Finally, Molly said, "I have to get some studying done. Got a victimology exam next week."

She disappeared inside. Rebecca said, "Anyone feel like coffee?"

Andrew declined, but Henry jumped at the offer with more life than he'd shown any other time this evening. As soon as Rebecca was inside, Andrew turned to his brother.

"Something on your mind, Henry?"

Henry said nothing for a moment; then, with his eyes still looking out into the darkness, he said, "The gun that Torrance found, the one he says killed Dave Bingham?"

"Yeah?"

"It's supposed to have that rich kid's prints on it. Zachary Barnes."

There was something in Henry's manner, in his voice, that Andrew didn't like. "And?"

"And it won't."

"You don't think it's the gun that killed Bingham."

"I'm not saying that."

Andrew closed his eyes as the truth began to dawn. He almost wanted Henry to stop talking. He wanted to pretend this conversation had never begun. But he said, "So what *are* you saying?"

Henry lowered his gaze. "It'll be my prints on the gun, Andrew."

CHAPTER SIXTY-TWO

"Did you hear what I said, Andy?" Henry asked quietly. "The prints on the gun are mine."

No, Andrew thought. *How could that be? Not Henry.* He suddenly felt feverish.

Then Henry began to tell the real story of what had happened the night his friend and mentor, Dave Bingham, died.

Bingham, who had retired from the force and gone private, was hired by Clifton Barnes to dig up dirt on the candidate who was in the lead for the elected position of Vermont Attorney General—Andrew Kane. It seemed that Barnes's rumored connections to organized crime might have been more than just rumor, and Andrew, who had promised a crackdown on mob-related activity in Vermont, was seen as a threat to Barnes and his associates in other states. So Barnes wanted ammunition he could use to derail Andrew's campaign. And because they were friends, Bingham warned Henry that he had found something, that there might be a bit of trouble on Andrew's horizon. In fact, he would be meeting with his client that night to deliver the financial records proving it.

"I don't know what Dave could have been referring to, Henry," Andrew said, truly perplexed, "but there was no dirt to dig up on me. I'm clean. Always have been. Well, until lately, anyway."

"Yeah, but Jared Schilling wasn't."

"What?" Schilling had been Andrew's campaign manager, with whom he parted ways after becoming attorney general. According to Bingham, Schilling had proof of payments he had received in exchange for promises that Andrew would be friendly to certain causes should the need arise. This was the first Andrew had heard of this. If promises had been made purportedly obligating him, he hadn't been aware of them—which was good because he wouldn't have honored them.

"It may have been Schilling doing it," Henry said, "but it would've looked like you were in on it. We both know that."

Though Andrew was surprised about all this, he had to admit that he'd developed a bad feeling about Schilling, which was why he'd severed ties with the man years ago. If Andrew wasn't so focused on Henry's confession, he would have been incensed about Schilling's actions.

From the corner of his eye, Andrew saw Rebecca appear at the screen door with a coffee mug in each hand—one for her, one for Henry—but she must have sensed something because, without a word, she backed away and disappeared into the house.

"So what happened with Dave?" Andrew prodded gently.

With his eyes still glued to the porch floor, Henry picked up the story again. He had followed Dave to the Rutland Projects, which had been closed for a few years and had become nothing but a place people went to do illicit things. Dave had a big envelope with him, the kind that could contain a file, and Henry confronted him while he was waiting to meet with Zachary Barnes, whom his father had tasked with obtaining the records from Dave. Henry tried to convince his old friend to forget about the case and bury what he'd found. He'd said Andrew would be good for the state, while Clifton Barnes was a thug in an expensive suit who only wanted to see Andrew lose the election so he could continue to do all the illegal shit he was doing. But Dave wouldn't hear of it. He said burying what he'd uncovered was the wrong thing to do, and besides, he'd taken the job, and he intended to see it through. He had a reputation in his business, after all. Besides, if Andrew was innocent of wrongdoing, which he probably was, the truth would come out. Henry said that Dave just wouldn't listen, and things heated up quickly, escalating shockingly fast given how close the two had been. Somehow—Henry couldn't even remember how—he ended up with a gun in his hand . . . not the service weapon that was still in its holster, but an unregistered throwaway. He wasn't even sure why he'd brought it with him that night, he said.

"While I was holding the gun on Dave, the door behind me opened, and I turned to look. I only had time to register someone coming into the building before I heard something and I turned back around, and it was Dave coming at me, going for the gun." He took a breath. Then another. When he spoke again, his voice was small. "It went off and . . . Dave went down."

Even though he'd known essentially what was coming, the words turned Andrew cold.

"I went right for the other guy," Henry said. "I wasn't sure why exactly, instinct, I guess, self-preservation, and we struggled for a few seconds until the door opened again, and *another* guy came in. I got distracted, the guy I was grappling with hit me, and I lost my grip. He took off and, seeing the first guy run, the second guy followed."

Henry looked up and, finally, met Andrew's gaze. His eyes looked almost empty. "I didn't know what to do. I should have stayed with Dave, I know that, but the two guys ran, and maybe out of habit or instinct or . . . I don't know, maybe because I was worried they'd seen my face, I chased them. They split up, and I followed one of them at random, but I lost him somewhere in the projects. I looked for a while, but he was just gone. So I hurried back to Dave and . . . he was gone, too."

He dropped his eyes again.

"I don't think it would've mattered if I hadn't left him," he said. "I really don't. He would've died anyway. Bullet caught him in the neck." He paused for several seconds, maybe half a minute. "I'll never forget the way he looked lying there."

Henry fell silent again. Andrew recalled how that night eight years ago seemed to change Henry. How he had struggled through a dark time from which it had seemed to take more than a year for him to emerge . . . and though Henry eventually seemed to reach the other side, Andrew had always thought he had lost a little something of himself along the way. Everyone naturally assumed it was because he had lost a friend, a friend whose body he had discovered. But Andrew now knew it had been more than that. He wanted to say something, to comfort his brother, but he said nothing. Henry needed to finish the story. They both needed him to finish it.

A long moment later, Henry said, "The envelope was still there, so I took it. I should have called the situation in right then, I know, but . . . well, I didn't want to be tied to any of it. For either of our sakes, you know?"

Even though he hadn't known about it at the time, Andrew was horrified to hear that he had any part in this, that Henry had done what he'd done, that Dave Bingham had died, to protect *him*.

"I was on my way back to my car," Henry went on, "when I heard something. I followed the sound, and coming out of another building was one of the guys I chased, one of the guys who saw . . . you know. I stopped him, and the thing is, he was high as hell, jittery, not talking coherently." He looked up. "Again, I didn't know what to do, Andy. I didn't know what he'd seen, but at the same time I doubted he'd remember anything he *did* see. I was standing right in front of him, and I didn't think he would've been able to describe me later. I had just decided to let him go and take my chances when I heard sirens, and the Rutland Police rolled up quick. Somebody heard the gunshot, I guess. So then

I *really* didn't know what to do. The cops saw me, their guns were out, so I identified myself, told them a man had been shot . . . and they just assumed I had the suspect in custody." He paused a long, long moment. "And I didn't tell them otherwise. Neither did the suspect . . . Kevin Austin. He wasn't in any condition to say anything."

Even given his accidental shooting of Dave, to Andrew, that might have been his brother's greatest sin.

Andrew closed his eyes. Not only was Henry his brother, he was his closest friend, and Andrew loved him dearly, despite all this. And to know that he was capable of such things . . . that he had done these things—some unintentional, but some definitely not—and kept it all inside . . . made Andrew heartsick.

"I gave my statement," Henry continued, "made up a bullshit story on the spot about Dave asking me to meet him there, and that was it. If they saw the envelope I was holding, they never asked me about it. I burned it later. I kept waiting for the cops to find Dave's work files or research on the case and come knocking on both our doors, yours and mine, but they never did. They had their shooter; they had the testimony of a state police detective. Case closed."

"And Kevin Austin . . ."

"Was a junkie," Henry finished for him. "That was all I saw," he added with a self-loathing shake of his head. "It shouldn't have mattered, of course, but at the time, I let it matter. I convinced myself that it mattered, that one junkie wasn't worth your career and all the good you were going to do as attorney general." He paused, then added, "And that he wasn't worth my going to prison for, either. At least, that was how I felt at the time."

He met Andrew's eyes squarely, something Andrew didn't think could have been easy for him in that moment. To be honest, it wasn't easy for Andrew, either.

"You don't have to tell me how wrong I was, Andy. And you won't believe this—no reason you should—but after that kid went to prison, every day he was behind bars, I considered coming clean. I thought about it every single day, all those years . . . right up until he died, and then it was too late." He gave a weak shrug. "I was kidding myself, though. I never would've stepped up."

Henry became quiet and looked out at the dark night. Andrew studied him and tried to imagine what it had been like for him to live for so long with what he had done. It was hard to feel terribly sorry for him under the circumstances. But then again, this was Henry. His brother.

"I always tried to tell myself that it probably didn't make much of a difference," Henry said, "that the kid would have OD'd somewhere along the line anyway, but I was just trying to justify something that was unjustifiable." He shook his head sadly. "It wasn't until I got home that night that I realized I didn't have the gun. I went back and looked for it a few days later, after everything died down at the scene, but I didn't find it. I always figured they'd find it and come knocking, but they never did. I never knew what happened to it. I figured some gangbanger had picked it up, and my prints would be wiped away."

He fell silent. He seemed spent, leaning forward in his chair, his arms resting on his knees, his shoulders slumped, his eyes on the porch floor again. He looked hollowed out. He also looked as though his story was finished. So, for the first time in several minutes, Andrew spoke. "I meant to tell you this earlier . . . I'm not even sure yet if I wish I had, or whether it's good that I hadn't . . ." He trailed off.

Without looking up, Henry said, "What is it, Andy?"

He took a deep breath, let it out, then said, "I'd asked Detective Ramsey to keep me informed on the Pickman case, and he called me this afternoon to tell me that the report on the gun Gabriel Torrance found came in. Ballistics matched it to Dave Bingham."

Henry nodded.

Andrew went on, "But they were unable to get usable prints off the gun."

He knew that the length of time fingerprints might remain on an object depended on a variety of factors, including, among others, atmospheric and environmental conditions where the item had been located, surface properties of the object, cleanliness of the fingertips at the time, and the unique condition of a person's fingertip skin. It was possible to lift fingerprints from objects that were decades old while failing to do the same with objects that had been handled recently.

Upon hearing this news, Henry looked up, and Andrew didn't see a trace of relief in his eyes, even though it meant there was no physical evidence to tie him to Dave's shooting. He looked out toward the darkness—they both did—and a heavy, uncomfortable silence settled on them. Andrew had heard too much. Learned too much. He still loved his brother and always would, but he wished Henry were the person Andrew had thought he was all these years.

Eventually, Andrew's mind began sifting through Henry's story, as much as he didn't want to think about it. "There's something I can't figure," he said after a long while. "Why would Clifton Barnes pay off Kevin Austin's father, fifty grand a year until Kevin died, if Zachary didn't kill Dave?"

Henry took a moment to answer, as though he needed a few seconds to change gears. "Maybe the old man didn't believe his kid when he said he didn't do it. Or maybe Cliff was worried about how his partners in organized crime would react if they even suspected that his kid had killed an ex-cop—those guys tend to want to keep low profiles, and they expect their associates to do the same—so he made his deal with Kevin Austin. If Kevin kept his mouth shut about Zachary being there that night, then Kevin's father wouldn't get hurt. In fact, he'd get paid. I'm guessing it wasn't hard for Kevin to do that, seeing as he probably couldn't remember much of that night anyway."

"Makes sense."

Henry thought for a moment. "I wonder what Pickman would have done if Torrance never found the gun."

Andrew said, "Grady Austin told us the answer to that, and it was confirmed by information in the binder that Pickman kept containing the details of his plans. Austin was insistent that they use the gun to take Zachary Barnes down. Torrance, who believed Barnes had committed the murder for which his lover was convicted, wanted that, too. They both wanted Barnes's actual fingerprints on the actual weapon to do him in. But if Torrance came up empty on the gun, Pickman was going to frame Barnes. The plans were all in his binder and files. The evidence, which he'd already manufactured, was in a closet in his basement. All he had to do was plant it convincingly, which, as we both know, was something he was good at."

Henry nodded, and they fell silent for a while. Andrew had no idea what his brother was thinking. Then Henry said, "It's all my fault. Everything that happened. Everyone who died, what Tyler went through, what happened to your career . . . all of it."

Andrew gave it only a moment's consideration. "I made my own choices, my own mistakes. You don't get to own those. The rest of it, though? Okay, what happened to Kevin Austin, yeah, that's on you. No doubt about that. I'm not telling you anything there you don't already know. But everything else . . . there's no way I'll let you take the blame for any of it. It was Grady Austin and Wyatt Pickman."

Henry didn't reply. Either he agreed, or he didn't have the strength or will to argue. Finally, he nodded to himself, drew a big breath, and said, "So, I guess in the morning, I'll turn myself in."

Andrew considered that. As he'd listened to Henry's confession, he couldn't help but wonder where things would go from here. He was glad that, finally, Henry wanted to do the right thing, even if it was far too late. Andrew thought about Henry in prison. He was aware of the generally accepted purposes for incarceration, which included locking up the offender so he couldn't commit another crime while behind bars; rehabilitating him; and punishing him as an effort to deter him from offending again. In Andrew's opinion, despite what Henry had done, such considerations didn't apply in his case. Henry would never commit another such crime. That was obvious. Similarly, he didn't need rehabilitating. Which meant his going to prison would be merely to punish him. And it sounded to Andrew like he'd been punishing himself for eight long years, and would be doing so for the rest of his life. His being in prison wouldn't bring back any of Pickman's victims. It wouldn't bring back Dave Bingham. And it wouldn't bring back Kevin Austin.

Andrew truly believed all of that. But if he were honest with himself, there was more behind his thinking. Because Henry was family. Henry was his brother. And though Andrew knew that almost no one else would understand . . . it was a blood thing.

"I don't want you to turn yourself in," Andrew said. Then he told him why. He also told him that he'd been a really good cop once upon a time and had the potential to be one again.

"We need good cops, Henry."

Andrew watched subtle changes ripple across his brother's face as it first displayed confusion, then introspection, then what looked to Andrew like resolve. Then, reluctantly, almost imperceptibly, Henry nodded. "So what now?" he asked.

"What now? Nothing, Henry. Life goes on. For us, anyway."

With those words, which would forever remain private, Andrew Kane issued another pardon.

They held each other's eyes for a long moment; then Henry nodded in understanding.

They sat side by side for a little while, staring into the darkness. Eventually, Henry said, "It's not *your* fault, you know."

"What isn't?"

"Any of it. I know you, Andy. I know you're probably not too happy with yourself. You probably think you made some mistakes of your own. But if you think you share the blame for anyone dying, you're wrong."

He was right. Andrew had indeed been thinking that.

"It doesn't matter that you pardoned anyone," Henry said. "Even if you hadn't, Pickman still would have gotten to everyone on his and Grady Austin's list. That's what he *did*. He devised plans and schemes. If you didn't do what he wanted, he'd simply have found another way."

"How about Kyle Lewis? If I hadn't pardoned him—"

"God, Andy, Lewis was *working with* Pickman."

"I just . . . I'm not sure . . ."

In Andrew's head, what Henry said made sense. But in his heart . . .

"Andy, if you're not gonna let me torture myself over the people Pickman killed, you sure as hell can't do it. *He* killed every one of them. Not you. *He's* responsible. He and Grady Austin. Not you."

Maybe after more time had passed, Andrew would see things that way.

"At least we did a little good," Andrew said after a moment. "We stopped him from murdering Jackpot Barker."

"I thought you were gonna tell me something good we did," Henry said, and Andrew felt the smallest of smiles crease his lips. Henry met his eyes and said, "Look, we're both gonna be thinking about all of this for a long time. And who knows, we may never again feel quite the same way about ourselves, or maybe even each other. I sure as hell have avoided looking in mirrors for the last eight years. But I want you to remember something, Andy—and I realize it's probably not enough, it doesn't completely balance the books, but remember this—no matter how guilty you feel or how badly you beat yourself up, if you hadn't done what you did, granted those pardons, Tyler would have gone to prison for the rest of his life. I believe that with all my heart. But now he won't. Because of you. I believe that with all my heart, too."

Andrew considered his brother's words.

"A lot of bad happened, Andy," Henry added, "stuff we'll probably never forgive ourselves for . . . but *that*, at the very least, is a good thing."

———

Less than a mile away, Tyler cruised along a quiet, moonlit road, his headlight stretching before him as he headed nowhere in particular, just enjoying the night ride. He hadn't been able to take his motorcycle out for weeks back when he was in trouble, and he'd missed it. In fact, he didn't even *have* it for a while. They took it. But they gave it back because he wasn't in trouble anymore, and he decided he'd ride it every day from now on. Every night, too. Now that he didn't have to stay home all the time, he found that he hardly wanted to be inside his house anymore. There were so many places to go. So much to see.

He rode through the crisp, cool night, smiling into the breeze that blew back his hair, thinking about how good it felt to be so free.

AUTHOR'S NOTE

When writers want to distort the truth—or perhaps even make up stuff entirely—they often rely on the concept of poetic or artistic license. It's an invaluable tool in a writer's tool kit, one of which I made good use in the writing of *A Blood Thing*. While I strive for accuracy whenever possible, sometimes facts must take a back seat to the story. Among the liberties I took as I wrote this book were my depiction of Vermont's clemency laws and its pardon process. Where I took the greatest liberty, however, was with the descriptions of recent corruption in Vermont's government and law enforcement agencies. In truth, I know of absolutely none. What occurred as backstory in *A Blood Thing* was pure fiction. Vermont is a beautiful, well-run state, and Vermonters are fine people. Indeed, those truths factored into my choosing Vermont as the setting for the book. For the story, I needed a state with certain kinds of clemency statutes, but I also wanted one in which government and police corruption would be truly shocking. Vermont is that kind of a state. There's a reason, after all, that it typically places near the top of every list of best US states in which to live. It's a terrific place.

ACKNOWLEDGMENTS

I usually begin by thanking my wife, Colleen, and I can't think of a reason to stop now. She's my first reader and biggest fan (or so she kindly claims), and I honestly couldn't do this without her. I mean that. Thanks go to my sons, too, who support me every day and think it's cool that I write books.

Heartfelt thanks to two of my siblings—Susan Hankins and John Hankins—both of whom read early drafts of this book. They are experienced lawyers, as is my wife, and the advice all three gave me improved this book immeasurably. The same goes for Mark Taylor, an esteemed state court judge who happens to be my brother-in-law, who also read an early version and gave me his valuable insight. If there are any errors, which I hope there aren't, they are mine alone, a fact of which I am certain they will remind me, if necessary. If readers noticed a theme in the book—family looking after family—I hope it is clear where it came from.

Thanks also to good friend Eric Stern, a talented musician, composer, conductor, and giver of advice about classical music.

Thanks, as always, go to my agent, Michael Bourret of Dystel, Goderich & Bourret LLC, for his many years of steadfast support and sage advice.

I am indebted to *everyone* at Thomas & Mercer who helped make this book happen, including (but certainly not limited to) Liz Pearsons,

Gracie Doyle, and Sarah Shaw. Thanks also to sharp-eyed editor Tiffany Yates Martin for making me dig deep.

My gratitude also goes to the former Vermont state police detective who chose to remain anonymous but still graciously answered my many questions.

To list the rest of the family members and friends whose love and support mean so much to me would require a book all its own, longer than this one. Just know how important you all are to me.

Finally, many, *many* thanks to those who use some of their valuable time to read my books, follow me on Twitter and Facebook, and reach out to me to let me know that they enjoy my work. I've said it before, and I'll say it again: it means the world to me. Truly.

ABOUT THE AUTHOR

James Hankins writes thrillers, mysteries, and novels of suspense, including *The Inside Dark*, *The Prettiest One*, *Shady Cross*, *Brothers and Bones*, *Drawn*, and *Jack of Spades*. He lives north of Boston with his wife and sons and can be reached through his website, www.jameshankinsbooks.com; on Twitter @James_Hankins_; and on Facebook at www.facebook.com/JamesHankinsAuthorPage.